NOWHERE

Also by Ryan Freerksen

Somewhere

NOWHERE

RYAN FREERKSEN

ISBN: 979-8-9903807-7-6 (Paperback)
ISBN: 979-8-9903807-4-5 (Hardcover)
ISBN: 979-8-9903807-6-9 (eBook)

Library of Congress Control Number: 2026900097

The story, all names, characters, and incidents portrayed in this production are fictitious. No identification with actual persons (living or deceased), places, buildings, and products is intended or should be inferred.

Front Cover Art by Anna Freerksen
Illustrations by Ryan Freerksen

First published in Bolingbrook, Illinois in 2026

Dedicated to Brittany, who threatened my life if I didn't publish my first novel, and to Tyler, who gave a voice to my characters.

CONTENTS

CONTENTS

This is the conclusion of the adventure that began with *Somewhere*. If you've read it, welcome back! If you haven't, I strongly suggest you pick up that story first. Our characters may be good and lost but there's no need for the reader to be.

When we left off, it was 1936 and Jack remained behind in the Kingdom with Annica, Ydoro, and a wayward Nel. Cyrus, meanwhile, banished his younger brother to an alternate reality for his attempted coup, then elected to follow after him. But wormholes are temperamental and Cyrus found himself trapped in a custom-made hell of Alec's design. Cyrus has become the leader he was meant to be, but does it matter now that he has lost everything? And Alec has finally succeeded in becoming the main character of his own story, but he just may have lost his soul along the way. All adventures must come to an end and our characters are careening towards their destinies already, whether they realize it or not…

NOWHERE

PROLOGUE

Somewhere, 1942

My how the Kingdom has changed." That was how his mentor had put it, wheezing and sputtering with his last gasping lungfuls of life. It was not meant as praise but rather a resentful, malicious commentary on the state of the world he had helped shape, and the paralyzing regret that he would never see it returned to its former glory. He would, for that matter, never see another sunrise. But his eyes hadn't shown defeat in those final seconds before they clouded over and rolled back into his skull, they had reflected hope. Hope that not only would his work live on, but that they were on the precipice of achieving their goal. He evidently did not need to see the end himself, for he had smiled contentedly as he passed.

Kero had grown much since that day, but he had to credit his mentor for introducing him to his new *family*. This family did not speak when out in public, nor give any acknowledgement to one another of any kind, but they had a deep bond that they shared. A bond that could only be revealed in secret, behind closed doors or more commonly under the dark cover of the forest. Anything beyond that would be far too dangerous under the new authority, and they had all seen what happened to those found guilty of treason. *New* authority was perhaps not accurate, they had been in power for six years now, and *my how the Kingdom had changed* under their rule.

Of course, back then, Kero had very little understanding or care for how the Kingdom was run. He did his duty, did what was asked of him, and lived his life. That was before he had been recruited. Before he had met *Vengeance*.

Vengeance is what they called *her*, in case their discussions were ever overheard by those loyal to the Throne. While many of their party led full lives within the Kingdom, enjoyed their freedom and the knowledge that they had a place in society, the same could not be said for Vengeance. She was a known fugitive, a wanted criminal by the King and Queen, and an outcast of the people. Breathing a word of her real name would bring the law down swiftly upon your head and land you an audience with the Crown. Many people didn't even know her real name, either because they had forgotten or never knew it. Efforts had been made to erase her presence from history, but six years was not that long ago, and time hadn't eroded her away quite yet.

With a name like Vengeance, Kero had expected a terrifying warlord of immense size and strength. What he had not been prepared for was a petite young woman with dirty-blonde hair and a welcoming smile. She had a story to tell; of ambition, entitlement, false-justification, and betrayal. When someone like that told you about their journey, how could you not follow them? Kero had bowed his head low in respect after that first meeting and pledged himself to her cause, but she had gently tilted his chin back up and insisted the fealty was unnecessary. She had then placed her finger over her lips indicating their pact of silence, extended her hand and shook his, saying, "I appreciate your support Kero."

Her ranks grew over the years, and the crown continued its hunt for her, oblivious to the fact that she had amassed a small but significant band of rebels who had infiltrated nearly every level of their infrastructure. Kero himself came and went within the new Temple freely. The rebels weren't ready, however. They had enough to make a declaration, but not enough to bring the establishment to its knees. And that is why it had been such a devastating blow when he had heard just this morning in the town square that Vengeance had been captured.

He hadn't wanted to believe it, but the streets were suddenly alive with throngs of people pushing and shoving their way towards the red Temple at the center of town, a monolithic beacon of strength for the Kingdom and the ruling seat of the King and Queen. The new Temple had been erected in the very middle of the Fire Fields with town proper extended out around it. As Kero ran out into the street, glowing mutely beneath his feet as the frozen fire pulsated benignly and ash kicked up into the air, he could feel the excitement and anticipation in the crowd. Everyone was converging on the Temple to see it for themselves; their very own boogeyman captured at last.

As Kero allowed himself to be pushed towards the Temple, like a branch caught in a current, he craned his neck and bounced on the tips of his toes to try and get a look ahead. It was no use with the dense crowd, but he soon found himself in the shade beneath the Temple and after a few more uncontrolled steps, he was in the entrance hall. It was a large, open-air room with enormous stone pillars flanking the sides and a solid wall along the back with a single door that led further into the fortress. In front of this door, and raised roughly ten feet off the ground on a stone landing that could be reached by a forward-facing stone staircase, were two large chairs. They weren't quite thrones, but they were close, and clearly ceremonial. It was from this stage that the King and Queen would often address the public or hear grievances from the people of the Kingdom. It was intended to stand in stark contrast to the kings of the past and their proclivity for instilling fear in the townsfolk, and in this effort it succeeded. But Kero also knew it made the rulers exposed, and therefore vulnerable. He had never been told the plan for taking over once the day finally came, but he had to assume it involved an assault from this spot.

For now, however, Kero looked around frantically, not willing to believe that their leader had been captured and their plans were at an end. Suddenly through the crowd, weaving authoritatively between the people, Kero caught sight of a familiar face. The Ambassador of the People was smiling from ear to ear and nodding his head encouragingly with the excitable crowd. He was working his way towards the staircase leading up to the royal landing when he noticed Kero and winked at him. "We got her," he exclaimed enthusiastically before reaching the base of the stairs. He and Kero had been working closely together for the last couple years. Of course, he was entirely unaware that Kero's loyalty lay elsewhere. The Ambassador ascended the stone staircase and made it to the top just as the far doors opened and the King and Queen made their appearance. They looked mildly shocked and ill-prepared for the mob before them as their Ambassador whispered something in their ears. The King looked out over the crowd with a fur-rowed brow, his eyes scanning the town below him, searching for some-thing.

The Queen stepped forward and finally spoke. "You'll have to for-give us; this is news to our ears as well. We hear one of our patrols made an exciting discovery."

The crowd began shouting and whistling and talking again and the Queen smiled at their enthusiasm.

"Let's see what they brought us, shall we?" the Queen said, and the people erupted in applause. "Garen, if you would be so kind."

This last sentence she yelled over the heads of the townsfolk, eviden-tially addressing one of her men all the way in the back. From his van-tage point, Kero couldn't see what was happening back there, but gasps from the outskirts of the crowd made his heart sink lower. Movement began to weave its way from the back of the masses towards the stair-case, like a serpent cutting a path through a patch of dense grass. From between the countless heads of the onlookers, Kero caught brief glimps-es of the royal guards dragging a prisoner forward; a prisoner with dirty-blonde hair.

The crowd had worked itself into silence by the time they reached the base of the staircase, and with an uncomfortable stretch of his neck, Kero was finally able to see the prisoner's face and confirm it was indeed Vengeance herself, finally captured.

The King took a step forward and looked down at his quarry, an ex-pression of shock and disgust shining through his features. "Nel," he exclaimed with a baffled shake of his head. "It's been a long time."

"Not long enough," Vengeance snarled. "What do I call you these days? Your *Highness*? Your *Royalship*?"

"Call me whatever you want," the King responded cooly, "you're here to answer to the people."

"Your people maybe," Vengeance hissed, "but you're forgetting about my people."

"You don't have anyone, Nel," the King retorted, "you're entirely alone now."

"Then you won't mind if I address everyone gathered here," Vengeance said.

The King smiled briefly, but it didn't fully mask his concern. "I think not, Nel." He then looked over her shoulder to the guards holding her and said, "Bring her inside."

As the guards forced her forward, Vengeance yelled back to the crowd, "Anyone loyal to me, the time is now! You know what to do, make me proud!"

The King and Queen looked alarmed at this outburst, but there was no perceptible reaction from the crowd. They all looked just as confused as Kero felt. Of course, unlike the majority of the onlookers, Kero *was* loyal to her, but he had never been told the plan. The crowd became boisterous and chaotic once again as Vengeance was led through the doors into the Temple with the King and Queen following. Kero turned to scan the area around him when a hand clasped his shoulder.

He barely had time to register the man's face before he leaned in close and grumbled in Kero's ear, "*the Guardian*, right now."

The man pushed through the crowd and was gone, but Kero had recognized the man as Lyman, one of Vengeance's followers, and shoved after him.

The Guardian was a reference to an enormous statue that had been erected in town square several years back. It depicted a man, standing high above the street with a staff clasped powerfully in his hand and a billowing cloak. His hair was frozen in a windswept billow around his determined face and a rough patch of skin patterned his right cheek and upper forehead. It was a man that many viewed as the savior of the Kingdom. But the statue stood over a stone base that contained a locked door, like the entrance to a crypt. A Temple guard protected this entrance day and night, but Kero never knew why.

Leaving the majority of the crowd behind at the Temple, Kero wove his way through the mostly abandoned streets until the Guardian came into view.

Kero picked up his pace to catch up with Lyman and whispered in his ear, "Do we have a plan? I was never told anything."

"You're being told now," Lyman replied without breaking his stride. He handed a small blade to Kero and continued, "Welcome to the big leagues, things are about to break wide open."

Lyman veered left before reaching the statue and the guard did not react, likely assuming he was simply returning home from the announcement at the Temple. Another man rushed out from one of the side streets and joined them as they walked.

"Do we have a plan?" the man asked Lyman. "Did she tell you anything before she was captured?"

"She told me everything," Lyman growled, "this was always the plan, it's just moved up now."

Several other people that Kero recognized as loyalists of Vengeance began appearing from the side streets, but it was far from an army. They each carried a machete or blade of some sort, but one man held what looked to be a stunningly large stone war hammer. This man nodded to Lyman, who nodded back.

Quicker than Kero could blink, Lyman had broken into a run and sprinted around the side of the statue, assaulting the guard from the rear and driving a long, narrow knife deep into the man's neck. The guard gasped and clutched at his bleeding throat, but he was losing blood by the gallon, and he soon collapsed onto the glowing earth. Lyman grasped the guard's legs and dragged him callously out of the way as the man with the war hammer strode forward confidently. He wound up his arms and smashed forward into the locked door with his weapon, shattering the solid wood and warping the iron hinges. He reared back and hammered again, this time tearing an enormous hole in the door. Lyman walked forward and fished his arm through the splintered wood, releasing the inner clasp and pulling the door open, which promptly fell apart into several twisted, ruined pieces. Kero squinted into the darkness beyond the stone doorframe to see what was housed within when a shout echoed from across the square.

The group turned to see the Ambassador of the People rushing towards them with two Temple guards at his side. The guards unsheathed their own weapons and ran to meet the group, who charged forward and hammered into them with machetes. The Ambassador, who Kero had never pictured as much of a fighter, pulled some sort of a bolt-launcher from within his cloak and fired two shots into his assailants. He only paused when he caught sight of Kero.

"Kero?" he stammered in disbelief. Kero just stared back at him with wide eyes as Lyman screamed, "Hold them off!"

The Ambassador seemed to shake himself back into action and charged the open doorway beneath the Guardian, yelling to his guards, "Stop them!"

The man holding the war hammer turned and forced his way through the shattered remains of the door and into the small crypt beyond. Kero, not knowing what to do, scrambled over the fragments of wood and followed him.

As his eyes adjusted to the darkness within, he at first thought the small room was entirely empty. There was nothing built within it, no benches, no tables, no shelves, nothing. But the man with the hammer was looking down, and as Kero followed his gaze, he saw what the guard had been protecting. A fragment of staff, roughly two feet long, lay on the ground as though it had been tossed aside years ago. It had a texture like burnt bark with deep fissures and cracks decorating its surface. From within these fissures, it glowed a ruby red, and the fiery ground beneath pulsated in a vibrant orange.

An arm grasped Kero's throat from behind and wrenched him backwards, attempting to pull him back out the door. Kero whipped around, more out of some survivalist instinct than anything else, and buried his knife deep into the abdomen of his attacker.

The Ambassador blinked in shock as he released Kero's throat and staggered, clutching at his bleeding torso.

"Stand back!" the man with the hammer yelled. He raised his weapon high above his head and brought it smashing down on the fragment of staff.

Something erupted behind Kero's sinuses. His vision clouded over and his head felt like a white-hot poker had been stabbed deep into his brain. He winced and tried to turn away, but his legs failed him and he fell hard onto his knees. The Ambassador stumbled forward and tried to push Kero aside, but in his injured state he only managed to collapse into him. Kero's fingers, hands, and arms were contorting painfully and he felt like he was being dragged backwards by something in the pit of his stomach. He squinted around wildly and realized that the man with the hammer was no longer behind him, but he did note that the staff had been shattered into several jagged pieces.

The Ambassador renewed his efforts and stumbled forward again, this time drawing a knife from his belt and stabbing it down into Kero's thigh as he crawled over him. Kero screamed and tried to roll out of the way, but he was still being dragged inexplicably deeper into the dark crypt. The last thing he saw before the void claimed him was the Ambassador reaching out and desperately clutching at the shattered remnants of the glowing staff.

The Ambassador's contorting hand managed to close around one small fragment before he was violently ripped backwards and followed both the man with the hammer and Kero through the newly opened *door* and out of their world.

For the first time in twenty-eight years, Ydoro had left the Kingdom.

CHAPTER ONE

OUT OF TIME

Upstate New York, 1971

G uy Michaelson sped down the rain-soaked autumn road at an admittedly reckless speed, weaving around corners and sliding slightly on the damp fallen leaves. It was becoming an unfortunate habit of his being late to his Monday morning lessons, and his class had begun to take notice. It was one thing for the occasional student to be late, but when the professor started to do it, it set a bad precedent. In fact, his ability to scold individuals who were tardy had become mostly nonexistent due to his recent custom.

His car screeched around the final corner and the campus parking lot came into view. He craned his neck out the side window, scouring the lot for an empty space when a man crossing the road made him slam on his brakes. As his car lurched to a halt, the man gave him a disgusted look but didn't linger, looking up at the lecture buildings with a somewhat lost expression. Guy rolled his eyes but waved a dismissive hand, having no time for confused students. He stomped on the gas again and roared around another bend in the lot until an empty stall appeared to him. His car tilted roughly into the space and Guy wrenched the gear shift into park.

Guy spilled out of the driver's side door and slammed it behind him, then realized he had forgotten his briefcase on the passenger seat and had to go back in for it. After a quick sprint through the front doors of the building and down the main corridor, he burst into his lecture hall with twenty seconds to spare. The restless class erupted in murmurs and tittering laughter, to which Guy, or Professor Michaelson as he would be known for the next hour and a half, smirked in response.

Guy's lecture came and went with mercifully few complications, and as the last of his students trickled out the exit doors of the lecture hall, he sighed deeply. He wasn't in the mood to teach today. This could partially be due to the gorgeous sunny morning that was unfolding just beyond the building walls, or perhaps the fact that Guy was nursing a mild hangover from the night before. Either way, his mood improved dramatically as he shoved the front doors open and breathed the cool, fresh air of the day. He strode through the parking lot and entered the grounds of the sprawling campus, his boots crunching off the fallen leaves strewn about the lawn.

As he entered the administrative building that held his office, ancient and weathered Professor Melner glowered at him unabashedly when he passed. Guy was never much bothered about what other professors thought of him, but especially so of Melner. He struck Guy as someone disapproving of everyone and everything younger than him, a category that included most people in the world, as Melner had to be pushing ninety-five. Guy continued down the walnut-paneled hallway, glancing absently at the many portraits of past professors lining the one wall. Most portrayed men and women around Professor Melner's age, but not all. There were a couple that showed youthful, bright-eyed young men that couldn't have been much older than Guy himself.

As he turned the corner to enter his tiny, cramped little office, he realized with a surge of exasperation that someone was already standing in it. How in the world could a student already need something from him, it wasn't even ten in the morning yet. But as the man turned, Guy realized it wasn't a student.

"Something I can help you with?" Guy asked with a grunt, somewhat annoyed by the audacity of the mystery person helping themselves through the door of his office.

"Sorry," the man said with a start, "I'm subbing for chemistry and maybe got turned around."

"Well these are administrative offices," Guy answered without hiding a baffled shake of his head, "you can find lecture halls in both neighboring buildings, maybe try one of them."

Guy brushed past the man to get to his desk, still perturbed that he had let himself in, whether the door had been open or not. As he eased himself into his chair, Guy realized that the man was the same one he had nearly run over in the parking lot this morning. Christ, he had looked lost then, had he just been wandering the campus this whole time? It was of no importance or interest to Guy, who pulled a pen from his desk and began to feign writing something in an attempt to end the conversation. It seemed to work, for the man thanked him curtly and left down the hallway.

Guy threw the pen back onto his desk and creaked back in his chair, watching the man walk the corridor at a complacent pace. If he were late and lost, why wasn't he rushing? The man even stopped to admire several of the portraits on the wall before finally disappearing around the corner. Where did the University come up with these people? No sooner had Guy looked down at his mostly empty desk than a knock came from his door and he glanced back up with a frustrated sigh. But it wasn't the lost substitute this time, it was Diana Rahm, the biology professor from down the hall.

"Hey Diana," Guy greeted her with a disinterested murmur. Diana was of the older generation of professors on campus. Not quite Professor Melner's age, but few living things were. She was short and just this side of being too skinny with grey streaks running through her badly dyed hair, and Guy never got the impression she had much use for him at all.

"Are you coming out this Friday?" Diana asked with a frankness that didn't quite disguise her lack of enthusiasm.

"What's this Friday, again?" Guy questioned with an absent shake of his head.

"Remember I mentioned a few weeks ago that I'm retiring at the end of this year? Well a bunch of the professors are getting together for a drink after classes on Friday."

"You're having a retirement party in November for a retirement in May?" Guy couldn't contain his thoughts on the absurdity of the concept.

"It's not a retirement party," Diana insisted, "just getting together for some drinks."

"I'll see if I can make it," Guy responded as politely as he could manage. He was someone who tried to spend as little time near campus as humanly possible when he was not working, and giving up his Friday night for a *pre-retirement* party sounded like the last thing he wanted to do.

"Sounds good," Diana answered with a lack of enthusiasm to match his own, and she shuffled off down the hall.

What was it with this day? Guy and Mondays had always had a hateful relationship, but it seemed like everyone needed something today. He put his face in his hands and ran his palms roughly down the sides of his cheeks. Coffee, that's what he needed to set his morning right. He heaved himself up to a standing position once again, his ancient chair groaning noisily as he did so, and exited his office. Hopefully if he hung out in the dining hall for a while, he would be left alone.

Guy began striding down the hallway, again glancing absently at the many portraits lining the wall, when one of them caught his attention. He backtracked, then stopped to face the grinning, youthful picture. It was one of the two younger professors memorialized on the wall, and he had never given any consideration to it until now. The man looked about his age at thirty-six, perhaps just a few years older, with stubble lining his cheeks and a piercing stare. But it wasn't his youthfulness that had stopped Guy. Unless he was losing his mind entirely, this very same man was the confused-looking substitute teacher who had just been in his office not ten minutes prior. He was under the impression that all of these professors were long dead. It didn't make a lot of sense to Guy.

It made even less sense when his eyes fell to the placard below the portrait, denoting its occupant... and the date of his death:

Professor Alec Dorn
1898 – 1935

CHAPTER TWO

THE POACHER

Jordan, Near the Coast of the Dead Sea, 1955

Nick Satterall looked down at his watch, squinting in the moonlight, and cursed. Where the hell was he? Of course, it was nothing new for Mauretz to be late, in fact he made a habit of it. But Nick was exposed out here, and out in the open desert with nothing but stars and sand to keep him company, there would be nowhere to hide if the authorities showed up. He looked down at his feet, the night sky casting the windswept dunes in deep blue tones, and busied himself with his flashlight, which he clicked on and off several times in annoyance. The harsh yellow light ruined his night vision, which only pissed him off further and caused him to start pacing with anxiety. Movement along the ground to his right caused him to start, and he clicked his flashlight back on to see a long thin snake as black as night slithering between a pair of dried-up clumps of brambles. There was so little life out here during the day that it was alarming to see anything that breathed. But night in the desert was always different. Full of wonders... and full of dangers.

Nick looked to his car, parked on the dune about a hundred feet from him, and considered packing up and driving away. If Mauretz was going to make him wait like this, it would serve him right if Nick were gone when he got here. In truth, Nick was not going to leave. He had a lot more riding on this deal than Mauretz did. He cursed again and kicked a small rock out of the sand, sending a bluish cloud up into the air as it caught the moonlight. Then he paused and cocked his head towards the sky. Had he just heard an engine? He remained silent and still until he was sure of what he was hearing, and finally turned to scan the horizon. Amber headlights could be seen, rocking up and down the dunes as they approached. Nick watched as they drew ever nearer, fairly certain that it was Mauretz, but how could he be sure? He reached around his back and put his hand on the grip of the pistol sticking out from the belt of his pants, just in case.

The engine noise tore through the soft night air with a grinding, horrible persistence that seemed wrong in such an untouched wilderness. Of course, the area wasn't untouched, it had just been forgotten in recent millennia. And that was exactly why Nick Satterall was out here.

With a sigh, Nick recognized Mauretz's car and released his grip on the pistol as the old vehicle lurched to a halt in front of him with a sputtering cough. The driver's side door flew open and a small, skinny man in his early twenties jumped out hastily.

"I know, I know, I'm late," Mauretz exclaimed with his hands thrown up in the air.

"Turn your damn car off," Nick demanded, looking around the rolling horizon warily.

"It's down the dunes a ways," Mauretz insisted, "another five-minute drive probably."

Nick rolled his eyes and walked towards the car. Mauretz gave a nervous hop and jumped back into the driver's seat.

"Headlights off," Nick said bluntly, leaning over and switching the dial on the dash instead of waiting for an answer.

"We could hit something," Mauretz complained, accelerating forward all the same.

"Use the moon," Nick growled, "I'm not getting arrested tonight."

An echoing metallic clank rang out from beneath the car as it bounced off a rock in the sand and Mauretz looked to Nick with raised eyebrows as if to say, 'I told you so.'

"So do we know what it is this time?" Nick asked. "If it's more tiny fragments of pottery, I swear to god…"

"They don't always tell me," Mauretz answered, "but I think it's a big one this time."

Nick looked to Mauretz apprehensively. "*Big* as in *size* or *big* as in a major discovery?"

"Major discovery," Mauretz confirmed, "They're trying to move fast on it. They don't get paranoid unless it's something real special."

Nick grunted in reply. Mauretz worked for an archeological excavation team in Jordan. He was no more than a hired hand when they needed extra diggers, someone to swing a pickaxe or work a shovel. He was paid little and worked like a dog. Nick, on the other hand, was what was referred to as a poacher. Not in terms of wild game, but a poacher of archaeological finds. He paid off Mauretz, who in turn would alert him when a site was discovered and provide him with the location of the treasure. The reason the scheme worked was that there were lines and lines of red tape to cut through before an ancient site could be dug. The scientists who made the discovery needed the permission of the local government, various antiquities societies, probably even the city museums for all Nick knew. It was not often a fast process, and it left small windows where Nick could swoop in and claim the prize as his own. Black market antiquities trade was not a new phenomenon, hell, the pyramids of Egypt were pillaged long ago, but it had certainly seen an uptick in recent years, particularly in this part of the world. Nick had buyers all over town, and in the next town over, and the town after that. Unloading his 'finds' was never the hard part. Getting in and out without being caught was the challenge, and an arrest would lead to a hanging.

Mauretz drove the car over the peak of a dune and it bounced precariously down the other side, the suspension creaking and moaning angrily. They picked up speed as they rolled downhill, skidding on the loose sand as Mauretz cut to the right. The brakes screamed weakly as they slid to a stop near some jagged, wind-sculpted rocks that stabbed out of the sand like blades.

Mauretz spilled out of the car awkwardly as Nick stepped out the other side and followed behind him.

"This is it," Mauretz confirmed, "there's an opening that leads underground."

Nick paused. "How far underground?"

"Not far," Mauretz assured him, "it's barely a chamber, just a shallow cave really."

Nick walked cautiously forward, taking the lead from Mauretz, his feet crunching absurdly loudly in the silent night air. The ground sloped downward towards the base of the rocks, and after clicking his flashlight on again, he could see the small opening ahead. He nodded to himself and took several more steps, but the descent was steeper than it had initially appeared, and he suddenly lost his footing. With a spray of sand, Nick fell to his hip and slid ten feet down the hill and through the mouth of the cave before coming to a stop. Nick swore and brushed his mop of overhanging dirty-blonde hair from his face. His flashlight had gone out in the fall and he rattled it until it sputtered back to life again.

"You alright?" Mauretz asked in concern, taking his own sweet time creeping down the hill.

Nick shook his head in annoyance and scanned the area with his flashlight, illuminating a scorpion creeping back into the shadows. He eased himself back to his knees, unable to fully stand in the low-hanging cave, and squinted around. Mauretz had been right, the area barely constituted a cave. It fed roughly seven feet back and culminated in a very solid-looking rock wall. The excavation team would likely dig further and see if an antechamber existed either beyond it or below, but not Nick. He was only here for the easily obtainable pieces. The quick money. But at first glance, there appeared to be nothing to find.

Mauretz had arrived at his side and Nick turned and asked, "You're sure this is the spot?"

"The permit request said lower left corner," Mauretz responded in an unnecessary whisper.

Nick shone his flashlight to the left and it illuminated what Nick had at first mistook for a rock. He shimmied closer, ducking his head lower and lower as the cave narrowed. The artifact appeared to be a clay jar of some sort, fairly nondescript and rusted brown in color. Nick wasted no time lifting it out of its sandy cradle and bringing it close to his face.

"At least it's intact," Mauretz offered nervously, clearly under the impression Nick would be disappointed with more pottery. But Nick had an idea what this was. He brushed at it with the backs of his fingers and carefully prized the lid from the base. The ancient clay crumbled along the top, a serious misstep for any legitimate excavation team, but Nick simply blew the particles away and tipped the jar sideways, releasing its contents onto the desert floor. It was a neatly rolled piece of parchment that the ages had loosened and crumbled into a substance that looked almost like a wasp nest, flakey and brittle. Nick's eyes lit up in hungry excitement and he teased the edges of the impossibly fragile paper open just enough to confirm the presence of Hebrew writing. Nick laughed aloud to himself and gently replaced the scroll inside its clay tomb.

"What is it?" Mauretz asked from behind Nick, unable to see past his shoulders in the tapering cave.

"It's a major paycheck," Nick responded with a grin, hoisting the jar under his arm and preparing for the steep climb back out. "When the religious nuts *and* the science nuts all get excited together, that's a good day for us."

With a significant amount of effort, Nick and Mauretz made their way out of the cave and back into the steadily cooling dry night air. Nick did a quick scan of the horizon just to confirm they were still alone.

"How long do you think until they realize it's gone?" Nick asked.

"Hard to say," Mauretz responded, "but I wouldn't hang onto it for too long. Like I said, they're pretty enthusiastic."

Nick nodded in understanding, still absently watching the rolling blue dunes. "I'm planning to unload it fast, and *not* here. I might take it north quite a ways. They'll definitely be looking for this."

A distant screech made Nick jump badly, but Mauretz just stared at him, being used to the sounds of the desert and recognizing it to likely be an owl. It wasn't like Nick to be this squirrely, but having this particular artifact nestled beneath his arm was making him paranoid, and he wanted more than anything to be well rid of it.

"Alright," Nick finally said, "take me back to my car. No contact for a few weeks, they'll be watching all the diggers closely. Trust me, they're going to be asking questions about this."

"I've answered questions before," Mauretz assured him, and he was right. This was far from the first time he had aided Nick in stealing a priceless artifact from beneath their noses. They would undoubtedly retrieve it eventually, once it had been sold a few times on the black market and resurfaced in a public-facing shop. By then, it would be far enough removed from Nick and Mauretz that whichever scientist, archeologist, or society had originally discovered it would have no choice but to pay the premium, buy it back, and move on.

The rocky car ride back passed in silence. Nick's initial excitement had quickly turned to stress and the piece was already burning a hole in his bag. He was considering driving north tonight, just to get it out of town as fast as possible, but that was likely unnecessary. Tomorrow would do just fine.

As Mauretz pulled up next to Nick's abandoned car, he gave a quick salute to Nick as he exited the passenger side. Nick put a finger to his lips as an unnecessary reminder to keep his silence and gave him a nod of his head. Mauretz put his car into gear with a metallic crunch and lurched away across the rolling sea of sand. Nick watched him go, shielding his eyes from the billowing cloud kicked up by the car, and stood out in the night air until the stuttering engine noises eventually gave way to complete, merciful silence. Nick patted the clay urn affectionately and looked up briefly at the starry sky above. This piece wouldn't make him rich, but it would be a hell of a payday. On top of that, Mauretz clearly didn't recognize the significance of the find they had just acquired, which meant he likely wouldn't notice if his cut of the sale was smaller than his usual thirty percent. In all, this was a good day for Nick Satterall.

CHAPTER THREE

THE HISTORY PROFESSOR

Southern Illinois, 2018

Katalina Killion sat up in bed with a start, throwing her new blankets and comforter aside with a flourish. Had she overslept? She pushed her wild tangle of auburn hair out of her face aggressively and looked at the time on her phone, then rubbed her eyes frantically to make them focus and looked again. No, she wasn't late quite yet. But she would be if she didn't get moving. She swung her legs out onto the floor and stood up, glancing briefly around the relatively large dormroom that still had incredibly minimal decorations displayed. She supposed that was to be expected in your first week of college, but many others on her floor had somehow managed to hang posters, family pictures, and quasi-inspirational quotes around their walls already. Overachievers, she thought. Kat was still getting a lay of the land and wouldn't even consider putting her personal stamp on her room until she knew the person she was going to be in college. Perhaps that sounded shallow, but she firmly believed that, after a rough tenure in high school, this was her time to reinvent herself.

A glance at her roommate's equally undecorated side of the room showed that she had left already, which was perfect because the shower would be free, and she couldn't risk being late to another class in her first week. Yesterday had been her first taste of college math, a prospect she had been absolutely dreading after her tumultuous relationship with the subject throughout high school. Luckily, Kat was attending an artsy college and they seemed to recognize that, while a number of prerequisites would of course be required, these students were just not into trigonometry and algebra. As a result, Kat had found a class titled "Math for Survival", which billed itself as logic-based math that the everyday person could apply in the real world. That hadn't sounded so bad to her, and yesterday's introduction seemed promising. That being said, she had made a terrible first impression by arriving fifteen minutes late, wheezing and out of breath after her sprint across campus, and then accidentally knocked a poor classmate in the head with her backpack as she was finding her seat. So much for reinventing herself.

She quickly showered, began to throw on whatever mishmash of clean clothes were at the top of her dresser drawers, then paused and decided to actually take an extra few seconds to find an outfit that matched. Once dressed, she grabbed her backpack and headed out the door, nodding awkwardly to a few dorm neighbors she passed in the hall. Kat didn't have too much trouble making friends, but she did have a tendency to start slower when first meeting new people, and these were *all* new people. Kat was short, and quite pretty in a girl-next-door kind of way, but an actual girl next door, not the ones you would see in movies. She had a tendency to put her head down and slouch as she walked briskly through the halls with her backpack, a habit that gave off a mousy vibe that she was trying to break herself of. She was certainly nerdy in terms of her interests, but being nerdy was the 'cool' thing these days, so that did nothing to dampen her social life. Mostly, she had to work on her confidence. With that firmly in mind, she stood up a little straighter, made a conscious effort to look ahead instead of at the ground, and smiled at anyone she locked eyes with.

It was a quick journey across campus, and she found classroom 312 fairly easily, but as she passed through the door, she initially thought she had walked into the wrong room. Unlike the sprawling lecture halls of her previous subjects, this room was stuffy and cramped with no windows to speak of and space for about fifteen people at the max, which was still more room than needed. Nine other students were sitting at their desks, some talking to one another while a few had their heads down, apparently trying to squeeze in a few extra precious minutes of sleep. In front of the class was a man who had to be in his thirties, but he had such a round, boyish face it was impossible to tell for sure. He had grown stubble around his chin and up the sides of his cheeks, likely in an attempt to make himself look his age, but it did little to help in this regard. Still, he had kind eyes that looked shrewd and analytical, the eyes of someone fascinated by the world. He smiled at Kat as she found an empty desk and sat down, then turned his gaze upon the class as a whole.

"Everyone found the place okay?" he asked, to which a few students nodded in silent, obligatory confirmation. "Good! I know it may not look like much, but I'll be honest, we're lucky we were given a classroom at all."

When several students furrowed their brows in mild, but still uninterested, confusion, the man continued, "I'll get to that. But first, let me introduce myself. My name is Dean Pyrene and I teach a number of history courses here. One of my most popular is 'History of the Ancient World', where we delve into Greece, Rome, Egypt, all of that. I offer an 'American History' class as well as 'The Origins of Humanity.' But this year, I had something special in mind. This is where my heart truly lies, and it did take a bit of convincing for the Board to agree to recognizing this as a history credit, but rest assured, it counts!" Mr. Pyrene paused and surveyed the room, the smile from his own joke refusing to leave his lips even as the room stayed silent and stony-faced. "But I do have to warn you," he continued, "this is anything but a blowoff class. This is a passion of mine, so please, I implore you, pay attention and I can teach you some incredibly cool pieces of history that you have likely never heard before. With that said, welcome to 'Cryptohistory', the study of all things lost, forgotten, sparsely studied, or poorly understood."

Kat nodded her head and smiled slightly. This sounded like exactly her sort of subject. Mr. Pyrene's gaze fell upon her and he smiled back in appreciation that at least one student was excited about his subject.

Mr. Pyrene continued. "All history starts out as a mystery. Well, actually no, all history starts out as modern-day events that eventually become buried and forgotten by the ages. But my point is that even the world history that we take as fact was once a big mystery that had to be painstakingly researched and unearthed, and that starts with forming theories. Take the eruption of Mount Vesuvius for example. The year 79 AD, one of the most devastating volcanic eruptions ever recorded completely decimated the Roman towns of Pompeii and Herculaneum, and we all know about it, right? There are exhibits in museums, historical tours through the towns themselves, even movies made about the disaster. But there was a time, when those ruins were first unearthed in the late 1600s, that we had no idea what they were. Theories were formed, excavations were started, and our understanding grew. But that's not always the case. Sometimes we don't have enough pieces of the puzzle to put together a factual picture, so we are left with theories only. That's what this class will be concentrating on. The history that we don't know for sure. Those questions that we may never know the answers to."

The class looked passive, if not outright bored, but Dean Pyrene did not look deterred. "Speaking of the late 1600's, let's dive straight into our first story. I refer to these as stories because sometimes they are little more than that. This particular one has plenty of cold, hard evidence throughout the centuries, but ends with a mystery. The year is 1695 and the waters surrounding Europe have become alive with merchant ships collecting valuable goods from overseas either via trade or more commonly gross exploitation. Of course everyone knows this as the days of pirates, but does anyone know what a 'privateer' was?"

Kat glanced around and saw no reaction from her classmates. She didn't know the answer either, but she wasn't shy about guessing. She raised her hand and Mr. Pyrene called on her with a smile.

"Were privateers the honest merchants?" she asked, "the ones who transported the goods back and forth for their government?"

Mr. Pyrene beamed at her answer but shook his head slightly. "You're on the right track, but not quite there. What's your name?"

"Katalina," she answered, "or Kat."

"Well good guess Kat," Mr. Pyrene said, "but actually, privateers were almost exactly like pirates, with the exception being that they worked for their government. You see, privateers carried what were called 'letters of marque', which granted them authorization to board, capture, and seize goods and ships that sailed under a different nation's banner. Essentially, legal piracy. At least it was legal in the eyes of their home nation. Pirates, on the other hand, would steal from anyone and were considered outlaws. You recognize the potential gray area, of course. If a privateer wasn't making enough profit from looting enemy nation vessels, it was real tempting to start looking at your own nation's ships. Well, it's hard to say for sure if this was the case with a Scottish gentleman named William Kidd, but it doesn't seem a stretch of the imagination."

Mr. Pyrene scanned the classroom for attentiveness, but undeterred by the sleepy faces that stared back at him, he continued. "Kidd sailed out from London in 1695 with his letters of marque and a heavily armed warship, the thought being he would be targeting pirates and enemy nation ships. He was backed by financiers in England and put much of his own money into the venture as well. But he fell on hard times and lost much of his crew due to raids and disease. Things were looking bad for him until he came across what he later claimed he thought was a legitimate quarry. It was a rich target, carrying gold and silver, and sailing under a French banner. Unfortunately for Mr. Kidd, while it sailed with French papers, the ship was actually an Indian vessel and was captained by an Englishman. This incident, along with other accounts of similar run-ins with Kidd's crew, led his financiers back home to become squirely, and he was declared an outlaw and a pirate. Knowing he was in trouble and the law was closing in on him, Kidd began traveling the coast of the eastern United States, making frequent stops and burying his loot. See, he was in possession of documents proving that his raid on the French ship was legitimate, but he refused to turn himself in with his fortune in hand, so legend says that he spread it out on various islands along the coast and drew himself cryptic maps to lead him back. He eventually surrendered himself in Boston, but those vital documents were confiscated and subsequently lost, leading to his being found guilty and sentenced to hang. Now here's where it gets real interesting; he wrote a letter to the Speaker of the House of Commons pleading for his life. He said he had what would nowadays be twenty-million dollars' worth of treasure buried, and that he could lead them to its location if he were to be spared. Well, he was not spared, he was hanged, and his claim became legendary. Supposed maps drawn by William Kidd himself have been recovered over the years, and teams still to this day search the shores where he was known to have sailed, hoping to come across his legendary treasure."

Mr. Pyrene grinned around the classroom, clearly quite impressed with the tale he had just presented, and Kat was happy to see that several of her heavy-eyed classmates had perked up a little bit during his story. But Kat herself was fascinated. Mr. Pyrene spent the rest of the class going through details of the various treasure hunts and projecting an assortment of pictures, some of which actually showed Captain Kidd's supposed treasure maps, and Kat happily absorbed it all.

By the time class was over, the only slightly more awake group of students began shuffling out into the hall, but Kat stayed behind a few paces and walked timidly up to Mr. Pyrene. He grinned as he saw her, clearly having noticed and appreciated her enthusiastic attention during his lecture.

"Kat!" he addressed her exuberantly. "How was your first day in Cryptohistory?"

"It was amazing," Kat gushed, and then, deciding she was coming across as a little too eager, she backpedaled and rephrased, "I mean, it was an interesting lesson."

Mr. Pyrene nodded enthusiastically and said, "You're going to love this class, Kat. The mysteries in our world are endless, you have no idea. I'll do my best to present you with all the best ones."

"Do you have a favorite?" Kat asked, "a favorite mystery you want solved?"

Mr. Pyrene grinned broadly. "Of course I do! An obsession, really. I've gone on trips around the globe looking for answers to this one."

"Really?" Kat wondered at him. "Looking for treasure?"

Mr. Pyrene shook his head, "Not treasure, not this one. More looking for knowledge I suppose. It'll be an upcoming lesson, I don't want to spoil it for you!" But he looked as though he could hardly contain himself, and he continued, "have you ever heard of 'The Hand of Jordan'?"

Kat furrowed her brow. "I don't think so."

Mr. Pyrene nodded in excitement and was practically bouncing on the balls of his feet. "Well I won't give it away just yet, but I personally think it is one of the most fascinating finds in our history, and the story surrounding its discovery is the stuff of legend. The look on your face today, that was the same look I had when I first heard the story of Nick Satterall!"

Kat and Mr. Pyrene spoke for a few more minutes before she thanked him again for the lecture and set out onto the bright, sunny grounds. 'Math for Survival' hadn't been bad, but 'Cryptohistory' had been amazing. She had never been a bad student, but it still surprised her immensely when she realized she couldn't wait for Dean Pyrene's next lesson.

AN ECHO FROM AFAR

1955

Y ou've gotta be kidding me," Nick Satterall grunted, extending his neck as far out as it would go and peering over the edge of the sheer cliffside. His stomach lurched as his gaze found the crashing waves hundreds of feet below and an image of himself falling popped into his head. There would be no surviving from this height if something were to go wrong. "Are you having a go at me?"

Mauretz, who was wisely, or suspiciously, standing a good five feet back from the ledge, shook his head and insisted, "I swear, there's a cave down there. At least that's what they're saying."

"Down where?" Nick demanded harshly, scanning what he could see of the rockface below through the darkness. "How far down are we talking?"

"It's only ten feet down or so," Mauretz said brightly with a confidence only afforded to someone who would not have to make the climb themselves.

It occurred to Nick that perhaps Mauretz had found out about receiving a lower cut of the last sale and was hoping to see his companion meet a grisly end, but how could he have found out? It was true that Nick had scored big with the contents of that clay urn a few months back, and Mauretz did not collect his fair cut in the strictest sense, but there was no way he could know that. Nick had driven four towns over just to unload the damn thing. He and Mauretz had gone radio-silent since that date, just as they said they would, until a tantalizing rumor reached Nick's ears. Mauretz reported that a small cave had been found in the side of a steep rock wall that overhung the unforgiving coast of the Dead Sea. How anyone had come across a cave in such an inhospitable place was beyond Nick's comprehension, but whatever artifact had been found inside was generating quite the fervor in town. Nick had even heard about it before Mauretz had contacted him, an uncommon occurrence. Just as they had done a few months back, and time and time again before that, Nick and Mauretz had travelled out to the site of the planned excavation in the dead of night, hoping to scoop up the loot before the proper permits had been obtained by the team.

Looking down at the roiling white waves crashing far below, however, Nick was having second thoughts about how profitable this rumored artifact could actually be.

"There's something down there, I promise you," Mauretz said, apparently correctly sensing Nick's trepidation and likely not wanting to miss out on his own payday.

Nick sighed heavily and began looking around. He would have to use the winch on the front of Mauretz's car to repel down, and looking over the rust-bucket of a vehicle now, Nick wondered if it would actually hold his weight. Nick swore under his breath and pointed a threatening finger at Mauretz.

"You damn well better be right about this," Nick growled, and he started preparing a rope into a makeshift harness.

It was another twenty minutes until Nick was comfortable with the knots he had secured around his body and fastened to the end of the winch. He gingerly tested his weight over the edge of the cliff, praying that the car was up to the challenge. A loud metallic groan as he leaned back almost caused him to lose his nerve, but the apparatus seemed to hold. He shot Mauretz one last withering look, gave a casual salute, and took his first backward step down the side of the cliff. The car remained mercifully quiet this time, so he took another step down, followed by another. There was plenty of moonlight bathing the bluff in a cool blue glow, allowing him to leave his flashlight tucked away and his hands, thankfully, free. But after about ten feet of downward climbing, he starting to consider abandoning the plan. What if Mauretz really was trying to get him killed?

No sooner had the uncomfortable thought popped into his head than his foot stepped down into nothingness. Nick's heart stopped for a moment and his body went rigid, but the harness held. He mumbled another curse and gathered his courage once again. If there wasn't stone below his feet, it must mean he had arrived at the entrance to the promised cave, even if he couldn't see it from this angle. With a deep, leveling breath, he restarted his rappel downward and found himself face to face with the black, yawning maw of a hole in the side of the cliff. Perhaps not quite a cave, but certainly an alcove at least. Nick sighed in relief when he was able to plant his feet on level ground again just inside the entrance and it was only then that he dared release his grip on the rope and un-pocket his flashlight. With an echoing click, the light turned on and bathed the stone room in a warm, albeit artificial, amber glow.

Unlike in the unassuming sandy hole that he had taken the clay urn from, he did not have to search for the relic in question. Nick approached slowly, dragging the ropes of the harness and the wire from the winch behind him. On the far wall of the cave was an extremely clear brownish-copper handprint with the fingers splayed out around it. He had seen cave art before, but this looked different. In fact, it didn't look artful at all, more like someone had been injured and leaned against the wall for support. But if it truly was made of blood, could it have survived the ages so well? And just below the hand, on a small outcropping of stone that served nicely as a natural shelf, were several objects all lined up neatly. What first struck Nick was how the artifacts had been *placed*. He would often find ancient objects strewn about or hidden, in various states of disrepair and in the process of being re-claimed by time. These objects before him now were *displayed*.

Nick squinted through the dusty darkness and crept closer, the incessant waves of the sea continuing to crash below and echo around the cave walls. They were figures of some sort, hewn out of stone and intricately crafted with crude yet exquisitely expressive detail. Two portrayed humans and the third some sort of bird-like creature. One of the humans stood up straight with his shoulders squared impressively and a staff clutched in one hand. There was something striking about this figure that set it apart from the others, a nobility almost. The other human was slighter in stature with a hood over his head and a scowl of defiance marring his features. He too held a staff although seemed to lean more heavily on it when compared to his counterpart. Rounding out the strange collection was a small fragment of burnt wood, an oddity that could easily have been dismissed as garbage except for its clear placement of importance amongst the figures. But was it burnt wood? As the beam from the flashlight danced along the rustic shelf, the fragment twinkled crimson in color, as though it held a secret just beneath its charred surface. Nick reached out, then paused. A strange sensation was overtaking him, almost like a whisper in his ear warning him not to touch the strange object. He shook his head but still held back. He allowed his fingertips to hover an inch from its surface as though feeling for an energy he couldn't see. Finally, he brushed its surface delicately, then lifted the piece from its ancient resting place with the tips of two fingers. He brought it to eye level and turned it over in his hand, allowing the light to trickle into its many divots and fissures. It was entrancing to stare at. While the outer shell on one side did indeed look like burnt bark, the rest almost looked to be made of ruby. It was unlike anything Nick had ever held before.

There came a sharp tug on Nick's harness, and it snapped him back to reality. He blinked and shook his head, then cursed Mauretz for his apparent impatience. He drew a small canvas pouch from his belt and collected the carved figures from their shelf. He tossed them unceremoniously into the bag and started to do the same with the ruby fragment, but then paused. He didn't know what it was he held, but he found that he strangely did not want to part with it. For the right price he was certainly willing to sell it, but a funny sensation seemed to accompany the artifact. It felt like he was holding something that he wasn't supposed to, that wasn't supposed to be here in the first place.

Nick shook his head to dismiss the crazy notion and rolled his eyes at his own superstition. And yet he didn't toss the fragment into the pouch. He scrunched the bag closed with the leather tie and returned it to his belt with the figures clinking mildly inside, and his other hand closed around the small ruby shard. This he placed into his opposite pocket. Perhaps he would reconsider its importance later when the daylight washed away the fanciful romance and mysteries of the night, but for now he intended to keep it only for himself.

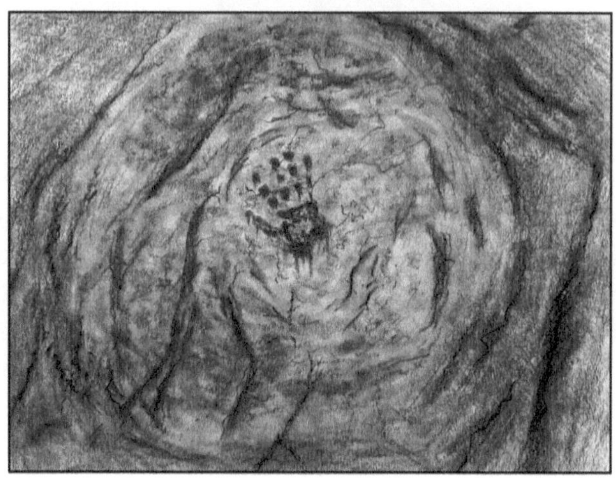

CHAPTER FIVE

THE HAND OF JORDAN

2018

A few months through and Kat had settled nicely into college life. She was doing well in all of her classes, had met a few acquaintances who were well on their way to becoming real friends, and was generally enjoying life. A party she had attended last weekend had not been the unmitigated disaster she conjured in her head prior to going, and it seemed to have given her social life an unexpected shot of adrenaline. Now people in the halls of her dorm and on the lawns of the campus would greet her enthusiastically, having formed some trivial bond by sharing a memory with her at the party. She accepted that universal social norm, and even found herself smiling at the flurry of attention, but she had always been someone who sought deeper bonds with those in her life, and each of these people would have to earn their place as a real friend. It was with that mindset that she found herself reflecting, with a certain degree of guilt, on the person she had bonded the most with over the past few months. Mr. Pyrene's Cryptohistory class had continued to fascinate Kat, and she had taken to hanging behind after her peers left to discuss various mysteries with her knowledgeable teacher.

As she shuffled into his now familiar cramped classroom, Mr. Pyrene gave her an exuberant nod of his head and a beaming smile while she found her seat. He pointed to the blackboard behind him which had written across it in a messy scrawl, '*The Hand of Jordan*'.

Mr. Pyrene announced the subject of the lecture with a dramatic flourish and then grinned at the dumbfounded lack of response from the sleepy class. "I know you've likely never heard of this piece of history, and I'm not surprised. It's a mystery that plagued archeologists in the Middle East, but it never quite gained traction in our history books. But this has been my obsession since I was very young, and it's maddeningly unsolved. The Hand of Jordan refers to a bloody handprint discovered in a cave overlooking the Dead Sea back in the fifties. It loomed over a small collection of artifacts; three stone statues, two of which were human and one of which was not. The human figures were examined thoroughly and while they could not be definitively tied to any leaders in history, experts agreed that their features were far too specific to have originated from imagination alone."

With an unnecessary amount of theatrical flair, Mr. Pyrene clicked a remote in his hand which ignited a projector behind him. The image showed a close-up of two ornately carved figurines in exquisite high definition. The two human statues immediately gave Kat the sense of nobility, but almost opposite ends of the spectrum. One stood upright while the other slouched, one wore an expression of regal defiance, the other a hateful scowl. But they both portrayed strength and conjured an image of supreme importance.

"What's the first thing you notice about these figures?" Mr. Pyrene asked the class, but his expectant eyes fell quickly to Kat.

Kat, who was by now used to being one of the only active participants in Cryptohistory, furrowed her brow and examined the image. She was ready to point out the juxtaposition of demeanor between the two when her eyes fell to the bases they stood on. Each one had a small yet unmistakable crown carved into the stand. It confirmed the regality she had so clearly felt when she first saw them.

"They're kings," Kat observed, "they each have a crown carved beneath them, but they seem to be opposites."

Mr. Pyrene beamed. "Very good, Kat! Yes that's exactly right, these artifacts do indeed appear to represent kings, and likely opposing sides as you rightly pointed out to us. But before we get too far into the weeds with dissecting their origins, I want to bring your attention to the third figure."

Mr. Pyrene changed the slide and an image of a carved birdlike creature filled the screen. It stood in a charging position, indicating powerful aggression, had enormous eyes that looked unnaturally large for its head, and an open hooked beak like an eagle on steroids. It was unlike any animal Kat had ever seen, leading her to one conclusion; this was a work of fantasy.

"Interesting creature, huh?" Mr. Pyrene asked. "Take a look at the base."

The base showed a horse head, which Kat found exceptionally odd. This was clearly not a carving of a horse.

"The horse denotes a knight in the game of chess," Mr. Pyrene explained in answer to the unasked question. "That along with the crowns on the first two figures... these are chess pieces. But again, experts agree the kings were based on real people." He switched the slide back to the image of the kings. "Look at the likeness in the faces. What else do you notice?"

Another student in class warily raised his hand and said, "That one has something on his face."

Mr. Pyrene nodded vigorously, "That's right! An injury possibly? A war wound? We don't know, but what experts *do* agree on is that the mark is intentional. The artist deliberately carved that rough patch into his face, again indicating a real-life person. It's not unusual for carvings from ancient history to be based on real leaders or deities of the time, but no record has been uncovered so far of a king with a facial wound of this type. It also makes one wonder about the staffs that the kings are holding. They seem to be identical, again indicating a dichotomy. And of course, if these two are based on real people, it begs the question..."

Mr. Pyrene changed the slide back to the birdlike creature, "what the hell is this thing?"

Kat stared at the creature for a good ten seconds, taking in the bristles along its back, the slit pupils, the muscular neck, and the horrible talons. Mr. Pyrene was right, it certainly seemed as though the artist had actually seen this creature. The idea sent a shiver down her spine.

"These artifacts were collected by a man named Nick Satterall. He was what's known as a vulture in archeology circles, someone unaffiliated with the excavation team who sneaks in and steals the prize before it can be retrieved by experts. While the artifacts can often be re-obtained on the black market, the site has been irrevocably damaged and so much of history is lost as a result. But here's where we enter into rumors and guesswork. According to local legend, Satterall also recovered a curious stone fragment from the site, and he became so enamored with the piece that he refused to sell it with the rest of his loot. Authorities became wise to his scheme, and his withholding of the odd artifact, but he wouldn't tell anyone what he had done with it." Mr. Pyrene paused for dramatic effect before concluding, "History doesn't know what happened to Nick Satterall. He vanished from all record after that, and the small fragment along with him."

Kat raised her hand tentatively. "Do we have any idea what the fragment was? How do we know it wasn't just a stone?"

Mr. Pyrene changed the slide and it projected a colored pencil sketch of a small piece of what looked like bark with red ribbons of ruby shining from beneath its fractured surface.

"We don't know who drew this, but it was obtained by the Museum of Antiquities in London after its discovery in an old law enforcement outpost in Jordan during a renovation. What is it? We don't know. Was it perhaps a precious gem of some sort? And if so, why not sell it? These are questions we may never find answers to. Then of course there's the bloody handprint that gives the find its name. When the excavation team was able to get to the site, it was the one thing Nick Satterall hadn't disturbed. You can now see the section of stone wall with the bloody handprint, along with the chess pieces, on display at the Museum of Antiquities in London. It's a small exhibit because most historians think of it as a mildly curious tale and nothing more. Present company excluded of course."

Mr. Pyrene finished his lecture with a broad, boyish smile, but the stuffy silence from the classroom made it clear that his passion for this particular story had not been as infectious as he had anticipated. Kat herself found the tale to be quite interesting, but her fascination was certainly dampened by the lack of resolution. Mr. Pyrene had warned the class up front that many of these mysteries would not have satisfying answers, but with this particular piece of history, Kat felt she had very little to sink her teeth into. There *could* be a puzzle to solve, but it could just as likely be nothing at all. Perhaps someone had simply carved some chess pieces and left them in a cave.

The lesson continued for another half-hour, with Mr. Pyrene examining various far-flung theories about the find and comparing the figures to other ancient chess carvings. As always, he did not allow the class's lack of enthusiasm to inhibit his own, indeed he seemed to become more animated the more he lectured on the subject. Kat found it endearing as always and felt perhaps a bit guilty that she was not as invested in this favorite mystery of his.

When class ended, Kat hung behind as she always did, but this time Mr. Pyrene did not wait for her to approach his desk before addressing her.

"I'm going!" Mr. Pyrene exclaimed, "winter break in a week, I'm heading to London! I've never actually seen the *Hand* itself, and it's time I changed that!"

Kat couldn't help but smile at his unbridled excitement, excitement that he was clearly looking for her to share. "But you said it was a small exhibit," Kat said, "you're flying all the way to Europe for that?"

As soon as she had said it, she felt immense regret for not faking her exuberance better, but to her relief Mr. Pyrene just grinned back at her. "I know what you're thinking," he answered, "it's not the splashiest mystery I've talked about, but I promise you, there's something to this story, I can feel it in my gut."

Kat laughed and shook her head, supremely thankful that she had not offended him. "What are you hoping the exhibit will show that you don't already know?"

Mr. Pyrene paused and tilted his head back and forth uncertainly, as though debating how to phrase something. "What I desperately want is that blood from the cave wall to be DNA tested." He seemed almost embarrassed to admit this. "Being able to identify what nationality that person was would go such a long way to better understanding that find. You see, Nick Satterall had trouble unloading the chess pieces because they didn't reflect classic artistic traits from the area. Generally, artifacts from a certain region and time period have an identifiable *style*, for lack of a better word, but those chess pieces did not match the area."

"Well you said the cave was along the coast of the sea, right?" Kat offered, "Maybe it was someone from elsewhere traveling by boat?"

Mr. Pyrene beamed again. "It's definitely a theory. One of many. But historians seem infuriatingly, stubbornly opposed to looking further into it. Sometimes I feel like I'm the only one in the world who cares about this mystery."

Kat smiled and bit her tongue, but Mr. Pyrene seemed to have noticed her look. He smiled as well. "Okay, okay," he nodded, "I see your point."

"It's too bad you can't get just a tiny swab of that blood," Kat said, deciding to throw him a bone, "you could send it to one of those genealogy labs and see where the owner came from."

Kat had meant this as a hypothetical dream rather than a real suggestion, but Mr. Pyrene lit up all the same. "That's not a bad idea!"

"But you can't get a swab of the blood," Kat reminded him, somewhat alarmed that he had taken the idea so literally.

"You're right, you're right," Mr. Pyrene said with a wave of his hand, but his eyes still looked entranced and dreamy. "You know Kat, it's students like you that keep me doing what I do. If I could have just one of you in every class who would really, truly absorb what I teach them and appreciate the history of the world in the way I do..." He shook his head with a grin.

"I can't wait to hear how your trip goes," she said.

"I don't know if I'll find any answers," Mr. Pyrene admitted, "but ya never know!"

The way he said this last part made Kat almost wonder if he had some plan up his sleeve, or perhaps some piece of information he was not sharing. Either way she just smiled back, once again enchanted by his endless enthusiasm for the subject.

CHAPTER SIX

BUYER BEWARE

1955

For the first time in his illustrious career as an artifact thief, Nick Satterall could not unload his loot. It had been a month since he had rappelled into that cave on the coast of the Dead Sea, and despite numerous meetings with various black-market dealers, no one was interested in the three enigmatic stone carvings he had procured. Nick was no historian, but to his eye, the small statues were captivating in their detail and mysterious in their creation. Apparently, that was exactly the issue these dealers were questioning. Three separate potential buyers told him the origins of the find were questionable at best, with one even stating directly that the artifacts were either staged or some sort of hoax. No one had been impressed with the bird-like creature, which he had been told did not match any known cultural lore, and the carving style was described as 'non-descript' or 'unfamiliar' when compared to the established historical techniques of the area. Furthermore, his last attempted contact had insisted the sculptures were crafted within the last twenty years or so, making them not historical artifacts but potentially the work of a local vagrant. None of this squared with Nick's view of the find in the cave, which he was certain held some significance, even if these uneducated wannabe-scholars said otherwise.

Now here Nick stood, in the dusty, dark back of a third-rate shop presenting the three carvings to the very last of his numerous contacts. Even before the wizened, wrinkled old shop owner proclaimed his thoughts, Nick could tell by his reaction that it would not be good news.

"I don't know what these are supposed to be, Nick," the shop owner croaked with a shake of his bearded, balding head. He put the piece that he had been examining down carefully, clearly trying to appease Nick rather than out of genuine concern for its safety.

"What do you mean?" Nick demanded, as though he hadn't had the same conversation near a dozen times in the last four weeks. "This is a major find, you'll wanna jump on this before someone else does. I have a lot of interest…"

With a shrug, the shop owner said, "Sell to them, if you've got offers out there. That's my advice to you. Because I don't know what these are, but they don't match any culture that I'm familiar with."

"Okay but doesn't that make you wonder?" Nick insisted with wide, hopefully entrancing eyes. He would have to push the narrative that these were mysterious to persuade of their value.

"It does indeed," the shop owner demurred with a slight raise of his bushy eyebrows. It was an accusation. He was insinuating that Nick was trying to pull one over on him.

"You should be thankful I even came to you with this you washed up old shit!" Nick snapped. "I shouldn't have even bothered stooping to this level."

"And why did you?" the shop owner retorted with a crooked smirk. "I didn't invite you to come here. It sounds like you've been turned down all over town."

"You're turning down a fortune old man," Nick growled, gathering the carvings up roughly. He turned to leave, but stopped. His pride got the better of him and he shoved his hand into his pocket, producing the small ruby shard and holding it up between his thumb and forefinger.

"This was found at the same site. Tell me, what local vagrant would have a gem of this kind in their collection?"

The shop owner squinted at the object and reached out to examine it, but Nick withdrew his hand. "Ah ah ah, you had your chance, old-timer."

The shop owner looked confused rather than disappointed, however. "It's a gem?" he asked. "It looks more like a piece of old bark."

"To your untrained eyes maybe," Nick laughed. "Just know you had a shot at this, but that's gone now. Good luck with your *shop*." He gave a condescending glance around the piles of dust-covered objects, pocketed the fragment, and stormed out into the dazzling sunlight.

Nick squinted this way and that, his eyes being forced shut by both the intense midday sun and the dust from the road being kicked up around him. The street was alive with hundreds of people jostling their way past each other, brushing shoulder to shoulder down the over-crowded corridor. Nick pushed his long curtain of bangs out of his face and began weaving his way back towards his car. If these artifacts really were worthless, perhaps he should just dump them. They were stolen pieces after all, and it wouldn't do to have them in his possession for much longer, especially if they weren't going to offer a payout. The fragment they were all wrong about, however. Something in his gut told him it held significance, even if he couldn't say why.

As he turned a corner down a side street, having to force his way against the flow of foot traffic, a man appeared up ahead that gave him pause. With the amount of people bustling about their days, it was surprising that any one figure would stand out, but this man had an authoritative way about him that screamed law enforcement. And he wasn't moving with the crowd either; he was standing back and surveying the passerby, as though searching for someone. Even so, it wasn't until his eyes locked on Nick that he recognized he was in real trouble.

"Christ," Nick muttered, and attempted to change course amongst the parade of people. Sure enough, the man started pursuing him, slowly at first but urgently nonetheless.

Nick glanced over his shoulder several times, confirming that the man was definitely following him, then quickly ducked down another street. This one was more sparsely populated, allowing him to pick up his pace, but the man emerged from the crowd moments later and suddenly broke into a run.

Nick cursed and bolted. His footsteps and those of his assailant echoed down the narrow passageway and several passerby watched the pursuit in alarm. Nick put on a fresh burst of speed, aiming for the next busy street and hoping to lose the man in the crowd. An old rickshaw with a missing wheel was leaning against a clay wall right before the entrance of the street and Nick decided to use it as leverage. He leaped onto the seat with one foot and launched himself out over the heads of the people before crashing down amongst them with his arms flailing. Several people spilled to the ground from being shoved but Nick didn't notice or care. He barreled onward, pushing people indiscriminately and forcefully cutting a path.

He crossed the street with immense effort and ducked through the door of a shop across the way. The owner looked shocked at his sudden appearance but Nick refused to break momentum and stampeded straight past him and into the connecting room with a back door. He stumbled through it into the back alley, but the situation was becoming dire. If the authorities were onto him, it was almost inconceivable that they would only have sent one agent, meaning others were likely stalking the neighboring streets waiting for him to be flushed out. It was a losing fight; his only hope would be to stash his loot until the danger passed.

Nick looked around wildly, searching for somewhere he could hide the carved pieces. It wasn't out of concern for their safety, as he was fast learning they were in fact worthless, but because being caught with them would condemn him. Without them, they couldn't prove anything. Out of desperation, he chose a bit of dusty piping sticking out of the side of a building to hide the artifacts. It protruded just above eye level, making them impossible to see if one were walking down the street. Besides, it wasn't permanent, he would be back for them as soon as he was out of trouble. He pulled the pouch containing the pieces from his pocket and moved to stash them, but paused. After a few seconds debate, he reached into his other pocket, pulled out the fragment of ruby bark and tossed it into the pouch as well. The entire package he then tossed onto the top of the pipe and began walking towards the nearest main street in a would-be casual manner. But it seemed his dropping of the loot was done just in time, for a shout from behind alerted him to the return of his pursuer. Nick bolted once again and wove onto the main thoroughfare, hoping one last time to ditch the man in the crowd.

Shoving a rickshaw aside aggressively, Nick turned down yet another alleyway but to his horror, he found the far end blocked by a beefy man with a neck the size of the average leg. Nick turned back the way he had come but his original antagonist had finally caught up with him and was walking forward tentatively.

Nick finally threw up his arms in resigned defeat and said, "Something I can help you boys with?"

"Nick Satterall?" the original man demanded.

"Ah no, you must be confused," Nick responded unconvincingly. "I'm just a tourist."

"Yeah, this picture says otherwise," the man said, brandishing a poor-quality copy of some sort of modern-day wanted poster.

"You got a badge or something?" Nick asked, "or are you just sheriff of your own volition?"

"We've been looking for you a long time," the man said, approaching closer.

"Now wait a minute," Nick began, scanning the surrounding area for an exit. "I'm sure we can work something out right here and now; there's no need to overcomplicate things. If its money you boys are looking for, maybe I can help you out with, let's say…"

"They're not letting you wiggle your way out of this one, Nick," the man cut in, "you're coming with us to the main office. After that, I guess it's up to you how cooperative you wanna be."

Nick held his hands out defensively as the man stepped closer and said, "Wait wait wait, I think I know who you're looking for. It's this man named Mauretz. He's been trying to sell excavation secrets all over town, let me walk and I'll tell you exactly where you can find him."

"Sorry Nick," the man answered, "this is the end of the line for you."

Nick turned on his heel and sprinted to the side of the alleyway with the intention of climbing up some exposed piping and onto the rooves, but the big-necked man had moved much closer than Nick realized and grabbed his forearm with a catchers-mitt of a hand. Nick turned and punched the man, but it appeared to have little effect. The man wrapped a python-sized arm around Nick's neck and easily held him against his chest, making any hopes of escape futile.

"Go to hell, the both of you." Nick yelled rather lamely, and the first man just smiled.

"I think you'll end up there first," the man smirked, and they escorted him back to his car and drove him out of town.

CHAPTER SEVEN

FRAGMENT OF THE PAST

2018

W hat in the world was he thinking? Despite that blaring, incessant question continuing to prod at the back of his subconscious, Dean Pyrene kept pushing it aside. He was a tenured professor of history and this was no way for a well-respected man of academics to behave. He probably wouldn't follow through with his ridiculous plan anyways, so it was likely best if he simply put it out of his mind. And yet, he had carefully packed a swab and a vial in his pocket when he had boarded his flight to London and had made sure it was still undisturbed when he entered the line for the Museum of Antiquities.

Now here he stood, watching the small throng of tourists and daytrippers scan their tickets and enter the museum, sweating bullets and shaking slightly, even though he knew he would probably lose his nerve and drop his asinine idea. When Kat Killion had mentioned the possibility of testing the blood from the Hand of Jordan through a genealogy lab, she hadn't been making a serious suggestion. And yet she was right, that was the simplest way to find out what nationality that blood was from. He would not have to resort to such measures at all if the rest of the historical community were to give even a shred of attention to the mystery. Here it sat, behind the imposing marble walls of the museum, in the lower level at the very far back corner, collecting dust and being visited by no one. At least that's how Dean imagined it. Perhaps he would find the exhibit bustling with excited visitors giving it plenty of well-deserved attention and he would find the excuse he needed to abandon his foolhardy plan.

Alas, after Dean finally entered the museum and wove his way deeper and deeper through its many mystical and enchanting halls, he found himself turning down a narrow corridor to a dusty exhibit tucked neatly in a back corner of a dimly lit room, facing at last his beloved mysterious relic, being visited by no one. The roughly four-foot by three-foot section of stone wall that had been exported from the cave in Jordan made up the majority of the miniscule exhibit, the faded copper handprint placed at an angle right in its center. Below the slab and off to the right were the three carved chess pieces, and to the left a plaque that titled the find and explored, in minimal detail, the story of its discovery.

Dean approached slowly before leaning in close to examine the chess pieces. They were smaller than he expected, but incredibly detailed. He was once again certain that the artist based these carvings on real people... and a real creature. His eyes wandered to the small plaque and scanned the words briefly with mounting disgust. Nick Satterall was not listed by name, only referred to as 'a thief', and there was no mention of the small shard he pocketed at all. Finally, Dean's gaze fell to the handprint itself, the centerpiece of the laughable exhibit and the only artifact on display with appropriate lighting. Dean was so ready to give up on his absurd plan that he was almost disappointed to find how easy it would actually be to collect a swab of the blood. The small section of cave wall that bore the handprint was mounted behind an equal sized sheet of plexiglass and not protected along the sides. The glass was meant to prevent some idiot from sneezing on it perhaps, but did nothing to stop someone from poking their fingers around the side and touching the stone itself. And if said fingers happened to be holding a

Q-Tip with a bit of solution to lift a tiny amount of blood from the imprint, it would do nothing to prevent that either.

Dean sighed and glanced shiftily over his shoulder. Was he really going to do this? No one was here to stop him. With his heart beating painfully fast and his hands shaking terribly, he reached into his pocket and withdrew the small vial, unscrewed the top, and produced the moistened Q-Tip from within. He did another quick scan over his shoulder to ensure he was truly alone, then began to lean in towards the exposed side of the glass display. His fingers barely fit behind the sheet but he ignored the painful scraping against his knuckle as he fed them in as deep as they could go, outstretching the Q-Tip as he went. He was almost surprised when he saw the tip of the tool reach the edge of the ancient, dried blood, having been certain some obstacle would present itself at some point during this scheme. Invested now, Dean touched the white tip to the dark blood and began to roll it, watching as the cotton discolored to a pinkish hue. Satisfied he had enough of a sample, he retracted the swab from behind the glass and hurriedly bottled it up and stuffed everything back into his pockets. An echoing laugh rang out from down the hall and Dean jumped about a foot in the air, but when he turned around, he realized it must have come from the next corridor down.

Deciding he had no desire to stay any longer than absolutely necessary with his nerves the way they were, Dean began striding in what he hoped was a confident manner down the hall and back up the marble staircase. He didn't dare breathe a sigh of relief until he stumbled back out the main double-doors and let the foggy dampness of the morning air wash over him. He did a final turn on the spot, just to make absolutely sure no one was following him, but of course no one was. It was as he had expected all along; nobody much cared for this particular mystery.

Dean looked down at his watch and was relieved to see it was only a quarter past nine in the morning. That was just about perfect. He had neglected to tell Kat the real reason he had decided to visit London on this particular date. Dean had found out that an elderly man had died in his home only a few miles from where he now stood; a man by the name of Mauretz Abernally. Though reports were vague, Dean was certain that this man was the very same Mauretz who had worked with Nick Satterall when he discovered the Hand of Jordan on that cliffside in 1955. History didn't know what became of Nick Satterall, but reports persisted of Mauretz's life. From what Dean had been able to piece together, Mauretz had emigrated to London at some point in the eighties and lived out a quiet life following his prior adventures with Nick. He had been the closest thing Nick had to a friend, according to reports, and could potentially have known what became of that mysterious ruby fragment. Dean always felt that, given Nick's complete and total disappearance from all record, Mauretz was the next logical lead.

Mauretz had died last week, however, taking many of his potential secrets with him. But perhaps not all of them. As it turned out, he had died a lonely man with no beneficiaries. That meant his house was being subjected to an estate sale to get rid of all his belongings, and the sale was occurring today, in a little under an hour. Dean skipped a couple steps at the thought and smiled to himself as he looked around for transportation.

*****

Dean's elation deflated the moment he stepped foot through the worn-down front door into the dingy, carpeted living room. Mauretz's estate was not what Dean had anticipated from someone so involved with antiquities in his past life. He had been expecting a house brimming with artifacts and treasures, mysteries and maps; what he found was something more akin to the hovel of a hoarder. Dean surveyed the front living room with relative disgust. Instead of relics from history, there were old newspapers and magazines, bargain-bin glassware and boxes of useless trinkets. There seemed to be every odd and end one would typically find at a local thrift store… except nothing of value.

He spent the next hour laboring through every box and rifling through every shelf, but to no avail. The two women running the sale seemed all too aware that there was nothing of value within Mauretz Abernally's peeling walls, for they were giving items away by the armful without much of a glance at the contents. Most of the potential shoppers wore the same look of wrinkle-nosed contempt as they poked around briefly at the myriad of junk before hastily exiting the premises. But not Dean. He would not be content until he had looked through every cabinet and every bin, just to be sure no artifact or clue existed.

Dean nearly tripped down the narrow staircase as he made his way to the second floor, weaving between overflowing boxes teetering precariously on each step. When he finally entered the deceased man's bedroom, a sour, heavy odor reached his nose that made him wonder if Mauretz had died in here. The room was far more empty than the lower level, leaving Dean to guess that everything had been boxed and moved downstairs for the ease of the customers. There were several empty cabinets, a dresser, a bedside table with a broken lamp, and a wall-to-wall carpet that showed a clear path worn into it leading from the bed to the doorway. Dean committed to spending as little time in the suffocating room as possible, but resigned to searching it all the same. He first started rummaging through the sparse belongings in the rickety cabinet, and became briefly excited when he discovered several chess pieces rolling around in the back of one of the drawers. Alas, they were plastic and stamped with a manufacturer date of 1991. Dean tossed them aside in disappointment and moved his attention to the dresser. Upon opening the top drawer, he was surprised to find clothes still jammed into it, forced in so aggressively that the drawer could barely slide out. He began throwing the assortment of tee shirts and socks onto the bed, at the very least insistent on seeing the bottom of each drawer before giving up hope. And then he heard it… a small stone clattering out of one of the balled-up shirts and bouncing across the bedroom floor.

Dean's eyes widened and he began scouring for where the stone had fallen, not daring to get too excited just yet. At that moment, a woman entered the bedroom and Dean tried to act casual, not wanting to draw attention to his hunt. But he had lost track of where the mystery object had bounced. He probably looked deranged with the contents of the man's wardrobe spilled out over the bed, but when he looked up to the woman and offered a friendly smile, he realized her eyes were locked onto the floor in the corner of the room. Dean couldn't see what she was looking at from his position, but his heart dropped all the same. Whatever it had been, and he was purposely stopping himself from fantasizing, the woman seemed to be intrigued by it as well.

Her eyes narrowed and she took a step towards the corner where the object had fallen. "Is that...?" She took another cautious step. "Is that some sort of gem?"

It was all Dean needed to hear. He barreled forward, all pretense of acting natural for the social interaction gone. He knocked the bedside table roughly with his hip and cut in front of the curious woman, reached down and snatched the small object from the ground without even getting a good look at it.

The woman looked affronted by the behavior but Dean found he could not care less. His heart was hammering almost painfully as he straightened up and opened his trembling fist.

Resting benignly in his palm was a small piece of what looked like burnt bark, but it was heavier than wood and felt much harder. And as he tilted his hand, the light from the hallway caught a ribbon of ruby stone twinkling from its core and confirming the truth of its identity.

"I was looking at that, you know," the woman said snippily from over his shoulder, but Dean ignored her. He was entranced by the tiny artifact. It was without a doubt the fragment that Nick Satterall had found in the cave alongside the chess pieces, and now Dean could understand why he had trouble parting with it. There was nothing inherently valuable-looking about the piece, but it had a quality to it that was undeniable, as if it held a long-lost secret so far buried that it was imperceptible to the modern eye.

"Am I gonna need to call someone?" the woman insisted again, and she held out her hand expectantly.

Dean looked into her pinched, scowling face for the first time and his patience with her did not improve. "Every police in the city couldn't pry this from me," he snarled against his better judgement, and he brushed past out into the hall and galloped down the stairs.

Once on the main floor, he glanced around quickly, looking for something to buy alongside the fragment. Paranoid though it may have been, he did not want to risk the salespeople questioning the value of what he was buying. His eyes landed on a mostly empty box with a snow globe and a dusty beer stein laying in it, which he snatched up hastily and tossed the fragment into. He brought the box of oddities to the table by the front door and offered a would-be-casual smile to the elderly woman staffing it.

"Find some good stuff, hon?" the woman asked conversationally in a gravelly, smokers' voice.

"I really did," Dean nodded and handed over his payment.

Once out in the dreary midday air, raindrops started pattering intermittently against his head, but nothing could dampen his spirits. He quickly reached into the box and extracted the priceless fragment, closing his fist around it greedily and glancing over his shoulder for that unpleasant woman from the second floor. Finding no one behind him, Dean identified the nearest trash bin and tossed the box into it, along with the snow globe and mug.

He put another block between himself and the estate sale before he dared another peek at his prize, but when he finally did, his eyes widened and glowed with wonder once again. He was holding a piece of history he had been studying as far back as he could remember. The chess pieces were the flashy part of the story, and the bloody handprint added a healthy dose of macabre intrigue, but the rumored ruby fragment that Nick Satterall had refused to part with, that was the source of Dean's obsession. It made no sense in the tale, and yet holding it now, Dean couldn't help but feel it made complete sense, in an incomprehensible way. As Dean gazed down at his newly acquired treasure, he strangely did not want to part with it either, even for the purposes of research. There was a feeling, an almost mystical energy, that surrounded the piece and made him want to jealously defend it from prying eyes.

As he closed his hand around the piece once again, he nodded to himself, promising to at least show Kat what he had found. She had earned that much trust by giving him the genealogy testing idea. But that would likely be it. The historic communities had long shunned this particular mystery and didn't deserve to be a part of this find. He would likely take the knowledge of the fragment to his grave with him, just as Mauretz had done.

CHAPTER EIGHT

END OF THE LINE

1955

G o to hell," Nick muttered, somewhat losing the edge of his aggression after several hours of questioning.

"Mr. Satterall, we're not going anywhere until you tell us what you've done with those pieces," the interrogator insisted.

They sat in a small, rundown room within an equally unimpressive security hut at the edge of town, the sunlight streaming in through the slotted blinds in dusty streaks. Nick had been deposited in a hard wooden chair upon arrival and cuffed around his back, his captors wasting no time in beginning their questioning. The two men who had brought Nick in stood in the corner while an official-looking man with a small stature and a bushy, untamed mustache grilled him. He wasn't getting anywhere and he knew it. The frustration was beginning to show on his splotchy, pink face, for his upper lip and right eyebrow had developed an unfortunate twitch. It was a comical tic that Nick was having a hard time ignoring.

"Do you hear me?" the small man demanded.

"I do," Nick responded flatly, "did you hear me?"

"Which part?" the man barked.

"The go to hell part," Nick sighed with a roll of his eyes. This man was not even smart enough to needle for enjoyment, not that Nick was enjoying any part of this. It was all well and good holding his own against these local authorities, but there was no telling which organization had put them onto his trail. If it were one of the various antiquities' societies, Nick could be in a very serious situation.

"Mr. Satterall," the man said, standing up straighter and attempting feebly to add an air of importance to his presence "if you don't start co-operating, things will get much worse for you. We know you stole several artifacts from a cave near the Dead Sea. We also know you haven't had any luck selling them."

"Hey, if I came across something in a cave, I can do what I want with it," Nick replied, "that's really none of your business."

"Perhaps," the man agreed, "but this cave you didn't just happen across, you *rappelled* into it. So why don't you try a different excuse."

"Hmm," Nick grunted, his eyes starting to glaze over. "Well I stand by my original statement, then. Go to hell."

"This is not the way you want to go with this," the small man threatened. "Because if you continue, I'm going to ask my two colleagues here to leave, and then no one will be around to report on... anything that were to happen."

Nick laughed humorlessly. "I'm not sure that's as intimidating as you think it is. Maybe Jolly Green over there would have better luck." He nodded his head towards the big guy who had helped apprehend him and said, "Ya know, I can't tell if you have too much neck or not enough neck."

The large man scowled at him and balled his hand into a fist threateningly, but Nick just grinned back at him.

The small, mustached man leaned in close, clearly under the impression that he was putting the pressure on, and said, "We have people scouring the streets of the neighborhood we chased you through; if you stashed those carvings, it's only a matter of time until they're found.

Why don't you help yourself out and tell us where they are. It will make this all much easier on you."

Nick smirked and replied softly, "Sounds like it would make it easier on *you*, actually. I'm pretty comfortable right here, and I've got nowhere to be."

The man's mustache gave its most prominent twitch yet and he growled under his breath softly. "Alright," he nodded, "take a walk you two."

Nick's two captors nodded obediently and moved towards the door.

"Don't go far ladies," Nick called out to them sarcastically.

As they exited the door, the small man followed them out, standing in the doorway and whispering something to them. Nick rolled his eyes at the incompetence on display. He slowly stood up from his chair, which they had neglected to secure him to, and carefully stepped over his cuffed hands to bring them to the front. The small man, taking no notice of the escape in progress behind his back, nodded to his companions and closed the door behind them.

"At last," Nick growled and hooked the chain of his handcuffs around the man's neck.

The man gasped and sputtered, reaching and flailing to fight off his attacker, but it was no use.

"Shush shush shush," Nick whispered casually as he put pressure on the man's throat. "When you wake up, you'll have a massive headache, blurred vision, and of course the burning question of how the hell you let this happen." As the man's arms began to tire and slow, Nick continued, "Rest assured it's not because I'm the best escape artist in the region, it's because you're a sorry excuse for law enforcement." The man began to slump towards the floor but Nick kept talking. "Wait, wait, before you go, I have one more bit of advice, and it's really important so listen carefully; shave that twitchy mustache, it looks ridiculous."

The man finally succumbed to the pressure on his neck and Nick released him, allowing his unconscious body to spill out awkwardly onto the floor. Nick inclined his head towards the ceiling and listened for a moment, making sure his two initial captors hadn't doubled back. Confident that he was alone, Nick reached down to the ring of keys hanging from the small man's belt and rifled through them until he found the one for the handcuffs. As he undid each wrist, he noticed a key on the ring with a Jeep logo, and a thought occurred to him. Was he bold enough to steal the man's car to get back to his stashed loot?

Nick gave a shrug and muttered to himself, "Why not."

*****

Nick blasted out of town and floored it down the dust-covered road back the way he had come. Now that he was guilty of not only poaching a historical find but also assaulting an officer, fleeing custody, and stealing an official vehicle, Nick would have to leave this area behind. Once he reacquired his hidden artifacts, he would perhaps try his luck further south. Admittedly, the artifacts were worthless according to every shop owner he had talked to, but on principle he couldn't just leave them. Besides, that little ruby fragment was stashed as well, and *that* he had no intention of parting with.

Nick's stolen Jeep blazed around a corner and he found himself near to where he had been captured earlier in the day. He parked the car carelessly and jumped out, tossing the keys across the street as he did so. He ran down several streets before he finally got his bearings and started to recognize certain landmarks. He had been in such a hurry he couldn't be sure exactly which alleyway he had hidden his treasure, but it had to be close.

Finally, he found the shop he had torn through and realized his prize was just out back and around the corner.

"Nick!" a voice called from off to his right.

Nick turned and was baffled to see Mauretz approaching him from between the crowd.

"What are you doing here?" Nick demanded, but then realized he didn't care. "Hey, I'm gonna be leaving town, things have gotten too hot around here. You know the drill, don't reach out, no contact."

"You're leaving?" Mauretz asked.

"Yeah, what did I just say?" Nick barked in frustration.

He made his way into the alleyway and began scanning the piping along the sides of the buildings.

"Where will you go?" Mauretz questioned.

Nick rolled his eyes. "What the hell do you care. I'm leaving. Good-bye. What else can I say?"

"We've just worked together a long time," Mauretz mumbled.

Nick finally identified the correct pipe and hoisted himself up, re-trieving the cinched bag with his other hand. "You'll get over it," Nick said as he jumped back to the ground.

"Smart," Mauretz nodded, acknowledging Nick's revealed hiding place.

"What are you still doing here?" Nick demanded. "I told you, get lost. This is goodbye."

When Mauretz just continued to stare at the bag in his hand, a reali-zation occurred to Nick.

"What *were* you doing here, Mauretz?" he asked, but he finally un-derstood. The small man from the interrogation had said they had peo-ple searching for the stashed treasure. He had also somehow known that Nick had rappelled down to that cave in the side of the cliff. There was only one person who knew he had done that. And the fact that Mauretz was now refusing to meet his gaze gave him all the confirma-tion he needed.

"You sold me out," Nick said in a threatening grumble, "after every-thing we've been through."

"It wasn't like that," Mauretz began, but Nick had heard enough. He reached around his back to grasp his ever-present pistol before realizing that his captors had taken it off him when they escorted him out of town.

Mauretz pulled his own gun from his belt and pointed it at Nick. "Hey, don't!"

Nick laughed. There was nothing funny to laugh at, except that this day was in such an aggressive nosedive it was becoming absurd.

"Have you even held a gun before, Mo?"

"Don't do this," Mauretz commanded, "just hand over the bag and I'll pretend I never ran into you."

Nick shook his head, still smirking. "So much for your loyalty. Apparently it comes cheap."

"Not that cheap, actually," Mauretz replied, still with his worn pistol aimed between Nick's eyes. "They were willing to pay quite a bit of money for information on you."

"And what about you?" Nick demanded. "You think they'll just let you walk after everything you've helped me pinch? Keep dreaming, they'll show you as much loyalty as you've given me."

"Save it," Mauretz snapped, "you were scamming everyone, I was no exception. Don't lecture me on loyalty."

"The real question you need to ask yourself," Nick began, "is who they're going to make an example of; a run-of-the-mill graverobber trying to make a buck, or you, the man on the inside hiring petty-thieves for his own gain." Nick adopted a placating, innocent voice and said, *"Mauretz was the mastermind behind the entire operation, sir, I swear. I never would have known anything about antiquities without him."*

Mauretz scoffed but Nick could tell that his point was well taken. A flicker behind his eyes had reflected the tinniest hint of fear.

"Oh what?" Nick continued, "that didn't occur to you? Maybe *mastermind* is overselling it a bit, they'll never believe that. I guess I'll have to think of just the right word to describe you."

Mauretz cocked the pistol, clearly becoming emotionally compromised by the exchange.

Nick smirked again. "I'm outta here, good luck to ya, you're gonna need it."

Nick turned to leave but Mauretz shouted, "Don't you move!"

Nick extended his arms out from his sides and continued to walk away. "Go ahead and shoot," he called over his shoulder, "see where that gets you."

White hot pain screamed through his shoulder as the bullet tore through muscle and bone. Nick hadn't even heard the gunshot but when he reached up to touch the area, his fingers came away bright with blood. The canvas bag had fallen to the ground beside him, a bit of blood decorating the edges. He turned, wide-eyed with shock and rage, and stumbled towards Mauretz.

"Don't!" Mauretz yelled, backing away from Nick's swaying advance. "Get on the ground now!"

Nick's fury broke and he sprinted towards Mauretz, ready to tackle the gun from the traitorous weasel and beat him to death with it. Mauretz flinched at the assault and moved to cover his head, but he let loose another round as he did so, and this one ripped into Nick's chest. He staggered back the way he had come then fell hard, slamming to his knees and trying hard to take in breath. He found this quite impossible, however, as though his lungs were actively deflating. A horrible wheeze escaped from his mouth and he twisted his face up towards Mauretz, a look of contempt settling in his eyes. He tried to force his lips to form a final word of defiance, but blackness was beginning to creep in through the sides of his vision. He wrenched his knee off the ground and slammed his foot down hard, but the blackness overtook him and he pitched sideways, crashing his head hard onto the pavement.

Nick's eyes had only partially closed by the time the life left his body, and he died staring blankly at the contents of the bag spilled out onto the road, a look of incomprehension permanently setting on his features. He did not live to see Mauretz rummage through his pockets and retrieve his identification to throw away, nor did he live to see him sell the three carved stone figures to the Museum of Antiquities in London, keeping the mysterious ruby fragment all for himself.

CHAPTER NINE

THE BOY FROM THE SEA

2018

K at simply laughed when Mr. Pyrene had regaled her with his tale of museum hijinks and the way he had practically shoved a woman out of the way at an estate sale to get his hands on the fragment of ruby bark. He had exuberantly unveiled his prize and tipped it lovingly into her outstretched palm, but she was embarrassed to admit that it did not hold the same charm for her as it did for him. She had prodded at it experimentally and arched her eyebrows towards Mr. Pyrene expectantly, but he could not seem to drop the smile from his face.

"Be that way if you must," he had said with a sigh, "but this is something, I'm telling you. Nick thought so too."

"Oh so you're on a first name basis with this guy now?" Kat had teased him.

But that was almost a month ago now, and finally, when she had entered his Cryptohistory class on a cool day in mid-March, he held up a large manilla envelope with some sort of official header printed on it and exclaimed exuberantly, "It's here!" Of course he didn't need to specify what *it* was; he had talked about little else since he had returned from his trip to London. The genealogy results on the Hand of Jordan had finally come in, and it seemed he had waited to open them until they could do so together.

Class seemed to drag on far longer than usual that day, and in a first, it seemed Mr. Pyrene's spirit wasn't really in his teaching today. He was clearly distracted, and while Kat was the only student who would know why, she also seemed to be the only one who took notice. Most of her classmates wore their usual blank stares as they watched him speak. It was with significant relief when he finally dismissed the class and came bounding over to her with the envelope in hand.

"Took them long enough, eh?" Mr. Pyrene said, sitting atop one of the desks and beginning to tease open the glued envelope tab. "I know, I know, it's unlikely this will tell us much, and who knows, the blood could be too far degraded to offer us anything, but maybe, just maybe, we can get an idea of the part of the world that blood was from."

As Mr. Pyrene pulled the papers out of the envelope, Kat asked, "So do you have any theories where the blood was from?" But he was looking down at the pages with a furrowed brow of confusion.

"I don't get it," he mumbled in disappointment.

"Doesn't show any heritage?" Kat asked, having assumed this would be the case.

"No it's... this can't be the right sample. There's a whole lineage here, a whole family tree. They must have gotten the sample mixed up."

He began rifling through the assorted pages, continuing to shake his head. "This isn't the right sample," he said again with increased frustration. But then a smile broke on his face and he laughed lightly, tossing the packet onto the desktop. "I guess we should have assumed something like this would happen, oh well."

Kat took the discarded papers and began flipping through them herself. "It looks like the sample points to this branch of the Evans family, in the early 1900's."

Mr. Pyrene looked over her shoulder and rolled his eyes. "You're telling me that blood was from the 1900's?" he asked in disbelief. "After all my theories, it's not even ancient history."

"Wait this is interesting though," Kat insisted, studying the lineage. "In this area of the family tree, there's only one member whose line doesn't continue. Randall Evans, born in 1898."

But Kat could tell that Mr. Pyrene was having trouble caring about these oddities right now. He was hiding it well with a casual smile and dismissive shrugs of his shoulders, but he was clearly bothered by the revelation that his prized mystery was not from the ancient world after all.

"So he became a drifter and made a home in those caves," Mr. Pyrene said with a shake of his head. "I guess the historians were right, there never was much to this mystery after all."

Kat however, was desperate to salvage some of Mr. Pyrene's passion. She whipped out her laptop and began an online search for Randall Evans. Nothing much popped up, and Mr. Pyrene seemed resigned to defeat. But Kat kept adding to her search, including parents' names and dates. Finally she came across something of interest. A more detailed family tree had been posted online, likely by a family member considering the amount of personal information added. Kat tracked the lineage back to 1898 and found the enigmatic entry for Randall Evans, which was underscored with the words 'lost at sea'. Upon further inspection, Randall's father Charles had the same designation.

"Lost at sea?" Mr. Pyrene breathed, peering over her shoulder with raised eyebrows.

"Could he have ended up in that cave after surviving at sea?" Kat theorized, but Mr. Pyrene was shaking his head.

"I guess possibly," he said quietly, "but look at the date of his father's presumed death. Randall would have been fifteen when they were *lost*."

Kat started a new search for Randall Evans including the words 'lost', 'sea', and 'death'. No further articles detailed the young teen who was lost at sea, likely because it was over a hundred years ago, but she did come across an obituary for a man named Randall Evans from the year 2000. He was an extremely elderly man judging by his picture, and she was ready to dismiss it as an unrelated person when she noticed his date of birth. He was born on the exact same date as the *lost* Randall Evans.

She looked to Mr. Pyrene, who was squinting at the obituary in confusion, having evidently noticed the unlikely coincidence as well.

"What are the chances?" Mr. Pyrene mumbled.

"You don't think this could be the same person, do you?" Kat asked. She was happy to see Mr. Pyrene engaging in the mystery again, even if this was a far cry from his original fascination with the find. It seemed, however, that his love for all things mysterious was getting the better of him, for his eyes were lighting up once again.

"It can't be," Mr. Pyrene insisted, "the guy would have been..."

"One-hundred and two," Kat answered, pointing at the article. She continued reading, noticing instantly that there was absolutely no mention of his family, either surviving or otherwise. In fact, the man seemed to have been such a loner that there was nothing about loved ones or friends of any kind. Except the obituary was clearly written by someone who knew him, not the typical generic one written by the local newspaper. Kat scrolled to the bottom and found the author listed as Cynthia Voigt, who identified herself as Randall's neighbor.

"Does it list where they lived?" Mr. Pyrene asked, pulling his phone from his pocket.

"Umm... it's an apartment complex in New York, upstate it looks like," Kat answered. After another quick search, she announced, "This place."

"You got a phone number?"

Kat read the number off to him, without any clue what he was hoping to accomplish by this, but Mr. Pyrene had already finished dialing and was holding the phone up to his ear. As he paced away to the other side of the classroom and began speaking into the phone, Kat started a new online search for Cynthia Voigt. Another obituary came up, along with many more pictures than Randall had. It was quickly apparent that she had been widowed before her death by a man named Richard Voigt, and before their marriage, she had been known as Cynthia Harlow. By all accounts they had lived a normal life together. Cynthia seemed to have remained near the same town most of her life, except for an unexplained gap in the 1930's.

Mr. Pyrene was approaching fast from across the room, now talking excitedly into his phone. He came up beside Kat and put his phone on speaker, announcing loudly, "I'm here with my associate Katalina Killion, can you tell her what you just told me?"

A brittle, ancient woman's voice spoke up on the other end, introducing herself as Betsy Wesham, the landlord of the apartment complex where Cynthia and Randall both lived. "They became quite close over the years, which is such a blessing when you get to that age. Especially for dear Randall, I don't think he had anyone else."

"Did Randall ever talk about his life as a young man?" Mr. Pyrene asked, "did he ever mention an ordeal at sea?"

"No, nothing like that," Betsy answered in alarm. "He was quiet, I don't think he was the type to have had many adventures."

"Was he from the area?" Mr. Pyrene asked. "His obit didn't say where he was born."

"I... I really have no idea," Betsy said, clearly becoming confused with the line of questioning. "I pride myself with my memory of people, but this was a long time ago."

"One more question," Kat chimed in, and Mr. Pyrene looked at her expectantly. "I can't find much record of Cynthia Voigt earlier in her life, did you know her well?"

"Oh sure," Betsy insisted, "Cynthia I knew very well, we were quite close."

"So she must have talked about her past life then," Kat pushed.

"Sure she did," Betsy confirmed. "You might not be finding her because she used to go by a different last name."

"No I know that," Kat said, still scrolling through articles online, "I know her maiden name was Harlow, I still couldn't..."

"Not her maiden name," Betsy interrupted, "her married name from her first marriage."

This Kat did not know. "Her *first* marriage?"

"Sure," Betsy said, "first she was Cynthia Harlow, at the time of her death she was Cynthia Voigt, but between them, she was Cynthia Dorn."

"Dorn?" both Kat and Mr. Pyrene repeated together.

"That's right," Betsy confirmed. "Poor thing too. Cynthia had a hard life before she married Richard. Her first husband was lost at sea if you can believe that."

A creeping, tingling sensation ran up Kat's spine at this revelation. She turned to Mr. Pyrene, who stared back at her with the same baffled expression. He must have been thinking the same thing she was; that there was no way these two disappearances at sea were a coincidence.

CHAPTER TEN

THE RIGHT QUESTION

S ir, I really am trying to help here," the wide-eyed young woman stated from behind the admissions desk, "I'm just not entirely sure what you're looking for. You want staff records from over a hundred years ago?"

Dean had finally given in to his persistent, nagging obsession and taken a plane ride to Dane University in upstate New York to visit the last-known place of employment of Dr. Cyrus Dorn, the first husband of Cynthia Dorn and the apparent victim of a tragedy at sea in the 1930s. He had no idea why this mattered or how it all connected to that mysterious ruby fragment that now sat in his desk drawer at work, nor how it connected to the Hand of Jordan archeological find, but he had become irretrievably obsessed with finding out. Kat Killion had implored him to bring her with, but it was out of the question. Not only would it likely be viewed as inappropriate but he would also certainly lose his job for bringing a student on an extracurricular cross-country trip. So here he stood, in the admissions office of Dane University, harassing the confused-looking receptionist with his unusual questions.

"It's a project I'm working on," Dean insisted, attempting to make his inquiries sound as normal as possible. "This professor was lost at sea, I'm sure the University must have some records of that."

"I mean… I don't know where…" the young woman stammered, looking more frazzled by the second.

From an office down the hall, a middle-aged woman with a short bob and a stern but somehow friendly face approached, offering a welcoming but forced smile. "I couldn't help hearing from my office," the woman said, "and I think I can be of some help, Mister…?" She raised her eyebrows questioningly for his name.

"Pyrene," Dean exclaimed, extending his hand to shake. "You can call me Dean."

The woman gripped his hand briefly before releasing it and told the receptionist, "That's okay Lauren, you can go back to what you were doing." She rounded the desk and said to Dean, "I'm Mrs. Barrett, now you were inquiring about Dr. Dorn?"

"That's right," Dean responded enthusiastically, "I know it was a long time ago, I was just working on this project and…"

Mrs. Barrett nodded before he had time to finish and said, "Well it was before my time, but everyone who has been here long enough knows the story. It sort of put our little university on the map for a while."

"So do you know what happened to him?" Dean pushed.

Mrs. Barrett pursed her lips almost pityingly and said, "Well honey, no one knows what happened to him. That's why people still talk about it. Why don't you walk with me."

Mrs. Barrett led him out of the admissions building and started to wander across the picturesque campus.

"He was well respected in his day, Dr. Dorn I mean. From what I understand, he was a real name in his field of theoretical physics. He was around forty when he was contracted to lead an expedition out to the Atlantic Ocean. That must have been… the 1930's maybe… sometime in there."

Dean was entranced. He couldn't even keep his eyes off the woman's prematurely lined face as she talked, causing him to nearly lose his footing more than once. "What were they looking for?" Dean asked in unbridled wonder. This talk of old-world expeditions was making him dizzy with excitement.

"It was something to do with a ship, as far as I can recall," Mrs. Barrett answered thoughtfully. "I can't remember if it was a crash site or if they encountered something in the water… it was along those lines, though."

They had arrived at a different building on campus, and Mrs. Barrett wrenched the heavy-looking door open with all her strength. It was only once she had gotten it open that Dean realized the gentlemanly thing to do would have been to help her.

"Lauren's a recent graduate," Mrs. Barrett explained as they stepped out of the sunlight into a long, wood-paneled corridor. When Dean gave her a confused look, she clarified, "the receptionist you were interrogating. But the staff here, they all know this legend well. It's always been one of those local mysteries."

Mrs. Barrett began leading Dean down the hallway, and he noticed that one wall was lined nearly its entire length with large-scale portraits of past professors. They must have all been dead because each bore a gold plaque with the occupant's name and a pair of years roughly spanning an average lifetime. Most of the subjects were ancient, with one in particular standing out as possibly the most haggard-looking individual Dean had ever laid eyes on. His plaque identified him as Angus Melner.

"Here we are," Mrs. Barrett said finally, stopping in front of one of the portraits. "Dr. Cyrus Dorn."

Dean looked into the eyes of the man and his intrigue was only piqued further. Cyrus Dorn had a wide, confident grin and old-fashioned good looks. He seemed somehow relevant even now, as an old portrait on the wall, in a way that Dean couldn't quite explain. He allowed Cyrus's unseeing stare to penetrate his thoughts and Dean tried to imagine what it was that this man had seen in the final hours of his life.

"So is the leading theory that his ship went down?" Dean asked, still not taking his eyes off the portrait.

"Actually the expedition vessel made it there and back," Mrs. Barrett explained, "it was his dinghy that vanished, according to eyewitnesses."

Dean nodded in understanding but his attention had been caught by the portrait directly next to Cyrus's. In it was a man of similar age, possibly a few years younger, with a more angular face, a bit of facial stubble, and a pair of piercing eyes. But it was his plaque that Dean found intriguing, for it identified the man as Alec Dorn, with a year of death that matched Cyrus's.

"Ah yes," Mrs. Barrett nodded before Dean had a chance to ask. "Cyrus's brother. They worked here together; close as can be from what people said. I'm sure poor Cyrus kicked himself for bringing his younger brother into harm's way."

"He was on the expedition as well?" Dean asked, noting an uncertainty behind Alec's piercing stare, but also a hint of fire.

"Oh yes," Mrs. Barrett confirmed. "The University lost two gifted professors to that ill-fated trip." As Dean looked back and forth between the two brothers, she continued in a wistful voice, "It certainly makes you wonder what happened out there, and what potential these two would have had."

"Ya know I saw him once," came a gravelly, guttural voice. Both Dean and Mrs. Barrett turned to see an elderly man with a pouchy face and a bulbous nose from excessive drink making his way down the hall towards them.

"Oh," Mrs. Barrett exclaimed with a dismissive wave of her hand, "Mr. Michaelson has been telling this story for decades."

"Doesn't make it any less true," the man said, finally reaching them and offering a gnarled hand to Dean. "Guy Michaelson," he grunted, "and I absolutely did see him, I'd stake my life on it. That younger one there, Alec."

Dean sized the man up and decided this was impossible. Guy Michaelson was certainly old, but he would have barely been out the womb when the Dorn brothers vanished.

"Dismiss me if you will," Mr. Michaelson said with a shrug of his shoulders, "But I saw him, in this very hallway. In fact, he stopped exactly where you're standing right now and looked at that picture."

"When was this?" Dean asked, unsure how much time to give this potentially senile old man.

"Early seventies," Mr. Michaelson answered with confidence. "And I'll tell ya the kicker, he was just about that age too." He pointed a sausage-like finger at the picture of Alec, and Dean's eyes followed.

"In the seventies?" Dean repeated, "that doesn't make any sense."

"Ignore him," Mrs. Barrett said with a shake of her head, "the Dorn's were long gone by that time."

"It was him," Mr. Michaelson asserted, "first found him standing in my own office like he owned the place. Said he was lost… but he didn't act lost. He strolled down the hallway like he didn't have a care in the world, like he had no place to be."

Dean furrowed his brow, intrigued by the story but baffled trying to figure out what to make of it. "But he was that age?" he pushed, gesturing to the picture.

"Best I could tell," Mr. Michaelson nodded, "give or take a few years. A young man still, that's for sure."

"He tells anyone who stands still too long about this," Mrs. Barrett explained, "don't feel obligated to believe him, nobody does."

Dean gave a snort of laughter at her abruptness, but Mr. Michaelson was undeterred. "Ya know who *did* believe me?" he pushed, "Diana Rahm." When Mrs. Barrett rolled her eyes, he turned his full attention to Dean and continued, "Now she was old by that time. Or maybe I just remember her like that because I was young. Funny how age does that. But she knew him, Alec I mean. They were friends when they taught here together. And she never dismissed my story."

"She's not around, is she?" Dean asked hopefully.

"Died a long time ago now," Mrs. Barrett explained gently.

"Here," Mr. Michaelson stated abruptly, "follow me, I have something to show you."

"Now Mr. Michaelson, our guest has to be getting back," Mrs. Barrett said placatingly, as though she were talking to an overexcited child, but Mr. Michaelson had already started down the hall, and Dean followed.

His office was small and dusty, but without much clutter. It had a fine wooden desk in the middle and cabinets lining the walls. Mr.

Michaelson bent with a grunt and retrieved something from a bottom drawer, placing it forcefully on the desktop for everyone to see. It was a framed degree from 1931 and it had Alec Dorn's name stamped into it.

Dean brushed a finger over a small crack in the glass and then looked up to Mr. Michaelson for clarification on what it was he was supposed to ascertain from this.

Mr. Michaelson smiled knowingly and explained, "About ten years ago I was rearranging my office, getting new cabinets when those ancient old ones were finally falling apart. This certificate here was back behind one of them, pressed against the wall. Must have fallen back there at some point." When Dean raised his eyebrows, Mr. Michaelson shook his head and said, "This was *his* office. Alec's office."

Dean nodded finally in understanding. "And this is where you first encountered him. He was standing in here."

"Exactly," Mr. Michaelson exclaimed in satisfaction. "He must've been looking for something. Or maybe just seeing how I'd changed the place, who knows. But it was him."

Dean, against his better judgement, was finally drawn in by this far-fetched story. Mr. Michaelson truly believed it, and old as he may be, he didn't come across as a crackpot.

"I don't know what he was doing here," Mr. Michaelson continued conspiratorially, "or how he got here, but I know for a fact he was here. Which means not only did he survive that incident at sea, but he didn't want anyone to know. He didn't return when he first went missing, and his brother was never heard from again, but Alec Dorn showed up here, forty years after he was declared dead... and he hadn't aged a day. Asking me why he was here or wondering if I'm just old and confused, those are the wrong questions." Mr. Michaelson lowered his guttural voice and widened his eyes in wonder. "The *right* question is to ask yourself what it is Alec Dorn found out there that he never returned from."

CHAPTER ELEVEN

THE EXILED KING

T he now familiar but no less uncomfortable sensation of having his sinuses explode behind his eyes came and went, and Alec Dorn, the displaced King of the West, strode through a *door* and back into his own reality in 1936 New York. 'Strode' was perhaps not the right word, for his painfully contorting limbs made anything more than a hobble impossible when passing through the anomaly, but Alec pictured himself striding nonetheless. Displaced he may be, but Alec Dorn had ruled over an entire kingdom at a time not too long ago, and he still very much considered himself a king. Of course, when he ducked out from under the canopy of trees in his backyard and looked up at his achingly suburban house, it told a different story.

It had been seven years since Alec had ridden his chariot into battle, and seven years since he had fought his traitorous older brother in the Fire Fields. Alec and Cyrus had once been close, but that was another lifetime. They had joined that fateful expedition as brothers; their heads swimming with dreams of discovery and fame. But their dreams soured when they found themselves stranded on an island in a reality that was not quite their own. The island housed a kingdom, at the time ruled by a violently eccentric tyrant named King Mora, who had essentially en-slaved the people and installed himself as their dictator. Cyrus and Alec had overthrown King Mora together, along with their crewmates Jack Viana and Nelida Yore, but taking control of the monarchy had not come easy and the Dorn brother's relationship had fractured under the pressure... then ruptured entirely. Cyrus had turned on him, and turned half the kingdom against him as well. Their ensuing duel had been a long time coming, the culmination of decades of buried history, and Alec was disgusted to admit that he let his brother get the best of him. In his rage, Alec had failed to recognize that Cyrus had made a significant discovery about the weapons that they each carried. Those enigmatic scepters evidently held a power that Alec never realized. When broken, they created a wormhole; a portal to another reality. It was through this that Alec, the once all-powerful King of the West, had fallen, bringing his reign to an end.

He had found himself choking and gagging in some middle-of-nowhere place in the ocean, and it looked briefly like his brother had actually managed to kill him. But there had been a cliffside nearby, and luckily Alec was a strong swimmer. He had made his way to shore, an incredibly difficult feat with a scepter still clutched tightly in his hand, and discovered before too long that he was back in his own, unremarkable world. As it turned out, however, it wasn't exactly his world, nor was it his time. Upon returning to his old home in New York, he was horror-struck to find that the year was not 1936 but seven years prior, and the life he had built for himself did not yet exist. Alec, however, had grown significantly in his time on the island, and where he once would have seen despair, he found opportunity.

As he walked up the sloping lawn towards the back door of his house, Alec reminded himself that this was all temporary, and that he *would* find his way back to his people... to his kingdom. Still, as he opened the door and let himself into the newly renovated kitchen and saw his wife Cynthia standing over the stove with the late-afternoon sunlight illuminating her beautiful features, he was reminded that his life here did have its modest charms.

Cynthia Dorn turned and smiled at him, offering a kiss over her shoulder as he passed.

"How was your day?" she asked in one of those painfully ordinary suburban rituals.

"Fine," he answered with a shrug, "still not much progress today."

Cynthia of course did not know what sort of progress he was trying to make. She was under the impression that he was still teaching full-time at the University, but in truth that job had lost much of its importance to him. There had been a morbid satisfaction in being able to steal the level of notoriety that Cyrus had once enjoyed on campus, but at the end of the day it was all temporary. The same, in fact, went for his life with Cynthia. There had been a time when he would have given anything to have exactly the life he was living right now; a prestigious job, respect from his peers, and Cynthia on his arm. But now he had seen something more... had *lived* something more, and there was no going back.

"I invited Cyrus over for dinner tomorrow," Cynthia called to him as he made his way deeper into the house. "He said you hadn't talked in a few days, I'm really worried about him. I think he's having a hard time adjusting to being back home."

Alec grinned to himself. Several weeks ago, Alec's monotonous domestic life had been given a much-needed shot of adrenaline. When he had found himself in the middle of the ocean seven years ago, he could not understand why he had ended up in that particular place, in that particular time. But he *did* know how to find that particular place again, and he wondered to himself if Cyrus would keep his word by following Alec through the wormhole. One of the last things his brother had said to him in the Fire Fields was to ask if Alec would join them if they were to find a way back home. If Cyrus did follow Alec through the wormhole like he had planned, why hadn't he shown up in the ocean with him? Alec didn't know these answers, but on a hunch, he decided to note the exact date that they had dueled in the Kingdom. After a seven year wait, Alec returned to that exact spot with a ship and a crew, and low and behold, there was Cyrus, the King of the East, flailing and choking in the water.

That had been three weeks ago now, and Cyrus was not taking kindly to his new place in this world. It was a fitting end to his insignificant reign, and now he was feeling the sting of second place. Alec had used his head start to take over Cyrus's old house, job, and even marriage, but he was getting off easy. He had essentially been relegated to Alec's prior status as the lesser Dorn brother; a place Cyrus always thought Alec should be grateful to have. Alec sneered thinking about the reversal and relished the idea of Cyrus coming to dinner and seeing his old life on display in someone else's hands. And he wouldn't be able to say a word.

"That okay with you?" Cynthia asked again, peering her head around the corner.

"Absolutely," Alec responded, shaking his head in apology for not answering her quicker. "Sorry, lost in thought today I guess."

"You're working too hard," Cynthia insisted wisely, "I know you're a hot shot at the University these days, but you might think about slowing down. You look stressed."

Alec nodded in agreement and put on a show that he would consider it. She was right, of course, about him working hard, but wrong in thinking it was the University monopolizing his time. For years now, he had been experimenting with his scepter and creating doorways to alternate worlds. The trouble was, the doors always seemed to open to the exact same location, albeit in vastly different times. This left experimentation rather limited, as he was only able to step into varying versions of upstate New York. It had, however, yielded some interesting results. In stepping through different doorways he created, he was able to visit Dane University campus at different points in different realities, a place where Cyrus and Alec had spent significant amounts of their adult lives. Sometimes he would end up in the past and sometimes the future. The future was especially interesting because he had discovered that in every single timeline he explored, himself and Cyrus always ended up on that island. Nowhere could he find a reality where the Dorn brothers continued to live out their lives teaching and growing old. Somewhere, somehow, in one of these alternate realities, Alec would find the key that allowed him to return to that island and his kingdom. So far, however, it had eluded him.

"It seems like you and Cyrus haven't been talking much since he got back," Cynthia observed, going back to chopping an onion on the counter. "You should make more of an effort, he doesn't seem like himself."

Of course he *wasn't* himself, Alec thought, at least not from *this* Cynthia's point of view, but he agreed all the same.

"I'm serious," she continued, "I think it might be survivor's guilt or something. Having been stranded on that island for so long, and it sounds like some of the team died too." After a pause, she pressed, "Has he talked to you at all? About his time out there I mean? Now he tells me he survived on a deserted island eating fruit, but when we first found him, he was rambling about kingdoms and creatures."

Cyrus had been fairly tight-lipped about his time in the Kingdom around Cynthia, but when he had first returned, he had divulged just a bit too much. He had later backtracked and insisted he was talking nonsense, but Cynthia had heard what she heard, and she wasn't in a hurry to forget.

Alec shrugged and said thoughtfully, "I think he probably had a touch of malaria or some other tropical fever. Those things can addle your brain."

Cynthia nodded but Alec could tell she wasn't entirely convinced.

"He'll be okay," Alec insisted. "Dinner tomorrow is a good idea, just remember not to be too pushy with him. No matter where he actually was, he's been through a lot. We just have to let him settle back into reality on his own terms."

As Alec turned away, his lip curled a bit at his own play on words. He felt just a little guilty toying with Cynthia in this way. No matter what his brother had become, Cynthia was a good person, and both this version of her and the version he had known in his own world were kind and supportive. He had courted her in this world not to seek revenge on Cyrus but out of an honest desire to be with her, so it pained him to admit that it wasn't enough for him anymore. She was mostly the same as he had always remembered her, but *he* was different. The world was different. He had discovered what real potential was in the

Kingdom, and everything else paled in comparison. That included prestigious careers, suburban houses, and even Cynthia.

CHAPTER TWELVE

THE MIGHTY HAVE FALLEN

C yrus Dorn was marooned. There was no other way of looking at it. He was marooned in an unfamiliar land, in an unfamiliar life, in an unfamiliar world. Once the indomitable King of the East, Cyrus had led an entire civilization as it rediscovered its strength, gave the power back to the people, and earned a place of legend within the Kingdom. The fateful duel in the Fire Fields had been seven long years ago for Alec, but only a matter of weeks for Cyrus. He had spent nearly every night since contemplating that discrepancy in time. Best he could figure, it seemed to have been caused by a small forgotten fragment of his scepter, which he had absent-mindedly left in his pocket when he stepped through the anomaly. A voice of counsel from his past had warned him about walking through *doorways* without a piece of the scepter on him, and it was advice he had only inadvertently heeded. Alec had passed through the anomaly without any such fragment, and evidently that caused him to become untethered from his own time. Unfortunately for Cyrus, however, Alec's time-slippage was only seven years, and he used that time to undo every accomplishment and every victory Cyrus had ever known. Now Cyrus was lost, without a life-raft, in Alec's newly created world.

Alec and Cyrus had once been close, at least in Cyrus's mind. There was a time when they worked side-by-side on campus, met for drinks most days after work, and had a real relationship. There was also a time when Alec had starting acting erratically in the Kingdom, but Cyrus had ignored the warning signs. Now, they were not brothers. They were bitter enemies, feuding kings who had become stranded together in exile. It was a bitter pill to swallow, but Alec had won, at least for now. He had found a way to take everything that Cyrus held most dear, and he had done so as retribution for being overthrown in the Kingdom. This last part made Cyrus smile, a rare occurrence these days. He smiled because if he had to do it all over again, he would. Cyrus's final act had been to protect the Kingdom from a truly monstrous threat, and even though it had cost him everything, the Kingdom was more important. His people were more important.

Cyrus stood, looked in the mirror, and fastened the last few buttons on his shirt, preparing to join Alec and Cynthia for dinner. Because enemies though they may be, appearances had to be maintained, and Cynthia did not know of the rupture in their relationship. Any attempt Cyrus made to reveal the truth only made him sound crazy, and he doubted very much that Alec would have any hesitation throwing him in the nut house if it came to it. So for now, Cyrus played the part, made nice with his brother and his stolen bride, and plotted his counterattack.

He glowered around the room searching for his keys. This was not his home, or any home he had ever lived in. This had been Alec's house in the world Cyrus had known. But not here. In this world, there *had* been a Cyrus living in this house, but it was not him. It was an alternate version of Cyrus who actually belonged in this world, who had never been married to Cynthia and never managed to attain as much professional success as he had hoped. Cyrus never met this man, and in fact to the rest of the occupants of this world, the transition from one Cyrus to the next had been seamless. The Cyrus of this world had joined an expedition, much the same way he himself had done, and was pulled through an anomaly out on the Atlantic Ocean. *That* Cyrus never returned. Then, five months later, a Cyrus did come back to this world, but it was not the one that belonged in this world. Only he knew the difference… himself and his traitorous younger brother.

Cyrus located his keys, unnecessarily as it turned out, because he walked out of the house without locking the door. What did it really matter, none of the belongings inside were his stuff. As he stepped onto the sidewalk, he glanced across the street at the outer perimeter of campus, still bustling with life as sunset began to overtake the day. Students ran back and forth, joking and laughing, living their lives without a care in the world. They didn't know the gift they had living here, not having to fight for their lives day after day. Cyrus shook his head, having lost his appetite for normal life as well as his ability to remain ignorant. He turned a corner and passed the old tavern that himself and Alec would frequent back home. He could pinpoint the exact table that they had shared when they first discussed the expedition. That was when Cyrus had convinced Alec to come. It had been their last night in their old lives. Looking at the table now, occupied by a college couple clearly on a first date, Cyrus noticed it appeared slightly different. Instead of a wooden surface like the one he remembered, it was grate metal, painted blue but faded badly from the sun. A glance up at the sign overhanging the area proved the name of the establishment to be different as well. This sort of variation had been alarming in his first week after returning, but now he was used to it. It was an *alternate* reality after all.

By the time he reached his old house, now inhabited by his brother, his stomach began to coil uncomfortably and his head gave an alarming spin. He steadied himself and took several deep breaths. He set his jaw and clenched his fist tightly. This was war, masquerading as a family dinner, and he had to be prepared for anything and everything that presented itself during the evening.

His knock at the front of the house was met swiftly with the door opening and a full-bodied hug from Cynthia.

"So glad you could make it, Cy," Cynthia insisted soothingly, as though he had anywhere else to be in this foreign land. "How are you holding up?"

It was one of those questions that seemed to come with every greeting and was always said in an incredibly careful tone. Cyrus just nodded in response and gave his obligatory reply, "I'm alright."

When Cynthia released him, Alec was standing behind her, holding out his arms to embrace his brother. The grin on his face dared Cyrus to decline the hug, something he had no intention of doing. He wrapped his arms around Alec and squeezed hard, satisfied when he heard a small pop in his brother's shoulder. He loosened his grip and brought a hand up to the base of Alec's skull, pulling his face in close to his own so that their foreheads were nearly touching.

"It's good to see you, brother," Cyrus growled, staring into Alec's cold, calculating eyes.

"And you," Alec answered with an undertone of superiority. "I hope you're settling well back into your routine. Just keep in mind, things will get easier... you have a whole lifetime ahead of you."

The threat of this last sentence was lost on Cynthia, who smiled at the two brothers being reunited and began to walk back towards the kitchen. "Have you gone back to work yet?" Cynthia called, "or are you still easing back into things?"

"Still adjusting," Cyrus responded darkly, still staring at Alec with contempt. "Life around here has just lost a bit of its luster somehow."

"Well you went through quite a lot," Cynthia insisted from the other room.

"You have no idea," Cyrus replied, finally passing Alec to follow Cynthia into the kitchen.

*****

Once dinner had come and gone, the dishes had been cleared, and they were sitting around the dining room table with wine glasses in hand, Cyrus found the evening much more palatable. Alec continued his attempts at goading him, but Cyrus found he did not much care. Alec could have this world, if that's what he wanted, Cyrus only cared about getting back to his own. Alec was currently regaling them with stories of his various achievements at the University and Cynthia was smiling proudly at him and nodding encouragingly. Cyrus took another lengthy sip of his wine and rolled his eyes slightly.

"It's just incredible what gifts the universe has given me," Alec wrapped up, a self-satisfied grin on his face. "I'm just thankful for the scientific minds that helped pave my way."

"Oh yes," Cyrus said while refilling his glass, "amazing what can be accomplished when you stand on the shoulders of greater men."

Cynthia furrowed her brow slightly at the comment but Alec just smiled. "I suppose that's why it's called the scientific *community*," he responded, "it's a give and take."

"Sure sure," Cyrus agreed, "and in any community, there's always that one who takes without giving anything." He rotated his glass absent-mindedly and watched the dark liquid roll around the interior before continuing in a disinterested grumble, "I believe that's the difference between a symbiote and a virus."

Alec's lip twitched slightly and Cynthia looked mildly confused. Cyrus smiled to them both in response and raised his glass. "To my baby brother, and everything he's worked *so hard* to achieve. May you receive *everything* you've got coming to you."

Alec and Cynthia toasted and drank before Alec asked, "So how's the house treating you, Cy? I always thought you'd want something bigger, but I suppose it's perfect for someone living all alone."

Cyrus, refusing to get riled by his brother's vain attempts to engage him, replied, "Eh, I like my own company. No regrets keeping me up at night."

"No regrets?" Alec repeated, "now that's interesting. I mean, not long ago when you first returned, you seemed positively addled with regret."

"Alec," Cynthia warned, appearing alarmed by his rudeness. But she seemed to be having trouble holding her liquor at this late stage of the night, and her eyes were looking a bit cloudy.

"Oh that's okay," Cyrus growled, "I'm happy to talk about regrets if that's what Alec wants. My own involve giving people chances who didn't deserve it. Granting people power who hadn't earned it. Not seeing clearly when people were beyond saving."

"Well saving people has always been your thing, hasn't it," Alec retorted as Cynthia's head began to droop slightly. "Even when people didn't want your help."

Cyrus took another long drink and said, "Well that's the thing about hopeless people, they never seem to know when help is needed or respect help when it's given."

Alec just gave a forced smile and replied, "Well I wouldn't know much about that, things have worked out pretty well for me."

Cynthia's head gave another twitch as she fought off her exhaustion and she announced, "I think all this wine has gone to my head, I might have to call it a night for myself."

Alec nodded and gave her knee a squeeze. "I'll be up shortly," he said gently.

Cynthia got unsteadily to her feet, bid Cyrus goodnight, and walked herself upstairs to bed.

As the door from the floor above closed, Alec smirked at Cyrus and said, "I'm sure you're wanting to start making your way home as well."

Cyrus instead reached across the table for the bottle of wine and, bypassing his glass entirely, took a lengthy swig. "I've got nowhere to be."

Alec glowered slightly but then gave a pitying laugh. "So your savage revenge is to drink through my wine collection, huh?"

Cyrus shrugged. "I can think of worse ways to pass my time. And since I'm stranded here with you…"

"*You* stranded us here," Alec clarified.

"And I'd do it again," Cyrus said in a disinterested grumble. "My place is between you and the Kingdom. As long as I'm still around, you will never see that place again."

Alec's expression soured but he didn't respond.

"Ya know, I've been wondering something," Cyrus continued, his words becoming slightly slurred from excessive drink. "This new world you've found, I know there was a different Cyrus living in it, and I know he went off on that expedition and never returned. But what about this world's Alec? You came here seven years ago, there would have been a version of you already occupying this world. What did you do with him?"

Alec's features darkened further and he glared back at Cyrus, but stayed silent.

Cyrus grinned. "Ah ha, you don't wanna tell me," he said, his words dripping with intrigue. "Must be something you're really conflicted about. Well if it helps, my opinion of you cannot sink any lower."

He tipped the remainder of the wine bottle into his mouth, tossed the empty vessel onto the floor, and asked, "You got any more of this stuff?"

Alec looked disgusted and replied, "I think it's time you were on your way."

Cyrus gave a short laugh, then stood slightly, reached across the table, and snatched Cynthia's unfinished glass for himself before slumping back into his chair. "No worries," he grunted, "I've found more."

Alec shook his head. "If only your Easttowners could see their king now."

Cyrus upended his glass and tossed it to the floor as well. "What's wrong Alec? Having me in this world isn't as much fun as you thought it would be? Maybe you should've just let me drown out there."

"It had occurred to me," Alec admitted venomously. "But I wanted you to see what had become of your life."

Cyrus gave a dismissive snort and leaned back in his chair, planting his boots roughly on the fine wooden table. "You're such an impossibly weak man."

A bit of Alec's old fire flared slightly behind his eyes and he curled his lip into a hateful grimace. "What I became on that island was beyond anything you could possibly dream of."

"Becoming a tyrant doesn't show strength," Cyrus growled, "quite the opposite actually, despite what your pitiful instincts may be telling you. But you never did have much sense."

"You'll want to watch your tongue, brother," Alec snarled. "It's a skill you'll learn in this world."

Cyrus studied Alec across the table for several long moments. "I am no brother of yours," he finally stated in a gravelly murmur.

With that, Cyrus lurched up and out of his chair, strode through the house and exited out the front door. Alec watched him as he went, an unreadable expression set on his face.

The brisk night air did wonders for his clarity of mind and Cyrus breathed deeply as he tilted his head up towards the mottled grey and black sky. He slowly descended the staircase and made his way to the public sidewalk just as a few droplets of rain began to patter lightly against his shoulders. He moseyed slowly through the neighborhood, a somewhat freeing sensation settling in his mind. His situation had become so absurdly hopeless that a strange calm had begun to overtake him. He was in no rush to go anywhere and he had nothing he had to do. He was simply existing in this world, and nothing more. A far cry it might be from his time as the King of the East, Cyrus Dorn finally had nothing left to fight for. He didn't hurry his pace as the sky opened up and a torrential downpour released from above. Instead, he slumped onto the curb bordering the street and stretched out onto the soaking brick sidewalk.

As a bit of distant lightning colored the clouds above, Cyrus found himself dreaming of far-off places. His mind soared out of the neighborhood, past the hustle and bustle of the New York docks and out over the Atlantic Ocean, deep black in the stormy night. He envisioned the abstract, twisted shipwreck lodged against its rocky cradle, and then past it to the Fire Fields of his Kingdom. He saw his friends' faces, so clearly they almost had to be real. He saw Ydoro, grinning broadly at him and talking about carving his historical chess pieces. He saw Annica, preparing for battle and giving him a wink. He saw Cain, bloodied and defeated but never forgotten. And he saw Jack, who gave him a smack on the shoulder and a reassuring nod. These were his people... and this was his home.

But lightning flashed again and erased the vision from his mind. He blinked slowly and willed the thoughts to return, but they had gone. And yet they had been so clear. Not for the first time since returning, he found himself desperately wondering what was happening at this very moment in his beloved Kingdom.

CHAPTER THIRTEEN

THE FINAL DAYS OF PEACETIME

J ack Viana woke to an empty bed, as he often did, dressed, and strolled over to the open window of his bedroom. From here he could watch town proper extend out from the Temple walls and spread to every corner of the Fire Fields like a weaving spiders' web. From his fourth-floor balcony, he was standing at the highest point in town, but it was admittedly far less grand of a view than that from the original Temple, which had towered over the surrounding area like a medieval castle of old. That was exactly the point in building a new Temple at the center of the Kingdom; to remove some of that separation between the people and the leadership. Prior leaders, namely Alec Dorn, King Mora before him, and King Irias before him, relished that separation and the drunken power that came with it. Cyrus Dorn showed everyone that there was another way of leading, and Jack made every decision with those teachings in mind.

Watching the town flourish below, the streets glowing faintly orange as particles of frozen fire were kicked up here and there, Jack couldn't help but feel that this was exactly the evolution of the Kingdom that Cyrus had envisioned. Easttown of course still functioned and thrived, as did Westtown, but they were simply extensions of the true center of civilization on the island. Once the location of the greatest duel the Kingdom had ever witnessed, the Fire Fields were now a symbol of peace and unity; a place of gathering and democracy, growth and innovation. This last part was evident even in the very building where Jack now stood. Where the past king's old Temple had taken great care to look like a fortress of the ancient world, this new one was a miracle of craftsmanship as far as Jack was concerned. It contained stone pillars, decorative flourishes, even a functioning stage on which to hold court. The builders had been immensely proud to show off their skills, both with the Temple and the statue known as the Guardian. Jack could see the monument from his balcony, although even from ground level it was difficult to miss. It stood twenty feet tall atop a small, crypt-like room, and depicted a windswept and steadfast Cyrus Dorn in all his glory. He clutched a scepter impressively in one wiry hand and glared out at the horizon with a set jaw and a fierce resolve. Of course, the real Cyrus Dorn would have laughed at the statue. He was nothing like the artificial hero hewn from stone to protect the town; he had been thoughtful, resilient, and, perhaps most importantly, moral. He led with a quiet strength, and had largely shed most of his ego by the time he left the Kingdom. But the people remembered him with the lens of mythology over their eyes, and there was nothing wrong with that. Everyone needed a hero.

As Jack made his way out of the bedroom and down the hall, an excitable young man of fifteen with a mess of dark hair and a wide, boyish face jumped out of one of the spare rooms and exclaimed, "King Jack!"

Jack just smiled mildly as he continued his walk down the hall, the young man bounding after him enthusiastically. "Mornin' Noma," he said with a laugh. "I've told you before, you don't have to call me that."

"Of course I do!" Noma insisted, "why wouldn't I?"

"Well for one, 'King Jack' sounds absurd," Jack answered in amusement, "and for another, I'm only king by association."

"King Jack has a nice ring to it," Noma pushed earnestly.

"If you say so," Jack grunted, but he smiled all the same. "Did you spend the night here again?"

"I did," Noma nodded vigorously, "I wanted to make sure I caught you early."

"I'm not hard to find," Jack reminded him, "you know I always have time for you."

"Good," Noma answered, "because I want you to come by the workshop when you have a minute, it's important."

Jack paused his stride and turned to face Noma thoughtfully. "Have you made progress on our little project?" he asked in a low voice, glancing down the hallway to make sure no one was around to overhear.

"I think so," Noma responded, "I'm not there yet, but I think I'm getting close."

"Alright," Jack nodded, still scanning the surrounding hallway apprehensively, "I'll be by later this morning. You're not telling anyone else about this, are you?"

"Of course not!" Noma exclaimed, "Only you and the Queen know about what I'm trying to do."

"Good good," Jack said with a pat on the shoulder, "let's keep it that way for now. I don't want the Kingdom working itself into a frenzy, we have enough of that going on right now."

Noma nodded so enthusiastically it was almost comical. "I understand King Jack. My lips are sealed!"

"Alright good," Jack said, stifling a laugh at Noma's undying excitement, "have you seen the Queen around?"

"I saw her head downstairs a while ago," Noma answered, breezing past any notion that some would consider it an invasion of privacy to be lurking outside people's bedrooms watching them come and go.

Noma was a trusted, although extremely junior, member of the royal court, and had unrestricted permission to roam about the Temple as he liked. Jack had known him since he was ten and had been present for much of his subsequent formative years. It was Noma's father who Jack had met first; an older man who had run a trinket and repair shop in town. But he had died four years ago now, and Noma was left to find his way on his own. Luckily, he was a resourceful kid and with a bit of guidance from Jack and others in the Temple, he had managed to flourish.

As they exited onto the main floor, Noma left through the front door with a nod, calling over his shoulder, "Please come as soon as you can, it's important, King Jack."

"I will," Jack promised, and he walked down the opposite corridor and out to an enclosed courtyard at the center of the Temple. It was here that he found his wife, as he suspected he would, leaning against the trunk of a tree and tossing a small stone up into the air distractedly.

"What's this?" Jack called out with a smile, "is our queen hiding away out here?"

Annica smirked and threw the rock playfully at Jack, who ducked out of the way as he approached her. She was a short, petite young woman with visibly toned arms and a near perfect face, at least in Jack's mind. Appearance-wise, she had changed very little since he had first met her near the hillside caves, back when he joined her working crew. As far as responsibility went, however, she was nearly unrecognizable.

"Just taking my time this morning," Annica answered, lifting another small stone from the ground and turning it over in her fingers. "I'm worried about everything that happened the other day," she continued, "and I know the people are looking to us to give them comfort."

Jack sat on the ground beside her and sighed deeply. "It's a heavy burden, I get it," he replied.

"How do you handle it, though?" she asked, "all these people looking to you for guidance?"

Jack thought a second before he responded. "People have always looked to you for guidance, Annica. You've been a natural leader for as long as I've known you. The only difference now is that you were chosen by the people this time. You were chosen to lead them, and I'm sure that comes with a lot of pressure for doing right by them."

"I mean, you're king alongside me," Annica pointed out, "don't you feel that same pressure?"

Jack shrugged mildly, "Certainly I feel pressure to lead them through these difficult times… but I wasn't elected by the people, you were."

Annica shook her head slightly and said, "They elected me, but they knew we were a package deal." After a moment's silence, she continued, "I just don't know that I'm cut out for this. Leading is easy when times are good, but what if I don't have what it takes to guide our people in what's to come."

Jack put a comforting hand on her thigh and said, "We don't *know* what's to come, but the people knew what they saw when they chose you. They knew you were up for the fight even if you doubt it yourself."

The turmoil that was currently torturing Annica had begun five days prior. A group of militants whose existence had gone entirely unnoticed by the Temple had made themselves known in a very public display, and the ramifications of their assault were not currently understood. It had started with the capture of Jack's old expedition mate and one-time acquaintance, Nelida Yore, who had evidently been living in the forest and recruiting to her cause under the name Vengeance. Despite how on-the-nose this moniker sounded to Jack, her goal appeared clear; to strike back against the new power in the Kingdom and those who had unseated her former ally, Alec Dorn. After the Dorn brothers had dueled in the Fire Fields, six long years ago now, and Alec had been banished to another reality, Nel had slunk off into the shadows and was never heard from again. Rumors persisted, and Jack certainly made it a personal mission of his to continue searching for her, but there was never any trace until this week. Jack had come to the conclusion that she must have died out in the wilderness, but now it was clear she survived with extensive help from well-placed allies. Those allies showed themselves when Nel was finally captured, likely feeling their hands were forced by the turn of events.

The fact that Nel, and by extension Alec Dorn himself, still had devoted followers amongst the citizens of the Kingdom was not the alarming, or even particularly surprising, part. What was so troubling, and currently weighing on Annica's shoulders so heavily, was their actions after Nel's capture. Her militants knew something that Jack had prayed would never be made public; the statue known as the Guardian was not strictly erected to instill awe. Cyrus's etched likeness certainly inspired the people, but beneath the monument's feet, housed in a stone crypt, was the secret to how Cyrus had banished his brother to another world. The scepters of the king, as Alec used to call them, were a matching pair of rustic, charred-looking staffs about five feet long that reacted violently with the substance known as frozen fire, the particles that made up the glowing Fire Fields beneath their feet. But they held another secret, one that had only been whispered about since its discovery. When left stationary for a period of time, the scepters ate away at the nothingness surrounding them, creating a sort of window to a different reality. This window could only be looked through, however, and was not an accessible gateway. When the scepters were damaged, however, and a fragment was broken off, a doorway erupted behind the shattered piece, which became a portal that one could navigate.

This all sounded so absurd, even as Jack reflected on it now, but he had seen these doorways open and close with his own eyes. It was the reason their expedition had ended up on the island in this reality in the first place, and how Cyrus was able to trick Alec into falling out of it. That had been at the end of their legendary duel, and Cyrus had elected to follow his brother into the unknown, forsaking his hard-fought claim to the Kingdom in favor of familial obligation. Jack felt Alec did not deserve the gesture and would have been happy to imagine the tyrant King of the West navigating an unknown world alone, but Cyrus had insisted. Upon leaving, however, Jack, Annica, and Ydoro had promised to keep the damaged fragment of scepter undisturbed and protected, lying exactly where it had fallen during the duel. This was important because, theoretically, if Cyrus had needed to return for any reason, he would only need to find the exact spot in his new world where he had been deposited, and that doorway would bring him back here.

After six years with no return, of course, it had to be assumed that Cyrus Dorn was living a happy life somewhere out there in another reality, so it wasn't the moving of the scepter fragment that concerned Jack now. Nel's group of militants had broken through the Kingdom's defenses, smashed their way into the guarded crypt, and further shattered that long-undisturbed scepter piece. This had opened a new doorway that two militants were able to travel through, along with an unwilling participant: the Kingdom's beloved Ambassador of the People, Ydoro. To what end they were traveling to that other reality Jack could not be certain, but his guess would be it involved retrieving their displaced King, Alec Dorn.

As horrifying as that prospect undoubtedly was, Jack's real concern was for the safety of Cyrus, as an assassination attempt could not be ruled out. Nel remained in captivity but had been persistently tight-lipped about their plans. Something would have to be done, but Jack hadn't quite decided what that was yet. So here he sat, heavy-shouldered and resigned beside his wife the Queen; each knowing that their times of peace had at long last come to an end.

CHAPTER FOURTEEN

THE DORN EXPEDITION

D on't tell me you believe the old guy," Kat scoffed, "I know you love a good mystery but this..."

Mr. Pyrene just laughed and shook his head. "You had to be there, Kat. This guy believes it though! He truly believes that Alec Dorn, *another* person lost at sea in the 1930's, was walking around his old campus in the seventies."

"He also said he hadn't aged a day, though," Kat pointed out, attempting to make him see the absurdity of the tall tale. "Just because he believes it doesn't make it true. You said it yourself, the guy was ancient."

The two of them had been debating the implications of Mr. Pyrene's visit to Dane University for the past ten minutes, and while Kat was certainly intrigued by this growing web of mysteries, she was having trouble seeing how they all connected. In fact, she was having trouble keeping track of which mystery they were currently talking about.

"Ancient doesn't mean senile," Dean exclaimed, "I'm telling you, this guy seemed sharp! And the admissions woman said he'd been telling the same story for decades. So his age really has nothing to do with it."

"But how does this relate to anything?" Kat asked, not rhetorically but out of genuine confusion. "I mean, I really can't keep this straight. This professor, Alec Dorn, is the brother of Cyrus Dorn. And Cyrus Dorn is the first husband of Cynthia Voigt, who is the neighbor of Randall Evans..."

Mr. Pyrene nodded enthusiastically and continued her line of thought. "And Randall Evans is potentially a kid who got lost at sea in the late 1800s."

"Potentially," Kat pressed. "All we know is that he had the same date of birth as the kid who got lost. But if it was him, why were the records never corrected? It seems like, as far as official records are concerned, the Evans boy and his father never returned. So why come back, rejoin society, and not tell anyone who you are?"

"Yeah I don't know," Mr. Pyrene admitted. "But by all accounts, his only close friend in his later years was this Cynthia woman. And it's just a coincidence that she also lost her husband at sea?"

"Maybe they bonded over that fact?" Kat offered. "I mean, it's possible we're thinking too much into this."

Mr. Pyrene, however, waved a dismissive hand and said, "That article you found, about the Dorn expedition, you're sure it didn't mention anyone named Randall?"

"No," Kat insisted, turning back to her laptop and scanning the online article, "and like I said before, it was a totally different time. Those disappearances were separated by thirty-some years." She squinted at the screen and began reading the article, dated from 1936, aloud for the third time.

"The Dorn expedition, led by renowned Theoretical Physicist Cyrus Dorn, set out from New York last year bound for a shipping vessel that had become incapacitated during a routine voyage on the Atlantic Ocean. Captain Robert Froescher described an unexplainable event that damaged his ship and warped its frame beyond recognition. The Captain's account was verified by every member of the crew onboard. When Dorn's expedition arrived at the site, inexplicable leadership decisions led to the investigative team boarding a pair of dinghies and attempting to traverse the rough ocean waters for reasons unknown.

The boat carrying Dr. Dorn, his kid brother Alec, the First Mate Jack Viana, scientist Dalton Sydney, and Field Equipment Tech Nelida Yore, seemed to encounter some trouble and presumably sank to the depth, carrying its occupants along with it. Cynthia Dorn, the elder Dorn's wife, insists this was not the case and that hope remains for the team to be found. 'They would have been in the water,' Mrs. Dorn is quoted as saying, 'how would five people simply sink to the bottom that quickly?' But Lieutenant Allen, the expedition's military escort, had a different perspective. 'Mrs. Dorn doesn't want to give up hope for her husband,' Allen explained, 'but I was in the boat beside her, and we couldn't see what happened. From what we could tell, Expedition Lead Dorn had become injured, causing Mr. Viana to attempt a rescue. By the time our boat reached theirs, it had sunk, and no survivors were left on the surface of the water.' Mrs. Dorn continues her relentless search of the surrounding waters to this day, her efforts admirable, if potentially misplaced. Captain Froescher, a man with a penchant for wild tales, insists that something supernatural happened to his vessel, but it has not prevented him from a life on the ocean. 'I don't know how to explain it,' Froescher said, 'but I'd never felt anything like it before, and I've never felt anything like it since. I suppose our world still holds some mysteries that just aren't meant to be solved.'"

Kat finished her reading and looked up at Mr. Pyrene, wondering if he had gleaned anything new from her retelling.

"See, that's not a normal boating accident," he insisted, "I mean, Cynthia Dorn is right, how are five people going to just sink in the ocean together that quickly?"

"That doesn't explain why Alec would show up decades later without having aged," Kat pointed out with a laugh. "Or how this all connects back to The Hand of Jordan."

"Yeah," Mr. Pyrene sighed, "The Hand of Jordan. Is that the key? Or just another mystery that became wrapped up in this one?"

He reached into his desk drawer and pulled out the small ruby fragment he had found at Mauretz Abernally's estate sale. He turned it over in his hand several times, then put it onto the desk surface and gave it a spin.

"It has to be connected," he said with a far-off look in his eyes, "Nick Satterall knew he had found something special, even if everyone in the historic community told him otherwise. Possibly the chess pieces were carved by Randall at some point, I'll concede to that, but then what in the world is this?" He flicked the fragment again and it spun in a shallow circle. "Nick didn't want to part with it, Mauretz didn't want to part with it… even Randall it seems held it in some importance. Enough to hide it away in some cave." He flicked the fragment again.

Kat plucked the piece from the tabletop and held it up over her head, allowing the light from above to trickle through it. "It's sort of a weird material, isn't it? I mean, we keep calling it ruby, but it's not. It makes you wonder, doesn't it?"

But Mr. Pyrene didn't answer.

"Mr. Pyrene?" Kat said, looking over at him.

Something was wrong. Mr. Pyrene wore a slack, vacant expression that chilled her to the core. His eyes looked unfocused, like they weren't seeing the world in front of him.

"Mr. Pyrene," Kat said again in alarm.

His eyes started blinking rapidly and she suddenly realized he must be having some sort of medical episode. She dropped the fragment from her hand and moved towards him, but a horrible wave of vertigo crashed over her. It felt like someone had upended the entire room and left her suspended upside down. She tried to shake the sensation but found her vision was too blurred to move. She tried calling for help but her voice never left her lips. She was sinking, melting, fading, and there was nothing she could do to stop it.

CHAPTER FIFTEEN

THROUGH THIS WORLD OR THE NEXT

C yrus Dorn was skulking, but he had shunned his pride a few weeks back so found that it did not bother him in the slightest. The Cyrus of old may have cared about such trivial things as appearances, but no longer. He damned this entire wretched world that he was trapped in, so if a passerby saw him and judged, so be it. But he was skulking with a purpose. Something had occurred to Cyrus that perhaps had taken far too long to sink in; Alec Dorn, the power-hungry force of nature that had nearly brought an entire civilization to heel, would never in a million years be content to live as a family man in a world as mundane as this. His continual boasting about his perfect life had fooled Cyrus for a time, but something was finally ringing false about the façade. With this conviction arming him, Cyrus had decided to follow Alec this morning, and to his surprise, Alec kissed his stolen bride goodbye, walked out of his house, down the sidewalk a block towards the University campus, and then doubled back. He gave his home a wide berth, ducked under a fence leading back into his own backyard and seemed to vanish behind his shed.

With the route he had taken, Cynthia would not be able to see him even if she happened to be watching out the back windows, which led Cyrus to the conclusion that the sneaking was for her benefit. He watched the shed from behind a tree across the street, but Alec never reappeared. He gave it a good ten minutes before deciding further investigation was the only way to get answers. He stepped back out onto the sidewalk, crossed the street to his former backyard, and squeezed through a small gap between the fence and a large oak.

Given that the yard had once belonged to him, he was quite familiar with how everything should look, so the differences were striking. The most noticeable was the shed that he was now creeping alongside. It was made of wood, and structurally quite similar to the one Cyrus remembered, but it wasn't quite right. It was built differently, had a slightly altered layout, and generally seemed to be of poorer quality. Of course this variation was easily explained, and to be expected now that he thought about it. The shed from his own world had been built by Cyrus himself. He had distinct memories of acquiring the lumber, pouring the foundation and constructing it piece by piece. But the Cyrus of this world never lived in this house. On its surface, this information seemed obvious and not overly interesting, but the more he considered the implications of this shed, the more intriguing it was. The existence of the shed seemed to indicate that Alec bought this house without it, just as Cyrus had in his own world, and had it built in the exact spot that he was familiar with. It begged the question of why. Sure, a shed was a useful addition to the backyard, but care had been taken to build this one as close to the original as possible. If it hadn't been crafted with his own hands, Cyrus would not have been able to tell the difference. It opened up the larger question of why Alec felt compelled to buy this exact house as well. There were far grander homes in the community, but no, Alec had wanted this one; he had wanted Cyrus's house.

As he made his way around the side and towards the barn-style doors of the shed, he found them closed and could hear no noise coming from within. He glanced up towards the house, wary of Cynthia spotting him creeping around their yard, but the dense foliage from the trees provided plenty of cover and he was largely obscured. Cyrus peered through the half-inch gap between the doors but couldn't see movement of any kind inside the shed. Very carefully, he teased the doors open a crack, and then a bit more. Finally, he opened the doors fully and discovered there was no one inside. Alec had certainly looked like he was entering the shed when he had snuck into the backyard, but there was no sign of him now. The answer to this particular riddle, however, was sitting right in front of Cyrus, leaning carefully against the far wall. Alec's scepter, the weapon of the King as he had been fond of calling it, was propped lovingly in the far corner, its charred-looking bark concealing the significant power it held within. Alec had fallen through the anomaly in the Fire Fields with his weapon in hand, and here it now stood, preciously cared after for the better part of a decade.

At the base of the scepter, easily missed by the untrained eye, was a small fragment of the staff and a heavy knife. This immediately confirmed two things for Cyrus; Alec had at long last discovered how to manipulate the scepters to create wormholes to other realities, and he had just now opened one and stepped through it. As he processed this information, his first reaction was panic. If Alec had learned the secret to creating *doorways*, as Cyrus had on the island, could he feasibly have found a way back to his Kingdom? But the more he thought about it, the more unlikely this seemed. Wherever Alec was going, and it seemed he had been doing this for a while, he continued to come back. If Alec had found a path back to the island, nothing could make him return, not even his twisted desire to torture Cyrus with his stolen life. It did, however, beg the question of where he was going. Based on Cyrus's experimentation with doorways created by the scepters, Alec could be anywhere, in any time, in any version of the world.

A sadistic thought occurred to Cyrus. He knew from experience that slightly moving the broken shard of the scepter in this world would cause the doorway in the connected reality to move exponentially, potentially hundreds of miles. If Cyrus were to give that tiny shard a small kick, Alec's conjoining door on the other side would move, and he would be trapped. There was a sick satisfaction at the thought, but Cyrus decided it would achieve nothing. His life had already been stolen in this reality, and there was nothing he could do to correct that now.

Marooning Alec in yet another reality would certainly achieve a modicum of revenge that Cyrus sorely desired, but any possibility at a happily ever after would remain out of reach.

Be that as it may, nothing was preventing Cyrus from following his brother through the newly created anomaly and perhaps discovering what he was up to. He took a step towards the fragment and began to feel that all too familiar pressure behind his eyes and up into his nasal cavity. But he stopped abruptly as something occurred to him. He dove his hand into his pocket and pulled out the tiny fragment of scepter that he had taken to carrying with him everywhere he went. The miniscule shard didn't look like much, but was the reason that himself and Alec became separated by seven years the last time they traversed a wormhole together. He moved to place it carefully on one of the exposed beams along the side wall but was surprised to find a similar shard already occupying the space. Cyrus prodded at it gently but then shrugged. Whatever the fragment had been set aside for, it was not Cyrus's concern at the moment. He placed his own fragment apart from it, exhaled in preparation for his journey, then took another step. This one was met with a blinding sensation that was nearly unbearable.

As he took his third step, Cyrus began to rethink his curiosity as he remembered what happened the last time he had followed Alec through a wormhole, but the thought came too late. As his eyes squeezed shut, he stumbled forward, being pulled further into the shed by the invisible strength of the anomaly. He would have been at risk of slamming into the far wall but for the fact that the shed would not be present on the other side. Indeed, as he floundered onward, his boot caught on what felt like a root and he pitched forward, landing not on the concrete floor of the shed but on freshly cut grass.

Cyrus winced and breathed in slowly, thankful at the very least that he had not been deposited in the ocean this time. He opened his eyes to a well-kept lawn and the sounds of birds chirping overhead. He shook his head to rid the disorientation and got wobbly to one knee before finally standing upright, willing his head to clear. He was standing near a tree, the owner of the root he had tripped on, that arched up and over a neatly manicured suburban yard. But it wasn't just any suburban yard, it was *his* yard. The yard he had just left, or at least a version of it. This variation of the Dorn house was painted a mildly hideous cream-yellow and had fake wooden shutters that contrasted poorly with the surrounding décor. The tree he stood under was the same as he remembered it, but larger, having clearly been given extra years to grow. The shed was absent entirely from this world and the surrounding fence was now made of metal. But the location was unmistakable.

How was this possible? Cyrus had always found in his own experimentation that these *doors* opened at random to any location on earth, yet this one seemed to have led to exactly the same spot, though clearly in a different time. Perhaps the scepters behaved differently away from the island. In the end, Cyrus decided it mattered little *why* it was happening, only that Alec was here, somewhere in this world and this time.

He ducked out from under the trees and started his way up towards the house when he caught sight of an elderly woman staring out the window at him. Her pouchy face glowered at him suspiciously and she raised her eyebrows in alarm as he started to approach. Deciding Alec must not have gone into the house with this woman on patrol, Cyrus hastily made his way to the gate and let himself out onto the public sidewalk. The best he could think was that Alec had gone to the University, though he could not think why, so he began heading in that direction, entering the campus after a short distance. It looked largely the same as he remembered, but how often would old buildings like these actually be updated? The automobiles lining the streets looked a bit more sleek, however, leading him to believe this was likely not the 1930's anymore.

Cyrus attempted to look authoritative as he traversed the campus, but it seemed to hardly matter; the students and teachers going about their daily lives paid him no attention at all. He scanned the faces as they passed, searching for any sign of Alec, but also realized it was unlikely he would be simply wandering with the throngs of schoolgoers. More probable, he would be in one of the many administrative buildings, perhaps the one that housed his old office. Cyrus spotted it across the walkway and began towards it when a woman caught his eye. She was exiting a neighboring building but had done a double-take when she saw Cyrus in the crowd. Cyrus squinted at her until recognition finally kicked in and he realized it was Alec's old friend Diana Rahm, albeit middle-aged at this point. It of course was not unexpected that he would run into alternate versions of the staff he knew, but it hadn't occurred to him until now that this was a reality where the Dorn brothers had likely never returned from their ill-fated voyage. Unfortunately, he had allowed his gaze to linger a moment too long and Diana's furrowed brow of confusion was slowly fading into a look of gaping awe.

Cyrus attempted to bow his head away from her and turned into the crowd of walking students.

"Hey!" he heard Diana call out.

Cyrus panicked and made his way to the nearest building, which happened to be the campus library. He heaved the doors open quickly and scrambled inside, scanning for a place to disappear. To his immense disappointment, the rooms were sparsely populated and there was no obvious group he could blend in with. He began hurrying down a corridor of bookshelves just as he heard the doors bang open again and a voice call out.

"Cyrus!?" Diana's voice shouted, causing several alarmed students to look in her direction.

Cyrus had managed to hide behind one of the shelves just in time, but he knew his spot would be easily found as she strode further into the library. He could see her through a gap in the books and she looked positively bewildered. Her eyes were wide and tearful as they desperately searched the area, and Cyrus felt a pang of guilt for allowing himself to be seen. He had no idea what year this was, but it seemed clear that the Cyrus of this world, and presumably Alec as well, had never returned, so seeing him was like seeing a ghost. The idea of giving her hope of seeing her long-lost friend again seemed so horribly unfair to Cyrus.

He was running out of shelf as she quickly made her way deeper into the library and he knew he was about to be discovered when the front doors flung open again with a loud clang. Diana glanced over her shoulder but then stopped dead in her tracks at seeing who the newcomer was. Cyrus peered through the carefully filed library books to see

Alec standing at the front of the room, looking mildly surprised to be facing his old friend at last. Diana was simply staring at him with her mouth agape and tears flooding down her face. She didn't seem to know what to do with herself as her lips formed several silent words that never became audible.

Alec walked towards her, a sheepish smile on his face. "I know this is a lot," he began to say.

Diana cut him off and began stammering. "I... I... What are you... How are you... You didn't... You never..."

Alec finally came to a stop in front of her and stared into her eyes.

"You're dead," Diana managed to say, "you never came back... it's been decades."

Alec reached out a comforting hand and placed it gently on her shoulder, but she flinched badly at the gesture. Suddenly seeming to lose control entirely, she broke down in loud, echoing sobs. She hugged Alec deeply and started saying, "There's just no way... you can't be here... I can't even... where have you been?"

Alec hugged her back and soothed, "It's okay, Di, I know. It'll be okay."

Suddenly Diana pulled away from his embrace as though she had finally processed the situation fully and stared uncomprehendingly into his eyes. "You can't be Alec Dorn. You look the same as I remember you."

"It's hard to explain," Alec conceded, "and I know it's a lot to take in. But I'm here now, that's what's important."

Alec glanced over Diana's shoulder in the direction of Cyrus, still peering out from behind the bookshelf, and shot him a murderous look. It suddenly became clear that Alec had not intended on being seen in this reality, and this reunion was not a part of his plan. Cyrus just shook his head in disgust at Alec's play-acting to Diana. It made him sick that he was feeding his old friend this bullshit about being back, when he obviously intended to leave again in a matter of hours.

"How do you look so young?" Diana asked, now stroking the sides of Alec's cheeks.

"I've been trapped on an island," Alec offered, at least admitting to a half-truth in this instance.

"But it's been so long," Diana pushed, with tears now freely flowing down her cheeks. "And your brother! I saw him! He's... he's... but his wife, she held a funeral... he never came back."

Cyrus felt as though a steel clamp were compressing his chest. He could not bear the thought of Cynthia searching for him and waiting for him, and eventually grieving for him. It was all too real, watching the people who had been left behind. A part of him wanted nothing more than to scour this world until he found Cynthia Dorn, return to her and live out his life with her. But he had to remind himself that this world's Cynthia was waiting for a different Cyrus, one she had shared a life with and made her own memories beside. It was semantics, maybe, and very likely that many of their memories of life together *would* overlap, but it felt wrong. This was not *his* world, and it would not be *his* Cynthia.

Alec was continuing to console Diana in as gentle a manner as possible, but Cyrus's stomach was coiling at the false comfort. He envisioned approaching this world's Cynthia in the same manner, offering her reassurance and hope only to abandon her again, this time by choice. It was sickening.

"Cynthia is okay, I'm sure," Alec was insisting to Diana. "It's been a long time, I'm sure she was able to move on."

Cyrus's gut twitched uncomfortably.

"She hired search parties," Diana said, "whole expeditions went out looking for your team. But it was all her. Her drive to find Cyrus was unbreakable."

Alec made a strange face, as though he were repressing a grimace. "Well apparently it was breakable in the end."

Cyrus snapped. Before he even knew what he was doing, Cyrus was barreling towards his brother like an uncaged animal, blinded by his half-buried rage finally rearing its ugly head. Diana looked up in alarm but Cyrus bypassed her entirely and tackled Alec bodily off his feet, smashing him through a nearby desk and sending a large, pull-chain lamp shattering to the floor. He punched his brother across the face sending a spray of blood misting across the ornate marble. Diana screamed out and Cyrus punched Alec again. Alec flailed wildly in the tangle of debris from the ruined desk and managed to unbalance Cyrus, finally connecting a fist with his jaw. Students at the far reaches of the library were staring in amazement, but no one made a move to step in. Alec attempted to right himself but Cyrus grabbed ahold of his shirt collar and flung him headlong over the remains of the table, sending his body careening into a heap on the other side.

"You son of a bitch!" Cyrus shouted at him, his powerful voice echoing off the vaulted ceilings of the torn apart room. "Tell her the truth you fucking coward!" He turned to Diana, still watching the violence with a hand clapped over her mouth, and yelled, "That's not the Alec Dorn you knew! That's the husk left behind after temptation consumed him!"

Alec was beginning to stand upright again, though unsteadily after his beating. He stayed hunkered slightly, like a cornered animal ready to strike out. And to Cyrus's surprise, he managed a grin, one that looked especially predatory with blood covering his exposed teeth.

"Now there's the Cyrus I remember," Alec sneered.

Cyrus just shook his head, but Diana was staring at her friend with renewed astonishment.

"He's right," Diana managed to say, "you're not the Alec I knew." As Alec continued to stare at her with an intensity that was difficult to read, she watched him for a moment before finally whispering, "What *are* you?"

Cyrus glanced sideways at Diana, suddenly impressed that she was able to see through her old friend's mask with such clarity. With his eyes locked back on his bloodied brother, Cyrus growled in response, "That right there is the monster within all of us, forever trying to claw its way to the surface. That's our darkness, at long last given human form."

Alec finally stood tall again and wiped the dripping blood from his chin. "What are you doing here, brother?" he asked in a low snarl, "this isn't your world."

"It's not yours either," Cyrus responded, "and I'll be damned if I let you infect another one."

"You couldn't stop me before," Alec said with a smirk, "it's possible you're not quite as strong as your people liked to tell you."

"Diana," Cyrus said, still not taking his eyes off Alec, "my brother and I are going to be leaving in a hurry in just a moment, and I want you to understand something." He could see Diana's attention turn to him out of the corner of his vision, and Alec gave a dismissive laugh, but Cyrus continued. "I want you to know that he and I are not a part of your world. We are best well forgotten by the time we leave, and I beg you to not spend too much of your life trying to understand what happened here today. It will be a waste of your happiness. All you need to know is that this is not your friend standing in front of you, and there was nothing you could have done to save him. Do you understand me?"

Diana made a noncommittal sort of noise and stammered that she didn't understand any of this. But Alec began to laugh.

"Still trying to save everyone," Alec taunted. "What makes you think we're leaving in a hurry?"

Cyrus gave Diana one last comforting smile, hoping that she would heed his advice, then turned back to Alec and said, "Because if I get back through that *doorway* first, I'm sealing it behind me… and you'll be cut off from your scepter, your one and only link to that island."

Alec's smile faltered, then slid from his face entirely. His eyes flicked briefly to Diana, then back to Cyrus.

Cyrus stared back at him, forced a smirk, and just to make sure he had his brother good and riled, he winked at him. Then he bolted.

Cyrus ran as fast as he could towards the exit of the library, and he could tell by the clambering footsteps echoing over shattered wood behind him that Alec had given chase. Cyrus flung the front doors open and sprinted across campus, praying that he was correct in thinking he was the faster of the two brothers. By the time he had reached the edge of the University grounds, Alec had closed the gap between them and was grasping at Cyrus's shirt sleeves. Cyrus turned and shoved his brother hard just as they entered the street, and the screeching of brakes announced a car approaching fast. As a maroon sedan lurched to a halt, Cyrus and Alec spilled onto its hood, both sets of hands still grappling at each other. Cyrus wrenched his brother up by his shirt-collar and slammed him back into the car, pushing himself back onto his feet as he did so. He lurched onward as Alec screamed something after him. A look over his shoulder showed Alec sprinting towards him with such ferocity that Cyrus's confidence faltered. If he couldn't get to the doorway first, he would be lost.

As the metal fence came into view, Cyrus didn't bother looking for the gate this time but instead used his momentum to launch himself up onto it and over the other side.

Alec was right on his tail. Cyrus didn't necessarily care about trapping Alec here as long as he didn't get trapped himself. He was practically on top of the tree root that had tripped him earlier before he felt the pressure returning to his sinuses. He breathed a sigh of relief as his eyes were forced shut and he allowed the anomaly to whisk him away.

Cyrus staggered hard into the wooden wall of the shed and knew he was back. A crashing sound from behind him announced Alec's return as well, who began scrambling around desperately to collect his precious scepter. He gave the shard on the ground a swift kick and it bounced off into the dusty corner.

Both brother's shoulders heaved up and down steadily as they struggled to catch their breath side by side, as strange as that felt to Cyrus. He glanced over at Alec who gave him a withering look, but then seemed to laugh slightly in spite of the situation. Cyrus straightened up and made his way towards the door, then remembered to pluck his own scepter fragment from the beam along the wall. Unfortunately, Alec saw the gesture. He intercepted before Cyrus had time to react and snatched the small fragment into his own hand.

"Where did you get this?" Alec exclaimed, seemingly mesmerized by the piece.

Cyrus had no more stomach for games. He punched Alec hard, who staggered into the wall from the blow. Cyrus was able to force the shard out of his brother's hand and he quickly deposited it into his own pocket.

Alec glared at him, but then shrugged in apparent disinterest. "What do I care, keep your little fragment. It's the closest you'll ever get to real power again."

Cyrus ignored the taunt but noted that Alec's eyes flicked to the other shard that had been placed on the wooden beam of the shed before Cyrus's arrival, seemingly verifying its continued safety. Cyrus turned and let himself through the door and out into the yard.

"What, leaving already?" Alec jeered after him, but Cyrus stayed silent. He had nothing worth saying at this point. "At least you've got some of your fight back," Alec continued to call, "god you were getting dull!" As Cyrus made his way to the gate and let himself onto the sidewalk, Alec shouted, "Oh, dinner this Sunday if you're around, Cynthia's making a roast." He laughed mockingly as he said it, but Cyrus wasn't fooled. Alec was bored in this world, and his only reprieve from the banality of the days was in his bitter nemesis, whom he had marooned himself with.

CHAPTER SIXTEEN

THE ALCHEMIST

Noma stood up in his cramped, endlessly dusty workshop and wove between the piles of strewn rubbish to the front window and gazed out of it hopefully. Still no King Jack. He turned back the way he had come and followed the narrow path he had created between the sea of trinkets. It was not a small workshop, but his ever-growing collection of tools, supplies, and experiments made it impossible to navigate from one side to another in a straight line.

Noma came to a stop facing the far wall and eased himself onto the debris-covered floor in front of his latest endeavor. Standing upright and harnessed into place atop a wooden stand was the top half of King Cyrus Dorn's scepter. The base of the wooden stand was bolted into the floor below, ensuring that the weapon could not move an inch. It had been secured in this way for several days now, as Noma continued his experimentation.

King Jack had approached him personally and asked that he look into the oddities and significant powers that the scepter possessed, hoping for a clue that could help him correct the debacle from several days' prior. Noma was young, but quite observant, and he could certainly note a buried sense of panic in the King's request. The King and Queen seemed to blame themselves for the assault that occurred at the base of the Guardian statue, and were desperate for the militants who had breached the crypt to be reclaimed. The trouble was, those militants had clawed their way out of this world entirely, and there was no telling where they had gone. That was precisely the task that had been set out before Noma. He had to gain a better understanding of the strange abilities of the scepters and find a way for the King and Queen to use them to their advantage. He had invited King Jack to come by the workshop and observe his progress, but so far he had not shown up. Noma had made a recent discovery that, while not a solution just yet, was intriguing.

In a tense trial just last night, Noma had found that the sandy particles known as frozen fire could in fact be manipulated. When the substance was superheated in a crucible and combined with liquid hot metal, it could be poured, forged, and hardened. Exciting as this was to Noma, Jack would likely not be overly impressed by the revelation. But the question that Noma now sought to answer was of much greater importance; given the scepter's almost magnetic attraction to the substance, could melted frozen fire be used to fuse broken fragments back together? They had seen the result of the staff being broken, but what would happen if one found a way to repair that break?

Noma regarded himself as an exquisite craftsman, having learned everything he knew from his father, and much of the town relied on him for general repairs. But the truth was, this particular innovation of essentially liquifying frozen fire was not his own. He had help, and it had come from the strangest of places.

No sooner had the thought entered his mind than the shuffling of footsteps announced the approach of his secret advisor. Noma looked up, and had anyone else been present it would have looked as though Noma was staring straight past the anchored scepter-half and into the empty wall five feet away. And that was precisely what Noma was doing, except that he knew the empty space was *not* in fact empty, and would not remain unoccupied for long.

Seeming to spontaneously materialize in the dusty workshop air before him, a cloaked man walked forward, gave Noma a warm smile, and eased himself onto the floor sitting across from him.

"Noma," the man purred, giving him a piercing stare from deep sockets within his leathery, warped face. This man was called the Alchemist, and he was a visitor from a far-removed reality. The Alchemist was unpleasant to look upon by any standard. His face was twisted and deformed; the results of a long-ago experiment gone horribly wrong. Lines creased his face not from age but from injury. Scar tissue built up several calloused patches that extended down his neck and, presumably, to the farther reaches of his body. His hands were clawed and grotesque, but still nimble enough for fine detail work, as miraculous as that seemed to Noma. The man was sharp, that much was clear, but his decades of work with unstable materials had taken a heavy toll. Noma would guess he was in his sixties, though the extensive disfigurement made it impossible to tell for certain.

"Hello sir," Noma greeted him, politely trying to stop his curious eyes from exploring the hideous damage to the man's physique.

King Jack had explained to Noma that the scepters were capable of projecting a view to another reality if left stationary for a period of time. This *window* only stayed open for as long as the scepter remained undisturbed, and would instantly close when the weapon was moved. So Noma's first experiment had been to secure the half-scepter to the floor, so that it was impossible to move without real effort. That was when the Alchemist had first shown himself, greeting him from a distant time and a different world. As it happened, the man was an innovator just like Noma, and he had been able to guide much of Noma's experimenting. The two had taken on a bit of a teacher and apprentice type of relationship over the past few days, and Noma was eternally grateful for the help. The Alchemist was from a more advanced version of the Kingdom and had advised Noma on the possibility of fusing the fragments of scepter back together. He had been patient in his teachings, and supportive of Noma finding his way, even if all he could offer was his words. This was the limitation of an open window to another reality; the worlds were overlapping each other in this particular spot alone, and the vision of the Alchemist sitting before him now was able to interact with Noma's world only within this small space.

"So what do we have on the agenda for today?" the Alchemist asked. He spoke in a smooth, liquid-like voice that dribbled each word out like melted butter.

"The King is coming by soon," Noma informed him, "to see the progress we made last night."

"The progress *you* made, son," the Alchemist insisted. "Don't be so quick to give away credit."

Noma brushed off the compliment and said, "I want to try actually fusing fragments together today."

"Patience," the Alchemist soothed, "don't start running before you've first learned to walk."

Noma thought it curious that a man so scarred by prior experiments would be cautioning against rashness, but perhaps that was exactly why.

"I just know how dire the situation is," Noma insisted, "I have to find answers for the King and Queen."

"You will," the Alchemist assured him, "when we spoke yesterday, you confided in me how important this is to you, to impress your king."

"Do you have a king?" Noma asked.

The Alchemist just smiled. "We all have leaders, but things work a bit differently in my time. We don't all have the benefit of Cyrus Dorn in our recent memory."

"He's long gone now," Noma reflected, "I was just a kid when he was around."

"You must remember something about him," the Alchemist pressed. "Was he as strong as they say? Or was it just circumstances that helped him rise to greatness?"

"I... I really don't remember," Noma insisted. But he felt he was somehow letting his newfound mentor down by not having more answers. "King Jack talks of him often," he finally offered. "They were close. To be honest, I think Cyrus Dorn left a bit of a hole in the Kingdom when he left. People don't talk about it, but you can feel it a bit."

The Alchemist smiled. "I know how important it is for you to prove your worth. I think this experiment of ours will do just that. What fragments are you going to test our theory on?"

Noma turned and retrieved a satchel-type bag from the floor behind him and stuck his hand inside. From within he pulled three small, jagged shards of the damaged scepter from the assault earlier in the week. According to the stories being told, the militants had smashed at the scepter-half with a war hammer to open a door to another reality, and these fragments were the result of that damage. The rest of that scepter-half still lay beneath the monument, for now undisturbed. Noma had thought it best to conduct his experiments away from the actual scepter intended for repair, at least until he knew what results could be had.

He lay the three fragments onto the floor in front of himself carefully, respecting the immense power they carried. The Alchemist's eyes brightened upon seeing them, apparently also taken with their importance.

"Funny how something so tiny can hold such power," the Alchemist reflected, narrowing his eyes to the small fragments on the floor.

"So how would this work, exactly?" Noma asked, his eagerness suddenly giving way to trepidation.

"Well," the Alchemist began softly, "the idea would be to fuse these pieces back onto the staff that they broke from. But for now, the initial test should be if the fragments truly can be fused. I would suggest attempting with two of the small pieces first."

Noma nodded, then looked at the man's ruined face and hands and began to recognize the danger of such boldness. He opened his mouth to voice his concern when a sudden knock came from the front door.

"That must be King Jack," Noma said, "I suppose our experiment will have to wait."

The Alchemist nodded his head in understanding and replied, "The King is lucky to have you. It's okay to believe in yourself."

Noma appreciated the statement but also found it odd for this particular moment. "I can introduce you, if you like," he offered.

The Alchemist shook his head slowly, "He might not understand. I would keep our conversations between the two of us, if I were you. I feel sure I'll meet him soon enough."

Noma understood his point, but another knock on the door cut the conversation short. "We'll pick this up later today," he insisted, to which the Alchemist agreed.

Noma stood up, dusted himself off and cut his way through the winding maze of his shop to the front door. He pulled it open and there stood the King, squinting in the afternoon sunlight. Jack did not look, or even particularly act, like an important king. He had a casual, apprehensive way about him that got in the way of his projection of authority. Noma supposed everyone had their own specific brand of leading, but found Jack's particular style left something to be desired. He certainly meant well, and that earned Noma's unwavering loyalty, but he had doubts that people would choose him as someone to line up behind.

Noma stood aside to admit him and closed the door softly once he was inside.

"Thank you for coming, King Jack," Noma declared, to which Jack just nodded in distracted response. "I was hoping to be a bit further along at this point, but I'd like to show you the discoveries I've made so far."

Jack agreed and allowed himself to be led through the shop to the back.

"Essentially what I am trying to do," Noma began as they walked, "is repair the damaged scepters with a method using liquified frozen fire. I have confirmed that the frozen fire can be worked with, so my next step is to attempt a repair." They arrived at the back of the shop, empty now that the Alchemist had retreated back into his own world, and Noma continued, "My next step is going to be attempting to fuse together these three fragments here." He gestured to the carefully placed pieces lined up on the floor, and then paused with a furrowed brow. His workstation remained intact, with the half-scepter still affixed to the stand, but on the floor beside it, only two scepter fragments now sat.

"Everything okay?" Jack asked.

"I… there were three pieces here… just a second ago," Noma stammered in confusion.

Jack shrugged slightly, understandably not recognizing the significance of the missing piece. Noma shrugged as well, though his own carefree gesture was forced, and decided to press onward. He proceeded to demonstrate to Jack how the frozen fire could be mixed with a soft metal such as bronze or copper and melted down. He further showed how this liquid combination could be poured into a mold or a concave made in sand, and that presumably, they could repair the fragmented scepter.

"When a piece is broken from the staff," Noma explained, "that piece is what tears a hole in our reality. But you have to remember, that specific break causes a wormhole to one specific reality. If you break a second piece, it opens a *new* wormhole to a *different* reality." He paused a moment to allow Jack's thoughts to catch up, then asked his burning question. "So what happens if you fuse those fragments back into place?"

Jack's head swayed thoughtfully, and his eyes narrowed a bit in concentration, but before long a smile began to decorate his features. "That's not bad, Noma." Noma beamed in response. "You think the repair may reclaim the people that were lost?"

"I think it's possible," Noma answered, "but of course I have no idea for certain. I think it's worth trying though."

Jack nodded enthusiastically. "I think it's worth trying too. How soon can you have this ready?"

Noma thought a moment and then responded, "It depends how much of a show you want to make of it. I can test it in here, although I don't know if it matters that it's a different location from where it was broken."

"I don't need an audience," Jack said, "but I think we should try it where Cyrus originally dropped the scepter. Give ourselves the best chance."

Noma agreed and the two talked back and forth planning out the far-fetched experiment. However, Noma didn't think it was as far-fetched as it sounded. After all, the idea was conceived by the Alchemist, who seemed fairly certain that it would work.

Noma's stomach squirmed slightly thinking of the Alchemist again. He was positive there had been three shards laid out on the ground; he could picture it clearly in his mind's eye. Had the third piece somehow gotten kicked under something when he stood up? He thought it was exceedingly unlikely given the care he had taken with them. The only conclusion he could draw was that the Alchemist had taken one for some reason. But for what purpose?

"Noma?" Jack asked, looking at him with mild concern in his eyes.

"Yeah, it's fine," Noma finally said with a dismissive shake of his head. "I was just thinking again how I could have sworn there had been three fragments. Must have miscounted."

But he hadn't miscounted, and it wasn't fine. Why in the world would the Alchemist want a fragment of the broken scepter? But admitting to Jack how much this worried him would require explaining that he had trusted the security of their kingdom to an outsider that he knew very little about. Only now, looking back, did Noma realize how foolish that had been.

CHAPTER SEVENTEEN

BYGONE DAYS

Cyrus had not been able to get that other scepter fragment out of his mind. The one he had noticed in Alec's backyard shed, placed with seemingly careful consideration on a support beam along one of the side walls. It was clear that Alec had been traversing multiple realities since he learned of the scepter's ability to open wormholes, so it stood to reason that small fragments of scepter would be scattered throughout that shed. But why was this particular fragment set aside? Perhaps it was simply placed there absent-mindedly at one point and forgotten, however the way Alec had eyed it during their scuffle over Cyrus's own fragment made him wonder. He had given it a day, but found his curiosity could not be abated. He also found that he did not have much care for the consequences of his actions anymore. With the prison Alec had constructed for him seeming completely and profoundly inescapable, it left him with little, if anything, to lose.

Alec had gone to his job at the University this morning, a rarity from what Cyrus could tell, though he supposed it was entirely based on his class schedule. This left the backyard, and the shed, unguarded for the time being. Using the opportunity to explore undisturbed, Cyrus let himself into his brother's backyard through the same gap in the fence he had utilized two days prior and made his way towards the heavily weathered barn-style doors.

"Cyrus?" came a voice from across the yard.

Cyrus winced but hoped he had disguised his regret quickly enough. He looked up to see Cynthia waving at him from across the yard and raised his own hand in greeting as he pivoted to meet her.

"What are you doing here?" Cynthia asked.

"Alec said I could borrow his shovel," Cyrus lied, pointing towards the shed.

To his immense relief, he noted that Cynthia had her purse slung over one shoulder and her keys in hand. She must be on her way out.

Cynthia nodded but stayed quiet a moment, analyzing Cyrus with eyes of searching concern. He would often catch her looking at him in this way, as though worried he may break down at any moment. From her perspective, of course, he had been through an ordeal at sea alone, and her caution with him was understandable. "How have you been holding up?" she finally asked.

As Cyrus answered that he was fine, it occurred to him that this was the first time he had found himself alone with his one-time wife.

"You don't always have to be fine," Cynthia insisted, peering at him like she was trying to see past a mask. "I know you try to stay strong around Alec, but I can tell how much pain you continue to be in. I won't pretend to know what you're going through, but I can imagine how foreign this place must feel after your ordeal."

Cyrus was baffled by the accuracy of her words, even if she herself didn't fully understand just how true they were.

"It's been a lot," Cyrus conceded, "and I wish I could explain better."

"You don't have to," Cynthia assured him, "you'll tell us when you're ready. But I can see you maybe starting to pull away from Alec a bit, and I just wanted to encourage you to lean on those relationships with the people who love you."

Cyrus was finding it difficult to maintain his composure at the absurdity of what she was unknowingly saying. "There are things you will just never understand," Cyrus insisted.

"You can try me, ya know," Cynthia responded comfortingly. "I'm a good listener, and I care about you Cyrus."

Being this close to his one-time wife and being asked to bare his soul was playing with his mind. It was so incredibly tempting to just start talking and never stop; tell her about everything he had been through, his fight to get back to her, and what had unknowingly happened to her life. But it wouldn't be right to put that on her, and it would solve nothing. That was the brilliance of Alec's takeover of this world; it left Cyrus carefully watched but unable to scream.

Cyrus nodded his head appreciatively and finally responded in a low voice, "Maybe some day, in another life, we'll have this conversation. On that day, I'll tell you everything I've been through. Everything I've done, the triumphs and the failures, the moments of doubt and the moments of joy. On that day, I'll tell you how much your kindness and compassion has meant to me, and how it kept me going in the darkest of times. On that day, you'll know who I truly am."

It looked like tears were threatening to form in Cynthia's eyes for just a moment, but they never fell. She almost seemed to appreciate the weight of what Cyrus wanted to tell her without truly understanding why. She smiled slightly at him and put a hand on his shoulder.

"I'm going to hold you to that, Cyrus," she said softly. "On that day… in another life… I look forward to meeting the real you."

Cyrus gazed into her eyes, searching for the tiniest glimmer of recognition from her that he knew would never come. "On that day in another life," he repeated to her, barely above a whisper.

"Well I've… I've gotta run," Cynthia said apologetically, "I'm sorry."

"I'll see you around, Cynthia," Cyrus said softly.

Cynthia turned and walked towards the gate, and Cyrus was grateful. He was worried that if he stared at her much longer, he would lose his conviction entirely and confess everything. He reminded himself forcefully, as he had done countless times by now, that that was not his Cynthia. His own Cynthia was out there somewhere, in another world, waiting for him to return. His chest swelled at the thought. He *would* find a way back to her.

But now, to more pressing matters. As Cynthia disappeared down the street, Cyrus turned and heaved the doors of the shed open. It was dark within, but narrow beams of light from between the warping slats of the walls illuminated the excessive amount of floating dust in the air, bathing the room with an eerie glow. He spotted the mysterious fragment right away, still undisturbed on the beam along the wall, and nodded his head. The fact that Alec hadn't moved it made his mission easier, though that likely indicated it was not of any significance after all. Cyrus plucked it from its resting place and noted a ring of dust from where it had been lifted. Apparently it had not been moved in quite a long time. He tilted it up to one of the many steams of sunlight filtering in from outside and turned the piece over in his fingers. At roughly an inch long and half-an-inch wide, it looked just as unimportant as his own fragment of scepter, but as always, the longer he stared into its ruby depths, the more entranced he became.

He finally pulled his gaze away and looked around for some sort of tool that would be strong enough to fracture it. If he truly wanted to find out if this specific *door* held any significance at all, he would have to step through it, and the only way to do that would be to re-break the fragment. He couldn't readily spot the knife Alec had used previously, but a heavy spade shovel leaned against the corner would do just fine. Cyrus snatched it into his hands and, with a slight shrug, tossed the scepter-fragment onto the concrete floor. He considered his plan for a moment, trying to decide if he was being reckless or not, and whether he cared. He decided that he did not. Bold was the only way forward in this unrecognizable hell.

Cyrus lifted the shovel up and stabbed down hard on the fragment. He had thought it might take several attempts, but a rupturing sensation behind his eyes told him that he had succeeded. Standing directly over the newly created doorway, Cyrus was pulled through almost immediately, shovel and all. He flailed slightly at the sensation of falling, but he felt solid ground beneath his feet before long and he was left stumbling, blind and throbbing, in this new mystery world.

There was loose rock below his feet, something he could both feel through his shoes and hear as his steps crunched beneath him. For a wild moment he pictured the Fire Fields and wondered if Alec had somehow managed to find a link back to a version of their lost Kingdom, but as he forced his eyes open, he saw the drab sun-bleached beige of unremarkable and familiar earthly rock. He lifted his gaze and scanned his surroundings. The first thing of note was that there was *nothing* of note around him. It was a slightly hilly landscape with trees dotting the area and giving way to a more substantial forest after a quarter mile or so. The clearing he stood in was mostly rocky with tufts of prairie grasses and yellowing vegetation somehow finding the nutrients needed to survive. But it was noticeably empty, and quiet. Sure, the occasional bird could be heard chirping on the breeze, and the wind blew lightly at the leaves of the forest, but there was a stillness to the world that unnerved him. It was like civilization had never reached this place.

Cyrus, recognizing the danger of losing track of the anomaly's location, lifted a large stick from the ground and stabbed it into the earth forcefully, leaving himself an easily identifiable marker to return to. He turned and began hiking towards the treeline, unsure of what he hoped to find and increasingly uncertain that he would come across anything of interest.

It was five minutes before he reached the edge of the forest, and again he was struck by just how quiet the area was.

"Hello?!" Cyrus called out, his voice echoing off the surrounding rocks and bouncing about into the distance. No reply came. Not even the flapping wings of a startled bird could be heard.

Cyrus continued to walk through the sparsely populated forest, giving a wary glance back towards the marker he had left for himself. If something were to appear dangerous, it would be prudent to have a clear path to his exit, though it was appearing increasingly likely this world was entirely uninhabited.

He took another few steps and then stopped suddenly. There was an animal up ahead, visible between the trees and low to the ground. Cyrus squinted in its direction, readying himself to flee. He couldn't make out any details about the animal, just that it was covered in coarse reddish-brown hair and stood about three feet off the ground. He suddenly regretted not arming himself before he began his trek. Even the metal shovel lay forgotten by the entrance to the wormhole. The animal was not moving, however, and seemed to have taken no notice of him at all. Remembering his newfound penchant for boldness, and praying he would not regret it, Cyrus began creeping towards the animal, slowly and steadily. He was approaching at an angle, hoping to give it a wide enough berth that it would flee the other direction if it became alarmed, but as he came ever closer, it struck him as increasingly odd that the animal had not moved at all. He furrowed his brow, took a deep breath, then crossed the final few paces assertively. Cyrus positioned himself behind the last clump of trees, still ten feet from the creature, and slowly peered around them.

It was immediately clear why the animal was not moving. It had not been alive for some time. It was an animal hide, in fact, dried out and heavily used, propped up on a low-hanging branch to warm in the sun. It wasn't the only thing set behind the trees, either. There was a small pile of blackened and charred wood, the remnants of a fire from the night prior, and several makeshift tools made of stone decorated the campsite. Cyrus had no idea what to make of it. It almost seemed to be from the time of early humans, but was that possible? Then a thought suddenly occurred to him.

Cyrus reached into his pocket and winced as he felt his own fragment of scepter within. He withdrew the piece with a shake of his head and looked down at it. He had forgotten to remove it when he had travelled through the wormhole, was it possible that was the reason for this strange world?

Something was not ringing true about this theory, but he was interrupted from exploring it further by a tingling sensation running up the back of his neck. Cyrus suddenly felt certain he was in danger. He looked up and began scanning the surrounding trees, still silent as a tomb. And then he saw it. His heart dropped. There was a man standing twenty feet from him, his arms hanging at his sides and a slight tilt to his head. The man was standing absolutely motionless. He was one of the slenderest humans Cyrus had ever laid eyes on, his exposed chest sunken in and revealing a sickeningly defined ribcage. His emaciated arms hung like strings at his sides and his pinched cheeks left his mouth slightly agape from malnutrition. An enormous beard covered the lower half of his face and his wild, filthy hair draped past his shoulders in knotted curtains. His eyes looked unnervingly empty as though he were not capable of higher brain function, and the way he looked at Cyrus was predatory and animalistic.

Cyrus wasn't sure he had ever been so unnerved in his entire life. Primitive though the man seemed, he was chilling to look at, and staring at him now recalled a sickly horror from within his gut that seemed to warn of primeval danger. He stared back at the man for a second more, then took a wobbly step backwards.

The man bellowed. It was the first noise he had made since appearing, and it was horrifying. Suddenly, the man broke into a run, charging towards Cyrus like a banshee out of his darkest nightmares. Cyrus turned to flee, nearly slipping on the loose rock below his feet. The man was nearly on him in no time at all, swinging a pair of stones connected by a tether made of browning sinew. He was deftly navigating the treacherous terrain with ease and Cyrus barreled through the trees towards the clearing and the marker he had stabbed into the earth, but it was still so far away.

Suddenly he was hit from behind by something hard. He careened forward, smashing to the forest floor and tumbling to rest in a heap near a pile of stacked firewood. As he scrambled to find his footing, he looked back and saw the man baring down on him, his eyes wide and deranged. Cyrus turned but was hit again. This time, his hand went down hard against the earth and he felt his wrist twinge badly. To his horror, the scepter fragment clutched in his fist, the one he had carried with him since exiting the Kingdom, released from his grip and bounced to the ground before tumbling away.

The moment the fragment fell from his fingers, a dizzying sensation began to overtake him. He wanted to turn and raise his arms against the next attack from the man but found he couldn't quite manage it. His vision was blurring and his head felt like it was splitting in two. Violent streaks of light began to overtake him and an enormous pressure behind his eyes forced them shut. His consciousness was fading, the terrifying man was closing in, and he was powerless to defend himself. His eyes flickered, he saw movement, then something beyond it. A light? Something glowing. Fire.

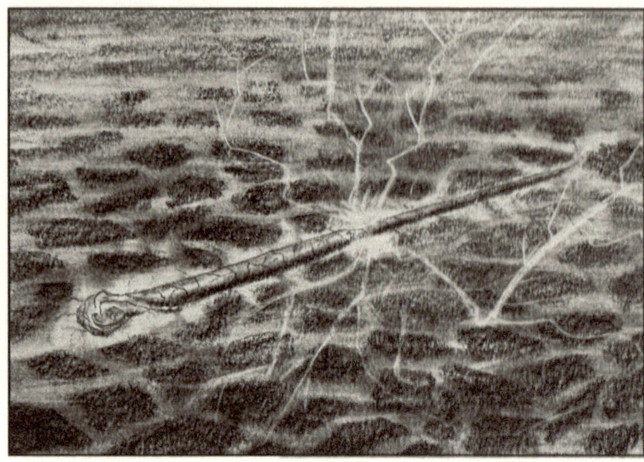

CHAPTER EIGHTEEN

FROM BEYOND

The weather in the Kingdom was mild enough, but the sky above was threatening to turn angry. As Jack looked up at the green-tinged clouds overhead, the wind beginning to snap at his clothes as he stood below the statue of the Guardian, he hoped the coming storm did not bode ill for their imminent experiment. The features of Cyrus Dorn's stone-carved face looming above seemed to darken with the sky, turning his expression from stoic to fierce. Jack pulled his gaze away and back down to Noma, crouched low at the base of the crypt with the shattered pieces of the scepter scattered out in front of him and a crucible of bronze melting away to his left. Annica stood next to him, an apprehensive look on her face as she watched the work unfold. A small group of loyalists had elected to show up as well, although how they became aware of what was being attempted was anyone's guess.

"You're sure about this Jack?" Annica asked, whispering slightly so that Noma would not overhear.

"Definitely not," Jack answered. "I have no idea what to expect here. But all we can do is try."

The frozen fire below their feet twinkled serenely as it always did, something they had become accustomed to since moving the town to the

Fire Fields. But where each of the fragments of scepter sat, it pulsated with an intensity that was almost blinding. Considering how strong the reaction was between the particles and the scepters, perhaps Noma's notion of using it as a binding agent wasn't so far-fetched after all.

"We're almost ready, King Jack," Noma called out, still busying himself with the fragments in front of him. "My plan is to bury the scepter partially in the sand, creating a cavity to work in. That way, we can mix the frozen fire into the melting metal and pour it directly into the hollow."

Noma began digging an outline in the ground around the perimeter of the top-half of the scepter, brushed away the particles within to create a negative, then set the scepter in place, shoring up the sand around it. He then did the same with the bottom-half, leaving room between the two for the individual fragments that had been shattered off. The full scepter now lay partially buried in the ground, appearing intact once again, except for the damaged mid-section, around which space had been left for the liquid metal.

Jack left Annica's side and walked forward, crouching down beside Noma and peering at his work. He understood the concept of the plan, and the logic behind the theory, but looking at the glowing contents of the crucible and the half-buried scepter in the ground, he found it hard to imagine it would work. After all, one of the first things the team had learned upon coming to this kingdom was that the reaction between the scepters and the frozen fire was not magic, it was science. And while Noma made this experiment sound both intriguing and hopeful, it struck Jack as more than a bit mystical as he watched it unfold.

"How violent is this reaction going to be?" Jack asked as he watched the melting bronze give an alarming sizzle.

"I don't know, to be honest," Noma admitted, but he sounded excited rather than apprehensive.

"I thought you were going to try with a smaller piece first?" Jack asked, "see how stable this stuff is."

"Have faith, King Jack," Noma exclaimed. "I believe the casting process will work. What we don't know… is what comes after."

Jack found that statement to be rather ominous, but Noma pushed forward all the same.

"Okay wait a minute," Jack finally insisted, "let's pause just a sec."

Noma did as he was told and looked up at Jack with an expectant gaze.

"What made you think to do this?" Jack asked. "I mean, did inspiration just come to you? What makes you so sure fusing the scepter in this way will bring our people back?"

Noma gave a deep sigh and responded, "To be honest, I had a bit of help. There's a man, he calls himself the Alchemist. He was able to guide me a bit."

"The Alchemist?" Jack repeated in confusion. "I've never heard of him. He's one of the townsfolk?"

"In a way," Noma said cryptically. "He's from a different version of our Kingdom, far in the future."

"Okay wait wait wait," Jack stopped him, quickly becoming leery of this entire operation. "You've been talking to someone from another reality? How?"

"Well you told me yourself how windows are created, King Jack," Noma insisted with an innocence that only partially hid his shame at not divulging this sooner. "He appeared to me and has been guiding me in my progress. He's done something similar in his world, and he said it was the key to controlling the anomalies."

"Be that as it may," Jack began with a shake of his head, "I don't like the idea of blindly taking advice from someone in an unknown world. I mean, they could be trying to..."

Noma let him trail off, leaving the potential repercussions left unsaid. "Look, I know we don't know him," Noma finally said, "but in a way I felt like I'd known him for years. I'm not sure why I am so certain this will work, but it just makes sense somehow. And this is Ydoro we're talking about, don't we owe it to our Ambassador of the People to try?"

Jack met Noma's piercing stare and couldn't help but be swayed by his belief. He nodded slowly and finally said, "I hope you know what you're doing."

Noma grinned in response. "So do I." He looked back at the buried scepter in front of him and began carefully arranging the small fragments in the cavity between the two halves of the staff. "You better stand back, King Jack. Just in case."

Jack put a reassuring hand on Noma's shoulder, then stood up and took his place back at Annica's side. Noma scooped a large amount of frozen fire particles from the glowing earth and dumped them into the bowl of superheated bronze. The mixture hissed angrily and released several alarming pops, but Noma just nodded his head undeterred. He stirred the mixture with a metal spoon and happily announced that it was incorporating well.

"I think we're ready," Noma declared, peering over the edge of the red-hot crucible with wide eyes. He pulled a pair of thick, hide gloves over his hands and scooped up a pair of metal tongs from the ground beside him. He then looked to Jack expectantly, awaiting his order.

Jack hesitated, scanning the makeshift workspace at the foot of the statue and trying to identify any potential risk that had not yet occurred to them. But he had to remind himself that it was just metal forging, albeit with different materials than he was used to. The process had been practiced for hundreds of years. So why did this feel so different? At long last, he gave Noma a firm nod of his head.

Noma took his meaning, shot him a smile, and clamped the tongs around the blazing crucible. He showed no hesitation as he lifted the vat of liquid metal from its cradle of flames, projecting the look of a hardened professional deeply invested in the task before him. His hands were steady as he moved the basin over the half-buried staff and paused directly over the mid-section with the fragmented damage. His eyes never moved from the yellow blaze within as he gently upended the contents, allowing the liquid to pour out and into the sandy mold below. As the glowing metal filled the cavity, it at first appeared to behave no differently than any typical metal. The liquid steamed and sizzled against the damaged scepter and began to settle into the low points of the hollow, absorbing each fragment as it did so.

Suddenly, a flash erupted in the middle of the staff where the metal had been poured and a sizzling snap followed. Yellow and gold sparks began popping incessantly at the repair site and Noma turned his face away to shield it.

"Noma get back!" Jack shouted, and Noma needed no further encouragement. The entire middle of the staff was now alight with flashing showers of embers that forced Jack to wince and avert his gaze. Noma dropped the tongs and crucible to the ground in a panic and scrambled away towards Jack and Annica. Through his squinting eyes, Jack began to see what looked like miniscule bolts of fine, amber-colored lightning shooting off from the repair site where the metal mixture met the scepter pieces, and it didn't stop. They seemed to be gaining both power and length with each flash, ripping up into the air with crackling sputters. But the bolts were not simply fizzling and dying. They seemed to be reaching out into the ether and then retracting back in, as though blindly seeking something from beyond the void. And then he saw it. If he had blinked, he would have missed it entirely. A tiny, inch-long fragment of staff suddenly materialized on the end of one of the ornate, reaching strands of electricity and flew through the air towards the still sizzling scepter, finding its place amongst the other shards with an explosion of light. But the fragment was not all that had been reclaimed. A person appeared out of thin air and plummeted towards the flashing staff. But instead of being drawn towards the weapon as the fragment had been, the person was ripped around in a circle as though caught in a funnel cloud orbiting the scepter. They skidded, flailing through the air before Jack rushed out and grabbed the person roughly to the ground and away from the continuously sparking vacuum that had been created. The man screamed, wincing in pain and confusion, and thrashing wildly. But Jack had no time to find out who the man was.

A second body suddenly entered the miniaturized storm, being pulled violently in the same manner as the first victim. Now Annica, Noma, and several of the onlookers began scrambling forward as Jack had done, clawing at the unknown woman as her auburn hair whipped around her head. She was likewise pulled hard to the ground to rescue her from the unyielding orbit as she kicked madly. A third man appeared, and then a fourth, and then a fifth. The entire area was suddenly alive with townsfolk ripping the newcomers out of the air like kites being pulled back to the ground. Every one of them wore the same look of horrified incomprehension as they tumbled to the earth and clawed their way clear of the sparking scepter, still half-buried and pulsating vibrantly.

The reaction seemed to lessen some after the fifth person was deposited, but thin tendrils of yellow lightning still reached out at random into the air, like they were searching for something unseen. Jack began wildly scanning the new faces. Each wore wide, terrified expressions, except one. From between several of the aiding locals, and wearing a look of utter disbelief, was Ydoro, their very own Ambassador of the People, returned at last. He looked the same as he had the week prior, but significantly shaken, visibly confused, and bleeding from the abdomen. Jack looked into the four additional faces and found that he did not recognize any of them. He looked down at the man that he had pulled from the air, still lying on the ground before him. The man looked back in bewilderment, his mouth opening and closing without any words forming.

"Are you okay?" Jack asked, but the man just continued to gape at him. "What's your name?" Jack pushed.

The man stammered and began blinking uncontrollably as he looked into Jack's eyes. "D... D... Dean," he finally stuttered.

Jack motioned for his surrounding companions to help him with the man, who seemed beyond the ability to stand at the moment, and made his way to the next stranger. This one was a young girl in her late teens who was similarly mouthing silent exclamations of terror. It was only with significant pushing that she identified herself as Kat. The next person who had come through appeared to be unconscious as Jack approached. Several of his people were attempting to render aid but it seemed the man had simply passed out from the experience. He was a short, slender man of about fifty with a bit of stubble lining his cheeks. Jack attempted to open the man's eyes but found them to be rolled up into his head, showing only white.

"Any idea who he is?" Jack asked his people.

"His name is Mauretz," came a bitter, jaded voice. Jack looked up to see the fourth of the strangers who had come through the anomaly. He was a tall man with a flop of dirty-blonde hair overhanging his chiseled features. His shoulder was bloodied from what looked like a gunshot wound and he wore an expression of poorly concealed contempt as he looked down at the unconscious man and finished, "He's the man who killed me."

Jack just stared at him, struck by his seeming disregard for having recently been pulled through a wormhole to another reality. "And who are you?" Jack asked.

The man grimaced as he extended a hand to shake. "Nick Satterall," he answered.

Jack shook the man's hand distractedly, then looked around at the rest of the group. His gaze finally landed on the scepter, half-buried in the sand, still sputtering and ejecting little fingers of electricity. It certainly did not appear stable yet, even with it having lost some of its volatility. He made his way to Ydoro, who was being well cared for by the gathered townsfolk.

"Are you okay?" Jack asked.

Ydoro gave a weak smile and said, "I'm good. How did you bring me back?"

Jack opened his mouth to respond when the scepter suddenly erupted with a fresh torrent of sparks and a loud crackle. A second staff-fragment fizzled into existence at the end of one of the reaching electric volts and rotated through the air before coming to rest in the mid-section of the weapon. Jack looked back the way the piece had flown, anticipating what was likely to follow.

A man materialized in the air, followed closely by a second, and then a third. But unlike their predecessors, they did not get dragged into a violent orbit. The bolts of energy seemed to retract back into the scepter before it gave a final, sparking shudder and went quiet. The three new-comers had fallen roughly to the ground, with one slumping to the right while the other two landed at opposite sides of the staff, now glowing mildly in its sandy cradle with its newly repaired midsection gleaming gold in the daylight. The first man had managed to land on one knee while the other planted his hands roughly to prevent himself from falling. They both heaved dramatically as they took in breath, grimacing from their journey.

It was a long moment before Jack realized that he knew the man with his hands pressed into the ground. He looked far older than Jack remembered him, though it was the sort of fatigue that came from distress rather than age. His eyes were winced shut but he still wore the same rugged beard and longer hair that curled down around his ears. His clothes were more pedestrian but the burn pattern around the side of his face marked him as the warrior the Kingdom remembered and the long-lost leader of the people. Jack's mouth fell open as he gazed upon Cyrus Dorn, the former King of the East.

It was only then, with a sinking sense of dread settling in his chest, that Jack allowed his eyes to wander across the twinkling scepter to the second man, still bent low to one knee. He knew who he would find even before his mind caught up to the realization. The man was regaining control of his breathing and had not taken his eyes off the faintly glowing Fire Fields beneath him. His face was alive with a yearning hunger as he reached out a shaky hand and brushed the frozen fire particles gently. He didn't look up, he barely moved an inch, but with a soft exhale of breath, Alec Dorn, the banished King of the West, bowed his head low and his features finally split into a wide, triumphant grin.

CHAPTER NINETEEN

LONG LOST

The last thing Cyrus remembered was falling to the ground near that crude, primeval campsite and feeling his wrist sprain painfully. But upon dropping the scepter fragment, his body seemed to tumble straight through the earth, head over heels, and his sinuses exploded in agony. The sensation was nothing new to him at this point, but he had no idea what could have triggered an anomaly so suddenly. The dizzying fall did not last long enough for him to panic, however, for he felt his hands slam hard into solid ground after a mere few seconds. But it wasn't until he opened his eyes, stinging through the dust and debris kicked up from his hard landing, that he realized the full magnitude of the wormhole he had just traversed. He thought it must be some trick of his mind as the cracked, glowing pattern of the Fire Fields came into focus, but the feeling of the coarse sand beneath his palms seemed to confirm its legitimacy. Feeling countless hands trying to help him, and hearing the jabbering shouts of a panicked crowd, he craned his neck sideways and finally looked up to find a person staring back at him... a person he had never expected to see again in his lifetime.

Jack Viana looked absolutely dumbfounded as he watched Cyrus on the ground, and Cyrus himself found he was entirely unable to hold a critical thought. His brain had become sluggish and mistrusting of reality, like he had somehow slipped into a dream without realizing. But Jack's focus had shifted away from Cyrus, and it was with a significant feeling of trepidation that he anticipated why. Cyrus followed Jack's gaze, and there, not ten feet in front of him, was his brother, reunited with his long-lost kingdom at last. Alec wore a broad grin on his face as he let the particles of frozen fire cascade through his fingers from a kneeling position. He looked up and his eyes caught Cyrus's, watching him intently. This wasn't a dream; Cyrus suddenly became sure of it. Something had happened that brought himself and his warring brother back to the Kingdom, and while he did not yet understand what that was, it was real nonetheless.

A commotion off to his left made him start and he pulled his eyes away from Alec to see a man fighting to free himself from several alarmed-looking townsfolk. The man wore an enormous beard and a wild mane of untamed hair, and it was only after a moment that Cyrus realized it was the very same nomad he had witnessed in the alternate reality he had just been pulled from. The man looked raving mad as he raged against his perceived captors, who seemed so stunned by his display that they were backing off in trepidation. He pulled free from the last of their hands, spun around and sprinted away from the circle of people making guttural, angry noises like a scared animal. No one called after him and no one gave chase. It was only then that Cyrus fully registered the strange group he was a part of. The locals were easy enough to spot, and of course he recognized Jack and Annica, but there seemed to be outsiders amongst their number, looking badly shaken and thoroughly out of place. There was a young woman with a tangle of auburn hair, who seemed to know the round-faced man sitting next to her, offering what comfort he could while shaking his head in confusion. There was a middle-aged man who had been rendered unconscious from his fall but was beginning to come to, and a rugged-looking man with blonde hair and a scowl standing over him. And then there was Ydoro, who seemed to be injured but pushing through.

Alec began to rise to his feet and Jack and Annica both stepped forward.

"We're gonna take it real slow now," Annica announced pointedly to Alec. "There's been plenty of changes since you were last here, and we don't need anyone upsetting the balance."

Alec was unarmed, and a quick glance around showed a kingdom that was vastly different from the way he had left it. While it seemed he did recognized these profound disadvantages, he began to step sideways all the same, like a predator suddenly on the prowl.

"Don't do this, Alec," Jack warned, tensing up for a struggle.

Annica was without a weapon, but she quickly remedied this by pulling the machete from a nearby guard's sheath and pointing it towards Alec.

Alec sneered and his eyes lit up dangerously. "This is my kingdom," he declared in a soft, threatening whisper.

Without warning, the townsfolk behind Alec seized him by the arms and several unsheathed blades to hold at his neck. Alec thrashed against them, but Jack just smiled.

"Things have changed, Alec," Jack said casually.

Alec's lip curled menacingly at hearing this. "You think you can hold me?"

"Of course we can hold you," Annica said, "you imagine this entirely new town was just built for show? You're in our world now, *my King*." She sneered the last part, likely remembering her early dealings with Alec and his insistence on being addressed as a monarch.

"You won't get away with this!" Alec roared, but Annica gave a dismissive wave of her hand and his captors dragged him backwards and away from the small ring of onlookers. They stopped a short distance away, letting Alec rage just out of earshot.

Jack walked over to Cyrus and helped him off the ground, fixing him with a searching expression that was hard to read. Cyrus stared back, unsure if this was the Jack he knew or an alternate one. But Jack's face finally broke into a disbelieving smile and he pulled Cyrus into a hug.

"You have no idea how good it is to see you," Jack exclaimed, releasing him and continuing to stare into his face. "I am so sorry to have pulled you from your life out there, I promise you it was not my intention."

Cyrus looked back at him and thought he perhaps appeared slightly older than he remembered. "So are you… the Jack I know?"

Jack nodded warmly and responded, "The last time I saw you was six years ago, standing in these very Fire Fields. You had just banished your brother… and chose to follow him into an unknown reality."

Cyrus shook his head remembering the preposterous decision and felt a renewed swell of gratitude for being brought back, however it had been accomplished.

"My King," Annica greeted him, hammering a fist into her chest with a bow of her head. "It's good to see you again. Welcome home."

Ydoro was stumbling towards Cyrus with wide-eyed wonder, practically tripping over the surrounding newcomers as he went.

"You came back," Ydoro said in a hushed whisper. "My King!"

Cyrus smiled and shook his head, reaching out a hand to pat his shoulder. "I'm not king anymore," Cyrus reminded him, "and one of these days I'll get you to stop looking at me with such reverence."

Ydoro shook his head vigorously, as though the notion were patently absurd. "You will always be my king," he insisted.

Cyrus just laughed lightly. "How did you do it? How did you bring us back?"

Jack stepped forward and pointed down at the mutely glowing scepter, half-buried in the sand between them. He spoke mostly to Cyrus, though the rest of the group continued to listen intently. "We had an incident, almost a week ago now, at this very spot. Our old pal Nel had managed to amass a band of rebels within the Kingdom, and they attacked the crypt that housed the scepter-half that you and Alec used to travel out of this world." He indicated a teenage companion standing respectfully beside him and continued, "This young man is named Noma, and he has been helping me to find a solution to this mess. We just completed an experiment that fused the broken scepter back together. We had hoped that might reclaim the militants who escaped; however it seems they are the *only* ones who did not return."

"That's what the fragment is from!" the round-faced man practically shouted, bouncing up and down on the balls of his feet. He had started vibrating with excitement about halfway through Jack's speech. He said it more to his young companion than the rest of the group, but he was pointing enthusiastically at the repaired scepter in front of them. "I can see it, right there in the middle! That's our shard!"

"You had a fragment of the scepter?" Cyrus questioned, suddenly recognizing a potential connection between the group. "Who are you?"

"I... my name is Dean Pyrene," he explained, "and this is my associate, Kat Killion." He indicated the young woman beside him, who looked just as wide-eyed but was perhaps not finding their situation quite as enchanting. "And you..." Dean continued breathlessly, now looking at Cyrus in amazement, "you're Cyrus Dorn, aren't you?" His mouth was hanging slightly open.

Cyrus furrowed his brow. "How do you know me?" He turned to Jack and said, "who are these people?"

Jack, looking just as unsure as Cyrus, simply shook his head.

"You're... the professor," Dean stammered, "and that was your brother."

Cyrus had no idea what to make of the man. "How do you know us?" he repeated.

"You were... you were lost at sea," Dean said, "we tracked you through history. Going back to a boy named Randall Evans from the 1800's."

Ydoro cleared his throat almost sheepishly. "There's a name I haven't heard in a long time."

Dean turned to him, surveying his passive smile. "It was you?"

"I haven't gone by the name Randall since before I came here," Ydoro answered.

"It was your blood, then," Dean continued. "The handprint on the cave wall in Jordan. That was you."

Ydoro looked back at him grimly, then lifted his shirt, revealing what seemed to be a very recent stab wound to his side. "You mean from this?"

The group was suddenly alive with concerned voices, but Ydoro brushed them off insisting that he was fine. As Jack instructed one of the guards to bring Dr. Garse, Dean began shaking his head.

"How can you… that's a fresh wound… the Hand of Jordan has been around for…"

He trailed off, but Cyrus suddenly felt a sick knot forming in his stomach as realization began to take hold in his gut.

"Dean, you said I was lost at sea," Cyrus started apprehensively, "how long ago?"

Dean shook his head in amazement. "That was almost a hundred years ago."

Cyrus stepped back a pace. He couldn't help it. "A hundred years?" He didn't know what the Hand of Jordan was, but he was starting to recognize what was likely going on. Dean was not from their time, and whatever had caused him to traverse this wormhole to the Kingdom, he was now displaced from his own reality.

"And you found a fragment of this scepter in a cave in your world, that's what you're telling me?" Cyrus asked.

"I believe that was my doing," Ydoro cut in. "When Nel's militants stormed the crypt and shattered the scepter, I managed to grab a shard, but it was too late. I was swept through the anomaly and away from the Kingdom."

Cyrus nodded thoughtfully. "That wormhole must have taken you to Dean's world. What happened to the scepter piece you were carrying?"

Ydoro shook his head. "I… I ended up in the water somewhere, swam to shore and climbed the side of a cliff. I emptied my pockets and began working out what to do, because I knew it must be a different world I was in. I put the fragment down on this rock ledge but… actually that's the last thing I did. As soon as I set it down, I was brought back here."

"So from your perspective, you were gone almost no time at all," Cyrus said, "but Dean, you found the fragment he left behind?"

"Not personally," Dean answered, "it was long before my time. It was found alongside some chess pieces and a bloody handprint… but the fragment went missing when a poacher looted the site."

The tall man with the blonde hair shifted uncomfortably and finally stepped forward. "Wait, wait, wait. You're talking about the find in the cave in Jordan? With the stone carvings and that little ruby stone?"

"Yes!" Dean exclaimed, "The carvings ended up in a museum, but according to legend, a man named Nick Satterall pocketed the ruby fragment."

The blonde man snorted with laughter. "Never been called a legend before."

Dean did a double take. "You're Nick Satterall?!" he practically yelled in excitement.

Nick just furrowed his brow with an uncomfortable smirk. "Who is this guy?" he asked the entire group in what Cyrus thought was a fairly demeaning tone.

"Okay so you both owned that scepter shard at one point in your life, that's what you're saying?" Cyrus asked.

Dean was nodding his head vigorously. "Kat and I have been studying it. Nick here stole the fragment from Mr. Randall Evans' cave, but I found it in the care of a Mauretz Abernally, he was Nick's associate."

The blonde man named Nick gave the small man still lying on the ground a swift kick in the ribs. "This is Mauretz right here." He gave him another kick for good measure and said, "he's pleased to meet you."

"Hey!" Cyrus commanded, and the group went silent. "I don't care what sort of issues you have with each other, you will conduct yourselves respectfully while you are here." As Nick rolled his eyes, Cyrus continued, "So every one of you touched that fragment at one point or another?"

The group all nodded in affirmation, and some further mutterings seemed to confirm that not only had each one of them touched the shard, but it was the last thing they remembered doing.

Jack was studying the group intently, slowly nodding in understanding. "And you Cyrus?" he asked.

Cyrus thought a moment. "I've had a piece of the scepter on me since that day I left the Kingdom," he said. "Last thing I remember is dropping it."

Silence fell over the group. Cyrus rubbed at the back of his head, then looked up for the first time since arriving. It was only then that it finally registered what was casting a shadow over their proceedings. Above the crypt they were standing in front of was a massive stone statue of a windswept warrior, gazing stoically at the horizon. It was with a mixture of pride and embarrassment that he realized the likeness was his own.

"That's new," he commented dryly to Jack.

"It's the Guardian!" Ydoro enthused, "It was built to protect the anomaly that you had travelled through, and keep a watchful eye on the town."

Nick was squinting up at the visage high above and raised his eyebrows at Cyrus. "That's you?" he asked skeptically.

"He's the King," Ydoro insisted to Nick. "He's the protector of this Kingdom and a legend in our society."

Cyrus felt a twinge of embarrassment at hearing Ydoro's gushing endorsement, but Nick just furrowed his brow further. "You're king?" Nick asked Cyrus, but before waiting for an answer, he finally asked the question that shockingly no one had yet said allowed. "Where the hell are we?"

Annica, who had been uncharacteristically silent for much of the conversation, finally smiled and stepped forward. She shrugged mildly and said, "Welcome to the Kingdom."

CHAPTER TWENTY

DEVIATIONS

Nick looked ill-amused at the vague response regarding their whereabouts and Kat was inclined to agree with him. This was terrifying. One moment she had been in Mr. Pyrene's classroom tossing around theories and stories and the next she was… here. But she had felt something right before. It was all blurring pretty quickly, but she remembered thinking there was something wrong with Mr. Pyrene. She had tried to help him but became disoriented and dizzy. Perhaps she had passed out and this was all an illusion? But no, looking around now she somehow knew this was real.

"Can someone please explain what's going on?" Kat practically begged.

The man who called himself Cyrus stepped forward. Apparently he was the elder of the lost Dorn brothers that she, along with Mr. Pyrene, had been tracking through history. Kat herself had never seen a picture of the man, but he looked about how she would have imagined.

"Look," Cyrus began, "I know this is going to be a lot to accept. You are in a place that is entirely apart from the worlds you know. And from what I'm gathering, it's also a vastly different time. My name is Cyrus Dorn, and I'm from the New York of 1935. Five months back, I led an expedition to a strange anomaly that was discovered in the middle of the Atlantic Ocean."

The man named Jack cleared his throat gently. "Actually, Cy, it may have been five months for you, but you've been gone from the Kingdom for six years now. Near as I can tell, it's 1942."

Cyrus blinked in apparent confusion but then elected to push past it.

"Okay, so six years," Cyrus agreed. "My team and I became stranded here, in an alternate reality from our own. This place is known as the Kingdom and... it's my home. As my friend Ydoro was quick to announce to everyone, I became king during my time here. I've relinquished that title since, but it doesn't change my dedication to these people. We will try to find a way to get you all back home, and with these new advancements with fusing the damaged scepter, maybe we have a shot. But for now, I need everyone to remain calm, be respectful, and let us try to figure this out."

Mr. Pyrene nodded fervently, absurdly accepting of this proposal, but Kat had tears in her eyes.

"We're stuck here?" she choked. "I can't stay here. I have a life... I have..."

Cyrus stepped forward and put a comforting hand on her shoulder. "It's Kat, right?"

"Kat Killion," she sniffed.

"Kat, we're going to try everything we can to restore you to your own place and time. I promise you that. Just work with us for a little bit. Let us try to figure this out."

Kat attempted to dry up her tears and nodded resolutely. "I'll try... sir... King..."

Nick snorted a laugh. "Just to clarify something, you're not *my* leader. I don't know you, or any of you. If you think I'm calling you *my King*..."

"I don't care what you call me," Cyrus cut him off, "but you will show all of us respect while you're here."

"Aye aye, sir," Nick said with a sloppy salute and a roll of his eyes. Kat thought to herself that this just might be the most unpleasant person she had ever encountered. No sooner had the thought occurred to her than he gave the man on the ground another hard kick.

"Hey!" Cyrus barked again. "Get him up."

The small man began to work himself into a standing position but Nick shoved him hard before he could manage it.

"What did I just tell you!" Cyrus demanded.

"Go to hell, the lot of you!" Nick snapped back. "If this isn't my world…"

"I don't care what world you're from," Cyrus roared, "you will conduct yourself respectfully while you are here!"

Nick puffed out his chest and squared himself up to Cyrus, who stared back at him with crippling authority. Nick seemed to deflate slightly at the challenge, for he put up his hands and shook his head in frustration. He backed off and retook his place in the group.

Cyrus turned back to his own people and Kat saw Jack give him an approving nod. They began talking amongst themselves and that debilitating fear began to wash over her once again. She found herself turning to Mr. Pyrene for comfort, though she knew he did not have any answers.

"Are we ever going to see home again?" Kat asked.

"I… I hope so," he responded softly, but then seemed to rethink his blunt response for he turned to face her and continued, "we will. I'll find a way to get you home."

Kat knew it was just empty promises he was offering and nothing more, but she appreciated the gesture. "How is this possible? What happened to us?"

Mr. Pyrene shook his head thoughtfully and said, "I wish I knew. It sounds like it was something to do with that shard…"

"Yeah explain that to me," came a voice from behind her, and she turned to see Nick Satterall joining the conversation. He wore a grim look on his face, as though his defiance for their situation were a weapon he could use against it. He looked angry and defeated all at once. "You wound up with that same ruby shard I found in that cave?"

"Yes," Mr. Pyrene answered, "but decades later. I mean, I taught about you in my history class. You're from a different time altogether."

Nick made a funny expression, somewhere between an eyeroll and a look of bafflement. "So when are you two from?"

"2018," Mr. Pyrene said, "about sixty years after you vanished."

Nick offered a whistle of surprise.

"So…" Mr. Pyrene began apprehensively, "when you said Mauretz was the man who killed you…"

"I mean he killed me," Nick stated flatly. "At least I assume since the last thing I remember is getting shot. Mauretz was my partner and he sold me out. Then when I confronted him about it, he thanked me with a bullet."

Nick looked down at the wound in his shoulder.

"But you don't actually remember dying?" Mr. Pyrene asked, "I mean, when you came here today… if you died, shouldn't you still be dying?"

"Buddy, do I know?" Nick responded in annoyance. "I don't understand any of this."

"Maybe I can help you with that," a comforting voice offered. It was the one they called Ydoro, a diminutive man with perpetually wide eyes and a kind smile.

"I don't know everything," he continued, "but I know how jarring it can be when you are *transplanted*. Especially in the way you were."

"Transplanted?" Mr. Pyrene asked.

Ydoro sighed and said, "As the King said, you're not just on an unknown island. You're also in a different time… and a different reality."

Kat felt her face go flush and a strange tingling began to play across her cheeks.

"Nick, you're not still dying because, strictly speaking, this version of you never did," Ydoro continued. "You being here means that you diverged from whatever fate was in store for you. Maybe Mauretz had another bullet for you, and an alternate version of you did take that bullet and die, but you, *this* you with us now, escaped that end."

Nick just stared back at him blinking.

"I came here when I was fifteen," Ydoro continued, "and that was years past now. I'd like to say that I come from your world, but I don't think that's strictly true. I must come from a similar reality, however, the same as our Kings."

"That's the thing," Kat pressed, "our world remembers Cyrus Dorn, and his brother. But they weren't kings, they were…"

Ydoro was nodding in understanding. "Seven years ago now, from *my* perspective at least, our Kingdom was ruled over by a tyrant known as King Mora. Things were bad, and our people were oppressed, but we had also fallen into a complacency that is difficult to excuse. And then a group came to the island, similar to the way all of you arrived. They were lost as well, ripped from their own reality just like you were. One of those men was Alec Dorn, a professor from another world, who saw opportunity where others saw defeat. He ended up bringing change here, but the thing about leaving your mark on history, it comes at a cost. His legacy is that of death… and destruction."

Kat, Mr. Pyrene, and Nick were hanging on Ydoro's every word, recognizing that they were hearing a story of great importance.

"I don't think he was always a monster," Ydoro said softly, nodding to himself. "In fact, I'm sure he wasn't. But he lost himself here, drunk on his own power. Luckily, another man from that group was Cyrus Dorn, Alec's older brother." Ydoro looked across the sea of people to Cyrus, who was still deep in conversation with Jack and Annica. "He never wanted to rule… and wanted no part of this kingdom. And yet, he became the leader we needed, and earned his place in our history."

"This statue is of him," Kat whispered in understanding, eying the towering monument above.

Ydoro nodded. "He saved us, not only from his brother, but from chaos and ruin as well. You see, he gave the people back their strength, their voice. And the peace has lasted, until very recently."

"So where do we come into this?" Nick asked.

"That scepter, it's an incredibly powerful instrument," Ydoro explained. "It is capable of ripping doorways from this reality to the next. Fragments broken from that weapon are what's responsible for bringing every single person here to this world. But several of those fragments have found their way out into those alternate realities. It seems that you, Mr. Satterall, were unlucky enough to find the one I left behind, and pass it on to Mr. Mauretz, and eventually to Dean and Kat."

Mr. Pyrene shook his head and exhaled deeply. "I've been tracking that fragment most of my adult life. I should have let the damned thing stay forgotten."

"The chess pieces," Kat asked, as something occurred to her, "you said those were they yours too?"

Ydoro smiled ruefully and nodded. "They're the Dorn brothers. I carved a whole set, years back. But the only person I used to play with was Cyrus. Once he was gone, I suppose I took to carrying a few around, just as a reminder of what I'd learned from him."

"But you left them behind in the cave?" Mr. Pyrene asked.

"Ydoro shrugged. "I remember taking them out of my pocket, along with that fragment, with the thought that I wouldn't need them if I were to be starting my life over in this new world. I knew I was trapped, so thought I would rid myself of those attachments to my past life... but then I was brought back."

"Okay but we found a version of you in our world that lived to be over a hundred," Kat insisted, "how is that possible if you're here?"

Ydoro looked extremely perplexed for several moments as his eyes darted around, as though attempting to solve an equation. Very slowly, he finally responded, still with a far off look on his face. "I suppose an alternate version of me *did* leave that cave and start a new life, just as I intended to."

"An alternate version?" Nick scoffed.

"That's right," came a strong voice from off to Kat's left. They all turned in unison to see Cyrus rejoining their conversation. He was accompanied by Jack and Annica, standing just behind him. Cyrus walked forward, seemingly weighing how to proceed. "I'm going to tell you all something that was explained to me in a time of great doubt in my life. All of this..." he waved his hands through the air in front of himself, "is not just nothingness. There are infinite realities passing by each other, never being seen or noticed by one another. I didn't fully appreciate what that meant at the time, but I think I do now. It means that there are infinite versions of me, and Alec, and Jack, and Annica, and all of you standing in this very spot and likely having this very conversation. But based on seemingly insignificant decisions, variations diverge, and what starts out as a small change becomes a life-altering deviation. Those parallel lives of ours are just as real as this one here. You just can't see them. I admit, the concept can make your head spin if you think about it too much, but consider how this has played out in your own world. Ydoro here feels that he left the Kingdom, landed in your world, then immediately returned here. That's *this* Ydoro's experience. Again, small deviations alter the course of these parallel lives. A version of Ydoro did rejoin society in your world and lived out the rest of his life in a world he didn't belong in. But that was a deviation from our Ydoro here."

Kat's mouth was hanging open and she knew it. It made her feel slightly better that Mr. Pyrene's was as well. A sad bit of understanding was also beginning to occur to her. Old man Ydoro who's obituary they had read lived out his life in a world he didn't know. No wonder he didn't have any friends or family to speak about him. The only person who had known him at all was his neighbor... Cyrus Dorn's wife. When he became marooned in a different reality, he must have sought out connections to the people he knew from the island. Maybe he was even watching over Cynthia Dorn out of loyalty to his old friend. What a lonely existence that must have been. Would that be their fate as well? Living out the rest of their days in a world they didn't belong?

"I know," Cyrus said softly, "It's hard to understand and hard to accept. What I want you to understand is this; I won't rest until I get you back home where you belong, I promise you that."

Kat found that, despite not knowing this man, she could believe his promises. Looking into his eyes, she found herself flooded with a strength that was hard to explain. She didn't know why, but she was grateful to have someone like Cyrus Dorn watching over them.

CHAPTER TWENTY–ONE

DEATH

C yrus felt impossibly overwhelmed. How could he not? He was trying to project strength and leadership to their terrified new companions, but in truth he hadn't fully processed for himself that he was back. He looked at the surrounding forests, the thatched roofs of the village, and the glowing ground below him. It was familiar, but he could see the growth of the six years that had passed. He peered down the streets of town spreading out around them. Each winding road twinkled faintly as they led away and an ornate-looking structure a ways down the main thoroughfare seemed to be the new Temple. It was made up of deep-red stone and clearly crafted by some truly gifted builders. In contrast to the stark utilitarianism of the original Temple, this was a work of art and presented more as a beacon to gather around rather than a fortress of war.

Cyrus watched Alec with unease, being held just outside the perimeter of the crowd gathered in the Fire Fields. He somehow couldn't quite make himself believe that the threat he posed was neutralized. He would feel far better when he was locked away somewhere.

"Well this is a bit awkward, my King," Annica started, stepping up alongside him, followed closely by Jack, "but I was actually nominated to lead in your stead, and Jack along with me."

Cyrus's eyes widened and he smiled at both of them. "I... of course. That's fantastic. I'm sorry, I shouldn't have..."

"My King," Annica interrupted, "I tell you this because the changes you made here survived. Your legacy lives on. The people chose me, and I will continue to live up to that, but you are a living legend in these parts. And you will always be my king."

Cyrus began to shake his head, but Annica nodded in insistence. Cyrus had never been comfortable with his own people's fealty and had long felt that the title fit him ill, like a uniform that had been tailored for somebody else. That feeling of being an imposter in the role had begun to ebb away during his short-lived reign, however, and now he felt strangely like that tailored uniform fit him slightly better.

He accepted Annica's words and replied softly, "I'll work on living up to that legend, but please don't take my presence here as a sign to step aside. The people chose you, and they chose you for a reason."

Jack reached over and gave Annica a reassuring squeeze, and it was only then that Cyrus realized the two must be a couple. The discrepancies in time were maddening to think about. From Cyrus's perspective, he had fought beside the both of them less than a month ago, but six long years had passed for them, and their lives had moved on. It was both comforting and horrifying all at once.

"Tell me more about this experiment that brought us back," Cyrus pressed, more to move on from the uncomfortable exchange than anything else.

It wasn't Jack that answered his question, however, but the young man named Noma. He stepped forward apprehensively, but anguish seemed to pull heavily at his features. Something was wrong.

"What is it?" Cyrus asked.

"It's an honor to meet you officially," Noma said morosely, "but I have to tell you something. This isn't how I was told this experiment would work."

"Told?" Cyrus questioned. "Who told you to do this experiment?"

"I... he's from another reality," Noma admitted.

Jack nodded and stepped forward. "He came clean right beforehand," Jack said, placing a comforting hand on Noma's shoulder. "It's okay. It may seem strange, but I think..."

"There's more, King Jack," Noma insisted, and his eyes fell uncomfortably to the ground. "He was curious about you, Cyrus. Kept asking questions about what had happened to you, what you were like. It didn't give me pause at the time, but why would he care so much about you? You were long before his time. And I think..." he took a deep breath as though willing himself to continue, "I think he stole one of the fragments from our world."

"He did what?" Jack exclaimed in alarm.

"I... I can't be sure," Noma stammered, "but... I think he did. Why would he do that?"

Cyrus looked at him anxiously. "What did he say about himself? His own world?"

Noma again looked down. "I... I guess not much. I should have asked more questions, I just... I was so caught up in finding a solution that would bring our people back."

This admission disturbed Cyrus more than he could say. It sounded as though the solution that Noma and Jack had been so desperate for had simply been handed to them on a silver platter. In Cyrus's experience, nothing came free, and world-saving answers didn't simply materialize out of thin air in the guise of a new mentor.

"What do you think it means?" Jack asked, noting the alarm on Cyrus's face.

Cyrus sighed deeply. "I think it means Noma's new friend *wanted* him to bring us back."

An alarmed shout cut through the air from behind Cyrus and disrupted his thoughts. He whipped around to see Alec having broken loose from his captors. He ducked under their grasping hands and dove forward onto the ground, seizing the repaired scepter from its cradle of fiery sand. He raked its head along the ground and scrambled back to his feet, causing a torrent of crackling fire to explode around him. The storm wasn't directed at anyone in particular but served its purpose well as a deterrent, for the entire group shielded their eyes in unison. Alec backed down a side street about ten feet before stopping, holding the scepter out in front of himself like a cornered animal.

"Don't do this, Alec!" Cyrus shouted.

"You think I'm going to a cage?" Alec snarled back. "This is MY Kingdom!"

Cyrus knew the damage his brother could do with the only remaining scepter on the island, but he was impossibly outnumbered. This was a move of desperation.

"Alec, this isn't the way," Cyrus called out to him, but Alec was looking less and less capable of rational thought. His eyes were darting back and forth, searching frantically for a way out of his position. The guards were beginning to spread out, machetes at the ready, hoping to flank him.

"Alec, let's talk," Cyrus said, attempting a different tactic.

"Okay, then hear this," Alec hissed, "if any of you make another move, it's over. I will take every single one of you with me."

Cyrus didn't want bloodshed, but Annica looked primed for a fight. She began looking to her guards, seeming to size up the situation from a strategic standpoint. Alec narrowed his eyes against her, then looked to Cyrus. If this were to be Alec's end, then so be it; but cornered animals are never to be underestimated. Alec slowly lowered the scepter head towards the earth. Miniscule particles of ash floated from the ground and began their ominous orbit around the staff head. And there he paused.

"Your move," Alec breathed threateningly.

An earth-shaking noise suddenly cut through the air, reverberating below the ground like a strike of lightning. Fifteen feet beyond Alec, in the center of the deserted road, the very molecules that made up the empty space seemed to rupture, eroding away violently like a burning curtain revealing the window beyond. Two figures strode onto the street, materializing suddenly from the newly created anomaly. One was a small, twisted-looking man with a face that appeared melted by some horrific incident. The second was imposingly tall, broad-shouldered, and domineering with a heavy brow and a slight sag in his lip, permanently exposing the edges of his teeth in an affixed sneer. He wore long, dark robes that looked shredded in certain areas for ease of movement and held two weapons that were unlike anything Cyrus had seen before. They appeared to be made up of countless pieces of the all too familiar scepters but had been fashioned into three-pronged nightmare instruments roughly the length of an average person. They had the same cracked-looking exterior but had been cobbled together using excessive amounts of melted bronze, resulting in rustic, warped-looking tridents.

Alec had turned where he stood and was eying the newcomers warily, who were now standing still as statues in the center of the street. Silence fell over the scene.

It was Annica that finally stepped forward. Her boots crunched loudly against the earth and seemed to practically echo to the far corners of town. "Who are you?" she called down the street.

But the two people did not move and did not respond. The anomaly appeared to close up behind them, becoming faint, blurry, and indistinct before vanishing entirely. But still the two people did not move. The tall man continued to stare in their direction with an almost tactical intensity, his wideset, penetrating eyes slowly scanning each and every person's face. There was something incredibly chilling about the man's features; a crudeness that only partially concealed the raw savagery beyond. His searching gaze seemed to stop just a bit longer on Cyrus's face than the others, and it caused the most horrible shiver to trickle down his spine.

"I asked who you are!" Annica shouted out again, her voice bouncing around the otherwise empty street.

Ever so slowly, the tall man moved his eyes to her, licked his lips, and finally spoke his first word in a soft, hoarse drawl.

"Death."

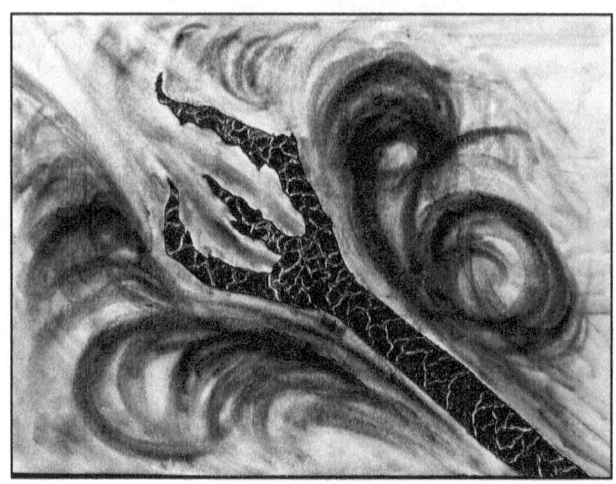

CHAPTER TWENTY–TWO

WHAT COMES AFTER

A lec Dorn backed up a pace. Where he had just moments before raised his scepter towards his old rivals, he now found himself with his back turned to them, sizing up the new arrivals with unease. The smaller of the two had an extensively scarred and burnt face that had long ago eroded away his more human characteristics, and yet it was the larger man that commanded Alec's full attention. He didn't know what it was, but there was something *wrong* with the man. Something unidentifiable. A minute ago, it would have been unfathomable for Alec to take his eyes off his brother and his band of loyalists, but they were an enemy he knew. Even so, he only had one thought in his mind. Standing within the borders of his kingdom once again, with the brilliant Fire Fields below and the mighty scepter gripped firmly in his hand, his old power was returning. It coursed through his bloodstream like pure adrenaline, focusing his mind and burning his caution.

"You're in the wrong world," Alec called out threateningly. He upended the gnarled top of his scepter towards the ground, drawing the tiny glowing particles from the earth up into the air and causing the staff itself to pulsate with a deep ruby color from within. "Go back the way you came," Alec snarled.

Yet the pair still did not move. And the way the tall man was staring at him was incredibly unsettling. Alec delayed only a moment longer and then boldness got the better of him. He swung the scepter forward in one swift motion, like a quick draw from the old west. A hurricane of burning embers blasted across the expanse between them, aimed straight for the tall man's chest. But the tall man was faster. He crossed his tridents in front of himself and the blast from Alec hit them dead center with an angry snap, fizzling out immediately after. Alec was dumbstruck. He had never seen the scepters do that before. His blood churned and then boiled over entirely. He raked his scepter towards the earth a second time, planning nothing short of an onslaught, but the man gave a swift tug on one of his tridents and Alec's weapon was wrenched entirely from his grasp. It flew through the air down the street and the man caught it deftly in one hand, letting one of his tridents drop to the ground in the process. Alec's mouth fell agape. Still fifteen feet away, the man looked down at Alec's scepter with an approving nod of his head and a placating smirk.

"Nice handywork," the man growled softly in his cold, measured voice. He was admiring the newly fashioned bronze repair site in the middle of the staff. He turned to his companion and asked, "Yours?"

The melted man shrugged slightly in confirmation and replied, "Who else."

The tall man nodded in mild interest, then tossed the scepter indifferently behind himself. Except it seemed the doorway they had just traversed through was still open, even without being visible, because the weapon vanished from the spot and seemingly fell out of this world.

The man planted his trident firmly into the ashen earth, clearly indicating his confidence that any danger had passed, and said softly, "You must be Alec Dorn. Am I right?"

Alec just stared back at him, entirely consumed by his shock and confusion. His rage was starting to ebb away slightly to be replaced with a crippling feeling of terror. Whatever power Alec had, this man's was greater. When Alec didn't respond, the man just nodded his head with a thoughtful growl.

"Alec Dorn," the man said again, but this time it wasn't a question. "The shadowy underbelly of the Dorn dynasty. The cast-aside failure of greater men."

Alec's rage returned in full, but it had nowhere to go. He felt naked and exposed without his scepter, and while every impulse in his mind screamed at him to attack, his body seemed to know better and refused to move. It left his roiling anger trapped within, and it was making him feel physically ill, like poison that he couldn't expel.

"And that must mean that one of you fine people is the elder Dorn, am I right?" the man said, drawing out each word like he was savoring its flavor on his tongue.

From behind Alec, he heard the crunching of footsteps and he was mildly surprised when his brother stepped forward and took a place directly to Alec's left.

"Aha," the man exclaimed, but it was grating in its falseness. "The great Cyrus Dorn." He gave a shallow dip of his head, like a bow that dripped with insincerity. "What an absolute honor it is."

"Who are you?" Cyrus commanded, and Alec despised how effortlessly powerful he sounded.

"It's of no matter to you," the man responded. "I just wanted a glimpse at history before we moved on."

Alec's heart leapt just slightly at the possibility that the pair would now be leaving.

Cyrus raised his arms slightly in a half-shrug and said, "You've seen us. Now move on."

The man laughed softly, more to himself than anyone else, and replied, "You misunderstand me, King Dorn. We are not going anywhere... I wanted a look at you before we moved on from the... pleasantries."

Alec shuddered at the way he said the last word.

The man stooped to retrieve his dropped trident and continued, "Now I realize this next part will be unappetizing for you, but just know that the more you resist, the longer you draw out your pain."

The rest of the group behind Alec began stepping forward, forming up together to stand in the way of this mysterious newcomer. The outsiders joined uncertainly as well.

"I am the ruling queen of this Kingdom," Annica called out. "This is your last chance to return the way you came."

The man smiled, and it looked like he was attempting to convey remorse, but it was a poor imitation of the real thing. "What a remarkable team you are. Stoic. Strong. Unyielding." He said the words in a tone that was somehow mocking and sincere. "Just understand, there was never anything you could have done to stop this."

Jack stepped forward to speak but the man shook his head before he could start. "As I said, the pleasantries are over. Now we move on to what comes after." He began raising his tridents into the air.

"What comes after?" Jack repeated.

The man looked back at him, his eyes projecting something almost like pity, but then his expression darkened, and a smile split his face.

"Fire," he said quietly.

He drew the tridents through the air and a terrible, low-register humming began emanating from within the weapons, and the sound seemed to be answered from below the ground itself. In their home world, one may have mistaken the shuddering beneath their feet as an earthquake, but in this one, a mist of frozen fire particles was lifting off the street and into the air, like an ashy haze overtaking a clearing. But the embers weren't burning out as they usually did. As the man rotated the tridents over his head, the glowing material all around them was becoming more vibrant... and more dangerous. The man gave the tridents a spin, not particularly fast or aggressive, more as though he were simply going through the motions. But the result was devastating. A cloud of the pulsating embers overtook a small house on the road to their left and the entire structure was incinerated in a matter of seconds. Fire tore through the thatched roof, wooden shutters, and heavy front door like they were a pile of kindling. The foundation ruptured beneath it and the dwelling buckled in on itself with a deafening crash. As the man moved the tridents through the air, the eye of the firestorm moved with it, consuming a second house in the process.

The group was yelling and screaming, many having produced weapons to try and fight this mystery person. But nothing was having any effect. Spears were launched in his direction, but he paid little attention as he continued to decimate the town.

"What do you want?" Annica yelled out, but she was ignored.

The man swung the tridents back the other direction, slowly and methodically, and more homes were swallowed by the inferno. People were now running freely through the streets, some carrying belongings while others shielding their loved ones from the flames. Screams of terror and pain were echoing out from every corner of the town, buzzing on the wind like a haunting swarm of insects.

The tall man finally looked back to them and said, "You may want to head on out now. This next part may be especially difficult for you."

With that, the man twirled the tridents casually in each hand, using far more flourish than he had displayed previously, and aimed both three-pronged heads down the long main thoroughfare. Alec followed the blazing storm as it roared across town and straight for the red-columned walls of the new Temple. Mortar and stone exploded outward from the structure several hundred feet down the road, launching foundation rocks the size of automobiles hurling through the air. Alec's mouth hung wide at the destruction, powerless to do anything to stop it. Even from this far down the road, people could be seen streaming out of the collapsing Temple, many batting at flames on their clothes as they went.

Jack made a move towards the building but was held back by Annica, who shook her head with wide eyes.

"Nel's in there," Jack exclaimed in horror.

The words were like a drop of lava in Alec's bloodstream. His mind suddenly seemed to clear and he had no more thoughts of anything other than his old ally.

"Where is she?!" Alec roared to Jack, who was looking absolutely beside himself with shock.

"The cell block," Jack managed to say, "in the lower level. But she must have…"

He had trailed off but Alec had stopped listening anyways. He snatched a machete from one of the nearby guards, who was too horror-struck at the surrounding carnage to notice or care, and began to sprint towards the burning Temple.

"Alec!" Cyrus bellowed from behind him.

For some reason, Alec did stop for a moment and turned back to look at his brother. Cyrus was standing amongst the rapidly deteriorating town, looking at him with an odd sort of expression. It was as if he wanted to tell Alec not to do anything foolish, but then remembered that the two were sworn enemies. Instead, he just gazed at his brother for a second longer before turning to his people and starting to order them to the edges of town.

"Make your way to the forest!" Cyrus could be heard shouting to the group, and Alec turned away. He ran as fast as he could over the burning ground, leaping over flaming pieces of wood as they spilled out into the road. More than once, a person stumbled out towards him, screaming for help or clutching an injury. Alec ignored every one of them, focused on one goal, and one goal alone.

As the Temple loomed close, it looked like an image pulled straight from the imagination. If one conjured a vision of the pearly gates of heaven, then these flanking deep-red columns crumbling in on themselves as flames consumed the inner doors must certainly be the entrance to hell. The heat coming from within was nearly intolerable and miniscule embers were stinging at his face and exposed hands. Alec winced as he ran up the ruined steps and entered the slowly collapsing fortress. The halls were empty, as he expected, apart from the destroyed bodies of the dead half-buried in the burning rubble. He spun this way and that, trying with all his might to identify a stairway that would lead to the lower level amongst the piles of shrapnel. He shouted out but no response could be heard over the haunting noises of the moaning structure. The interior rooms were quickly becoming unidentifiable as they imploded and soon there would be nothing left but a mountain of rock.

A nearby column gave way and smashed to the floor directly in front of Alec, causing the ground beneath his feet to sink down an extra foot.

His knees buckled and he caught himself on his hands. This was becoming hopeless.

"NEL!" he called out in desperation.

He climbed over the newly fallen obstacle and scanned anxiously for any sign of a stairway, but the truth was any such entrance was likely long buried already. A fiery wooden beam detached from a wall above and crashed into his shoulder, burning his shirt badly and expelling embers into his face. Alec cried out in pain, but his scream wouldn't stop. He had been so close to reclaiming everything he had lost, and now he felt as powerless as ever. His scream turned to a bellow; a roar of defiance to the gods for stripping his power away after offering him a small taste.

The sound of tumbling rocks echoed out from his left and Alec winced, predicting a full cave-in. But when he turned to look, his chest gave a painful spasm as a person climbed into view. It was a woman, and she had crawled through a small hole from within the piles of enormous stone. She was covered head to toe in white ash and soot, a decent amount of blood shone brightly from her temple and decorated the front of her shirt, but it was a face Alec would recognize anywhere.

"Alec?" Nel whispered with unrestrained shock in her eyes. "How… how are you…"

Alec ran to greet her, putting his hands up to her face and looking into her eyes. He wanted to ask if she was okay, or even say something clever about his own return, but instead he just stared at her. And she stared back. As was the case seven years ago, looking into Nel's eyes filled him with an inexplicable confidence that was almost painful. He felt like he could do more, was capable of more, as he allowed her gaze to infiltrate him. The reflection of the surrounding flames flickered and danced in her eyes as her open mouth finally curved slightly into a baffled smile.

A wall collapsed behind them and shook the earth so violently that Alec almost lost his footing. Their brief moment over, Alec grabbed Nel's wrist forcefully and dragged her back the way he had come. Pushing through the stinging of embers and roar of the surrounding inferno, he ducked his head and led her through what was left of the front entryway and out into the deteriorating town.

Alec could no longer see the area where the group had stood, nor could he find the mysterious man with the tridents, but the black smoke rising from the streets was so thick and merciless that identifying anything more than broad shapes was impossible. He led Nel down a side street, weaving his way towards what he hoped was the edge of town. There were no more people present, as everyone still alive had likely evacuated long ago. It was eerie and claustrophobic as they navigated the devastation, every so often having to step over a body. It was with significant relief that they found the treeline and clambered out of the Fire Fields and into the merciful cover of the forest. There was a dampness to the air within that can only be found in the natural presence of trees, and it soothed Alec's dried-out lungs therapeutically. After several sputtering coughs, Alec managed a half-smile to Nel, who just continued to look at him in shock and wonder. Her skin was greasy and blackened from soot and a fresh layer of powdery ash was clinging to every inch of her body, but she smiled back at him all the same, albeit in a pained sort of way. She didn't ask him how he had returned or how he had found her, she likely figured there would be plenty of time for that later. Rather she just nodded her head and looked at him expectantly. Alec, looking just as battered as Nel now that he had time to examine himself, nodded back at her and drew in a ragged breath. He put a hand on her shoulder and began to walk, moving deeper and deeper into the freshness of the forest, leaving the heavy, sticky smoke and the flaming town behind.

CHAPTER TWENTY–THREE

WE PROTECT OUR OWN

K at was still blinking back a thick, blinding layer of tears nearly an hour after the devastation in town. They were mostly caused by the choking black smoke they had run through to enter the woods, but she didn't kid herself that the air quality was the only reason for her leaking eyes. She didn't know what to think or feel and certainly didn't know how to act in this new world, one full of kings and queens, temples and ruins, heroes and villains.

Herself and her fellow newcomers had been led hastily away from the burning town by the King and Queen, but it was Cyrus Dorn that held her attention the most. He didn't look or act like someone displaced from the life he knew. He exuded a power that was hard to deny, and there was an authority about the man that was unwavering. The locals referred to him as their immediate past king, and it was clear that they looked at him with extreme, almost mythical respect. But reconciling this with the way history remembered him from their own world was nearly impossible. Not that he lacked respect as a professor lost at sea, but the man before her now seemed comfortable as the leader of a people, and it was hard to argue that he looked like he belonged here.

Cyrus was currently busy strategizing with the King and Queen. There were many others as well, streaming in from the surrounding woods and looking to the trio for guidance. The group's numbers were swelling by the minute and it was leaving Kat, along with her stranded cohorts, pushed to the side. This wouldn't have been so bad on its own, but the small bits of conversation they were overhearing were utterly terrifying. This society was talking about going to war and if Kat and the other transplants weren't careful, they would get caught up in the crossfire.

Nick was looking more skittish by the minute. He had taken to pacing around, shaking his head and muttering about how none of this was possible. Kat could sympathize, of course; the idea of multiple realities was horribly dizzying.

The man named Mauretz began to shuffle towards them, and Nick shot him a murderous look. "I *know* you're not coming over here," Nick threatened. "The next time you're within my reach it's over for you."

"Nick," Mauretz began, raising his hands in surrender, "I know we've had our differences…"

"Oh, like how you murdered me?" Nick snapped. "You're a goddamn traitor. You'll stay the hell away from me if you value your pathetic life."

Mauretz cowered slightly and abandoned his approach, ambling off into the steadily growing crowd.

"Do you think he can actually get us home?" Kat found herself asking Mr. Pyrene.

"Nick?" Dean practically laughed.

"No, Cyrus," Kat clarified. "There's something about him."

"That *something* is arrogance and self-proclaimed rank," Nick insisted as he passed by them during one of his many shallow laps.

"Oh come on," Kat pushed, "I don't think it's like that. He seems to genuinely…"

"There's nothing genuine about this place," Nick snapped back, finally stopping his stride. "I don't buy into any of this."

Mr. Pyrene furrowed his brow. "Buy into what? You don't believe they're telling the truth?"

"Look," Nick responded aggressively, "last I remember I was getting shot. I think that's a little too convenient. Who's to say I didn't just die and this is the afterlife?"

"You're not in the afterlife," came a voice from behind them. They all turned to find Cyrus watching them carefully.

"My King," Kat stuttered, though she immediately went red in the face at using the title.

Nick rolled his eyes. "He's not a king," he laughed, "let's not forget where he came from."

Cyrus smiled mildly but ignored the jab. "Well you haven't died, Nick. At least not here. This place that you've found yourselves in, it may seem foreign, but I assure you, it's as real as your world. When I first came here..."

"No offense, *Professor*," Nick interjected, "but I don't want any part of this."

"Part of what exactly?" Cyrus asked.

"This," Nick answered, waving his hands wildly. "All of this. Alternate versions of past leaders and revolting societies and ALL OF IT! It doesn't involve me at all!"

The hostility was likely coming from a place of distrust and fear rather than anger, but Kat still found it distasteful for him to be shouting at a king who was only trying to provide them with answers.

Cyrus raised his eyebrows and responded, "You're not wrong. The Kingdom history does not involve you... yet. But we've just been attacked, and even with your eyes stubbornly shut, I know you saw what that man can do. So when you say you want no part of it, that's fine. But it won't shield you forever... and it won't save you."

Cyrus's last statement hung in the air for a moment. Nick finally shook his head dismissively. "I don't need to be saved. You're not my king, these are not my people, and this is not my world." Nick had begun to spin in a shallow circle, surveying all of the shocked-looking locals around him. His gaze finally landed on Mr. Pyrene and Kat, and it appeared this was the final straw for him. "I mean, you say the last thing you remember is touching that ruby stone? The last thing I re-member is DYING!"

The word echoed throughout the forest and left a heavy silence in its wake. Kat noted Mauretz shrink slightly, further withdrawing into the gathered crowd.

"Ya know what," Nick finally continued, in a softer but no less an-guished voice, "I've already died once, what's the worst they can do to me? You fight your fight Professor, best of luck to ya."

Nick turned and began to cut through the crowd, heading off into the forest.

"Where are you going?" Cyrus called after him.

Nick turned without breaking his stride and extended his arms out from his sides. "I've always done better on my own, that's just the truth of it. Leave me out of your games." He shoved roughly past the outer-most members of the audience and vanished beneath the shadows of the trees.

Kat bowed her head from the awkward exchange, silently wondering if any of them would ever see Nick Satterall again. Cyrus let the silence draw out for a while before finally breaking it.

"He's not wrong," Cyrus began, not as an announcement to the crowd but in a soft, intimate way to the remaining three transplants. "This isn't your home, and this isn't your fight. I can't promise your safety, but I can promise my protection for as long as I'm able to offer it."

"You can count on the same promise from all of us," Annica stated, making her way through the crowd. "We protect our own, and if you stay with us, you're one of us."

Kat couldn't help but feel slightly better. Cyrus Dorn had a presence that was easy to put your faith in, but Annica was no commoner either. She had a fierceness in her gaze that betrayed the fighter buried beneath the surface, despite her diplomatic exterior as the ruling queen. She held Kat's gaze a few seconds longer than the others, and it filled her with some much-needed confidence.

Mr. Pyrene seemed to have lost his voice entirely, and Mauretz stayed stubbornly silent, further cementing Kat's perception of him as possibly the least impressive person she had ever met. But Kat felt bolder than she had felt before. She nodded to herself, took a deep breath, stepped forward and stated firmly, "We're with you."

CHAPTER TWENTY–FOUR

WHAT THE WORLD LEFT BEHIND

I t was intoxicating being around Nel again. And yet, there was a strange, detached feeling that accompanied the reunion, something that he couldn't quite put his finger on. Perhaps it was simply being back in his kingdom again after so many years, and having it taken away just as suddenly. Either way, with each story he told to her, Alec felt more like himself, and a half-buried sense of power and purpose snarled to life once more. He left out many of the more intimate details of his exile, particularly regarding his marriage to Cynthia. Not only did he sense Nel would not appreciate hearing about the passions of his new world, but she would likely find it somehow low that he had taken over Cyrus's life so completely. That would be her own ignorance of course, as she never truly appreciated the simple fact that Alec had met Cynthia first and she had been stolen from him by none other than his own brother. But this was all ancient history now, and if he were being honest with himself, at the current moment he was not missing Cynthia all that much.

"Seven years," Nel nodded in understanding. "That's about how long you've been gone from my end as well. I think it's been six years here."

"You were locked up," Alec said in concern, "what did they do to you?"

Nel smirked and shrugged, "Oh not much. The new monarchy doesn't take kindly to followers of Alec Dorn. I haven't been a welcome face in town since the day you left."

Alec at once felt a sting of rage at the treatment of his closest ally, but also a swell of gratitude for her unwavering loyalty, even after so long.

"You still have followers," Nel insisted, "even if they don't make themselves known. They ache for your return and are ready to stand with you."

"Without my brother, I would have expected Easttown to crumble," Alec said bitterly. "I can't understand it."

"There is no Easttown and Westtown anymore," Nel explained, "at least not like there was. Those days are long gone. The Queen wanted everything equalized. One big, happy society." She said the last part in such dripping mockery that Alec smirked. "I swear, you wouldn't even recognize the Kingdom these days."

Alec snorted slightly thinking of the current wreckage in the Fire Fields. "Whatever Jack, Annica, and the rest of those fools built in my absence, it seems like it's long gone now. The man with the tridents saw to that."

"What did he look like?" Nel questioned. "You didn't recognize him from anywhere?"

Alec had started shaking his head before she had finished her sentence. The mystery duo was of course the first thing Alec had told Nel about once they had trekked far enough into the forest. She had not been able to see any part of the assault from her cell, only the horrific aftermath. "He wasn't from this world," Alec insisted, then rolled his eyes in a conceding sort of way and clarified, "I know none of us are, but he didn't *belong* here by any stretch of the imagination. It was like an invading power making a play for the Kingdom."

"Can we use him?" Nel asked with a devious cunning in her eyes.

"Not this man," Alec answered. "The way he spoke, it was like he was above it all. Like we were all just predictable obstacles for him to move aside."

Nel put a hand up to his cheek and bore into him with her intoxicating gaze. "Don't let it get to you. You're back to claim your crown, he won't be in your way for long."

There was a time when Alec relied on such gestures to boost his confidence, but that seemed like a long time ago now. Instead, he reached his own hand up to hers, pulled it from his face, and leaned in to kiss her. There was also a time when Nel would have decided in the moment whether she was going to return his affections or not, but that also seemed to be a relic of the past. This kiss she returned with a fervent longing he had never felt from her, and she bit his lip to the point that he grunted slightly in pain. When they parted, she grinned at him widely and that old fire within him roared happily. It felt toxic in the absolute best way.

"We need to decide our next move," Alec said. "I don't think we have time to waste."

"Perhaps this will help you find your footing," Nel said, and she indicated over his shoulder with a tilt of her head. It was then that he registered the crunching of footsteps and wheeled around in alarm.

Several people were approaching from beneath the shadows of the forest and Alec, despite Nel's relative calm, found himself scanning wildly for a weapon. Nel put a reassuring hand on Alec's shoulder and whispered, "It's okay my King. These are your people."

Two things struck Alec about her statement. The first was the humbling phrase 'your people.' He had of course relied on the forces of Westtown when the East invaded his lands, but that was six long years ago. The fact that he had supporters even now was something different, and the gratitude he felt was a new sensation. The second oddity about her wording, and something he found he wasn't opposed to, was Nel referring to him as 'my King.' His subjects had certainly used the title when he was in power, but Nel was his equal in every sense of the word, so her use of the label was not out of fealty. It was almost like she saw him as more now, and it made him want to *be* more.

Alec scanned the newcomers, five in all, and nodded his head appreciatively.

"We are grateful to you for finding us," Nel said to the group. "The day we have been waiting for has finally arrived. Our king has returned."

It was suddenly strange to Alec how much he had truly missed in his time away, and the thought came with the realization that these were more Nel's people than his own. They all fought in his name, and revered him as their leader, but it had been Nel actually leading them.

"Thank you for coming," Alec finally managed.

"These are some of your most vigorous supporters," Nel stated, looking to them fondly. "Lyman here led the assault after I was captured, and Tytus has managed to infiltrate the new Temple's security forces."

"My thanks," the man named Tytus said with a shallow bow of his head. "Vengeance has made sure we kept the faith."

"Vengeance?" Alec asked with raised eyebrows.

Nel shrugged and responded, "I needed something they could call me that wouldn't draw attention. After you left, I think Jack and Annica assumed I had died out here. Which suited me just fine."

"Have you seen what's become of the town?" Alec asked Tytus.

"We have, my King," he responded. "As far as I'm concerned, that Temple was a mockery, the ruling seat of the imposters. Your Kingdom is well rid of it."

Alec nodded in agreement but didn't voice aloud his trepidation about whose hand had destroyed it.

"I actually come with news, my King," Tytus insisted. "Or rather, an opportunity, if you were so inclined."

"Oh yeah?" Alec questioned, his interest piqued. "What's that?"

"I think it's best if I show you," Tytus answered, "if you would be willing."

Alec looked to Nel who nodded her approval. He was long past needing her validation for his decisions, but the truth was he did not know this man, and he could only be trusted if Nel said he had earned it.

"It's not far from here," Tytus continued. "Perhaps a mile's walk to the north."

Alec agreed and it wasn't long before the group was hiking north into unknown territory, following no path or trail that Alec could identify. It wasn't a part of the Kingdom that he recognized, but of course he had spent very little time in the heart of the forests. As they walked, he turned and realized that Nel was staring at him.

"What?" he questioned.

"It's just been a long time," Nel answered. "We've been waiting for this moment for almost a decade."

"So have I," Alec declared. "It's just... strange... if that makes sense. I've spent so long searching for a way back here, and then it seems I was suddenly *drawn* back by something out of my control. I've dreamed of little else, but it feels so different than what I hoped."

Nel lowered her voice even below a whisper and said, "I want you to lean on me for such feelings, but I have to advise you not to show trepidation amongst your followers." She glanced around at their five companions, seemingly looking for eavesdroppers, but the team was fairly spread out. "It just wouldn't do to have your authority questioned; they need someone to believe in."

Alec bristled at the insinuation. "My authority questioned? I'm their king. And anyone who thinks otherwise..."

"You can't afford to be this naive," Nel interrupted. "If Cyrus has returned as well, like you say, that's a problem. Because his legacy amongst the people has gone more or less unchecked. In fact, Jack, Annica, and Ydoro have elevated him to practically divine status over the last six years, making him a significant problem for you. Your legacy is tarnished, if I'm being honest. You need to remind everyone of your strength."

"If my legacy is tarnished, you allowed that to happen," Alec snarled.

Nel stopped her walk abruptly and wrenched Alec's arm around to face her. "Look at me right now," she hissed, "I've been a fucking fugitive for the last six years because of the choices you and I made. I don't regret a single one of them, but you abandoned me here."

"I didn't have any control…" Alec began but Nel pounded a fist into his chest, commanding silence.

"No," she cut him off, "no, you don't get to do that. I put it all on the line for you, and I was forced into exile for it. I've built what I could given my circumstances and guess what, it resulted in you coming back. But you have to accept reality that Cyrus's legacy outshines your own. I've kept your memory alive, but did you expect me to have the keys to your kingdom waiting on a silver platter when you returned? You have to seize your own mantle, and I can't do that for you. If you're incapable of doing that, then you shouldn't have come back."

Alec was cowed into silence. Their surrounding comrades had stopped walking and were milling about awkwardly, pretending to not hear the exchange. He felt an incredible anger at being scolded in such a way, and yet he could recognize the truth in her words.

"I'm sorry," he finally managed. "I am grateful for what you've done for me. I couldn't have done any of this without you."

Nel finally smiled again and responded, "Damn right you couldn't. And don't you forget that again." She shoved his chest playfully, gave him a wink, and turned to continue walking. It was one thing that had not changed about Nel; she was able to switch the tone of an exchange at the drop of a hat, usually when she got what she wanted. In this particular instance, it helped Alec push aside his guilt for snapping at her when she had so clearly been fighting in his name every day since he vanished.

It was another ten minutes before Alec began to recognize the gentle incline of the landscape and the rough clearing beneath the trees ahead. Six years of foliage growth had nearly reclaimed the once prominent path they walked down, but now that he knew what to look for, it was hard to miss. Alec allowed his gaze to travel up the trail, past the clearing, and finally land on the imposing stone walls of his once magnificent Temple, glowing slightly orange in the powerful afternoon sun. This commanding fortress had been the seat of Alec's power during his relatively brief stint as leader, as well as his home. In days gone by, one would have been greeted with guards at the entrance and spears pointed down from the battlements above, but no longer. The structure now presented as a shell of its former glory, beginning its slow deterioration into disrepair as the world gradually left it behind. Gone were its days of prominence, it now belonged only to history and lore.

As they approached, almost apprehensively on Alec's part, he saw that the heavy double front doors stood open wide, but beyond them was just darkness, heavy oppressive darkness that gave the impression of an endless chasm. The torches that had once illuminated the great halls were long extinguished, leaving behind a damp, murky feel that emanated out from the entryway and almost seemed to warn of death and decay.

"One moment, my King," Tytus said, and he brushed past Alec and vanished into the blackness beyond the doors. Alec looked to Nel questioningly, who simply shrugged. It certainly brought back a flood of memories from his time in power, but he was failing to see the importance of returning to the structure now. Sure, it could provide shelter in the days to come, but without the guards, the weapons, and the workers, it was nothing more than an empty building. Tytus returned with a flaming torch in hand, which Alec had no clue how he had managed to light, and beckoned them all inside. As he stepped through the threshold, the darkness extended out around them like a fog, obscuring anything and everything that may be inside. The flickering torchlight illuminated the floor in front of them, but its brilliance was nowhere near strong enough to touch the distant walls or the cavernous ceilings. It left Alec with the feeling of being watched from just beyond the orb of firelight.

The group's bootfalls echoed around the room with haunting clarity, wet and gravelly against the long-forgotten stone floors. As they favored the left side of the room, Alec could see the doorway swimming out of the shadows that led down to the dungeons below and the cell block that had once housed the past king Irias, Nel, and eventually Jack. Continuing on, they came to the far wall and another door that led deeper into the Temple's abandoned depths. There were windows in some of the upper levels of the structure, but down here on the ground floor, the torch offered no reprieve from the crushing black.

A small stone kicked by one of their party skittered across the floor with alarming clarity and to Alec's horror, the noise was answered by the swift padding of fleeing footsteps just beyond their range of view. Alec froze, as did the rest of the group. It was too quick to be human and he shuddered to think what sorts of creatures had made this dank forgotten place their home over the years. The footsteps circled off to their right and Tytus attempted to track them with his torch held high. A low, guttural wheeze met the unwelcome gesture followed by an aggressive, rattling hiss. And suddenly Alec knew what was stalking them in the dark. His heart hammering, he lifted the torch out of Tytus's grip and crept forward slowly, his other hand raised against a potential attack.

"Alec," Nel warned in a whisper of apprehension but he simply raised a finger to her indicating to give him a moment. With his hand shaking badly, he suddenly started rifling in the folds of his shirt and produced the pendant that he had been wearing for seven years; a metal claw clutching an orb that looked like an eye. He had never taken it off during his exile, even in his most defeated of times. It was a reminder of his lost power and the kingdom that awaited him if he could find a way to return. It wasn't necessary for Alec to expose it now, the creature could smell its pheromones through his clothes, but it gave him some comfort all the same.

He took another shaky step and then another. Finally, a shape began to form from the shadows and two enormous glowing eyes came into focus, reflecting the torchlight back at him with eerie definition. Another hiss met his ears and sent a shiver down his spine. Alec closed his eyes for a moment, then flattened his fingers and extended them into the blackness, reaching out and praying this wasn't a bridge too far. A sharp snarl cut through the air and Alec flinched badly, but he didn't move. He kept reaching, ever so slowly and steadily into the unknown. The snarl ebbed away slightly into a low-register growl; uncertain but not aggressive. And then a tentative footstep crept forward and Alec saw the hooked beak and scaly face of the Neodactyl finally come into the light. Its yellow eyes were searching and predatory but the quills along its feathery back were beginning to relax. It took another cautious step and sniffed in Alec's direction. Alec allowed his fingers to drop slightly and the animal extended its long, wiry neck to reach them. Its face brushed gently against the very tips of his fingers and the low growl slowly receded into something more akin to a cooing sound. It finally folded its quills back down into its plumage and relaxed its bristling feathers, accepting the return of its long-lost owner.

Alec breathed deeply and brushed carefully at the animal's colorful coat, allowing it to close the final steps between them in its own time. Alec turned and the rest of the group was grinning, no one more widely than Nel.

"You've still got it," Nel exclaimed, and he wasn't sure if she was referring to the pendant around his neck or his ability to control the beast.

Alec smiled as he turned to face the group, allowing the Neodactyl to slink to his side just like the old days. The group looked awestruck by the display and were nodding their heads in approval. Alec approached Tytus with a new air of confidence and placed a hand on his shoulder. Tytus shuddered slightly at the gesture, eyeing the King's creature apprehensively, but Alec smiled at him.

"Thank you for this," Alec said benevolently. "You have proved yourself to be a true loyalist. You have a place at my side when I retake this Kingdom."

Tytus's mouth was hung slack, his eyes showing a mesmerized wonder that was causing Alec to swell with self-importance. The man finally blinked rapidly, as though awaking from a stupor, and bowed his head low.

"Thank you, my King."

CHAPTER TWENTY–FIVE

THE UNKNOWN

Having his old ally and former leader back was a funny thing. There was a time, ages ago by Jack's counting, when Cyrus had been his rival. Nemesis was too strong of a word, but Jack did not think much of the man when he had first encountered him. Cyrus Dorn had been belligerent, headstrong, and egotistical when he had first boarded Jack's expedition vessel, and his arrogantly barked orders and showmanship had done little to sway anyone's opinion. He was a poor leader when he started the journey, there was no doubt about it. He inspired little to no faith in his abilities, and the chest-puffing was a weak façade to hide his insecurities. Of course, Jack had not made it easy on his new leader. Jack had spent much of his adult life taking orders aboard various shipping vessels and he had had his fill of inexperienced, under-qualified captains. But people are not always who they first seem. This place had awakened something in Cyrus that was impossible to ignore. It was easy to equate his unprecedented rise to Alec, and call it simply a reaction to his brother's catastrophic fall, but Jack knew better. Cyrus never wanted to be a leader, not really, and that was exactly why he was so good at it.

In the end, Jack had learned much from Cyrus Dorn, though he wasn't likely to be admitting that aloud anytime soon. But when Cyrus had gone, following his brother through that anomaly, Jack was left to pick up the mantle from him. Not that the people had asked him to lead, he was only their king now because of his marriage to Annica, but he had still felt a responsibility to see that Cyrus's democracy survived. He had been methodical in placing layers within the hierarchy, a crucial step that Alec had failed to do, and he had done so in the hope that his teachings would live on after his departure. They had lived on, Jack had made sure of it. But how does one continue to lead when your long-lost predecessor suddenly reappears? Jack felt like he should be handing the crown back to Cyrus, but that was absurd. Annica was queen now, elected by the people once Cyrus had stepped down. Anything less than that would be an assault on the very foundation that Cyrus had built. So Jack maintained his title of king, despite an awkward nagging in the pit of his stomach.

It had now been three days since the new Temple had been burnt to the ground and the rest of the town razed around it. That meant three days that the entirety of their population had been living in the forest, strategizing and scheming, but defeated nonetheless. Perhaps 'entirety of their population' was not an accurate assessment; there were still countless numbers that lived in former Easttown and Westtown, and Jack knew of no reason they would have had to vacate their homes. But this man, this mystery assailant who had suddenly appeared in their streets, along with his scarred and warped companion, had ensured that the center of power within the new kingdom had been reduced to ash. Where had he come from? How did he know of Cyrus and Alec? Where had he learned the power to control frozen fire in such devastating fashion? The man had wrenched Alec's scepter out of his hand with such ease that it appeared like an afterthought. As though Alec, the Western King of such immense power that he had nearly decimated the Kingdom over a feud with his brother, was little more than a nuisance to be tossed aside. It terrified Jack to his core, and he found himself looking to Cyrus once again for guidance and strength.

In true Kingdom fashion, the builders and masons of the town had wasted no time in crafting makeshift campsites for the homeless towns-folk now residing in the forest and the area now resembled a rustic village, tucked away under the trees. Canvas tarps had been procured from the worksites in the west to create shelters and each occupant now had their own small segment of land to call their own. Of course privacy was a thing entirely of the past, for there had not been nearly enough material to provide walls for everyone. They had tried to insist that the Queen and King, both current and former, should have more elaborate sites than the rest, but it was Annica who had eventually talked them out of it. This was not a permanent settlement, and would never serve as such, but it would have to do for now while they regrouped and decided how to deal with their new foreign invader.

"King Jack," came a mild, slightly quaking voice that nevertheless made him start. He had been so absorbed in his own thoughts that he had not noticed Noma's approach.

"Hey Noma," Jack responded, "how are you settling in?" It was a weak attempt at normal conversation but his heart wasn't in it at the moment.

"I... I've brought this down on all of us." Noma looked positively stricken when Jack finally looked him in the eyes. "The man with the melted face, he's the one who convinced me to try that experiment to bring our people back. He... he wanted this to happen."

He looked relieved when Jack just nodded his head in understanding. "It's an important lesson, Noma. You choose who you trust. You need to learn to read people." When Noma continued to look down in shame, Jack took pity on him and decided to pivot away from the lesson he sorely wanted to give. "I don't understand how him stealing a fragment of our scepter would have allowed them to come here. Did he ever mention those new weapons during your talks?"

"No," Noma answered, "he only told me that he was from a future version of our world, and that advancements had been made."

Jack sighed deeply, trying his hardest to not snap at Noma, who he had to remind himself was incredibly young. "What do you know about the man?" he finally asked.

Noma seemed relieved to be asked a question he had a solid answer to, for he began talking with a bit of his old confidence again. "He calls himself the Alchemist. He runs a repair shop in his kingdom, very similar to mine. I should have known not to trust an outsider, he just seemed to understand me so well, and seemed so genuine in his desire to help. I'm sorry, King Jack."

Jack just patted him on the shoulder and said, "No more time for what-ifs. Now we need to find out more about his leader... and the world they come from."

Noma appeared far lighter after their talk, nodding appreciatively and bowing his head, but Jack was feeling like he needed to take action. He began weaving his way between the sea of tents and tarps, looking for Cyrus. The beginnings of a path had already been tramped down by the constant flow of foot traffic and it was giving the settlement a slightly permanent look that unsettled him. He passed the newcomers Kat and Dean, both of whom looked thoroughly out of their element even three days on. They were consulting amongst themselves in low whispers and broke off abruptly at seeing Jack pass. Dean offered a strange, nervous salute that made Jack smirk slightly, but he returned the gesture all the same. When he finally came upon Cyrus, he found Annica there with him, reporting on something in urgent fashion.

"Jack," she beckoned quickly as she saw his approach. "I've just been filling in Cyrus, the first of our spies have returned from the Fire Fields."

It had been Annica's idea to send reconnaissance missions back to the now destroyed town proper and bring back reports on what their new arrivals were up to. Their missions had strictly been to observe and report, not to engage.

"Tam has been watching their movements for days," Annica said, "but our mystery guests are doing very little. There have been no attempts to build anything or recruit anyone. They've simply been... waiting."

"Waiting for what?" Jack asked with a cold shiver.

Annica just shook her head in response.

"He must want something," Cyrus growled thoughtfully. "What reason would he have for coming here otherwise?"

Annica stayed silent once again but her clever eyes were narrowed and searching. It was disheartening to know so little about their antagonist.

After a long pause, Jack finally said bluntly, "Is there any possibility of an assault?" When his companions just stared back at him, he continued, "I know it's crude, but we outnumber them by the hundreds. We have trained fighters..."

"The one thing of note that Tam did report," Annica began softly, "was that a townsman attempted to sneak back into the ruins of the town. He got within fifty yards before the tall man raised those tridents into the air. He was annihilated before he could even rethink his decision. There's no fighting this man, not with brute force alone. Two men, ten men, a thousand men, it won't make a difference, they'll all burn the same."

It was a sobering statement, but undeniably true. An army marching on the ruined town square would only result in the total destruction of said army. "What then?" Jack asked. "What's our move?"

But Both Cyrus and Annica had stopped listening and it didn't take Jack long to realize why. The surrounding village had gone eerily silent. For just a moment, it seemed as though the very forest were holding its breath, with every bird, mammal, and insect retreating into their homes. And then the whispering of dozens of panicked voices began to roll towards them as the townsfolk collectively shuddered and gasped. Jack turned slowly, his head hung low and his eyes squinted warily. Along the worn-down path, people began withdrawing from the thoroughfare and into the mouths of their tents. It was then that Jack saw the approach of a group of people, striding with the same importance that the former King Mora had once projected with such ease. Alec Dorn was at the head of the brigade, cutting through the camp like a dagger through flesh. He was flanked by Nel on his left and a Neodactyl on his right. Five armed loyalists formed up behind him, scowling apprehensively and gripping their machetes tightly. It had been six years since Jack had seen the nightmare pet of the King and his breath caught in his throat at the sight. Nel was eying the camp with mild interest, but to his surprise, there was no hint of superiority in her eyes. As for Alec, his jaw was set and his gaze was focused, but some of the desperate madness he had shown beneath the Guardian had subsided. He looked strong... and determined.

Cyrus stepped forward, blocking both Jack and Annica from following suit and planted himself firmly before his brother.

"You're not welcome here, Alec," Cyrus commanded with such quiet authority that Jack could swear he saw Alec's stoicism falter behind his eyes.

Alec stopped his approach and his party did the same. There was silence for a long time as the two stared at each other. The memory of their last devastating confrontation in the Fire Fields seemed to hang over the meeting like a shadow, and Jack fidgeted uncomfortably. It was with significant worry that he realized Cyrus was currently unarmed. But when Alec finally broke the taut silence, his voice sounded cautious rather than hostile.

"I don't want to be here either," Alec declared, "but circumstances have changed, brother. I think it's time we had a talk."

CHAPTER TWENTY–SIX

COMMON GROUND

Annica snapped her fingers and a guard scrambled forward to offer her one of her custom-built bolt-launchers, which she grasped quickly. She never gave an order, there was no need to. Her people knew her leadership style well and knew her to be a person of action. She aimed the weapon straight at Alec's heart and cocked her head.

"I will not hesitate to kill you, Alec," she called out. "As your brother has stated, you are not welcome here."

"I just want to talk," Alec insisted, but his history of butchering their people made the request far less reasonable. Annica just continued to glower at him.

The Neodactyl at his side gave a crackling hiss but Alec brushed his fingers gently over its neck and it relaxed slightly. "We have a common problem," Alec began. "I know you recognize it as well as I do, our desires are more aligned than they have ever been before."

"Our desires, sure," Jack retorted, "but our means of achieving them, not so much." He turned to Cyrus and Annica and said, "You see what he's doing here, right? Without an army at his command and no resources to speak of, he wants us to clear the way for him to take control of the Kingdom again."

Cyrus cocked his eyebrows and looked back Alec's way. "He's not wrong, Alec. I'm not seeing a reason we need your help at all."

Alec considered the accusation momentarily, then nodded slowly. "Okay then answer me this; why have you not made a move? It's been three days and it seems your people are settling into a new colony out here. Are you simply content allowing that man to take your hard-fought town… your home?"

Jack rolled his eyes slightly and said, "I'm sure you'll be arriving at your point soon."

"The point is you're hardly thriving out here," Nel sneered, "so let's dispense with the posturing."

Annica narrowed her eyes and fought hard against the urge to bury a bolt into Nel's throat. But the point was a valid one; they were no closer to taking their home back than they had been when the newcomer first arrived. She lowered her weapon slightly and said, "Okay, let's hear it then." When Alec and Nel just stared back at her, she continued, "You must have a plan, if you were willing to stroll in here. So what is it? What have we not considered?"

Alec looked around at the slowly gathering crowd and raised his arms in a dramatic sort of shrug. "Do you have somewhere we can talk?"

"We're talking now, Alec," Jack declared. "But if you're referring to privacy, I think not."

Alec snorted incredulously. "What do you think I'm gonna do, as-sassinate all of you once we're alone?"

"That sounds precisely like something you would do," Cyrus an-swered, and Alec fell silent. "You've burned all faith any of us ever had in you, and we certainly don't trust your ability to make rational, calcu-lated decisions. You wanted to talk, we're talking. If you have a plan, let's hear it. But stop wasting our time masquerading as a reasonable man. That time is long past… and you're not fooling anyone."

Alec's eye twitched slightly and an expression of darkest loathing briefly rippled across his face. But it didn't last and he kept his composure, like someone recalling an exhaled breath. He smiled coldly and nodded. "Okay, have it your way, brother. We can talk here."

Annica let her weapon fall slightly, but not much. She had no intention of letting her guard down around Alec Dorn, no matter what assurances he gave. He seemed to take note of the continued aggression for he smirked at her in a rather condescending sort of way.

"You can't beat him the way you want to," Alec began. "Without a scepter of our own, I don't think we have any weapons that can stand against that pair of tridents he carries."

Annica found it laughable that Alec was entirely dismissing the fact that he himself had gotten the last remaining scepter taken, and even more absurd that he was already referring to himself as 'we'. But she bit her tongue and let him continue.

"You have probably also realized that attacking him with sheer numbers won't do any good. What he did to your new Temple will dissuade you from that I would think. So we need to be tactical."

He paused and looked around at the group as though this were a revelation of some sort.

Cyrus rolled his eyes. "You're not telling us anything new here. Do you have a plan or not?"

Alec grinned. "He knows us, brother. You and I. And he looked more than a little curious to meet us the other day. What that tells me is that you and I are the *only* people who can approach him without being obliterated on sight. He's too curious."

Annica glanced at Cyrus, who looked like he was trying to find a piece of the statement that he disagreed with. Eventually he nodded his head in acceptance. "Okay, I'm inclined to agree. But I know your plan can't be to just walk up to him with a machete. His *curiosity* won't last long if we're armed."

"Of course not," Alec nodded, "we won't be armed. But we also won't be alone."

"Will you stop talking in damn riddles," Cyrus said roughly, "get to your point."

Alec looked put out by the interruption but kept calm. He reached out his hand and patted the Neodactyl gently on the neck. "This is how we get to him. We bring the Neodactyl, leave it hidden in the trees. Then, at my call, it'll come running. It can cover that distance infinitely faster than a human; he won't know what hit him."

Cyrus weighed this in his mind, but it was Jack who spoke up. "Do you think we're insane? Walk up to him yourself if you are so certain it will work."

"What's your objection?" Alec asked impatiently. "You're not risking your people. In fact, I'm the one positioned to lose something here. The only thing you're risking…"

"Is our king," Annica finished before she could stop herself. "Why would we risk that?"

Alec's eyes darted from Annica, to Cyrus, to Jack, to Ydoro, and back. He seemed unable to figure out who he should be addressing, which made sense given his blatant lack of understanding for a sustainable leadership structure. "Am I understanding this right, Cy?" Alec finally asked, landing on his brother as the top authority figure. "You wouldn't risk your own life to save your people?" When he was met with only silence, he continued, "Because that's all your risking. This plan involves nothing from anyone else. It's you and me. Just like it always was before."

The last sentence was not a sentiment coated in nostalgia; it was sneering and hateful, and Annica felt sure it was intended as bait.

The silence drew out painfully before Jack finally spoke. "You never answered my question; why not go by yourself? If you are so certain this man's curiosity will stay his hand, why is Cyrus needed at all?"

Alec's expression slid just slightly and a bit of his smarmy resolve seemed to ebb away. "It was Cyrus that intrigued him, not me." It was an admission that appeared to pain Alec to say aloud, but he continued in a low growl that had lost all pretense of self-righteousness. "He wants you Cyrus, I could see it in his eyes. He hungered for you, like an animal. He knows you from history and thinks he can learn something. I think you're the reason he's here, in this place and this time."

Jack began to cut in to disagree, but Cyrus held up his hand to stop him. His brow was furrowed and creased with contemplation and his shoulders suddenly looked like they were supporting the weight of the world again, as they had during his reign as King of the East. Alec was looking expectantly, as though he knew there was nothing further he could say to make his point resonate.

"You can't be considering this," Jack urged Cyrus. "Your brother can't be trusted."

"I'm not trusting my brother," Cyrus finally answered, almost somberly, "I'm trusting what I saw, and I fear Alec may be right." When Jack looked incredulous, Cyrus continued, "It can't be a coincidence that this man shows up within minutes of my coming back. Alec's also not wrong; we're out of options at the moment."

Alec grinned, nodding his head approvingly but also allowing his contempt to creep back to the forefront. "Now there's the Cyrus I know," he hissed. "All you've gotta do is check that ego of yours and you can save your people. Maybe they'll even build another statue of you."

Cyrus, instead of being drawn in by the mockery, responded, "I'll go with you on one condition. If I'm putting my life in the hands of you and this creature, I wanna know, here and now; how are you controlling it?" When Alec hesitated, Cyrus continued, "No games, no excuses. Explain it to me, and we have a deal."

Alec's lip curled in disgust and it was clear he was trying hard to weigh his options. Finally, he sighed, reached beneath his shirt and withdrew a small dangling pendant from a chain around his neck. "This is how I control it," Alec admitted, and there was no lie in his eyes. "It was King Mora's, and Irias's before him. It emits a pheromone that the Neodactyls can smell. It denotes me as the trainer they originally imprinted on, their master."

Cyrus narrowed his eyes at the slowly rotating glass orb and nodded his head with a half-smile. "Simple… and smart." He looked impressed at the obviousness of the deception. "Okay, then we have a deal. We can leave within the hour."

Alec grinned again, stowing the pendant back beneath his shirt. "It'll be just like old times. Storming Mora's Temple and taking the spoils for ourselves."

*****

Cyrus went to work almost immediately preparing to leave, during which time Annica felt it was her duty as queen to inform their *guests* that they were not welcome to linger within the perimeter of the makeshift village. She had thought this command might be met with resistance, but Alec's company nodded rather agreeably and withdrew to the far edges of the clustered tents and awnings. The plan seemed to be for his people to journey back to wherever they had come from and await Alec and the Neodactyl's return. Annica felt she could trust them to follow through on this because Alec would not want to risk his precious few loyalists by bringing them to confront the mystery assailant.

After verifying that they had exited camp, Annica made her way back to Cyrus's tent where she found him already surrounded by a chattering group consisting of Jack, Ydoro, and Noma. Jack was attempting to talk Cyrus out of this venture, but the other two were nodding at their prior king's conviction with excitement and wonder. Cyrus was getting a daypack ready and slipping a rusted machete into his belt. As Annica closed the distance between them and nodded wordlessly at the weapon, Cyrus explained he intended to drop it at the treeline before entering the remnants of town. This told Annica that the machete was a deterrent against his brother, not for the newcomers.

"I just think this should be discussed further," Jack was insisting. "Yes, we've been brought down, but that doesn't mean that you have to singlehandedly fix everything yourself."

"Something my father always used to say to me," Noma chimed in with a slightly inappropriate level of excitement to his voice, "is that you can't fix everything, but you can damn sure give it a try."

Jack gaped at him with a look of puzzlement that was almost comical. "Noma, remember how we've discussed when to speak up and when not to?"

Annica smirked at the odd father/son dynamic that the two shared, but her levity didn't last.

"I understand what you hope to accomplish by this," Jack continued towards Cyrus, "but you're being rash. You've just come back, and I don't want..."

"Exactly," Cyrus interrupted, dropping his preparations and turning fully to face his friend, "that's why it needs to be me. You've kept our legacy alive here, the both of you. *All* of you. Yes, I was their onetime leader, but you're their leaders now. I'm a remnant of a past time. A time, with a little luck, that can be forgotten eventually. Or at the very least, slip into ancient history. Our work can't all be destroyed now because of one man. We risk very little by me going, but Alec could be right and this could be how we take our kingdom back. I have to try."

Jack was shaking his head but seemed at a loss for rational arguments. "I don't like it," he finally landed on.

Cyrus nodded amiably, "You don't like it because it's coming from Alec." When Jack didn't deny it, Cyrus smiled. "My brother doesn't scare me. This is desperation, him seeking us out. He's running scared and he knows that we're his only chance. But don't worry, I haven't changed my mind about what he is."

Jack still didn't look convinced as Cyrus slung his pack over one shoulder. "This is Alec Dorn we're talking about," Jack finished, "don't you forget it."

Cyrus grinned. "Never."

He turned and gave one last scan of his allies, an odd expression on his face.

Ydoro, wide eyed with awe, said, "Give him hell."

It was the same three words that Jack had said to Cyrus before he faced his brother in the Fire Fields six years ago. Annica doubted whether Ydoro had been familiar with the expression before hearing it then, and it made her smile realizing where he must have adopted it from.

Cyrus nodded in appreciation, turned, and strode away along the path and out of sight.

Jack turned to Annica, almost looking for permission to follow as he watched his friend be led into the unknown once again by his traitorous younger brother. She just shook her head. "You can't. You can't save him. Cyrus has to choose his own path."

Jack nodded, but his eyes tracked apprehensively up the trail.

"Don't worry, my King," Ydoro said quietly, joining his gaze, "this is Cyrus Dorn we're talking about." When Jack looked his way, Ydoro met his eyes and smiled. "And don't *you* forget it."

CHAPTER TWENTY–SEVEN

MAGNUS

When Cyrus joined Alec at the edge of their temporary village, the rest of his company bid them good luck and hiked off to the north and presumably back to where they had come from, just as promised. Nel gave Alec a quick kiss before they parted, leaving Cyrus with just a hint of unease. He intended to move extremely cautiously around Alec and had no plans of letting his guard down while they were alone. He knew Jack worried of the wisdom behind this expedition, and while Cyrus couldn't say that he wholeheartedly blamed him, he knew Alec at this point and knew how his mind worked. Yes, Alec very likely had the intent of betraying him at some point on their journey, the trick would be anticipating when. With this in mind, Cyrus had insisted the Neodactyl prowl on ahead so that he wouldn't have to worry about it doing anything unpredictable. It was only reluctantly that Alec had agreed.

It was five minutes of trekking in silence before Alec finally spoke up. "You must be thrilled, returning here to find your beloved empire intact." Cyrus ignored him. After another minute of quiet, Alec tried again. "You know, your people are counting on you. If you show up again having failed, it's hard to imagine them allowing you to stay in power."

"I'm not in power," Cyrus retorted dryly, half kicking himself for being drawn in by Alec's statements at all.

"Okay," Alec said in a sarcastic sort of concession, "maybe not officially, but they built a statue of you. You're still their leader whether you want to be or not. And the truth is, Jack or Annica or whoever else plans to take your place won't be able to rule from beneath your shadow, not while you're still here."

Cyrus turned, scanning the intentions behind Alec's fake smile, and offered a smirk. "You'd like that, wouldn't you. Me stepping aside and leaving my people to contend with you."

"I'm simply saying that…"

Cyrus drew the rusted machete from his belt in a quick, fluid motion and brought the tip of the blade up to Alec's throat. Alec stopped walking immediately.

"I know what you're saying," Cyrus growled, and Alec just stared at him. "You're *harmlessly* trying to make me second-guess what's best for my people. *Innocently* suggesting that for democracy to work, I need to step aside. You've lost your subtlety, brother." He allowed the point of the blade to graze the stubble under Alec's chin. "You're scared of me, even more than you're scared of our mysterious newcomer. And you should be. They built a statue of me because I defended them from you. I continue to be your worst nightmare and while I stand, you will *never* rule again."

Alec grinned. "There's that ego."

"Play all the games you want," Cyrus threatened, "they'll get you nowhere."

The machete made a soft tinging noise as Cyrus brushed the very end of Alec's chin with the blade and slipped it back into his belt. He began walking again and Alec only paused momentarily before following. It was another few minutes before the silence was broken.

"You certainly think a lot of yourself, don't you?" Alec goaded.

"Standing next to you," Cyrus answered, "it's not hard."

The rest of their journey remained quiet between the two of them, making their bootfalls against the forest floor sound deafening. In truth, Cyrus was nervous. Alec's carefully hidden lack of confidence was his weakness and stoking that particular facet of his personality was not difficult. But dismissing his volatility because it was born from emotion would be a mistake. He was an unpredictable and dangerous opponent, perhaps even more so now that he had lost much of his power. And the familial ties that had colored much of their original conflict had all but dissolved. This was not an Alec that he recognized anymore, and Cyrus would use every tool at his disposal to prevent a repeating of history.

He heard the Neodactyl give a soft hiss around a bend in the trail ahead and upon rounding the corner themselves, it was clear why. They had arrived at the Fire Fields and what was left of the town square. Many of the dwellings were burnt and collapsed, either reduced to piles of debris or incinerated from the inside leaving the ashen husk of the exterior behind. It was from between the charred remains of these last standing houses that the wind could be heard whistling, creating an ominous symphony of droning hums and groans. No life was visible in the town from where they stood at the treeline, but Cyrus somehow knew that the newcomers were still close.

Alec stooped slightly to communicate with his creature, which cooed receptively as though it understood perfectly what was expected of it. Cyrus caught a glimpse of the pendant hanging from his brother's neck, obvious now that it had been pointed out to him, and again admired the simplicity of the trick to controlling the creatures. As Alec righted himself, the Neodactyl stalked off to the left and disappeared into the shadows of the forest.

"It'll come when it's called, don't worry yourself," Alec responded to Cyrus's unasked question. His apprehension must have been showing on his face, but he took a deep breath to try and settle his nerves. Was he putting too much faith in his ability to read Alec? He *knew* Alec meant to betray him at the opportune moment, but he had to think that their goals were aligned until after the newcomers were eradicated. He felt certain that Jack was right; Alec wanted to use the Kingdom's resources no longer available to himself, namely Cyrus, to eliminate a very clear threat. Only after that would it make sense for a double-cross.

"So what d'ya think?" Alec asked, studying his brother's face with a probing smile. "You ready for this?"

Cyrus unsheathed his machete and flipped it down into the ground where it stuck, vibrating just slightly. "Let's find out," he answered.

Alec grinned more broadly, and it gave Cyrus just a bit of extra strength seeing the reaction to his resolve. The two strode out into the open air, shoulder to shoulder, cutting their way through the sickly black layer of smoke, dust, and ash that still clung to the ground like a ghostly blanket. It glowed just slightly from the particles of frozen fire that made up the earth below, but the dark cloud was trying its best to stifle that as well.

A loud crunch made Cyrus jump badly, but it turned out to be the snapping of a former wall support under Alec's boot, made brittle by the inferno. The unnatural quiet in the air was playing tricks on his mind. He yearned for a weapon. His scepter would be best, but he would take his machete gladly. In truth, he just wanted something to hold, a conduit for his desperately needed confidence.

"Now I had my doubts," came a hoarse, drawling voice that seemed to pierce the silent air like a spear. "I thought to myself, did I make enough of an impression that the two Dorn brothers will actually stand together?"

Cyrus scanned his surroundings wildly, at first unable to discern where the voice was coming from. But then he saw a form, opaque and featureless in the mist, sitting casually on the remains of one of the collapsed houses. It was the larger of the two men, but his companion appeared to be skulking just behind him.

"And here you are," the man continued, "impossible as it had seemed to me."

Alec and Cyrus had stopped their approach, noting wordlessly that the man's tridents leaned against the wreckage nearby. The man looked their way, his face still eerily devoid of detail in the haze, and stood up. He was a hulking beast of a man; tall, broad-shouldered, and incredibly strong. His head dangled to the right slightly as though he were permanently ducking under a low doorframe, and he looked at them through the tops of downturned eyes.

"I'm honored that the great and powerful Dorn's would take the time to come see me personally," the man said, "rather than just the spies I've seen slinking about in the forest."

Cyrus squinted, attempting to read the man. His eyes looked hollow, almost dead, and the way he talked in a would-be-casual way was not only disingenuous but gave the impression he was attempting human conversation for the first time. There was a sterility to his words that was so impossibly cold. Cyrus scanned the burned remains of the house that the man had been sitting on, and he took notice.

The man raised his eyebrows and said, "Like what I've done with the place?"

"Why did you come here?" Cyrus finally demanded. "You came, you destroyed, and now you're just… waiting? What are you waiting for?"

It was the answer he had been dreading, but Cyrus still found himself caught off guard hearing it spoken aloud.

"You," the man growled with a smile.

Alec looked sideways to Cyrus, who stayed quiet, studying the situation.

"I understand your apprehension about me," the man said, as though burning the town to the ground had somehow been misinterpreted, "we haven't even had proper introductions yet."

The man took a step forward and his companion with the melted face followed in his wake. Cyrus noted that both tridents had been left behind. The man extended his arms outward in a congenial display and tilted his body into a shallow bow. "My name is Kysaar Magnus, and I come from a place not so different from your own." He straightened again and clarified, "Similar place, different time." He began to pace forward a bit, furthering the distance between himself and his horrific weapons. "You see, I know you both from my own people's history. The Dorn brothers were legendary, as was their feud to control the Kingdom. It brought conflict and violence and death… but it also brought greatness." He paused, both his pacing and his speech, and studied Cyrus. "It mattered, what you did here. And it lasted. I do hope you can take some comfort in that."

That horrible coldness tainted every word the man spoke. Even a supposed message of comfort came out as a hateful taunt from the tongue of Kysaar Magnus. Cyrus had a vision of a fish being slowly reeled in on a line.

"I'm not buying it," Cyrus finally answered, and the man scowled slightly. "You say you came here for me, but it sounds like I was long before your time. What is it you're hoping to gain by coming here?"

Cyrus didn't actually care about the man's response; he wanted him distracted so that Alec could call his creature. But Alec had been frustratingly quiet for the entire exchange. As Kysaar Magnus began to talk again, Cyrus whispered out of the corner of his mouth, "Now."

But Alec didn't move. He almost seemed enthralled by the man.

"Call it now, Alec," Cyrus hissed.

When Alec still did not move, Cyrus began to panic. But then, to his immense relief, he heard footsteps approaching from the left.

Magnus, who had been elaborating on the prosperity of his own kingdom, seemed to register the noise as well. But the footsteps weren't running, they sounded calculated and cautious. And human. Their group of four turned in unison and Cyrus's heart dropped at the sight of the new arrival.

"And who might you be?" Magnus asked in a mildly interested growl.

"You can call me Nel," Nel responded with a soft bow of her head.

Cyrus looked to Alec, who wore a self-satisfied smirk. His heart began hammering painfully fast.

"I come in peace," Nel said, exposing her hands to show she was not armed.

"We both do actually," Alec announced, and he took a step forward. "We recognize your power, and I admit it to be far superior to my own. I have a proposition for you, if you'll hear it."

Cyrus glared at his brother, who did not return his gaze. Magnus looked from Alec to Nel, nodding silently to himself.

"Alec Dorn," Magnus finally said, savoring the words in his mouth. "History doesn't speak kindly of you. Cyrus Dorn was the dawning of a new age but the writings about his younger brother are mired by his failures." When Alec stayed respectfully silent, Magnus bore into him, as though examining a newfound species. "But history doesn't account for everything, does it? After all, you were the spark that ignited Cyrus's Kingdom. He found his way because *you* pushed him. I think that bears remembrance, celebration even. He couldn't have flown if you hadn't first taken him over the cliff."

Alec inclined his head in an appreciative nod but still did not speak. He had finally learned restraint.

Magnus let the quiet draw out for another moment. At long last, he said, "Okay, let's hear your proposition, Alec Dorn."

Alec bowed his head again in a gesture of thanks and said, "You speak kindly of my brother and his impact on your history, but in truth you can't think much of his teachings if you were willing to burn his dynasty to the ground. I think you're curious to know what would have happened if he hadn't won the duel in the Fire Fields. I can't rewrite history for you, but if you want my brother, what I propose is that you take him and go. He can answer for what he's done in your world, and you can give *this* world a shot at something greater. An alternate course for history. Leave this world to *me*, and I'll make sure history remembers how you tipped the scales. Kysaar Magnus will be remembered."

If Cyrus still had his machete, no force on earth could have stopped him from burying it in Alec's neck. As it was, he had no weapon to strike with and was left balling his hands into such painful fists that they were beginning to turn white.

Magnus nodded his head thoughtfully, then turned his sights on Nel. "And what's your take on all this? You agree with this path?"

Nel offered her most placating smile and nodded. "Your power is undeniable. And I'm looking for change."

Magnus adopted a thoughtful expression and wobbled his head back and forth in a show of contemplation. "Interesting," he said, "very interesting."

"I thought you'd want to hear what I had to say," Alec responded.

"No," Magnus said, still seemingly debating with himself, "what you had to say wasn't interesting in the slightest." Alec's smile faltered. "What I find interesting is that you so freely offer up your brother but then expect me to trust your loyalty." Magnus smiled to himself. "It's actually quite amusing."

Alec turned a deep shade of red and Cyrus could sense the blood boiling beneath the surface.

"Perhaps I haven't been clear about what I want Cyrus Dorn for," Magnus continued, taking several more steps forward, and away from his tridents. "I care not what your feud did to your history or mine. I came here, to this specific reality at this specific time, because in all the worlds I've seen, and they truly are countless, this moment stands out. In every world where you stay away; where you duel, share parting words with your people and leave, your kingdom thrives. Cyrus Dorn's teachings live on and the two of you pass into legend. Your rule was never meant to be long, just powerful. *This* moment, right here and now, in this very specific reality, is your kingdom at its very weakest. It's an anomaly that I've been searching for a very long time. Nothing bends the will of the people quite like watching their hero fall. I'm not here to take Cyrus Dorn away, I'm here to *break* him."

The speech took the air out of the conversation entirely. Alec looked just as dumbfounded as Cyrus felt and the whistling of the wind through the surrounding mangled houses was the only sound in the world. Kysaar Magnus stared back at them expectantly, like a spider that had just caught a fly in its web. But as far as Cyrus was concerned, there was one last move to play. He took a single step forward.

"Now look at that," Cyrus said, projecting as much confidence as he could muster. "You've come all this way, through countless realities as you claim, searching for this exact moment. And what do you do?" Cyrus smiled. "You overplay your hand. ALEC NOW!"

Despite whatever Alec had planned when they first walked into the Fire Fields, Cyrus knew this was not what he wanted. Alec whistled loudly. Almost immediately footsteps could be heard racing across the expanse of burnt debris. The man with the melted face seemed to cower slightly and Magnus turned wildly to identify the incoming threat.

Alec grinned. "Maybe you picked the wrong reality after all."

Magnus turned swiftly towards his tridents but at that moment the enormous bird sprinted into view, closing the distance between them at a horrifying rate. He would never reach his weapons in time. The Neodactyl let out an echoing screech as it charged, fifty feet away, then twenty-five. It was within ten feet of its prey before Magnus abandoned his search for a weapon and faced the creature head-on.

"NO!" Magnus shouted, and to Cyrus's utter disbelief, the Neodactyl slowed down, cocked its head, and skidded to a halt. It chirped mildly and sniffed in his direction.

Alec looked baffled. His mouth hung open in horror and betrayal. Magnus reached forward and ran his fingers gently over the bird's quills. And he smiled.

Magnus reached into the folds of his cloak and produced a pendant on a chain, identical to the one Alec was currently wearing. "This just isn't your day I'm afraid," he growled mockingly. When Alec just stared, he continued, "I wish you could see your face, I really do. You must have thought yourself special, controlling those birds and making your people cower. But all it takes is this. No skill, no power, just this little pendant. And when you've seen as many realities as I have, they come easy."

Alec looked too stunned to move. Cyrus imagined his brother suddenly felt as naked and helpless as he did. Alec attempted a whistle to call his creature, which did cock its head at the noise, but Magnus wove his hand into the bird's plumage and grasped it dominantly.

"I think not," Magnus sneered. "Bring me a tie."

At first Cyrus was unsure who he was speaking to, but then the man with the melted face came forward and produced a length of rope, which he fed around the creature's neck and tied to a large section of damaged house. Cyrus kept forgetting that the second man was here; easy to do given how he seemed to remain creeping beneath the larger man's shadow. Despite his horrible appearance, he had such a lack of presence that he just naturally seemed to fade into the background. This likely made him a particularly valuable, and particularly malleable subject.

"I'll ask you to do the same with our guests here," Magnus said to his counterpart, who turned to retrieve more rope. Cyrus thought of running but knew there was no use in such an open area. "You understand, don't you?" Magnus said, "I take no pleasure in bringing such legendary rulers low. I mean not to degrade you, but I can't have you running off." He turned to Nel, who still stood a distance away, still as a statue. "And what about you? Do you plan to join them?"

Cyrus found himself praying that Nel had brought a weapon, perhaps concealed somewhere behind her back. But her reaction of confusion told him not.

"You're giving me a choice?" Nel asked with a hint of a humorless laugh.

"Well certainly," Magnus answered. "The Dorn's fate was sealed the moment I stepped foot into your world, but you I don't know from history. I can see your loyalty lies with the younger, but I also wonder how that has worked out for you so far?"

Nel just stared back at him. The man with the melted face had returned carrying not only a large amount of rope but one of the tridents as well, which he handed respectfully to Magnus. No move was made to use the weapon but having it in hand was a powerful statement all the same.

"Am I wrong in guessing that you originally followed Alec Dorn because you thought him the stronger?" Magnus asked. When Nel didn't answer, he continued. "You thought he was going places, and would take you with him. But then he vanished, didn't he? And you were left to defend a legacy that was indefensible. Extreme though his methods have been, you were willing to overlook them if it meant establishing your place in power. But you tied your chariot to the wrong horse, didn't you?"

Alec had started to step forward, his face distorted with hatred and anger. Magnus casually pointed his trident Alec's direction, never actually turning or even looking his way, and Alec stopped.

"These can't have been easy years for you, Nel," Magnus pushed on. "I imagine you a bit of a pariah in the Kingdom once your beloved leader abandoned you. But you told me you were looking for a change. Tell me honestly, is that what you really want?"

This time he did wait for Nel to respond, who looked entirely incapable of forming her thoughts into words. Something in her eyes was undeniably shifting. Instead of her unflappable, stony resolve, there was a new energy that Cyrus could sense, even from this distance. Certainly confusion. Perhaps also regret? Alec looked wounded beyond measure by her silence. His ever-present anger was cracking a bit, and true, honest sorrow was taking its place.

Nel looked at Alec but averted her gaze hastily. "I don't quite know what to say," she finally croaked, and Magnus smiled.

"Well if you had known what to say, then I wouldn't have trusted it," he responded. "But you do have a choice ahead of you. Do you want Alec Dorn? Or is it power you want?"

Nel met his eyes and Cyrus could swear he saw flames reflected in them, though nothing burned nearby. But she still didn't answer.

Magnus nodded in understanding and approached her. "I can understand your hesitation, and that's exactly what makes me believe you. If it helps, I don't mean to do Alec any harm. He is a loose end that I cannot have running around my kingdom, but Cyrus is my quarry." He stopped within several feet of her and bore into her eyes. "What is it you want, Nel?" he asked in a low growl, "because what I am offering you is nothing more or less than a second chance. Do you want it?"

He extended his hand out to her, palm up. An invitation.

Nel stared back at him in silence, trembling slightly. Then, slowly, she reached out and placed her own hand in his.

Cyrus shook his head in profound disappointment. Alec quaked next to him and allowed his gaze to drop to the ground in defeat. It seemed the fire within Alec Dorn had finally burnt out.

CHAPTER TWENTY–EIGHT

TIDINGS FROM A CONQUERER

S omething was wrong, Jack knew it in his gut. It had been nearly twenty-four hours since Cyrus had left camp with Alec and the Neodactyl, and there had been no word from them since. Cyrus was being foolish trusting his brother, and even more foolish if he believed he could anticipate a double-cross before it came. Jack had felt power-less to stop him, but could he have done more? Could he, as king, have ordered Cyrus to abandon the plan? Indeed, did his position as the cur-rent ruler eclipse Cyrus's own as the former king? The fact that Jack did not know the answer to that question likely gave him his answer. Be-sides, himself and Cyrus had never worked that way together. Despite their explosive arguments prior to their original journey, Cyrus as king had never given Jack a command. He had ruled by talking things through.

"It's been too long," Jack announced without prompting as Annica joined him near the edge of camp.

"I know it," Annica expressed somberly and Jack's concern only grew. She had staunchly insisted up until this moment that Cyrus knew what he was doing and would return to them victorious. "I had one of our men track Alec's people after they left. He just reported in. Alec's allies returned to the old Temple… but they can't find Nel."

Jack's eyes widened. "You don't think…"

"We don't know what's happened," Annica insisted, "but something's not right. And I think it's time we stop waiting."

"Whatever Alec and Nel have done," Jack began fiercely, but Annica shushed him quickly, looking over his shoulder.

Jack turned to see Dean and Kat approaching timidly, their eyes studying the interrupted conversation with trepidation. Annica offered a warm smile and greeted them as a compassionate and comforting leader. Jack himself shot them a frustrated glance before a look from Annica reminded him of his duty as their king. He forced a smile just a bit too late.

"We don't mean to interrupt," Dean said respectfully. "The truth is, Kat and I are just feeling a bit useless around here. We wondered if there was anything we can do?"

Annica was never one to shy away from assigning work but seemed a bit too preoccupied to consider the offer. "It's really appreciated," she responded, "we'll certainly let you know."

Dean looked mildly dejected and turned to walk away but Kat remained where she stood. "Is something wrong?" she asked with a bluntness that Jack found impressive. "It's just, we're sort of playing catch-up here, taking what we know from our world and applying it to the dynamics here on the island. But Cyrus hasn't come back. And I hope it's not out of turn to say that I don't trust Alec with him. I saw his speech yesterday, but I didn't believe him. He spoke with… other intentions. Like there was a poison behind his eyes that he was trying to cover up."

Annica stared at her inquisitively, reading her eager expression, and nodded her head. "A lot of people would have been taken in by his words. Indeed several of my own fighters have come to me over the last day expressing relief that Alec and Cyrus would be working together again. But you didn't buy it, huh?"

Kat shook her head slowly.

"Neither did I," Annica answered. "Alec Dorn is not to be trusted. Is *never* to be trusted."

"Then why did Cyrus go with him?" Kat asked, and again there was a sincerity in her demeanor that was quite disarming.

"Cyrus has a hard time being objective when it comes to his brother," Annica answered in a calming, almost motherly way. "Cyrus himself doesn't see it I don't think, but it clouds up his judgement."

"You almost seem like you hold that against him," Dean replied.

Annica sighed and Jack wondered how much she was planning to share with these newcomers. "I think he can be better. I think he has a gift for leading people, but if he's not careful, he'll lead them somewhere they don't want to go. He rules with emotion, which makes him unique, but having Alec around has always complicated his resolve. He could be more, if he tried."

Jack nodded in general agreement. For all of Cyrus's strengths, he was confident that Annica was astutely identifying his greatest weakness.

"Ya know, it's funny," Dean began in a way that served as a forceful reminder that the place he truly belonged was in a classroom, "I think you have a very different perspective of Cyrus Dorn that maybe affects *your* judgement of him."

Annica raised her eyebrows at the accusation but offered a smile and a nod for him to continue.

"You know Cyrus Dorn as the ruler, the king, the man they built a statue of. And maybe that's why you expect more of him. But I think what's hardest for Kat and I is reconciling this mythical leader of yours with the college professor from a small-town university in the States. Of course I can see that this place changed him, and maybe for the better, but I can't even imagine being pulled from my own world into this foreign one, and then having the resolution and purpose to lead an entire society of people whose lives you barely comprehend. That's incredible to me. You know him better than I do, there's no denying that. But I know where he comes from. I think that's crucial to understanding anyone, great men and women included."

Annica nodded with an expression of deep respect on her face. "I can see why you were a teacher, Dean."

Jack suddenly cocked his head. He thought he had heard something, footsteps possibly, approaching from around the bend in the path. Kat seemed to have noticed something similar.

"I think someone's coming," Kat whispered and Dean and Annica suddenly fell silent. Annica pulled a bolt-launcher from her belt and aimed it in the direction of the noise.

"Identify yourself!" Annica commanded.

"Alright, alright," came a sneering female voice from just around the corner, "don't shoot, I come in peace."

Annica lowered her weapon only slightly as Nel walked into view, moseying with so little urgency that it bordered on disrespectful.

"What are you doing here?" Annica growled. "We haven't heard back from Alec and Cyrus, so if that's what you're..."

"No, and you won't be," Nel stated as she closed the distance between them and stopped walking.

Jack's chest tightened horribly and Annica recentered her aim directly between Nel's eyes. "Explain," she demanded.

Nel smirked and extended her arms in a lazy show of peace. "I'm not the enemy here, I assure you. But we do have one. So do you wanna hear about it or do you wanna kill me?"

Annica raised her eyebrows as though the latter option was desperately tempting, but conceded and dropped her weapon to her side. "Okay let's hear it."

"First, a confession," Nel began, "I didn't go back with the rest of the crew yesterday. I followed Alec and Cyrus to the Fire Fields."

"We figured that," Annica responded curtly, "give us something we don't know."

"The man now holding both your king and mine is named Kysaar Magnus," Nel said with a mix of satisfaction and apprehension in her voice. "And believe me when I tell you he is not to be underestimated."

"Is Cyrus okay?" Jack asked, his fear getting the better of him.

"For now," Nel confirmed, "but he won't stay that way. It seems our new guest wants to make a public show of breaking your beloved leader."

"To what end?" Annica asked, her militant persona winning out over emotion for the time being. "What does he want to accomplish by taking Cyrus?"

Nel paused, biting her lip as though debating her next sentence. "He says he wants deliveries to start. Food, water, supplies… and workers."

Annica's eyes widened. "You spoke to him."

"Only briefly," Nel insisted. "Alec and Cyrus were already captured when I approached. I thought maybe I could diffuse the situation but Magnus was in no mood for further discussion. I'm lucky I was able to walk out of there with my life."

"Lucky us," Annica responded dryly. "So Cyrus is being held to force us to comply?"

"I suppose," Nel shrugged, "but this man is too dangerous to negotiate with. Your people are strong, I say you go in there with everything you've got. He's powerful but he's only one man. Well, two technically."

"The day I ask for military advice from you is the day I step down as queen," Annica hissed. "You can go now."

"I can help," Nel insisted, stepping forward, but Annica raised her bolt-launcher and she stopped.

"We don't want your help, Nel," Annica said. "You have our thanks for bringing us this information, but that's all. You're still not welcome here."

Nel looked exasperated at the dismissal. "Where am I supposed to go?"

"How 'bout whatever hole you crawled out of before," Annica stated bluntly. "There's nothing for you here."

Nel nodded with a smile that looked more like a grimace. "At least someone around here is comfortable giving orders. Poor Jack seems more like a bodyguard than a king. Guess we can't all be Cyrus Dorn, eh Jack?"

Jack just shook his head, unimpressed.

"Yeah," Nel laughed to herself, "I guess the strong silent type suits you. Go on continuing to protect your queen."

Annica firmed up her grip on her weapon, still aimed at Nel's head. "I don't need protecting Nel," she said dismissively, "off you go."

Nel rolled her eyes and backed away down the path, her hands still partially raised against the weapon. She remained casual in her retreat, as though it was beneath her to be threatened by them. Finally she turned and disappeared into the forest.

Annica's demeanor changed abruptly the moment Nel was out of sight. She spun around to face Dean and Kat, who looked utterly bewildered at the entire situation. "You want something to do? Find me Ydoro, now. There's no time to waste."

As Dean practically tripped over Kat rushing to deliver on the command, Annica turned to Jack, her eyes finally betraying her anxiety and fear. "We are not giving in to this," she stated firmly. "I'm not condoning a head-on assault like Nel wants, but it's high time we fortified ourselves. If he wants a reaction from us, he'll get one."

"We don't have enough weapons," Jack said, startled. "We lost most of them when the Temple burned."

Annica shook her head. "I've had weapons caches stored throughout these forests for years now, we're more prepared for this than you think."

"Why?" Jack asked, but then he rephrased when he realized how petulant the question sounded. "Why didn't I know about this?"

"It was before I was queen," Annica insisted, "I never trusted this peace, and honestly, it's lasted longer than I could have hoped. I thought the danger would be from Alec's supporters or even Alec himself. But either way, we *are* ready to defend what's ours."

Jack studied his wife with more than a bit of apprehension. She had mellowed quite a bit from her take-no-prisoners attitude as a laborer, but she still maintained an undeniable revolutionary streak. She wore the crown of queen well and was far better at projecting strength for the people than Jack would ever be. But lest he forget, it was by Annica's own hand that Westtown fell. Cyrus was given credit for saving the Kingdom and banishing the King of the West, but it was Annica and

Cain who had started that rebellion. Looking at her now, eyes sparkling with resolve and her face a stony mask of defiance, it was incredible that he had ever forgotten her strength. It was suddenly easy to remember just how powerful the will of the people could be.

CHAPTER TWENTY–NINE

OUR CHOICES SHAPE THE WORLD

I t had been an extraordinarily uncomfortable night trying in vain to find a soft spot on the hard, damp stone floor of the ruined Temple. Doubly so because every time Cyrus moved, the heavy iron clamp around his ankle jangled loudly against the chain tethering him to the remains of the structure wall. The weight of the cuff was so great that he had horrific dreams of pressure and suffocation brought on by his inability to move one leg without serious effort. It was debilitating in every way and now that a new dawn had arrived, he felt as helpless as ever. As he squinted through the piercing glare of the morning sun, he saw Alec was already awake, chained in similar fashion directly across from him, no more than seven feet away. Their manacles made it impossible to reach one another physically; perhaps Kysaar Magnus recognized the very real possibility of one of them murdering the other given the chance.

They had been escorted to the remains of the new Temple the day before and their only weapon, the pendant to control the Neodactyl, had been confiscated. Without the ornate necklace around his neck delivering pheromones into the air, Alec would no longer be recognized by the Neodactyl, leaving him to fear the creature just like everyone else. Cyrus supposed there was a grim satisfaction in that, but at the moment it felt like nothing but another devastating blow. The brothers had been bound in an area that was not quite indoors but not quite outdoors. Cyrus imagined the chamber had likely been a strictly interior room while the dwelling still stood, but with the damage caused by Magnus's fire display, all that remained was a leaky, cracked roof, several of the heavier stone columns to support it, and piles upon piles of rock. It could be an open-air sunroom if not for the violent scars decorating every surface. Magnus was nowhere to be seen but he was never far away. Himself and his quiet companion made frequent walks around the perimeter, always glancing through one of the many gaping ruptures in the walls to ensure the Dorn brothers were still captive.

Cyrus rubbed his face forcefully and glanced in Alec's direction, who looked puffy eyed with purple shadows consuming his youthful features. Cyrus wondered if he had slept at all. As he scooted himself into a sitting position, the iron chains scraped loudly against the floor causing the man with the melted face to briefly glance through from outside before continuing his patrol.

"Well look who's awake," Alec grunted. It was likely meant in a malicious way but the defeat in his voice made it come across as indifferent.

"I don't wanna hear it, Alec," Cyrus growled in reply. "You got us into this mess. I knew you would betray me, but I guess I didn't count on you screwing us both over so profoundly. I mean really, most creatures on the planet have a persistent survival instinct that prevents them from making such stupid decisions. How you continue to find your way around that evolutionary gift is staggering."

"Yeah, keep talking from your high horse," Alec hissed, and there was at least a touch more venom in his voice, "if you were so confident in your own decisions you would never have followed me here."

Cyrus nodded. "You're right, you've made fools out of both of us. Congratulations."

Alec didn't have a snippy retort for this and instead elected to feign deafness, gazing up at the ceiling in disinterest. But Cyrus was having a hard time staying silent. Perhaps it was simply having Alec as a captive audience for once, but he couldn't resist the urge to continue poking him while he was down.

"You do understand that you've already lost, don't you?" Cyrus asked, trying to will Alec to meet his gaze. "I mean, talk about overplaying your hand, you've tried *everything*. And you could have been running a kingdom right now, but instead you overreached, went to war with your own people, lost that war and found yourself exiled." Alec stirred a bit, shifting his weight and developing a twitch under one eye. But he still stared stubbornly at the ceiling. So Cyrus continued. "And I gotta say, your exile was better than you could ever have hoped for. You managed to steal my wife, steal my entire life in fact; job, house and all, and you could torment me until the end of your days. But that still wasn't enough. You overreached *again*, searching for ways to get back here only to succeed and set another trap for yourself. Haven't you ever stopped to think that maybe the problem is you? Maybe you're the poison that makes every life you live rot around you? I mean, you couldn't find a single world that you visited where you were happy. Doesn't that tell you something?"

Alec finally returned his gaze, and his rage looked hot enough to burn the entire Kingdom around them both.

"Don't talk to me about other worlds," Alec whispered in a rough growl, "I've seen them all. You think because you found a way to banish me that you understand these wormholes, but you know nothing about it." His face looked warped and creased with anger but his voice never rose above a whisper, even as tears watered the folds of his eyelids. "I've visited countless worlds, countless times, countless realities. And do you know what I've found? Loops. Endless, never-ending loops." He seemed to compose himself just slightly and wiped his eyes. Cyrus thought for a moment that he was done talking, but after a brief pause, he continued, steadier now. "In the world we originally came from, you and I fell through an anomaly that connected to the Kingdom, but only that exact anomaly from that exact world should lead to that exact Kingdom. But I've visited our old university campus too many times to count and in every single damn one, you and I aren't there. Do you know where we are? Presumed dead; lost at sea after our dinghies vanished. Without exception. So that same anomaly occurs in *every* world. But does it lead to *our* Kingdom? No, it leads to an alternate version of the Kingdom where an alternate version of you and I may still be." Alec looked half-mad as he expounded on his theory, like a frayed rope about to snap. The tears had returned to his eyes but they now darted around the room, like he barely cared that Cyrus was present to hear his ranting. "But you recognize the strangeness about that, don't you? That anomaly apparently opens in that same place in every single version of our world. Meaning someone *always* breaks a piece off Mora's scepter in the Kingdom, a wormhole *always* opens in the ocean, and you and I *always* fall through it. It's an endless loop and it makes you wonder if there's any fucking free will at all! Or are we just destined to be caught in this loop forever?"

Silence settled between them like a dense layer of fog, the air thick with anger and accusations. Cyrus did feel for Alec's hopelessness, but this was a person he could never have compassion for again. However, in all of Alec's raving words, Cyrus found that he only had one question he wanted an answer to.

"What did you do with your other self, Alec?" Cyrus asked softly. When Alec looked his way with a furrowed brow, Cyrus continued, "Your original self, the one that occupied the world we were trapped in together. Whose life you stole. What did you do with him?" Alec refused to answer yet again, looking carefully at the ground. "You killed him, didn't you?"

Cyrus couldn't be sure of the accusation, but it felt somehow accurate. And Alec didn't utter a word to deny it. Cyrus shook his head in disgust. He could understand the reasoning behind the move, but to kill one's own self from an alternate reality, dashing all possibilities from their future seemed so incredibly sick.

"Then let me ask you a different question," Cyrus said, and Alec looked back up at him. "You had a way back to the Kingdom. When you let the Cyrus of that world travel through that anomaly, why not join him? You could have started over, corrected your mistakes and had it all. Why didn't you?"

Alec considered his answer, something Cyrus was surprised by. When he finally spoke, it was with a stronger, more resolute voice. "That wouldn't have been my Kingdom. The moment we got there, it could have been me with a scepter buried in my neck instead of Dalton. Hell, you saw the alternate world we were marooned in together. The storefronts were different, the trees in the yards were different, even the people were a bit off. Tiny variations can have drastic impacts on the flow of the world. I couldn't guarantee *that* Kingdom would be the same, or that things would happen in the way they had happened before. It was a risk not worth taking."

Cyrus nodded his head thoughtfully. "Fear, in other words. Fear of losing the control you had. It's pathetic." When Alec didn't disagree, Cyrus did feel a slight pang of guilt for his harshness. "But you did just answer your own question, brother. We *do* have free will. Otherwise, we wouldn't be able to make those tiny variations. I think that's more evidence than has ever existed before that we do control our own destinies. Our choices shape the world."

Silence reigned once again. It was only broken once the man with the melted face came tottering into the room carrying several pieces of barely ripened fruit.

"Breakfast," he croaked, tossing one to each of them. He looked like he intended to leave without further interaction, but Cyrus spoke up.

"What is it you do for Kysaar Magnus?" Cyrus asked. It wasn't meant to be goading but was an honest curiosity.

The man turned, the unnaturally smoothed skin of his face catching the light and projecting an unpleasant sheen. "Whatever he wants of me." He said it with a hollowness that contrasted dramatically with Magnus's own drawling but passionate speech patterns.

"Do you have a name?" Cyrus pushed.

The man offered a smile and the damaged skin along his cheek stretched horribly. "They call me the Alchemist."

"And why do they call you that?" Cyrus asked.

"Because I can do things that others cannot understand," the man responded, a bit more passion now bleeding into his quiet words.

"Magic powers and the like," Alec grunted in sarcastic disinterest.

"There's nothing magic about my work," the Alchemist purred, "but it is certainly beyond the skill of most. People assign the label of magic to things they don't understand. Am I wrong in guessing that you thought the scepters magic the first time you saw them?"

"Well they do open portals to alternate realities," Cyrus offered.

"Alternate realities exist whether you were aware of them before or not," the Alchemist insisted, "those scepters are simply a tool for navigating them. My work, boiled down, deals with finding the right tool for every job."

"Ever encountered a problem you couldn't find the right tool for?" Cyrus asked.

The man smiled again and shrugged his shoulders. "Something my father used to say, you can't fix everything, but you can damn sure give it a try."

With that he turned and ambled out of the room, leaving Cyrus with little in the way of new information.

Cyrus lifted the violet-colored fruit up to his nose and gave it a sniff. It was odorless, and likely tasteless as well. Meager rations for the conqueror's captives. He sat a moment longer considering the Alchemist's words. At least he had been willing to have honest conversations with Cyrus; something Kysaar Magnus had thus far refused.

CHAPTER THIRTY

THE QUEEN'S REQUEST

Dean had rushed to find Ydoro, just as Annica had instructed. Following a brief meeting between the two, loyalists were sent into the surrounding forests to gather weapons that had been hidden throughout the Kingdom, evidently waiting for things to go bad. Because one thing was increasingly clear the longer they stayed in this foreign land; things *had* gone bad before. Thanks to a brief history lesson from Ydoro, Dean and Kat had learned about Alec Dorn's violent reign, the Battle of Westtown Square, and the banishing of a king by his own brother. The pieces were beginning to fill in, even to an outsider, and Cyrus Dorn's place in these people's history was becoming clearer than ever. But how had he managed it?

Dean himself still felt like a lost child amidst the building of fortifications and gathering of weapons. The Queen was preparing for war and Dean's only job seemed to be staying out of the way. Yet Cyrus, an outsider of similar circumstances, had somehow scorched such a permanent mark on history in only a few months' time that he had attained legendary status. Dean shook his head at the daydream; even in his own world, he wasn't the type of person to be remembered. Sure, he had fantasies of discovering the origins of the Hand of Jordan and that mysterious ruby fragment, but he had wanted that knowledge for himself. He never needed the fame that went along with such conquests. With his nose firmly in a book was where he felt most comfortable, and that was the type of person who would never make history. He wanted to get home; to his couch and his collection of history texts, and it seemed Cyrus Dorn might be the person who could get him there. That was the best he could hope for. Still, he wished he wasn't feeling so *useless*.

"Don't you think we should be helping?" Kat asked Dean as though she were reading his thoughts. They were walking through camp aimlessly, as they often did; an alternative to simply sitting beneath their tarp and watching the world go by.

"I'm not sure how," Dean answered. "I think we're just in the way, to be honest."

Mauretz Abernally's campsite came into view ahead and Dean briefly considered changing course to avoid him. Mauretz had proven to be a bit of an oddity since coming to the island. He rarely ever spoke to anyone, averted his gaze when people looked his way, and spent most of his time hunkered beneath his tarp. The few times that Dean had attempted contact with the man, he had seemed tragically uncomfortable and incapable of continuing a basic conversation. Or perhaps he was just out of practice. From the little that Dean had been able to ascertain about Mauretz's life, it seemed he had been a scrappy young excavation digger working in Jordan when Nick Satterall had first preyed on him. *Preyed* because Nick knew full well he was taking advantage of a poor, impressionable youth. Despite Nick's outburst about being betrayed and murdered, he had not been the victim in that relationship until the very end. Mauretz was manipulated and used for years to line Nick's pockets, and while he certainly benefited himself from the criminal enterprise, he had no exit strategy as Nick did. When things got too hot in Jordan for Nick, he made plans to uproot and leave without regard for his longtime companion and the lack of similar opportunities available to him. Mauretz eventually made the decision to sell Nick to the authorities hunting him in exchange for his freedom, but when their standoff ended with a murder, Mauretz used what money he had saved from their dubious ventures and set sail to England to begin a new life. But beginning a new life in a foreign country wasn't easy for a person like Mauretz, who had spent the entirety of his life to that point living in such desperate poverty that he barely knew how to function in a society. He became a recluse, settled into middle-age collecting trinkets and hiding behind closed doors, and eventually eased into his twilight years without any real human contact. The Mauretz Abernally with them now was not quite elderly just yet but wasn't far off. Dean supposed the reason for his slightly more youthful appearance was likely connected to the last time he had actually touched the small ruby fragment that Dean had uncovered in his dresser drawer. If the last time Mauretz had touched the fragment was decades back, it meant that *this* Mauretz diverged from his life in the States at that time. It also meant that he didn't know how he had spent the remainder of his years.

Dean gave him a nod as they passed, which Mauretz quickly ignored by averting his eyes to the ground. Kat shot Dean an apprehensive look as though she didn't understand why he kept trying. She was young, after all, and could be forgiven for not recognizing the sadness in what had become of a potentially promising youth.

"Dean! Kat!"

Dean spun in a clumsy circle looking to identify the voice. No one had wanted or needed him for anything since their arrival, so it was jarring to hear his name called so forcefully. His eyes fell to the Queen, Annica, who was approaching with such commanding swiftness that Dean had the briefest urge to run. Her face was friendly, however, and put him at ease fairly quickly. He bent his neck into an awkward bow, still unsure how he was supposed to be addressing such *royalty* within the Kingdom. Kat did not follow suit.

"You gave me a good idea the last time we spoke," Annica said, a small grin playing at the sides of her lips. "You still want to be useful?"

"Absolutely," Dean stated immediately.

"Good," Annica replied, "then follow me, both of you."

She led them to an area behind her own quarters that, while not quite private, was a bit removed from the hustle and bustle of the main drag.

Waiting for them were Jack, Ydoro, and Noma, all of whom looked up expectantly at their arrival.

"So, you know what we're up against," Annica began pointedly to Dean and Kat, "and I think you know what's at stake. Stated plainly, I can't go to war with this man. We have the numbers but not the firepower, even with our stockpiles. And in truth, I don't know enough about our enemy to make a calculated decision. But doing nothing is not an option. I will not leave our former king to whatever fate this Kysaar Magnus has in store for him. Am I correct in assuming the two of you do not have combat training?"

Dean blinked awkwardly and looked at Kat. "I... I... well..."

"We do not," Kat answered bluntly for both of them.

Annica smiled. "That's okay. I mean no offense, but we figured as much."

"Are we going to be fighting?" Dean asked in alarm. Despite hearing consistently about a possible war, he had assumed he would take no part in such things.

"That's not what I'm looking for from you," Annica said bracingly. "You made an interesting point the other day, Dean. You told me I didn't know the true Cyrus Dorn because I didn't have an understanding of where he came from. And you were right. I've lived on this island all my life, and the particulars of his world and yours are lost on me." She paused, perhaps attempting to read Dean and Kat's reactions to her words. "I think the same applies to our new friend Kysaar Magnus. We have no idea where he comes from or anything about his world, just that he cut a doorway out of it to get here. But something stood out to me when we first encountered him in the street. When he took Alec's scepter, he threw it behind himself... where it vanished, presumably through the door and back into his own world. That tells me the doorway is still open."

Jack, Ydoro, and Noma were all watching Dean and Kat with rapt attention, leading Dean to realize they had already been briefed on this theory. This meant their interest was solely on whether Dean and Kat would take the assignment request that was undoubtedly about to follow.

"I want to know what's on the other side of that door," Annica said fiercely. "I want to know where *he* comes from. But I can't spare any of my fighters, in case things devolve sooner than expected. What I would ask of you, Dean and Kat, is to traverse into that unknown world, use whatever means you have to, and bring me back something real that I can use against Magnus. I need to know how we beat him. And maybe the only way to know that is to understand where he comes from."

Dean was too stunned to speak. He opened his mouth and closed it several times, unable to make his lips form words. When he did attempt a response, his throat had become inexplicably dry and he began coughing uncontrollably.

"I know what I'm asking of you," Annica continued sympathetically, "and I'd be lying if I said it wouldn't be dangerous. It's not fair to ask this of you, and I recognize that. This isn't your world and this isn't your fight. But we need this. I can get you in. Then it'll be your job to get back to me."

With Dean's coughing fit beginning to subside, he planned to argue that Kat was only a student and that he had a responsibility to keep her out of harm's way, but Kat spoke up before he could.

"I'll do it," Kat stated firmly, and Annica smiled.

"You'll what?" Dean practically shouted. "Kat, I can't let you…"

"This is all real," Kat shot back, "isn't it? I mean, you and I tracked this place through history without knowing what it was we were following. But this is all part of something real, and too big for us to turn our backs on. We can't choose to just *sit it out*. That's not the way real life works. Besides, if you're ever going to get back to your classroom and I'm ever going to get back to my life, then *we* need to win. The Kingdom needs to win."

Dean had stopped his sputtering about midway through Kat's speech and was now looking at her with a mix of respect and horror in his eyes.

"She's not wrong," Annica said, still gently. "We are going to do everything we can to get you both back to where you came from, but we can't do it without a scepter. And by my count, two are in the hands of the enemy and one is through that door. Help us so we can help you."

Dean was now stubbornly shaking his head. He wanted to present a logical, educated argument but his words were failing him. When the group just stared, apparently waiting for him to regain his composure, he took a few deep breaths and steadied himself out.

"Why us?" Dean finally asked. His voice came out as calm, but internally he felt close to cardiac arrest. "Sending us on this mission simply because you don't want to risk your strongest fighters isn't a compelling reason. In fact, it sounds like a death sentence. By your own admission, this will be dangerous. Why not send someone better prepared to face that danger?"

Annica took a step forward, and there was a steadiness in her demeanor that somehow did infect Dean with the tiniest modicum of strength. "I didn't choose you because you're expendable. I chose you because you're an observer. You see to the truth of things, both of you. Kat, you were able to see right through Alec's proposal when many of my most trusted warriors could not. And Dean, you were able to see the truth of the burden that Cyrus carries when the rest of us missed it. Your power is your ability to see people. See things that others can't. *That's* what I need. Someone who will see through whatever they first encounter on the other side of that door. We need you."

Dean was lost for words again, but this time it wasn't due to obstinate denial. No one had ever spoken to him in this way before. He had never been truly needed before, and he hated himself for feeling weak and so incredibly useless during their time of need. But he wasn't an adventure seeker and he never would be. Dean Pyrene followed the rules and stayed on the straight and predictable path, not inviting danger into his quiet life. But then he remembered how he had snuck into the Museum of Antiquities in London to swipe a sample of blood from a priceless artifact, and how he had been willing to tear Mauretz Abernally's house to the foundation in his search for the scepter fragment, and he thought maybe he did have an adventurous side after all, buried deep. He had never taken many risks in his life and always considered himself a fairly mild and perhaps even cowardly sort of man. But looking into Annica's fierce eyes now; the face of a queen going to war for her people, Dean thought maybe, just maybe, he could change.

LEGACY

Cyrus could hear the crunch of footsteps approaching across the decimated Fire Fields long before he could see who they belonged to. Sound carried strangely across the wasted landscape, echoing ominously in the taut, painful silence. Apart from the moaning wind and the occasional Shrieking Bat call, silence reigned, and footsteps stood out as unnatural and violating in their audacity.

It was hard to tell if the oppressive white blanket still covering the surrounding area and obscuring the distant treeline from view was lingering smoke or in fact ash at this point, but through the haze, walking with a confidence so casual that it was disgusting, came Nel. She had been gone a full day since swearing her allegiance to Kysaar Magnus and accepting her first mission. Because sound cut through the silence so easily in the area, their conversations had not been difficult to overhear, not that Magnus seemed to care. He made no attempts at keeping his voice down for the benefit of Cyrus and Alec, still chained within the remains of the Temple. He had instructed Nel to walk back to Annica and Jack's camp with a message that Cyrus Dorn had been captured, and if they valued his life, they needed to begin deliveries of supplies along with workers to rebuild. It was a rather insipid request in Cyrus's mind and made him think it was likely given simply to ensure that Nel could, and would, follow orders. As she returned now, he could see Magnus walk to greet her, extending his arms outwardly in a showy display of affectionate welcome.

"Our envoy has returned," Magnus bellowed in his hoarse rasp of a voice.

Alec could not see the reunion from his vantage point, but he perked up noticeably at the announcement. He glanced Cyrus's direction briefly, then let his eyes fall back to the floor.

"How did they receive our message?" Magnus asked.

"They didn't give a direct response to it," Nel explained. "They were more interested in the reasons you were here."

"And did you tell them?" Magnus asked.

"I did," Nel answered, "just as you instructed me."

"Good girl," Magnus growled. "Not the most glamourous assignment I know, but we had to start small. I have big plans for you."

Nel smiled and gave a respectful nod of her head.

"What do you think their next move is?" Magnus asked her, and the way he studied her face made it clear he was looking for more than just an educated guess; he wanted to know how *she* would think the situation through.

"Well, they won't attack you directly," Nel offered, her eyes narrowing in determination to propose a useful answer. "But they also won't simply bend to your will. These are a people that rose up from the ashes of nothing to fight off the West. And they've had six years to convince themselves that they deserve their hard-won freedom. The most difficult thing to break will be their sense of justification. A people oppressed are easy to keep oppressing. But a people who have wrenched their freedom back from their overlords... that's something else."

Magnus nodded slowly, then smiled. "That's not a bad answer," he growled. "Far better considered than I would have expected. I can see you're not just the muscle to Alec's ambition." Nel looked incredibly pleased with herself. "But you didn't answer my question. What *will* their next move be?"

Nel's eyes dropped to the ground, almost as though she were embarrassed. "Apologies," she said, and took a breath. "I believe they will search for a way around your defenses. They know how powerful your weapons are, so they will attempt to take you when your defenses are down. Our weakness is in our numbers. With only the three of us, the chances of militants sneaking their way in is high. And only you wield the tridents, making this area only secure as long as you are awake and watching."

Magnus laughed. "Another excellent answer. And, if I'm not mistaken, one laced with the seeds of your own ambition, am I right?" When Nel seemed lost for words, Magnus continued, "Is that not the reason you mention the tridents? You'd like to wield them yourself?" He laughed. "All in due time, child. You'll prove yourself soon, I have no doubt."

The two began walking together and Cyrus tracked their footsteps until their voices faded away. He sighed heavily and glanced at his brother. Alec was slumped slightly, leaning against the far wall, and if Cyrus didn't know better, he could have been sleeping. But Cyrus did know better and beneath the surface, Alec was boiling... at least he hoped. Alec's defeat seemed so incredibly real. Since returning to the Kingdom, he had lost his scepter, lost the Neodactyl, and now lost his closest ally. Cyrus did not care in the slightest about Alec's feelings, but his loss of hope was not something Cyrus could use.

This line of thinking was interrupted when Nel abruptly entered their makeshift cell, followed closely by the Alchemist. Alec stared up at her with wide eyes, but she pointedly avoided his gaze.

"Big man wants to see you Cyrus," Nel stated matter-of-factly.

"Well he knows where to find me," Cyrus responded dryly.

Nel grinned. The Alchemist walked forward and stooped over Cyrus's leg, crunching a key into the iron lock and twisting. The clamp sprang open and fell to the ground with a heavy thud.

"What is it he wants with me?" Cyrus demanded.

Nel shrugged in disinterest. Alec was still staring at the back of her head, either willing her to turn and face him or attempting to burn a hole in her skull. But she took no notice of him whatsoever.

Cyrus, free of his bindings, stood up, and he was happy to note that both Nel and the Alchemist took small steps backwards in his presence. A prisoner he may be, but he was still a considerable physical threat to both of these captors. Nel waved her hand toward one of the largest holes in the wall indicating for him to lead the way out.

The first thing of note upon exiting the Temple ruins was the Neodactyl, released from its tethers and prowling ominously over the piles of shattered stone with incredible ease. It looked Cyrus's direction with its enormous eyes and released a rattling snarl. Beyond the creature stood Kysaar Magnus, his hand grasping one of his tridents while he leered at Cyrus. The old town road could still be made out, winding away behind him, but the structures flanking it had been all but obliterated. Homes and storefronts towards the outskirts still stood, but the life within them had flickered out. The enormous statue of Cyrus himself also remained intact, now looming over the decimation of his once mighty Kingdom in a horrible parallel to real life.

Magnus smiled broadly as Cyrus approached, one side of his mouth drooping slightly as it always did.

"There he is," Magnus exclaimed in a horrific bastardization of the common greeting. "I thought we could walk. Get to know one another." He wasn't trying to hide the insincerity of his words; he was relishing it. But Cyrus joined him all the same, with Nel, the Alchemist, and the Neodactyl following from a distance. They began walking slowly, with Magnus looking around as though taking in the sites.

"I know what you're thinking," Magnus began. "You're wondering how to get out of this. How to pull one over on me. How to turn the tables in your favor." He reached into his pocket and produced the pendant that he had taken from Alec. His own still hung safely around his neck. "This was a smart idea," Magnus continued, "I truly admire your resolve, but I assure you, you are truly beaten. You think I would traverse countless realities just to blunder and let my guard down now? Granted you don't know me very well... but I think you're getting there."

Magnus dropped the pendant to the ground where it rolled slightly before falling still. Cyrus had the wild urge to dive and grab it for himself but resisted the suicidal temptation. He glanced at the trident in Magnus's hand, the first time he was able to get a good look at the weapon up close. As he had suspected, it was comprised of many, many smaller fragments of scepter all fused together with ribbons of gleaming bronze. Unlike the scepters that Alec and Cyrus had once carried, this weapon was *made*; hewn into this specific shape for a specific purpose. And its purpose seemed to be destruction. Magnus took note of his interest and smiled.

"Impressive, isn't it," Magnus said. "Forged by the Alchemist. The man knows his stuff. Too modest for his own good, in my opinion. He always loved tinkering; he just needed someone to *direct* his craft."

Magnus extended the trident out in front of him, moving it over the earth in a slow, sweeping motion. The ground fizzled and crackled below with tiny embers exploding into flames before their eyes. As Cyrus watched, the fire engulfed Alec's fallen pendant, which spat and hissed angrily before rupturing and turning to black.

"Truly an artist he is." Magnus brought the weapon vertical again and stabbed the base into the remains of the pendant, extinguishing any hope that it had survived the demonstration. "Perhaps it would be wiser to abandon your thoughts of escape," he growled quietly.

He continued walking with Cyrus following in his wake. Magnus was right, there was no move Cyrus could make to turn the tables. Even the desolation of the town now provided an open wasteland impossible to run through without detection. So few objects remained standing that the crumbled Temple he and Alec were being housed in had become an island amidst an open sea. It was like the expansive yards of a prison that proved to be as much a deterrent to escape as the cellblocks themselves.

"I'm aware of how highly your people regard you," Magnus began, almost conversationally. "I wasn't lying when I said that history remembers you, Cyrus Dorn. But you're a smart man; you must realize by now that your legacy is built on timing rather than ability. The people needed a hero to look to after your disastrous predecessors. Irias was calculating but ultimately weak. Mora was strong but ultimately over-confident. You..." Magnus glanced sideways at him, "well you were fair… but ultimately blind." They were approaching the statue of Cyrus, casting an enormous shadow over the surrounding area. Magnus was looking up at it with reverence. "I actually saw this statue, in my own world. It looked much the same as it does here. That should provide you with some pride knowing that it stood for decades after your reign ended. Of course I was also witness to it being torn down. Legacy doesn't last forever I guess."

"You talk a lot about legacy for someone well on his way to leaving nothing behind," Cyrus finally retorted. "You only have a legacy if there are people who remember you. If you end up king of the ashes, you'll eventually fade away."

Magnus nodded, still looking up into the statue's stoic face. "Your people will break, you know. Right now they are concocting some ill-conceived plan to retrieve you. Predictable as clockwork. But their hope won't last long, it never does. When you break, they break. And then they're mine."

Cyrus laughed slightly and Magnus looked at him in surprise. A boldness was suddenly overtaking Cyrus that was difficult to rationalize, but he began talking all the same. "For all your reality-jumping and all you've seen, you don't understand my legacy at all, do you?" Cyrus turned to face Magnus head-on, feeling suddenly braver than he had in weeks. "My legacy isn't about me, it's what I left my people. Maybe they did need a hero to put on their shoulders, but having that hero is what gave them the strength to find their own footing. They don't need me anymore. In fact, this statue of their savior is a fiction, and they likely know that. He's cold and resilient and impressive… and infallible. Inspired by a man perhaps, but not a man himself. That's what a real legacy is, and it's something you'll never have for yourself." Magnus shifted slightly closer to Cyrus, squaring himself up in front of him. Cyrus smiled. "Maybe you're the one who's ultimately blind."

Magnus continued to stare at Cyrus, practically nose to nose, but he lifted his trident horizontal again and the ground beneath them began to quake and moan. With an authoritative wave of his arm, Magnus released a hurricane of fire towards the statue. He was almost casual in his action, but the fizzling, snapping, and popping while the statue was engulfed was impossible to ignore. This was a battle of wills, however, and Cyrus understood that. As Magnus refused to turn away from Cyrus's gaze, Cyrus must do the same. Turning to look at the destruction of the monument would be a show of defeat in this man's eyes, so he met his unblinking stare, clenched his jaw, and stared back. An eruption burst from the base of the statue as the stone became superheated to the point of obliteration. The earth shook beneath their feet as enormous pieces of rock burst outwards and white-hot embers exploded into the air. Cyrus, at the very edges of his vision, could just barely register the collapse of the beloved monument as the base lost all structural integrity and buckled beneath the weight. The Guardian tipped forward, slow at first then gaining speed as a trail of flame followed it like a comet. When it finally struck the ground, Cyrus's knees buckled from the tremor and threatened to spill him off his feet, but his balance remained true even as glowing ash peppered his cheek painfully.

Magnus had not looked away either, still glaring straight into Cyrus's eyes, scanning for weakness. As the last vibrations from the collapse thundered out and quiet overtook the Fire Fields once again, Magnus smiled approvingly and nodded his head.

"You have courage, I'll give you that much," Magnus said. He studied Cyrus for a moment longer, then his smile grew into a wide, toothy grin. "Good," he growled. "When a weak leader falls, the world feels the tremor. It passes through everyone like a cold shiver, cracks the foundation, and then fades. But when a strong leader falls, a chasm opens. The world gasps and that void becomes eternal."

"I built this Kingdom to last," Cyrus responded, "or haven't you been paying attention? My people will live on long after I'm gone."

"They will indeed," Magnus said, "but *your* people they'll no longer be. It's human nature to try and fill that void, even if all logic and reason screams against it. Mark my words, it will be shocking how quickly your people slip under an authoritarian regime once again."

Magnus turned to walk back the way they had come but for some reason, Cyrus couldn't shake the urge to continue his argument.

"They'll surprise you," Cyrus called out.

Magnus stopped and spun on his heel to face Cyrus again. He waved his hand casually and both Nel and the Alchemist began walking forward to take him back into captivity.

"I can't be surprised," Magnus said, almost as though he regretted the truth of the statement. "I will never understand people who think that we alone are immune to the cyclical trajectory of history. Humans aren't complicated. They make the same decisions over and over and over again through the ages and each time they are certain it's new ground they navigate. History is our greatest roadmap for the future… but you have to be paying attention."

Nel and the Alchemist each grasped one of Cyrus's arms roughly and began to haul him back to the remains of the Temple. As they passed Magnus, he grinned in diabolical enjoyment.

"I'm thrilled that you disagree, I really am," Magnus yelled after him. "The stronger you resist, the more spectacular your fall."

Cyrus wanted to convince himself that the reason for the forceful end to the conversation was Magnus no longer wanting to spar with such a skilled opponent, but that would be a lie. Cyrus had seen too much within his own world to dismiss Magnus's view of history. Perhaps it *was* human nature to repeat the same mistakes. His people had been made strong; forged in fire and conflict, but would it be enough now? Their hard-earned strength was formidable and resilient to be sure, but largely untested. It was with a horrible sense of trepidation that Cyrus realized how soon it would be put to the ultimate test. So far, no one and nothing had been able to stand against the power and brutality of Kysaar Magnus.

CHAPTER THIRTY–TWO

THE DOORWAY TO NOWHERE

With every step closer to the Fire Fields and the remnants of town square, Kat's heart hammered in her chest all the more painfully. Committed though she was to taking on this assignment for the Queen, she was certain she had never done anything so reckless in her entire life. This was a life-or-death mission where any wrong step could bring it all crashing down. What a strange concept that was. A few weeks ago, she was worrying about her grades and whether she was integrating well enough with her college peers and now she was sneaking into an unknown alternate reality to bring down a tyrant threatening the democracy of a strange kingdom in yet another alternate reality. It spun the mind just thinking of such things but as Mr. Pyrene let out a strange labored noise beside her, somewhere between a groan and a whimper, she thought maybe she was handling the situation reasonably well.

Annica had been able to talk Mr. Pyrene into joining the expedition in the end, arming them each with a rusted machete to tuck into their belts, but it hadn't been easy. He had thrown up every roadblock he could think of to argue against the mission, but Kat suspected it was her own insistence on going that eventually convinced him. As terrified and resistant as he was, he did seem to feel a genuine responsibility to protect Kat, no matter the danger. It was incredibly touching that he was willing to step so far outside of his comfort zone for her, but in truth she didn't feel she needed the protection. Young though she was, she felt strangely ready to seize this adventure. It was like the proven existence of alternate realities had lit a fire beneath her and she suddenly felt exceptionally small and insignificant. Not in an existential crisis sort of way, more as though her mundane daily actions were of little to no consequence in the end. That was quite a freeing thought when you got down to it, and it seemed to be giving her carte blanche to make her actions count. While school, and friends, and her life and future seemed impossibly far away and trivial right now, her actions today *did* matter. She was determined to seize on that.

They arrived at the edge of the Fire Fields and Mr. Pyrene made a slight gagging noise as though he were about to vomit. Annica, the Queen herself, was leading them to the hidden doorway but she had brought along several of her militants as backup. It was a small group, however, with the thought being they needed to avoid all detection. This was a stealth mission after all, not an assault. From their current position they were carefully shielded from view, but through the dense foliage town could be seen and the wasteland it had become sprawled away to the southeast. Annica had said the best landmark for finding the invisible doorway would be the statue of the Guardian, as they had been standing beneath it when Magnus and the Alchemist had entered their world. The problem was immediately evident, however; the statue no longer appeared to be standing.

"It's gone," Annica whispered, surveying the wasted landscape, "he tore it down."

Mr. Pyrene shook his head vigorously. "This is a bad idea."

Kat followed Annica's gaze and found that people could be seen standing outside the formerly picturesque Temple off to their right.

"I see Magnus..." Annica began slowly, squinting through the haze. "The Neodactyl's there as well, that's not so good. The Alchemist, and someone else... oh hell, that bitch. Nel's with them too."

She withdrew from the treeline and squatted on the forest floor, Dean and Kat following suit.

"Okay so the old Temple, that must be where Cyrus and Alec are being held," Annica reported. "That works well for us because this is *not* a rescue mission, not yet. The Temple is a ways down the road from our doorway so I think we can sneak in from the east undetected. We're going to bring you there, right up to the door, see you through it, and retreat back into the forest. It will be your job to find your way back. Do you understand?"

Mr. Pyrene shook his head and mumbled something but Kat nodded. She was terrified but also felt exceptionally ready.

"I'm counting on the two of you," Annica said, "that means you don't have the luxury of dying over there. Whatever you face, you fight it with everything you've got. You fight your way back to me, do I have your word?"

Kat smiled slightly and nodded again. "You have it."

Mr. Pyrene's head gave several strange wobbles but then he did nod as well. "I swear it," he responded.

Annica smiled wickedly and grasped each of their hands. "Then welcome to the war." She stood abruptly and unsheathed a bolt-launcher from her belt. She waved to her three companions who drew their own weapons and moved to flank Mr. Pyrene and Kat. "We move quick and we move smart," Annica instructed, "stay close and step lightly."

They crept along the treeline just within the forest for about ten minutes before finally stepping out into the Fire Fields. They crouched low and kept themselves hidden behind half-standing buildings and debris when possible. Annica moved like a cat, barely making a sound as her feet crept over the glowing earth. Kat felt significantly less inspiring as one of her boots caught on a shattered piece of wood and almost tripped her.

As they drew closer to what remained of the statue, their options for cover became more sparse. They were now in the very heart of the destruction and every former dwelling now lay in ruin. Luckily, the road could still be identified, even covered in charred debris, and Kat thought she could see the spot where Kysaar Magnus had stood when he rained fire on the Kingdom. Annica, looking at the same spot, caught Kat's eye and nodded. They were crouched behind a bit of stubborn foundation that hadn't fully collapsed and their target, the invisible doorway, was about twenty feet in front of them. Beyond that was the pile of rubble that had once been the Guardian statue, and several hundred feet beyond that was the ruined Temple and Kysaar Magnus. It was a good distance away but Kat knew how far his tridents could reach if the team was spotted.

Annica leaned in close and began whispering into Kat's ear. "That's the spot, it has to be. From my understanding, you'll start to feel it when you get close. Don't back away, though. When you feel it, walk forward. We've never seen one quite like this, just keep a calm head and get your bearings once you're through."

Kat nodded soundlessly, her chest beginning to tighten even further.

"We'll cover you from here, good luck," Annica said and gave both of their shoulders a squeeze.

Mr. Pyrene looked petrified but allowed himself to be ushered forward all the same. Kat led the way, keeping as low to the ground as possible. She moved slowly, one foot in front of the other, attempting to avoid any potentially noisy objects in the road. As they drew closer to their mark, the rubble that used to be the statue of the Guardian also came into focus. The head was still intact, lying on its side and staring blankly forward. Several other larger pieces remained but much of it had been reduced to shapeless piles. There was something incredibly ominous about seeing the former king's likeness in such a dilapidated state.

"Oh my god," came Annica's voice, breaking the silence. It wasn't her words that sent a shiver down Kat's spine but the volume at which she spoke. If she wasn't whispering, something had gone terribly wrong.

Kat looked back at Annica who had her eyes on the horizon behind them. "RUN!" she screamed.

Kat turned wildly. Roughly fifty feet beyond the shattered statue was Alec's creature, the Neodactyl, sprinting towards them with horrific velocity. Kat had a split-second decision to make; run forward blindly towards the supposed door and the approaching talons of the creature or abandon the plan and flee back the way they had come. Kat reached out and seized Mr. Pyrene's wrist, pulling him roughly forward. She could hear Annica scream her name but her choice had already been made. She groped out madly at the air in front of her, praying to feel something. The Neodactyl let out a screech that was unlike anything she had ever heard in her life. It was twenty feet from them now and closing. Annica and her team released a torrent of bolts from their weapons, but they seemed to have little effect. Kat scrambled, her ankle twisting terribly on a rock, but she couldn't slow down. She heard Annica draw her machete, the metal singing as it scraped her belt. This was it. They had seconds left to find the door or parish.

"HERE!" Annica shouted, rushing forward to intercept the beast.

Kat stumbled again on the loose rubble and her hands hammered into the ground. But she suddenly felt something; a quiet tingling behind her eyes. It tickled at her sinuses and extended up into her eardrums like warm water filling her head. Heeding Annica's orders, Kat shoved herself forward, still reaching at the nothingness with her outstretched hand. The sensation grew and a dizziness began to wash over her, but the creature had to be close. As Kat looked back, the world seemed to be literally dissolving around her. The Fire Fields and the sky above them were darkening into streaks of color, somewhat like a fresh painting that's had water poured over it. There was suddenly a liquidity to the entire world that made it seem somehow thin and temporary. The last thing she saw was Annica, her machete raised against the charging Neodactyl, now five feet from her and launching itself through the air. The world closed in around itself and was gone, the last blurred lines of light giving way to crushing blackness.

Kat fell hard onto her back, her head cracking painfully against the ground. She didn't need to wonder if Mr. Pyrene was still with her; she had not released his wrist since first grasping it. She opened her eyes slowly, though she had no memory of having closed them, and looked around. They were inside, that much was clear, and weak, muddied beams of sunlight were attempting to penetrate the walls through narrow gaps in the wood slats. It was dusty and dirty within showing no signs of life or habitation. Her gaze fell to Mr. Pyrene beside her, who grunted in pain and attempted to sit up. As he locked eyes with Kat, he gave a weary smile.

"You've got some nerve, kid," he said in exasperated fondness, "but let's not do that again."

"Agreed," Kat responded, sitting herself upright and easing into a standing position. "Do you think Annica will be okay?"

Mr. Pyrene shook his head. "We can't think about that right now. We have a job to do."

As Kat nodded in agreement, she scanned the room, attempting to get her bearings. It was entirely empty apart from a single object lying on the ground against the wall. As she stooped to inspect it, she recognized the long, charred staff of the repaired scepter that Magnus had taken from Alec. She lifted it into her hands and ran her fingers over the foreign material.

"Should we try to send this back to the Kingdom?" Kat whispered.

"With what we just saw?" Mr. Pyrene answered with a shake of his head, "we could be further arming the enemy."

He was right of course; they had no idea what was currently happening on the other side of the door. If the Neodactyl had spotted them, it was only a matter of minutes before Magnus would come running. The Queen and her men could already be captured... or worse.

"So we take it with us?" Kat asked. She was feeling the pressing need to verbalize each of the doubts within her head.

"I don't think so," Mr. Pyrene said, "we have no idea what's on the other side of these walls, what sort of world we're walking into, but that scepter is not subtle. If we are here to gather intel, then we'll want to blend in, and that weapon is a dead giveaway that we don't belong."

"Okay," Kat agreed, "so we leave it here, take it back with us when we leave."

Mr. Pyrene nodded silently but it was written all over his face that he wasn't certain they *would* ever leave.

"It's quiet, isn't it?" Kat asked. "I mean, I don't hear anything outside. No footsteps, voices, birds."

"Quiet works just fine for me," Mr. Pyrene grumbled.

Kat moved towards the door on the far wall, attempting with all her might to show strength. She grasped the cold, worn handle firmly, took a deep breath, and pulled softly. The door creaked angrily as it opened and Mr. Pyrene winced at the noise, but he need not have worried. On the other side of the wall was nothing of particular interest. They seemed to be in a town, but one that had long since been abandoned. Kat recognized the twinkling Fire Fields comprising the road beneath them but every one of the dwellings on either side of it seemed lifeless and barren.

Kat stepped forward and walked a few paces down the street. Mr. Pyrene began to follow her but then turned abruptly and walked back to the door of the building they had just exited. He picked up a small rock from the ground and dragged it across the wooden door leaving a chalk-white line.

"So we can find our way home," Mr. Pyrene said with a shrug.

Kat nodded and continued walking. Their footsteps were so incredibly loud in the silence that anyone nearby would surely hear them, but that didn't seem to be an issue. There was nobody.

The sky was heavy with cloud cover and quite colorless, casting a drab blanket over everything below. The town was different from the one they had just come from, even when it still stood. No statue of Cyrus Dorn loomed above and there was no sign of a Temple. This town didn't look to have been destroyed in any way, simply left to rot and decay. It was eerie.

Ten minutes on and they were finally approaching what should have been the treeline, except there were hardly any trees to speak of. The Fire Fields came to an end but instead of the beginning of a forest, there were just exposed hillsides, some tenacious shrubs, the occasional dried-out tree, and plenty of rocks. Anything natural about the area had been sucked out and bleached by the sun leaving seemingly endless nothingness.

"No wonder Magnus wanted to leave this place," Kat whispered.

"Well we *all* want to leave this place," came a scratchy, taunting voice. Kat jumped in alarm and turned to see three people approaching from behind one of the rickety houses. "But it seems old Magnus is the only one who's managed to succeed."

Mr. Pyrene put a protective arm in front of Kat but stopped short of actually placing himself between her and the danger.

"What do you want?" Kat demanded, her hand dropping to the handle of the machete at her side.

"Well that depends," the man in front responded, "who are you with?"

"With?" Kat asked. "It's just me and my friend, and we're not looking for trouble."

All three of the strangers laughed. "I mean who do you serve?" the man asked. "Which king?"

Kat's stomach squirmed slightly. The only time she knew of in the Kingdom's history when two kings ruled was the brief reign of the Dorn brothers.

"We serve no king," Kat responded. "We're on our own."

The group laughed again. "Now that's not something you hear people admit every day," the man said, and he began to slowly approach.

"Hey hey," Mr. Pyrene exclaimed, putting up his hands. "What do you want?"

"Well," the man said sneeringly, "we wanted to know what you were doing in our territory, but since you claim to have no allegiance to anybody, I suppose we have no quarrel with you."

Kat breathed a soft sigh of relief. "Good," she said, "then if you'll let us…"

The man started tisking before she could finish. "You don't seem to remember the rules around here, little one… and it's gonna cost you."

Kat backed up a pace but bumped into something large. She attempted to turn but an arm wove its way around her throat from behind and locked her in place. She immediately began writhing and thrashing but her unseen assailant seemed enormous. Mr. Pyrene moved to intercept but a woman from the original group seized him.

"Let's everybody calm down now," the original man said casually, "we don't plan to hurt you, but I guess that's up to you."

"What do you want?" Mr. Pyrene yelled again, "we have nothing."

The man walked close, reached down and pulled the weathered machete from Mr. Pyrene's belt. "This is something."

"We need those," Kat insisted rather lamely as her own captor took her machete for himself.

The first man sighed. "Take this as a lesson. This is a dangerous place to be wandering by yourselves, and if you haven't sworn fealty to anyone... well then no one's going to come running to save you."

Kat's captor abruptly released her and gave her a shove. The woman holding Mr. Pyrene did the same.

"Town is that way," the man said, pointing west. "Without representation, I'd suggest you stay within its limits. It's a good thing we found you before others did." He signaled to the rest of the group, who all withdrew into the alleyways between the buildings. He gave Kat a wink and said, "You take care now."

The group was gone as quickly as it had appeared. Kat was shaking and Mr. Pyrene looked a sickly green color. Neither of them spoke as they walked briskly away from the area heading west. It was ten minutes before either of them worked up the nerve to say something aloud.

"They took our only weapons," Kat said, keeping her voice as low as possible.

"We're not prepared for this," Mr. Pyrene agreed, "I don't know what we were thinking coming here."

"They need us," Kat insisted. "We just have to stick together... and get to town fast."

"What sort of Kingdom is this?" Mr. Pyrene asked. "I thought these would be Magnus's people, but this just seems like... anarchy."

Kat gave him an apprehensive look but didn't respond. This was not what she had expected on the other side of the door. It was like society had crumbled altogether leaving no structure in its wake.

The next thirty minutes passed without another confrontation, but Kat still breathed a sigh of relief when they finally came upon the described town and found it bustling with inhabitants. Kat had never been to Westtown within Cyrus's Kingdom, but she had to imagine this was its counterpart in this alternate reality. There were wagons and rickshaws, workers and oxen, storefronts and taverns. Only something wasn't quite right about the place. Upon closer inspection, the town didn't seem to be functioning with any real semblance of civility. It was chaos. People were asleep in the road and drunkenly brawling right out in the open. It was noisy, filthy, and crowded like an old-timey pirate's port. Mr. Pyrene shot Kat a terrified look but then attempted to recompose himself. She wasn't sure she had ever seen a person so far outside their comfort zone in her entire life.

A bottle flew over her head and shattered against the wall of one of the dwellings, spraying glass everywhere.

"We need to get off the street," Kat insisted.

"We can't just go wandering through different buildings," Mr. Pyrene whispered in response.

Kat bit her lip and scanned the various establishments. The only one that's function seemed obvious was the tavern; a run-down clay-colored hovel with a rounded open doorway and dancing torchlight within.

"Come on," Kat said, "in here."

Mr. Pyrene protested but followed all the same. Kat had been worried upon entering that they would find the source of the ill-tempered drunks, but it seemed they had all taken to the street to fight. The tavern itself was fairly empty and quiet. A barman stood hunched behind the stone counter, a group of three whispered conspiratorially in the corner, and a blonde-haired man sat by himself with a drink in his hand and his foot up on the table. It was this man that looked up when Mr. Pyrene and Kat walked in, and he practically spilled his drink down his front when he saw them.

"Son of a bitch," Nick Satterall grumbled, setting his mug down with a heavy thud.

Kat just stared back at him, trying to comprehend seeing a familiar face in such a foreign land.

Nick shook his head in annoyance and brushed the overhanging hair from his face. "Now just what the hell are you two doing here?"

CHAPTER THIRTY–THREE

THERE WAS A TIME

T he silence was unbearable. Cyrus picked up a small stone from the ground and tossed it at Alec's chest where it bounced off and clattered loudly against the floor. Alec glowered at him but did nothing.

"You're gonna take this?" Cyrus asked him. "Nel betrays you and you're just going to roll over and die?"

Alec lifted his leg slightly showing the large iron clamp around the ankle but said nothing.

"Uh huh," Cyrus continued. "So the almighty King of the West is officially defeated, is that right?"

Alec just shook his head and shrugged. "You're not faring much better."

"Maybe not," Cyrus admitted, "but I haven't given up either."

"Keep telling yourself that," Alec muttered in disinterest, "I'm sure your calvary will be coming over the hill any minute now."

Cyrus studied his brother, taking in the premature lines on his youthful face and the hollowness that had settled in his eyes. This place really had extracted its toll from him. It had offered everything he ever wanted in the world, then dared him to shoulder the responsibility that came with it. Alec Dorn had failed, in every way imaginable, and for this failure he had been stripped of those dreams. But his desperation to retain that power had consumed him so entirely that his grasp on it had become a stranglehold. As Alec's power waned, so did he.

"You used to be something," Cyrus said, "do you remember that? When your reach didn't exceed your grasp?"

Alec laughed hollowly. "Advice from the great Cyrus Dorn; dream smaller. Nobody else is worthy of living in the stratosphere like you."

"You think this comes easy?" Cyrus snapped. "My people respect me because I treat them with respect. But I work hard to make sure I'm doing right by them. *Not* for myself."

"I do think it comes easy," Alec grumbled, "just like everything has come easy for you. You were handed a kingdom; I had to fight for mine."

"Bullshit," Cyrus retorted bluntly. "We took this kingdom together, you and I. Or perhaps you've forgotten. Because there was a time when we supported each other. When we covered each other's backs. Went to war for one another."

"And I know that helps you sleep at night," Alec snarled, "but I hope you're not actually buying into this legendary savior nonsense that your people are peddling. It's useful to them now; gives them an idol to worship. But what did you *actually* do for them? Really think that over. Because I find it hard to believe that you built all those Easttown houses with your own two hands, your diplomacy with the trade road failed miserably, and I don't remember seeing you at the Battle of Westtown Square. While your people fought for their sad little town, you stayed behind, keeping your hands clean. Some legend."

Cyrus wanted to argue, but there was a bit of truth in Alec's words, and it had been eating away at the back of his mind since returning from his walk with Magnus. Honestly, he didn't feel he *had* earned the pedestal that his loyalists now placed him on. It's easy for people to love a savior when that savior is nothing more than a memory. But their idol had returned, and that meant Cyrus suddenly needed to justify his legendary crown. What had he truly done to deserve such respect? He banished Alec during their duel in the Fire Fields, but was he not also responsible for creating Alec in the first place?

Cyrus sighed heavily. "Look, I don't like this prospect any better than you do, but we need to put our differences aside and find a way out of here. This isn't about me and you, not right now."

Alec laughed hatefully. "Differences," he repeated.

"Are you capable of that or not?" Cyrus demanded, "because the way I see it, you can either plant your heels, shut me out, and prove everyone right... or you can prove everyone wrong and show that you do still have a modicum of common sense. That you're willing to put aside personal grievances to ensure everyone's survival." Alec looked up at him. "So what's it going to be?"

Alec studied him for a long moment and Cyrus wondered the last his brother had held his gaze for more than a second. Alec finally smirked with a look of extreme superiority. "You must be loving this, having me here to scold like a petulant child."

Cyrus simply raised his eyebrows at the accusation, feeling that arguing with someone acting like such a petulant child was useless. His lack of verbal response seemed to work, however, for Alec nodded and said, "Okay, what's your plan?"

Cyrus glanced out the side of the building, though there was nothing much to see at the moment. "Well, these shackles are only our first obstacle. There's far too much open nothingness surrounding us to be able to flee on foot."

"Did you bring a vehicle you forgot to tell me about?" Alec grumbled in agitation.

"You heard what happened earlier today," Cyrus continued, undeterred, "*someone* tried to cross that expanse and the Neodactyl ran them down."

"That's what it sounded like," Alec agreed.

"What that tells us is they have that creature watching the perimeter. If we attempted to flee, we'd be killed instantly, and that's only if the Neodactyl spotted us first. They're all watching."

Alec made a disgusted grimace and flicked a pebble in front of him, which bounced into a crack in the floor and disappeared into the chambers below. Cyrus knew he was thinking about how quickly he had lost control of his creature.

"Best I can think is that we make a run for it after dark," Cyrus said.

Alec shook his head. "The Neodactyl would still smell us, not to mention the fields cast a light of their own. Sundown doesn't provide us much cover." Alec smiled, much to Cyrus's surprise. "Besides, my plan to get us out of these shackles is dependent on mealtime."

"You have a plan?" Cyrus asked.

"The Alchemist holds the keys to these manacles," Alec whispered, "he also happens to be the one who brings us food... and he's physically the weakest of the three."

"You think we could overpower him," Cyrus nodded before pausing. "Even in chains?"

"Alone maybe not," Alec agreed, "but together we could. It would need to be carefully coordinated. He'd see an attack coming, but if I waited until he was right over me, then unbalanced him just enough to push him towards you, you could subdue him."

"We'd have to be real quiet about it," Cyrus said warily.

"No," Alec smiled, "we'd want to be loud about it. Once we're free of the chains, we want them coming in after us."

"It'd be a massacre," Cyrus insisted, "or if we fled, they'd run us down."

Alec shook his head. "We're not fleeing out into the fields."

"Where then?" Cyrus asked.

Alec tilted his head upward towards the ruined ceiling and the spots of exposed sky beyond it. "We go up," Alec answered.

Cyrus followed his gaze and studied the ruins of the Temple. The red stone walls, once beautifully marbled and gleaming, were now reduced to splintered pieces of stone and dust. Enormous chunks of rock balanced precariously along the edges of the walls, the last remains of the upper levels. There was something comforting about seeing daylight shining through the many holes and cracks, but the freedom that it represented still seemed impossibly far away.

"It's a risk," Cyrus finally said. "We could end up trapped, and we wouldn't be out of their reach for long."

"We don't need long," Alec hissed, and a bit of his hungry resolve began to show through. "Magnus is so arrogant, he can't imagine anyone finding a way to outsmart him..." Alec grinned broadly at the feeling of his old strength again, "...but he'll never see this coming."

CHAPTER THIRTY–FOUR

THE ORDER OF DISORDER

N o, no, stop talking," Nick demanded in frustration, "it wasn't an honest question, I don't give a shit what you're doing here... no don't sit down, oh c'mon."

Dean and Kat had rushed over to Nick's table in the tavern as soon as they recognized him and helped themselves to the two vacant seats despite his incessant protests. Dean was beyond caring about politeness and determined to get answers.

"How are you here?" Dean asked in amazement, "and you know us? I mean, you're not... this isn't your world I take it."

Nick scoffed. "My world? How the hell would this be..."

"How did you get here?" Kat interrupted him. She reached across the table and snatched the drink he had set down, gulping several mouthfuls greedily.

"Oh c'mon!" Nick exclaimed again, snatching the mug back. He paused a moment longer, seemingly trying to decide if it was worth his time explaining himself or not. "I came here after I left camp, alright. I saw that staff vanish and figured maybe that anomaly led somewhere. Guess I was right."

"This is where you wanna be?" Dean asked with raised eyebrows.

"It's not ideal, I'll give you that," Nick responded with a shrug, "but I'm not big on the whole team spirit thing, maybe you noticed."

Kat snorted in exasperated laughter. "So this was the better alternative? It's a wasteland, and a dangerous one from what I've seen. I mean, do you have a death wish?"

Nick rolled his eyes. "Is your new kingdom much different? It's all chaos, and one person trying to fuck the other over. That's the world, no matter which *world* you're in apparently." He paused and took a long swig of his drink. "And no, I don't have a death wish... I'm just not all that crazy about living."

Dean watched Nick for a moment; the man he had studied endlessly throughout his career, whose impulsive decision to keep that fragment of staff for himself had brought all of them here in the end. What a disappointment that such a man would end up being nothing more than a common criminal; someone with no morals and no desire to change his own fate.

"What's happened here?" Dean finally asked. "These don't seem to be Magnus's people, who do they..."

"I'm gonna stop you right there, D-man," Nick interrupted, "I'm not getting into this with you. I don't care what's happening with your kings and I don't care what you're doing here. You want answers, ask around, but fair warning; they're not the friendliest bunch."

At that moment, a rowdy group of four locals staggered loudly into the tavern. They all wore machetes at their sides but were nothing like the Temple guards or Annica's militants. They walked with a swagger that exuded authority and confidence but the lack of discipline amongst them was notable. Judging by the slurred speech of the woman currently talking to her cohorts, they had been drinking heavily just like everyone else in the town, yet they strut in a way that seemed to invite a challenge. This wasn't simply an after-hours excursion; it was a statement to all that they were ready for a fight.

As they collapsed against the bar and the barman began pouring drinks, Dean leaned towards Nick and whispered, "Who are they?"

Nick backed away from the table and shot them both a look of warning. When they attempted to scooch forward themselves, Nick stood up and pivoted away to a different table, turning his back on them entirely and slumping into its chair with his drink in hand.

Before Dean could show his disapproval at the rudeness, one of the women from the group called out, "What's this then?"

Dean looked at Nick, who was blatantly ignoring everyone with his head bowed over his mug and his shoulders hunched.

"How come he moved away from you?" the woman demanded, one of her eyes drooping slightly from excessive drink.

"I… I… I don't know," Dean answered honestly.

"You know him?" one of the others asked, pushing away from the bar and swaying towards them with one hand resting ominously on the hilt of his machete.

"We thought we did," Kat answered, "must have been mistaken."

"Who are you?" the woman demanded.

"Nobody," Kat said, "just passing through."

The group seemed to find this hilarious. They guffawed and stamped their feet and smacked each other's shoulders in amusement.

The nearest man came level with their table and rested his knuckles roughly on its surface. The smile had left his face as quickly as it had come. "Nobody passes through here," he growled. "Who are you with?"

It was the second time someone had demanded to know where their fealty lay, but Dean didn't have a better answer than the last time. As he stammered, the man leaned closer, the rough skin around his face looking like the hide of a rhino. He was pockmarked and weathered with a hideous scar running from his brow down past his mouth. He made a soft growling sound indicating he wanted an answer.

"They're with King Noros down south," Nick grunted from his table.

"Noros?" the man questioned, his apelike brow pulling down even further.

"He's new," Nick growled, finally looking over his shoulder, "but gaining a reputation. So I wouldn't if I were you."

"Oh you wouldn't?" the man repeated, standing upright and walking towards Nick's table instead. "And what about you? Who are you with?"

"King Tyka," Nick answered quickly. "Northeast of here."

"Hmmm," the man responded. His companions had begun losing interest and were milling their way back to the bar. "Tyka, eh? Now that's one everyone knows." As Nick just stared back at the man, he nodded his head in apparent deep thought. "Ya know, I passed a few of Tyka's men just down the road from here. Maybe I should bring you to them, see if they recognize you."

Nick's eyebrows raised. "You lay a hand on me it'll be the last thing you do. Bring them here if you want, but I'm not moving. Who knows, maybe they're in a playful mood and won't kill you for approaching."

The man looked murderous, but his companions began calling him from the bar. "It's not worth our time," the woman insisted. "I'm ready to go anyways."

The man's lip curled as though he were examining a particularly ugly bit of roadkill. "You disgust me," he finally growled.

Nick snorted a single note of laughter. "And yet you're the one whose face looks like the underside of a truck."

The man clutched the handle of his machete, almost compulsively, but didn't draw it. Instead, he staggered backward towards his companions. "You better watch yourself, boy, there's plenty of open land between here and your territory. Something bad could happen to you."

"Can't wait," Nick retorted dryly, raising his mug in a disingenuous toast before bringing it to his lips again.

The man's friends pulled forcefully at his shoulders until he finally turned away. He swayed alarmingly as he joined them, then marched back out to the street without another word. His companions followed without a backwards glance.

Dean wasted no time in rushing to Nick's table and seating himself at the other side of it, Kat joining to his left.

"Oh C'mon!" Nick scoffed again.

"Who's King Tyka?" Dean demanded, ignoring Nick's squirming. "You're with him? Is he..."

"I have no idea who he is," Nick spat in frustration, "all I know is that he's one of the bigger ones."

"Bigger whats?" Kat asked.

"Bigger kings," Nick reluctantly explained. "Apparently you're not getting the picture yet, they're a dime a dozen around here. This isn't your pal Cyrus's Kingdom with his rules and his laws. This is chaos. You wanna be a king around here? No problem, get a couple strongmen to salute you and you're a king. Might even last a few days before you're overthrown by your own men."

"But… this can't… this is all that's left?" Dean stammered.

"There's simple rules to survival around here," Nick said, downing the last of his drink, "stick to town, that's the main one. It's the only neutral territory on the island, if you can call it that. It won't keep you safe, but it's been generally established as belonging to nobody. All are welcome here, but anything goes if you know what I mean. Someone wants to murder you here, not a soul's gonna stop them. That is unless you belong to one of the kings. Retribution is swift around here, and each faction will gladly go to war with their neighbors over the slightest offense."

"How many kings are there?" Dean asked in amazement. "How many factions?"

Nick thought a moment. "By last count I think it was seventeen." As Dean and Kat balked, Nick corrected himself, "No sixteen now. King Ruhan was overthrown this morning from what I heard."

"No queens?" Kat asked.

"Oh plenty," Nick answered, "they call 'em all kings around here, male or female. I think eight of them are women. But I stay out of it, stick to myself and stick to town. Keep a low enough profile and nobody bothers you."

Kat looked like she was struggling to form her thoughts into words. "This… this isn't… this doesn't work. This is no society."

"Hell no it's not," Nick agreed, "this is the wild west."

Dean was shaking his head in disbelief. "How does that even… I don't…"

Nick leaned forward over his empty drinking vessel and offered a smirk. "Welcome to Nowhere. This is the ruin that Kysaar Magnus left behind."

CHAPTER THIRTY-FIVE

RUN

It was showtime, and Cyrus was impossibly nervous. They could well be careening towards their doom; this foolhardy bid for freedom the final undoing of the Dorn brothers and their short-lived reign. Cyrus had made his peace with this possibility, at least that's what he was trying to convince himself. He had faced death many times before, several at the very hands of his partner in this escape, but this felt somehow different. The odds were stacked so thoroughly against them that it seemed impossible to attain victory, yet there was no thought of turning back now. Cyrus refused to be the puppet of Kysaar Magnus; tortured and broken and paraded around for his people to lament. He couldn't bear the thought of being used in that way; death seemed the better alternative. Of course, death was not plan A. Alec had become increasingly confident in their mission, though he had refused to share what gave him such confidence. Cyrus thought perhaps it was simply having a task before him that accounted for the shift in his demeanor.

"You ready for this?" Cyrus whispered across the room to Alec. The Alchemist would be wandering in any moment now to deliver their dinner, and once they made their first move, there would be no turning back.

"Don't worry about me," Alec grumbled. He looked anxious as well but was trying hard not to show it. "Just follow my lead and I'll get us out of here."

Cyrus just nodded in response. He felt sure Alec was relishing the idea of Cyrus following his orders, but he was in no position to argue. He looked apprehensively up to the exposed sections of sky above, turning a rust orange in the waning afternoon light, and wondered what victory would truly look like. Was this a foe they could realistically defeat? There was a time when Cyrus thought he was done with such adventures, if one could call them that. He had thought he was stepping out of the Kingdom and back into a boring world of normalcy and repetition, but fate had other plans.

The muted crunch of approaching footsteps made Cyrus jump slightly and he gave his cheek a few light smacks to restore his resolve. He looked to Alec who nodded wordlessly and clenched his jaw. Sure enough, the footsteps proved to belong to the Alchemist, who stepped through one of the holes in the wall and entered the room. He looked tired in the way he carried himself, his shoulders heavy and his eyes blank and passive. Cyrus was struck with the impression, not for the first time, that this man did not share the same vigor for the mission that Magnus did. Indeed, his exhaustion seemed more than skin-deep, and Cyrus wondered if the morals of this hostile takeover were playing a role.

The meal tonight seemed to be some sort of bread which the Alchemist was delivering on makeshift plates made of scrap wood, no doubt debris from the many destroyed homes. He wasted no time in dropping Cyrus's portion on the ground in front of him before turning towards Alec to do the same. This was it.

"Why do you go along with all this?" Cyrus asked him, attempting a distraction. "You can't believe in Magnus's way of ruling, can you?"

The Alchemist placed Alec's plate and turned his head towards Cyrus. "You speak of things you don't..."

Wham!

Alec had kicked off from the ground hard and rammed his shoulder into the Alchemist's back. The man careened towards Cyrus in a free-fall, attempting to turn wildly to face his attacker. Cyrus stood up in one swift motion and punched the Alchemist across the face, who pitched sideways from the blow. He fell to his hands and knees and attempted to scramble across the floor in retreat, but Cyrus grasped one of his ankles before he was entirely out of reach and wrenched him backwards. The Alchemist yelled out but Cyrus wrapped an arm around his neck and began squeezing as tightly as he could. He had never actually attempted to render someone unconscious before but was confident this was how it was done. The man thrashed and kicked in desperation, however, and Cyrus instantly found the process taking far too long. As the man squirmed and Cyrus began to lose his grip, he released his hold entirely and punched the Alchemist hard across the face. He went instantly limp, falling to the ground like a log with a dull thud.

"The keys!" Alec hissed, looking wide-eyed at their handiwork.

Cyrus stooped and attempted to reach the unconscious man's pockets but found it impossible with him face-down. As he heaved him onto his back, footsteps could be heard rushing towards their makeshift prison.

"Hurry!" Alec whispered frantically.

Cyrus dove his hand into the Alchemist's pocket and pulled the keys from within. There were only three on the ring, but it meant trial and error would be the only way to find the correct one for each lock. Cyrus shoved the first into his own manacle's keyhole, but it didn't budge. Cursing, he attempted the second and was relieved when the enormous hinge crunched open. He wasted no time in tossing the set to Alec who began trying his own in visible panic. Cyrus stepped out of his bindings and wheeled in a circle, trying to decide which direction the approaching footsteps were coming from. He desperately wished he had a weapon but other than the occasional rock, there was very little to be used.

"C'mon!" Alec shouted and Cyrus was surprised to find him already free of his chains.

Alec ran to the far wall and launched himself upwards, grabbing hold of a piece of rocky overhang that led to the exposed sky above. Cyrus raced after him and grasped his brother's foot firmly, shoving him up with all the strength he had. The boost worked and Alec was able to pull his legs the rest of the way to the top of the shattered stone ledge. He rolled onto his stomach and extended his arm downward for Cyrus, his hand outstretched. But time had run out and the Neodactyl came charging into the room with a high-pitched bellow. Cyrus panicked and, abandoning his brother's offered hand, he bolted towards the adjoining wall and leaped up, his fingers just barely managing to grip the rough surface above. He was dangling by the very tips of his fingernails, but it was enough. Feeling the bones in his hand scream in protest, Cyrus was able to get a palm over the ledge, then a forearm, then an elbow, and finally his chest with an almighty hoist. The creature was bearing down on him below and would be on his legs in seconds if he couldn't manage to pull himself up. Cyrus howled in pain as he forced his body up and over the shelf, his shirt and abdomen shredding badly against the rock. The Neodactyl threw itself into the air and snapped at Cyrus, but he pulled his legs up just in time and the creature fell back to the ground with an angry hiss.

Both Alec and Cyrus were now balanced on the remains of the Temple walls, navigating the precarious and narrow rock ledges like gymnasts on a balance beam. There were pieces of ceiling still in place and from this vantage point roughly nine feet off the ground, the remnants of the second floor were partially visible. But everything was shattered and unidentifiable, mostly made up of rubble and a few large chunks of column that hadn't fully made their way to the ground. Cyrus danced along the top of the wall towards Alec, praying his brother had a second part to this plan.

Voices rang out from below and as Cyrus looked down, Magnus and Nel sprinted into the room that himself and Alec had just climbed out of. With the Neodactyl eying them hungrily from the ground, it took them no time at all to identify where their captives had escaped to. Nel looked baffled but Magnus smiled greedily, one of the tridents grasped in his hand.

"Where do you think you're going?" Magnus taunted.

Alec, looking down at their pursuers with unbridled hatred, prowled along the narrow wall like he was examining a bit of prey. "I told you before, you've come to the wrong world." He seemed to be eying the various bits of shattered rock balanced dangerously around the wall and the remains of the second floor. He looked at Cyrus briefly and gave a subtle head jerk indicating for him to follow.

"Look who's got his teeth back," Magnus laughed. He extended his trident out from his side and it began to glow burning gold. Flames began to uncoil from the Fire Fields outside and snake in towards the weapon.

Alec finally stopped walking near an enormous boulder roughly four feet around that was balanced tentatively between the edge of the wall and a bit of remaining column.

"You planning to crush me with that rock?" Magnus sneered. He stepped forward and placed himself directly beneath it, extending his arms out. "Let's see what you've got. In fact..." Magnus grasped Nel firmly by the shoulder and pulled her close. "Let's see if your ruthlessness matches the legend. Give us your best shot."

Alec paused, looking down at Nel who stared back at him with unreadable eyes. This would never work, Cyrus thought to himself, and Magnus was baiting him. Was Alec foolish enough to take the bait?

"Alec," Cyrus whispered, but his brother was just staring down at Nel with contempt. He seemed frozen facing her, and Magnus was loving it.

The tendrils of flame were beginning to enter the room below, drawn to the tip of the glowing trident and waiting to be launched.

"What do you say, King Dorn," Magnus goaded, "shall we see who's faster?"

Alec's eye twitched. His lip moved convulsively. His hand closed into a fist. Magnus had him... there was no turning back now.

Alec let out a roar and shoved against the boulder with all his might. Cyrus threw himself bodily into its side as well just as Magnus dragged his weapon through the air and sprayed a torrent of flame their way. The rock crunched free of its cradle and free-fell towards Magnus and his firestorm. As the fireball consumed the descending boulder, Magnus and Nel stepped easily to the side and out of its way. Cyrus thought this was the end of it, until the stone reached the ground below and shattered the floor with such power that the earth shook. The boulder had punched straight through the already damaged ground level causing a catastrophic collapse of the floor. The ground ruptured beneath the feet of Magnus, Nel, and the Neodactyl, becoming a chasm of shifting stone and debris as the entire area was swallowed into the subterranean level below. The Neodactyl was claimed by the void first, hissing and screeching as it was dragged to the shattering depths. Nel and Magnus attempted to dive towards the edges of the widening mouth but the avalanche that had begun could not be undone. With the trident still drawing tentacles of flame, uncontrolled explosions of fire were now erupting as they splashed against the tumbling cave-in.

It was then that the entire wall Cyrus and Alec were standing on gave a heart-stopping shudder. Cyrus looked down in terror just in time to see the stone form a devastating fracture beneath his feet. The wall buckled, finally succumbing to the widening abyss below, and began to freely crumble.

"MOVE!" Cyrus shouted and Alec turned to flee.

There was nowhere to run that wasn't being sucked into the maw but there was also no time to think. Both Cyrus and Alec propelled themselves as far as they could along the shattering wall before throwing themselves out into the open air with outstretched arms. The ground came to meet him fast and Cyrus's chest slammed hard into the pebbly surface of the Fire Fields. He gasped in agony as the air left his body entirely. A horrible wheeze escaped his mouth as he rolled onto his back and attempted to crawl away from the collapsing building.

Tremors were reverberating through the earth as the endless tons of stone finally settled into their new resting place. Alec coughed deeply beside him and went limp from exhaustion. The sky above had turned a drab grey as evening set in, but it came with the promise of renewed freedom. It had worked, and Cyrus couldn't believe it.

No sooner had the thought entered his mind than an explosion burst forth from the edges of the rubble and ignited the darkening night air. It seemed Magnus had managed to reach one of the connecting rooms below before being crushed by the cave-in and the power of his trident would make quick work of his rocky tomb. With several more sizzling flashes, Magnus climbed unsteadily into view, the side of his face bleeding badly and a look of raw hatred in his eyes.

"RUN!" Cyrus yelled and he and Alec turned tail and fled across the wasted landscape. Magnus let out a thunderous bellow and raised his trident into the air, drawing fire and ash towards its head. As he twisted it in a wide circle, flames erupted from the ground and began lashing across the path along which Cyrus and Alec ran. Sparks sizzled against Cyrus's cheek and his eyes watered, blinding him from his progression. With a horrible lurch, he felt his foot inevitably catch against a piece of debris and he skidded to the ground. As he looked back, Magnus was abandoning his firestorm and began sprinting after them like a deranged animal. But he wasn't alone. To Cyrus's horror, the Neodactyl was now freeing itself from the same hole Magnus had climbed out of and rabidly joining the pursuit.

Cyrus clambered to his feet and began running after Alec towards the treeline, but he wasn't going to make it. He ducked low and grabbed a fist-sized stone from the ground and continued his flight, fully aware that it was going to come to a close-quarters brawl. Alec had arrived at the edge of the forest up ahead and sprinted into its shadowy depths, leaving Cyrus to deal with their attacker on his own.

Magnus's footsteps were drawing near and Cyrus knew he had only seconds. Chasing a wild impulse, he sidestepped at the last moment, leaving Magnus to overshoot just slightly. With his pursuer off-balance, Cyrus barreled forward and smashed the stone in his hand against the back of Magnus's skull. He crashed to the ground and Cyrus dove after him, smashing his head with the rock a second time. Blood poured from Magnus's temple but his eyes were mad with rage. He punched Cyrus across the jaw and used the momentum to kick hard into his stomach. Cyrus buckled. He had expected the Neodactyl to join the fray but, to his surprise, the creature bypassed them entirely, racing towards the forest. Cyrus looked up. Alec had reappeared at the treeline and was carrying the machete that Cyrus had dropped on their way in. He held it forward like a warrior out of ancient times, but he had expected to battle Kysaar Magnus, not his beloved Neodactyl. His stoicism faltered just slightly but he raised the blade all the same. It was an impossible fight and Cyrus knew it. He attempted to hit Magnus with the stone a third time but his advantage had been used up. Magnus clobbered him with his fist, his bloody teeth bared like a lion over a fresh kill. Cyrus hit him back with the majority of his remaining strength and attempted to get his feet back under himself, but Magnus seized his leg in a glove-sized hand and dragged him back to the earth.

"ALEC RUN!" Cyrus called, recognizing the futility of their situation. The only remaining hope would be for Alec to get back to their camp and return with an army.

Alec hesitated and for the briefest moment Cyrus wondered why. It should not have been a hard decision for Alec to leave his brother to die. With the Neodactyl only a few paces away, Alec gave a final look at Cyrus, then turned and fled into the forest. The creature gave chase, but only briefly, for Magnus whistled and it abruptly turned back the way it had come.

Magnus looked down at Cyrus and his expression was wild and predatory. Blood was flowing freely from his head and trickling into his eye below, forcing it shut.

"That was a mistake," Magnus snarled. "I guarantee you will come to regret what you did here today."

Cyrus looked up at him; up into his bloodshot eye, at his drooping mouth and exposed teeth and knew he had to destroy this man. Kysaar Magnus would not rest until the entire Kingdom had been brought to heel, and then he would decimate everything that Cyrus and his people had built. Town proper was only the beginning.

"And I guarantee I'll make you regret ever coming to this world," Cyrus growled back, borrowing his brother's threat. "You think Alec is ruthless? You haven't met the real me yet."

Magnus smiled broadly. "There's the king I've read about. But you're too late. I'm sure your brother thinks he's bringing the calvary now… good! When they arrive here tomorrow, they'll find your beloved statue in ruin. And in its place? They'll see you… hung by the neck… their *symbol* just a memory… and your legacy extinguished."

Magnus punched Cyrus again and as his head lolled to the side, he could just barely make out Nel, slowly approaching from the ruins of the building. She looked entirely worse for wear, covered in soot and blood, but her expression was dark and hateful.

"My dear, we have a structure to build," Magnus announced to her, getting heavily to his feet, "something easily seen from all sides. I want it towering over the field and commanding the attention of everyone who sets eyes on it. It should be grand. It will be the final resting place of a king, after all." He looked down at Cyrus with revolting superiority. "An end befitting the great Cyrus Dorn."

CHAPTER THIRTY-SIX

THE COLLAPSE OF A WORLD

K at didn't like the idea of leaving the perceived safety of the tavern any more than Mr. Pyrene did, but they had promised Annica they would bring back answers. Nick had exhausted all usefulness quite quickly and resumed his mission of drinking himself into oblivion, so the only real option was to start asking questions of the rest of the locals in town. The obvious issue with this plan, of course, was that everyone in town seemed to be about as pleasant as the man with the scar who had harassed them at their table. They tried the barman but were stonewalled instantly when they mentioned Magnus's name, so that left them no choice but to attempt poking around outside. Mr. Pyrene, or *Dean* as he insisted on being called now that they had traversed two alternate realities together, was patently against the idea.

There was no other way of describing it; this town was a scary place. Most of the citizens ignored them entirely, wrapped up in their own arguments, conversations, or fights, but every once in a while they were met with a suspicious glare as though it were clear they didn't belong. They avoided the larger groups and anyone who looked too unruly or particularly militant, but this left shockingly few individuals. As they quickened their pace to scamper past a boisterous and violent cluster of six, Kat began to wonder if anyone would be safe to approach. She averted her gaze from an exceptionally murderous looking man and found herself staring at a wizened and feeble old woman sitting with her back against one of the outer walls of a building. Her leathery skin had more lines than an old suitcase and her sunken eyes had a passive but somehow knowing look to them. With impossibly few options, Kat seized the opportunity and planted herself next to the woman along the wall. The woman looked mildly alarmed at her new company but made no move to leave.

"This may sound odd," Kat began, "but can you tell us about this place? About this town?"

The woman looked skeptically from Kat to Dean and back. "Bring me an ale and we can talk about whatever you like," she croaked.

Kat nodded vigorously and said, "We can go to the tavern if you…"

"I said *bring* it to me," the woman insisted. "I'll wait."

Dean looked confused but Kat nodded to him and he begrudgingly began walking back towards the tavern to retrieve a drink for the old woman. Kat stayed behind, hoping she could coax the woman into talking, but she staunchly refused until Dean returned and her beverage was placed in her hand.

"Not from here?" the woman wheezed as she took a healthy gulp of her drink.

"We're not," Kat admitted, "we come from elsewhere, but we're trying to understand this place."

The woman rolled her eyes slightly. "Not the nicest world to find yourselves in. Not sure what there is to tell."

"Well we understand that there are multiple rulers currently in place," Dean questioned, "why is that? Isn't there a better way to govern?"

"Govern?" the woman scoffed, "you really aren't from around here. We used to have a singular ruler; they were elected by the people. Laws were written, rules were followed. But that was before."

"Before what?" Kat pushed, "What went wrong?"

"A man took over," the woman grumbled ominously, "and once democracy is undone, it can be near impossible to bring back."

Kat looked at Dean warily. She didn't need to ask who the man was. "Kysaar Magnus," Kat breathed.

The woman shot her a hateful look. "Strange you'd know a name like that, not being from around here." When Kat didn't explain, the woman shrugged. "Law and order became privileges of the past real quick. The thing about Kysaar Magnus is he doesn't know how to lead, he doesn't know how to conquer, he doesn't even know how to rule. He stripped the Kingdom, overused every resource, and sucked our lands dry."

Dean shook his head in disgust. "So all of these new kings, and different factions…"

The woman laughed, a horrible creaky noise. "That's the irony of it all. We thought things were bad under Magnus's rule, but the real nightmare started when he vanished. Once the Kingdom was depleted, he recognized the end of his reign, must have moved on. Nobody quite knows what happened to him, but the power vacuum he left was catastrophic. Gone were the days of elections and voicing your opinion. Those that wanted power started seizing it, and stability collapsed within hours. It was actually rather shocking how quickly things went awry."

Kat was horrified at the old woman's tale, but she was still left with one burning question. "How did Magnus ever get voted for in the first place?"

The woman looked at her with such apparent pity in her eyes that Kat had trouble meeting her gaze. "Oh honey," she answered, "Kysaar Magnus wasn't elected, he tore his way into our world with a pair of tridents."

Kat's mouth fell open. This wasn't Magnus's home world. Why hadn't she considered that before? She suddenly looked again at her surroundings, at the people fighting in the streets, the militants each serving a different king, everyone searching for a power grab, and a horrible realization washed over her; this place used to be just like Cyrus's Kingdom. They had laws, security for their people, elections, and a forum for debate. Magnus had ripped into this reality just as he had ripped into theirs, and this was the result. He had left a depleted world behind, not only irreparably fractured but also profoundly inhospitable. It was a sobering glance into their future, if he couldn't be stopped.

"So you have no idea who he was before?" Dean questioned, "or where he came from?"

Kat thought it was a valid question but the woman seemed to tense up a bit. Her brow furrowed and she adopted a look of extreme distrust. "You have a lot of questions about Kysaar Magnus."

As a pack of unruly locals thundered past and one of them released a cackling, drunken laugh, Kat jumped, suddenly ill at ease. "We're just curious is all," Kat insisted.

"I'm sure you are," the woman answered, but it was no longer an earnest conversation. Some part of this woman was shutting down, hastily walling herself off from the interrogation.

"We don't mean any harm by our questions," Dean said, recognizing the shift in the woman's demeanor.

"Mmmhmm," the woman said with a nod of her head. Without ever turning away, she suddenly called out with a much stronger voice than Kat would have thought her capable of, "Kingsmen!"

The laughing group that had passed moments earlier all turned in unison, their smiles still plastered on their splotchy, intoxicated faces.

"These two have quite an interest in Kysaar Magnus," the woman reported, her eyebrows raised so high they risked disappearing beneath her thinning hair.

"That a fact?" one of the men from the group snarled as the entire band, probably a dozen in all, began walking back down the road towards them.

"No, we were just curious," Kat said again, her eyes now growing wide with fear.

"Nobody's just curious about Magnus," another from the group said with a sneer. "What are you really up to?"

Dean got hastily to his feet and Kat followed his example. These people did not seem interested in a rational explanation, not to mention they were heavily armed. The man in front seemed to be the leader, or at least the highest-ranking within his present company. They all wore machetes on their belts but his more closely resembled a sword. It was longer than his counterparts, still with a curved, broad blade but lacking the rust. The handle was ornate cast bronze and seemed to be decorated with an assortment of symbols. He leered at them, his towering physique casting both Dean and Kat in shadow.

"Who do you serve?" the man demanded.

Dean began to sputter again but Kat started searching her brain for the names Nick had used to get out of trouble in the tavern. "King Tyka," she finally stammered.

The group all erupted in boisterous laugher.

"It's true," Kat pushed, attempting to project strength, "and if we have any trouble, then you can explain it to him."

The group laughed even louder.

"What's funny?!" Kat snapped.

The leader shook his head in dismay and took a step forward. "Well for one, King Tyka's a girl." Kat felt the blood drain from her face. Her mind scrambled to find a way to course-correct, but then the man continued, "And for another, Tyka is *our* king. And curiously enough, we don't know you."

Kat's heart fell. She looked desperately to Dean, but he just stared blankly back at her. The man unsheathed his machete, definitely more of a cleaver-style sword now that she could see it, and held it beneath her chin. "Now you're in some trouble, my dear."

"Okay wait," Kat said, raising her hands in surrender, "the truth now. We're from another world, actually two other worlds, and Magnus has come to our kingdom now, that's the only reason we're here, we're not looking for…"

The man struck her across the face. Kat's vision went blurry and she staggered sideways from the blow.

"Hey!" Dean yelled but the man leveled his weapon against his chest and he went silent. Kat had never been hit before and it made the situation feel suddenly, desperately real. It was like the man's strike had suddenly knocked this bizarre adventure into the real world for her.

"You're in the wrong place if you think talking will save you," the man stated roughly, all hint of laughter entirely gone from his features.

"You must have known that using King Tyka's name for protection would catch up with you in the end… you must also have known that it was a crime punishable by death."

"We didn't know," Kat answered with a jerky shake of her head. "We swear we didn't know."

"That makes you either dumb or a liar," the man said, "either way, it'll cost you your head."

"We've told you we're not from here," Dean began again.

"Right," the man said stroking his chin theatrically as though he were thinking, "which leads me to believe you were sent by Magnus."

"No!" Kat practically screamed, "he's our enemy too! We're here looking for ways…"

"If he's your enemy and he's come to your world, then what's to stop him following you here?" the man questioned, but he wasn't looking for an answer. "That buys you nothing. Goodbye, enemies of Magnus."

The man drew his sword, stepped forward swiftly and swung it straight at Dean's neck, who was too dumbfounded to move or even react. But Kat was faster. In a moment of incredible stupidity fueled entirely by desperation, Kat leaped forward, bouncing off her tippy-toes, and punched the man square in the cheek.

Silence fell. The man did not seem overly hurt by the attack, but stunned. The act had managed to off-balance him at the last second and his sword had missed Dean by inches. Now he stared down at Kat like a bug that needed to be crushed.

Kat raised her hands again. "Please," she said. She tried to adopt her most innocent, wide-eyed look. "Please."

The man smiled pitilessly and stepped towards her. Without a word he suddenly reached out and grabbed her throat with a gigantic, meaty hand and lifted her from the ground. Kat gasped and choked, her eyes bulging in terror. Suddenly she was no longer a young girl; she was a wild animal ensnared in a cage. She twisted and kicked, rolling around in the air like a fish on a line. She lashed out with her hands, clawing and ripping at his face until they found something to grasp; his ear. She buried her nails into its soft underside and wrenched towards herself with all of her strength. Using the only weapon she had available to her, she sunk her teeth into the fleshy appendage and began tearing like a lion out of the Serengeti. The man screamed and attempted to throw her to the ground but she just wrapped her hands all the more tightly around his head and shredded at his skin, feeling a piece of his ear come clean from the side of his face. The man roared and finally managed to pull his head free, using the leverage to fling her from himself.

Kat landed on the ground lightly, turned to Dean and yelled, "Run!"

The two turned and sprinted back the way they had come, having no idea where to flee to or where to hide. The rest of the group had seemed too aghast by Kat's sudden attack to stop her, but now they could be heard barking orders to one another and giving chase.

Dean and Kat rounded a corner and found themselves back where they had started, just outside the run-down old tavern. The area was mostly empty apart from one individual staggering unsteadily towards a far wall, doubled over and clutching his stomach. He looked like he was going to be sick. Kat searched the area wildly for an escape but it was already too late; the group had caught up with them and was fanning out in the street, blocking their way. Gone was the chuckling and jovial banter amongst the group, they now all wore expressions of deepest fury.

The leader swayed to the front, one hand grasping his sword, the other clamped over his ruined ear. Blood soaked down the side of his neck, discoloring his shirt and pattering into the sand. Kat was more scared than she had ever been in her life. She began to raise her hands in surrender one more time but paused when she realized it was no use. Instead, she looked to her right and saw the drunken man, leaning heavily against the wall with his head bowed low, and thought of one last, mad idea. She scrambled towards him and gripped the machete tucked in his belt. The man barely seemed to notice as she pulled it free and, with a rather forced twirl, she squared herself up against the wall of foes before her. They each tittered briefly at the display but she was happy to note that her savaging of their friend's ear had at least earned her the respect to not be outwardly laughed at. Dean looked stunned and shook his head at her, but what other options did they have? If she was going to die, she planned to at least die swinging.

The leader strode slowly forward a few paces but then paused. With the side of his face now fully covered in blood, he turned to his party and motioned to several of them to move against Kat in his stead. She smiled briefly at his hesitation.

His companions moved forward fast, their weapons already drawn and ready. Dean backed up a few paces and Kat, armed with her single rusted blade, braced herself for the attack. The nearest of the assailants drew close, flourished his weapon and slashed hard towards Kat's head; but rather than parry his swing, Kat ducked. It was incredibly effective. The man's arms overextended and it seemed to take some real effort for him to regain control of his wild blade. He cursed and swung again but again Kat danced out of his reach just before his weapon could make contact. The man's fury broke and he began swiping at random, left, right, and center as Kat bounced just out of reach. The man cried out in frustration and wound up his arms over his head, slicing downward in what should have been a devastating hit. But his anger had made him slow and predictable, and instead of hopping out of the way, Kat dove forward into a crouch and ran her machete along the side of his thigh, carving open a small but significant gash. The man screamed but Kat had no time to waste. Suddenly every single member of the group was seething forward, their weapons swinging every which way in an attempt to take her down. She bounded in and out between the angry mob like a mouse flitting under heel, always just out of reach of the hacking blades. The street had become chaos, with the militants having as much chance of killing each other as Kat, but she knew she couldn't keep up the tactic for long. Spotting Dean near the outskirts, she flung herself towards him, seized his arm and raced through the only doorway open to them.

They found themselves in the dusty tavern once again, but it was only a second before their pursuing horde came spilling in after them. Kat seized a heavy clay mug from a nearby table and, barely registering Nick Satterall's cry of protest, she launched it at the approaching group where it shattered against one of their heads. The barman entered a state of panic at the violent eruption within his establishment and began yelling for order, but it was no use. Dean, finally appearing to accept their dire situation, upended a table and held it aloft like a shield, charging forward into the group with its broad top serving as a battering ram.

As Kat ducked out of the way of yet another blade, she saw Nick pushing himself out from behind his table in confusion and withdrawing into the corner.

"Oh yeah, don't help, we've got this!" Kat called after him sarcastically.

Nick shook his head, possibly too baffled to react but also likely attempting to protect his image as a local. Kat rolled her eyes in disgust just as the group's leader lurched into view from between the crowd. His ear was still bleeding freely but he released the wound in favor of a two-handed grip on his sword. Kat was happy to see, at the very least, she finally warranted a real combat stance from him. She raised her own tragically inferior weapon and prepared for a final showdown. The man smirked briefly, squared his shoulders, and charged.

Suddenly the machete was tugged out of her hands from behind. Kat turned wildly. Nick was standing beside her. He twirled the blade loosely with his wrist and threw it headlong towards her attacker where it impaled deep into the man's chest. He staggered sideways into a table where he collapsed, splaying out onto the ground with the machete twitching where it had stuck. Nick rushed forward and wrenched the blade free from the body and threw it to Kat. He then stooped and retrieved the broadsword from the floor.

"Guess we're in it now," Nick yelled with a shrug. He gave the sword a quick spin through the air and nodded in approval. Without another word, he raced forward to the defense of Dean, who was in the process of holding three assailants at bay with his table-shield. Nick mowed down all three in a matter of seconds, using the sword like it were an extension of his arm. Kat just stared at him in amazement. As it turned out, Nick Satterall was an excellent fighter. In fact, he was far and away the best combatant in the room, something the militants were quickly beginning to realize.

As Nick sliced through two more, he turned to Kat and shouted, "Oh sure, don't help, we've got this!"

Kat came back to reality with a start and sprinted forward into the fray. She positioned herself behind Dean and his table, stabbing out over the top when a target would present itself. But the fighting didn't last much longer. Their scrappy trio had managed to kill eight of their men and the remaining few were starting a panicked retreat out onto the road. Nick raced after them, slashing and hacking as he went. By the time he finally skidded to a halt in the sand outside, only two of the original company remained and they had long since dropped their own weapons in favor of a quicker departure. Nick looked reluctant to let them go but had likely decided a pursuit would not be worth his time.

As the last of the fleeing footsteps faded away, Nick gave his new blade a fancy twirl and looked down at it with a broad grin. He then looked up at Dean and Kat, who had joined him outside the tavern, and said, "So how did you manage to make so many friends so fast?"

Kat and Dean both launched into explanations, each talking over the other, but Nick put up a hand to stop them.

"Okay okay okay!" Nick exclaimed, rubbing his temples. "I get the idea. Well the bad news is, you've blown my cover. Word of this will spread. The good news is, drinking yourself to death is shockingly boring, so I've got nothing else to do but help you."

"Where did you learn to fight like that?" Kat asked in amazement.

Nick chuckled. "I've been fighting all my life. It was just a part of growing up where I come from."

"That wasn't just street fighting," Dean insisted.

"No," Nick agreed, casually walking between the fallen bodies and examining each of their dropped weapons. "I've seen some real action as well. That's also a part of life where I come from. Mostly firearms in battle but I'll tell ya, when things get messy, as they always do, it's good to know how to handle yourself up close and personal if you know what I mean."

He finally seemed to identify a machete that he liked the look of, for he scooped it off the ground and began running his fingers carefully along the edge. Satisfied with its sharpness, he tossed it to Dean who looked so shocked at the gesture that he nearly dropped it.

"That should do for you, D," Nick said, "but as for you…" he pointed at Kat, "you can really handle yourself."

Kat smiled slightly and felt herself go red.

"I mean, your form's a mess," he continued, "and your stance is sloppy, but you've got serious spirit. Hell, these kingsmen didn't even know what to do with you."

Kat wasn't sure if she should take this as a compliment or an insult, but she stayed quiet.

"I think for you…" Nick began slowly, scanning the remaining weapons in the road, "yeah, this'll do you." He seized another off the ground and tossed it to her. She was exceedingly proud of herself for catching it without fumbling.

"So where are you headed?" Nick asked.

"I… well we don't know," Kat admitted. "We were sent here by the Queen to learn more about Magnus's past…"

Nick looked entirely perplexed. "But you didn't have a plan? You just hoped to wander the streets and ask people?"

It felt painfully foolish when Nick said it like that.

"We need a way of defeating this man," Kat insisted defensively. "Civilization is falling rapidly in the Kingdom, and if we don't come back with something, it's only a matter of time before it becomes… well, like this."

Nick appeared to appreciate the directness of her statement. "Alright," he nodded, "that I can get behind."

"So now you're helping us?" Kat asked, more than a bit wary of his sudden reversal. "We're grateful for the help but what changed? When Cyrus asked for your support, you turned your back on him."

Nick rolled his eyes. "You guys have to complicate everything, don't you." When Kat just stared at him, unsatisfied with this answer, he sighed heavily and continued. "At the rate you two are going, you'll be dead by day's end. I can either let that play out or I can offer my services." Nick flipped his sword into the air and caught it deftly with the other hand. "Lucky for you, I'm offering my services. You want 'em or not?"

Kat smiled at his confidence in spite of herself. "Yeah, we want 'em," she answered.

"Good choice," Nick said, tucking the sword into his belt. "First order of business is getting off the streets. Murder's not exactly frowned upon around here, but a massacre of this size… people will be talking."

"Where to then?" Dean asked.

"Well that's the other reason you're lucky to have my services," Nick answered with a wink, "I know just the man for you to talk to."

CHAPTER THIRTY–SEVEN

SOMETHING APPROACHES

J ack woke with a start. What had awoken him? A noise in the forest? A dream already forgotten? Or anxiety for the unknown road ahead? As he rolled from his cot and placed his feet against the blanket spread over the ground serving as a floor to his tent, he thought he knew the answer. The darkness surrounding him, stifling and oppressive when he had first opened his eyes, began to ease away just slightly, forming images of ghostly grey objects as his vision adjusted to the night. A glance at the sky showed the usual explosion of stars beginning their slow retraction from the world as the first imperceptible hints of the new day whispered their way in. Camp was quiet, silent in fact, and not even the birds had begun to wake just yet. It was peaceful in its own way, but Jack found himself dreading its inevitable tarnishing that no doubt would come.

A glance behind him showed Annica, sleeping well despite a miserable start to the night. Dr. Garse had tended carefully to her injuries and insisted they would be mere memories before long, but seeing his wife with such horrific wounds had churned Jack's stomach. She had limped her way back into camp after delivering Dean and Kat through the doorway and into the unknown, but promptly collapsed upon arrival.

As her closest allies rushed to their queen's aid, her companions described the gruesome attack that had nearly claimed all of their lives as well as their desperate flight back to the protection of the forest. Evidently the Neodactyl was now under Magnus's control as well, and it had set upon them instantly when they were spotted in the Fire Fields. It chilled Jack's blood to think how close he had come to losing Annica, but tough didn't even begin to describe her. She insisted that the gory ruin of her left shoulder and arm was a fair price to pay for information on how to reclaim their kingdom. Jack heartily disagreed, but Dr. Garse insisted that a salve of his own creation would be sufficient in healing her quickly.

Jack stood, stretched, and ducked out from beneath their shared canopy only to again wonder why he was awake. In truth, he hadn't slept well in quite some time and he thought he knew why. It had been six years since Alec Dorn had taken him prisoner from the Westtown plaza, locked him in a cell, and used him as a bargaining chip to gain the upper hand over his brother, but Jack hadn't forgotten the helplessness he had felt in those days. Cyrus had risked open war with the West to get him back, and now Cyrus himself was someone's prisoner, waiting and hoping for a rescue that might never come. He deserved better from his friends, much less his Kingdom, but the truth was the current situation looked grim. Many of the people were in favor of storming the Fire Fields to reclaim their former king, but it was Annica demanding patience. She wasn't wrong, of course; any direct assault on Kysaar Magnus was a suicide mission, but it still left Jack with a sick, guilty feeling in his stomach.

As Jack wandered his way through the dark, shadowy camp, he realized his guilt extended far beyond his abandonment of his friend. These were his people, homeless and scared, scattered to the forest without the most basic of belongings. He owed them stability, and it had been taken from them in the most violent of ways. One day they would have real peace, he had to believe that.

Jack arrived at the edge of the encampment where a single guard stood on watch duty. The man turned to Jack and smiled drowsily.

"Couldn't sleep, my King?" the man asked.

Jack shook his head with a grunt. "Something woke me, not sure what." As he felt the cool morning air brush against his face he scanned the darkness ahead, the shadows finally beginning to reveal their secrets as dawn threatened to arrive. "A feeling maybe," Jack mused, slowly. "Anything of note last night?"

"Very quiet," the guard reported. "Although in the last five minutes I've thought I heard snapping twigs more than once." As Jack turned to him, he kept his eyes trained on the trees. "Could be nothing... could be something approaches."

Jack turned back to the forest, suddenly far more ominous in its appearance, but couldn't hear anything.

"Don't worry my King," the guard said congenially, "there are many noises in these trees at night, they never prove to be anything. A passing animal perhaps."

But Jack was disturbed by the account all the same. The last time he had awoken without explanation, he had left bed to discover Annica and Cain had declared war on Westtown. With his sickly feeling refusing to subside, Jack crept forward a pace.

"My King, you shouldn't," the guard insisted, "it's not safe."

Jack just shook his head and continued slowly into the trees. He didn't plan to go far; he just couldn't escape this strange feeling, a feeling that they were perhaps being watched. As he got about ten paces away from the edge of camp, however, he still had yet to come across anything of interest. He stopped, slowed his breathing, and listened.

Snap.

A twig broke, somewhere up ahead, and Jack's skin began to tingle all over. It could have been an animal... but it could have been a person. The guard suddenly arrived at Jack's side and, with a bolt-launcher firmly in hand, he said, "My King, I have to insist we go back. We don't know..."

Jack put up his hand abruptly and the guard stopped speaking. He had just seen something, though not in the direction of the cracking sticks. Off to their left, roughly fifty feet away, Jack could swear he saw movement. Now, everything looked as still as glass, but no, something was out there. Jack stared into the trees, willing the shadows to ebb away just the tiniest bit more and illuminate what they were concealing. He leaned forward as though the extra several inches would help. There *was* something out there. Was that a tree trunk? His eyes traced the outline; nondescript around the base but strangely curved near the top. Not a tree. Perhaps a plant? Were those leaves? No, Jack realized with a start, it was hair.

His heart began to hammer and he tried to slow his breathing down. There was a person standing out there, but they weren't moving. They were standing perfectly still, like a sentinel surveying the area. Jack tilted his head, trying to force the details to form in the lightening darkness, and thought he could finally make out a person's face. It looked strangely nondescript, and suddenly Jack realized this was because the person wore a long beard and a wild mane of hair. Their clothes were dingy and dirty, helping them blend into the rugged terrain beyond, and as he watched, the person turned and looked directly back at Jack. He could feel their eyes lock, even from this distance, and he practically gasped. But the person did not move and did not react. Instead, they slowly lifted a hand up to their face and lay a single finger over their mouth, demanding silence. The action made Jack tremble, though he didn't know why. Suddenly he realized he had seen this man once before. He had inexplicably come to the Kingdom the same day the scepter had reclaimed Alec, Cyrus, and the others.

As Jack watched, the man lowered his hand once again and turned his head away, looking out into the forest in the direction Jack had heard the cracking twig.

Snap.

This time it was clearer and much closer. The bearded man wasn't the one making the noise, which begged the obvious question; what was out there approaching their camp? Another glance at the mystery man showed him staring intently in the direction of the cracking twigs, almost entranced. Whatever was out there, this man could see it.

Snap.

The guard beside Jack stepped in front of him, extending a protective arm out to block him from danger.

Snap. Snap.

The guard raised his weapon. "Show yourself!" he called out.

The footsteps stopped. Jack waited for something to jump out, but nothing came. Finally, he sidestepped the guard and began to walk forward briskly. The guard, looking alarmed at his boldness, followed. The trees ahead rustled and Jack vaulted around a clump of foliage to face their approaching visitor.

"Alec!" Jack exclaimed in shock.

Alec stood in the dark forest, bloodied and dirty, with his hands up in the air and wide, unblinking eyes. He was shaking his head rapidly before Jack had even asked him any questions.

"It's not what you think," Alec insisted.

Jack grasped Alec roughly by the collar and began dragging him back towards camp, the guard tracking him with the bolt-launcher.

"No please," Alec begged, "let me explain!"

"Where the hell is Cyrus?" Jack demanded.

"It wasn't my fault," Alec pleaded, "I didn't have a choice. I had to leave him."

"Leave him where?" Jack snarled, hoisting Alec bodily over a fallen tree in their path.

"With Magnus," Alec explained, "I promise, I didn't mean to."

"Right of course," Jack responded sarcastically, "because you're the picture of nobility, I almost forgot."

Jack stopped, suddenly remembering the bearded man watching from the shadows. He turned and was slightly surprised to find him still there. He was watching the proceedings with such rapt attention it was slightly chilling.

Alec went silent as well upon seeing him. "Who is he?" Alec whispered.

Jack shook his head. "I have no idea."

He thought of calling out but it seemed somehow wrong to do so. Like it would violate the man's clear desire to be passed over and forgotten. Still, there was something horribly targeted in the way he looked at them. It wasn't passive observation; it was emotionally charged. Jack didn't know how he could discern this from such a distance, but he could.

Slowly, the man began to back away, before long becoming lost in the reaching shadows of the forest.

"Friend of yours?" Alec asked Jack.

Jack wrenched Alec violently forward in response, continuing the short walk back to camp. Once they had crossed the outer perimeter, Jack threw him forcefully to the ground and said, "Speak! What happened?"

"I… I… Look, you have to understand," Alec began to stammer.

People started curiously poking their heads out of their tents at the commotion. Ydoro and Noma had joined them within seconds of their arrival.

"You sold him out, didn't you?" Jack spat. "I warned him not to go with you."

"I didn't, I swear," Alec responded, "we escaped, together. We were out, but Magnus caught up to him and… I tried, but…".

Jack bent and grabbed Alec's collar again. "Enough lies," he roared, "what did you do with your brother?!"

"Alec," a voice exclaimed from behind, and Jack turned to see Annica having joined the growing crowd.

"You have to believe me," Alec said, "he told me to leave him. It was the only way."

"Why would he do that?" Jack demanded.

"To warn you," Alec answered, "Magnus won't stop at the Fire Fields. He'll bring this entire Kingdom under his command. And I think he plans to execute Cyrus… he wants an example made of him."

Jack released Alec and let him fall back to the dirt. "When?"

"I… I don't know," Alec admitted, "but his power is growing. He has the Neodactyl, and Nel has betrayed me… betrayed us."

Jack rolled his eyes. "Now there's a shock," he spat. "Why should we believe a word you say?"

As Alec stumbled over his words, Annica stepped forward, still gingerly cradling her injured arm. "I think he's telling the truth," she said slowly, examining Alec with extreme care.

"Why do you think that?" Jack asked skeptically. "This could all be an act; he could be leading us into a trap."

As Annica studied Alec, she said softly, "Because Alec Dorn's greatest weakness is his inability to show weakness. He would never allow himself to project defeat, even in a ruse to obtain victory. Victory without allowing his strength to be known would taste bitter and hollow in his mouth." She stepped forward several paces, still watching Alec carefully. "No, if he's coming to us *like this*, pleading with us, it's because he's suffered a real defeat. It's desperation."

Alec looked ill; his face pinched as though he were sucking on something sour, but he said nothing.

Annica knelt beside Alec, her face a mask of authority and strength. "So what would you have me do, Alec?"

Alec shook his head. "I don't know what to do," he admitted, "but I know that Magnus will be expecting you to come, which means whatever his plans for Cyrus are, he'll move fast."

"If we leave now, we could arrive just before midday," Annica said, "but without a plan, I'm not sure our odds have improved."

Alec looked back into her eyes. "I don't know," he said again, "but by midday, it could very well be too late."

CHAPTER THIRTY–EIGHT

EXECUTION

There was no sleep to be had for Cyrus Dorn. How does one sleep the night before their own execution? It seemed he should be absorbing every feeling, every miniscule detail of life before it was ripped from him. It seemed he should be picturing Cynthia's face and holding it close as the end drew near. It seemed he should be observing the stars above and reflecting on the enormity of the world… and the tiny section of it he had carved out for himself. None of these feelings came during his final night, and as the sun inevitably broke over the horizon and bathed his surroundings in a beautiful, tangerine glow, he felt nothing but a strange emptiness that it should end like this. A part of him felt certain this couldn't be the end; that someone or something would swoop in and rescue him from his ironclad fate, but perhaps that was simply denial talking. Alec had run off, presumably to alert Annica and Jack of his swiftly approaching demise, but even if Alec had trekked through the night and the army was on their way, Cyrus would be long dead by the time they arrived. The sun had just entered the sky after all, and with the new day came the promise of his end.

Magnus had been furious with their attempted escape the night before, and doubly so with the near deaths of his few followers. Alec's plan had been a good one, and the cave-in of the Temple ruins had come very close to claiming every one of their enemies to the void. Unfortunately, all had escaped with relatively minor injuries. Even the Alchemist, who Cyrus had been sure was crushed by the falling rock, had regained consciousness and lived to see another day.

Cyrus was not the only one unable to sleep through the night. Magnus, Nel, and the Alchemist had worked by torchlight erecting an enormous structure out of scrap wood and stone on the former site of the Guardian statue. It was not overly grand or particularly artful as Magnus had initially demanded, but Cyrus supposed it would serve just fine as the site of his execution. The structure seemed designed to hoist him off the ground and display him high above the surrounding clearing. Hanged by the neck, that was Magnus's plan, and watching the trio examining their handiwork in the daylight, Cyrus could think of no way to stop it.

Cyrus was tied now to a piece of remaining foundation, his original cell having of course been obliterated during their escape attempt. It wasn't a permanent or overly dignified setup for a captive, but he supposed it didn't have to be. It actually reminded him a bit of his treatment of Nel during his time as king. She had been captured by his people and he had elected to tie her to a post outside for all the town to see. Cyrus rubbed his temples now, reminiscing of all the terrible things they had all done to one another.

As he watched Nel now, smiling to Magnus approvingly while they inspected the structure they had built together, he just lowered his head in disgust. He should have been able to see all of this coming. He had expected a double-cross from Alec and known Nel was prone to following power, but how had he let it come to this? Had he just been so certain that he could outsmart everyone else? Was it that old bit of arrogance shining through; a persistent gift from his former self that had never quite died? Perhaps he still craved that praise from the people that would follow if he were to single-handedly neutralize the threat to their kingdom once again. He wasn't sure he believed that, but there *was* a truth dancing just out of his reach; some painful but undoubtedly accurate realization that his mind was resisting.

The Neodactyl prowled near to Magnus, seemingly calm as long as he remained calm. 'They're emotional creatures' he remembered King Mora saying. God, that seemed like a lifetime ago. Back before his relationship with Alec had fractured, and before he had become a king. Did he regret what had happened? It was an interesting thing to reflect on as his final day blazed toward its finale. It had seemed so very important to leave this place, this island, and return to his own world, even when it meant traversing an unknown reality to get there, but now he did wonder. What if he had convinced himself he was running towards something so he wouldn't have to face the uncomfortable fact that he was actually running *away* from something? What if, in some dark recess of his mind, he was fleeing from the person he was supposed to be. He closed his eyes heavily. There was some truth in that, he could feel it. Maybe his destiny was here, and as agonizing as the prospect was of losing his former life, *this* was what he was meant to be. That was it. *That* was the truth that his mind was resisting. He had been running from that prospect since they first arrived on the island, but here at the end, it seemed so vividly clear.

Cyrus opened his eyes again, a strange sense of purpose washing over him. This knowledge did nothing to help his current situation, but perhaps it didn't need to. Perhaps it was enough simply knowing one's self at the close.

Nel laughed; a flirtatious, carefree type of noise that danced across the field and made Cyrus cringe. As he glared at her, she brushed a hand against Magnus's arm the same way she used to do with Alec, then ran it up to his face in an incredibly familiar way. Revolted at watching how shameless she could be, Cyrus allowed his gaze to land on the Alchemist instead. He sat on a bit of debris slightly removed from his companions; his disfigured face hung low as he stared at the ground. Cyrus was struck once again by this man's lack of enthusiasm for the mission at hand. Perhaps it was a weak spot in the group that could be exploited. As he watched, however, the Alchemist raised his head, noticed Cyrus's gaze, and glared back at him with such perceptible venom that his former thoughts vanished. In fairness, Cyrus had knocked the man unconscious just last night.

With the sun now screaming across the open field, dawn was now in full force, and Kysaar Magnus turned to face Cyrus.

"Well here we are, King Dorn," Magnus exclaimed, extending his arms outward. He started approaching, slow and deliberate, relishing his power. "This isn't how I wanted things to play out, but you forced my hand. Truthfully, there's not much your miserable band of loyalists can do even if they did somehow get here in time. I'm sorely tempted to let you live until then; let them watch you die with their own eyes. What d'ya think?"

The prospect of postponing the execution, however briefly, made Cyrus's heart leap just slightly. At the very least, it would allow time for further possibilities to present themselves, but as Magnus stared at him with raised eyebrows, he understood that he was simply being toyed with. Magnus was hoping for him to beg for his life and was excited at the opportunity to deny it. So Cyrus remained silent.

"Ehh," Magnus said finally, acting as though he were only now reconsidering his proposal, "I think not. Seeing your body will just have to do."

Nel, the Alchemist, and the Neodactyl all followed in Magnus's wake, each with their own brand of hunger in their eyes. Cyrus was forcibly reminded of a pack of jackals descending on an injured gazelle.

The Alchemist produced a length of rope and handed it to Magnus.

"My dear," Magnus drawled, turning to Nel, "if I were to ask you to personally carry out the execution of your former companion, would you accept?"

Nel looked positively ravenous in her response. "I would be honored."

Magnus smiled broadly. "Inspiring. But alas, I have a different task for you. I want you near the treeline, ready to sound the alarm should any of his loyalists attempt to stop us." When Nel looked mildly disappointed, Magnus continued, "Chin up, my dear. You've proven your loyalty and demonstrated your passion for my reign. I don't doubt your hatred for this man, but I fear seeing his demise up close could prove challenging, even for you."

Nel bowed slightly.

"That's my girl," Magnus growled with a smirk. "Would you like to say goodbye?"

Cyrus was disgusted by the entire display. Magnus looked positively gleeful as he paraded Cyrus's impending death before his own eyes. He almost appeared to be stalling the act, squeezing out every drop of misery he could. Cyrus didn't plan to give him the satisfaction.

Nel walked forward, a horrible smirk on her lips and pure hatred behind her eyes.

"I suppose this is it, Doc," Nel said silkily, adopting the mocking title she used to call him by when they first joined the expedition together. "I wish words could do justice for just how much I despise you. You led our expedition to ruin, then had the audacity to name yourself a king. You were always arrogant, but then you became truly insufferable. You couldn't stand Alec making something of himself so you rose up to stop him. It will end up being your undoing." Nel was quite close now, bent to look him in the eyes. "You remember what I said to you on that hillside? When we first came to this place? I told you to back down and find happiness playing second fiddle." She grinned. "I'll bet you wish you had listened to me now, eh?"

Cyrus hadn't planned to respond to any of them, but having Nel distort the past in such hideous fashion was more than he could bear.

"And what will your undoing be, Nel?" Cyrus snarled, "because the way you move through kings…"

Wham!

Nel hit him across the face. He wouldn't have guessed she still had a nerve to hit, but it seemed he was wrong. Nel looked murderous. She crouched in front of him and grasped his hands in her own.

"I want you to remember my face," Nel hissed, "remember that it was me who put you in the ground. Because you could have made it here, if only you'd learned to adapt. But no, not the *great* Cyrus Dorn. Goodbye Doc, I will make sure you're forgotten."

Nel dropped his hands and stood up, smirking down at him in self-satisfaction. But something was different. An object was now in Cyrus's hand that hadn't been there before. As Nel patted Magnus on the shoulder and began her retreat to the treeline, Cyrus felt at the object with his fingers, trying to figure out what it was. He turned it over and suddenly knew. The object he held in his hand was the pendant, *Magnus's* pendant. A quick glance at the man's neck proved the absence of the chain, and he hadn't yet noticed.

As Magnus ordered the Alchemist to untie Cyrus, his mind reeled. He looked after Nel, walking confidently away from the group, and realized she must have snuck it off him while she was stroking his arm. He then looked at the Neodactyl, still staring at him hungrily… but no, not hungrily, *expectantly*. Cyrus, not Magnus, was now in control of the Neodactyl. And Magnus had no idea.

The Alchemist pulled Cyrus roughly to his feet and presented him to Magnus. The Neodactyl hissed just slightly but did nothing. They were emotional creatures after all, and while Cyrus was calm, it remained calm. Magnus pushed Cyrus ahead, forcing him onward towards the newly constructed gallows, and the creature followed. Of course Magnus hadn't noticed the change in the creature's loyalty, how would he? While in a group, the Neodactyl was passive in the presence of its master. Cyrus glanced again at Nel's back, now fifty feet away, and was suddenly struck by the brilliance of her plan. Nelida Yore may yet save them all.

Magnus gave Cyrus another forceful shove and the Neodactyl hissed more angrily at the aggression. The façade would not hold up for long; it was time to test the power this pendant held.

With the gallows now looming only several paces away, Magnus shoved Cyrus again and, praying his desperate theory would hold true, this time Cyrus allowed himself to fall. His palms slammed into the rocky earth and Magnus laughed, but Cyrus had gripped a small stone in the process. As Magnus bent to pull him upright, Cyrus spun wildly and struck him across the face, the stone connecting firmly with his cheekbone. But Magnus had been ready for the attack and easily wrestled the weapon from his grip, flinging it off into the field. He then lashed out and grabbed Cyrus by the throat.

He pulled him close and growled, "I hope that was worth it. Your final act of defiance."

Magnus was barreled off his feet, his body disappearing entirely as the Neodactyl tore into him with slashing talons. He screamed in agony as blood sprayed into the air, his limbs flailing madly in every direction. The Alchemist attempted to draw a machete from his belt but Cyrus sprinted towards him like a charging silverback and tackled him around the midsection. As he fell, the weapon skittered away across the ground and Cyrus punched him hard in the face. Nel was racing back towards the action but she still had fifty feet yet to go.

A whelping noise came from behind, and Cyrus turned to find Magnus having buried a small knife into the Neodactyls brilliant plumage. It hissed furiously and coiled its neck in defense, but it was clear the injury was bad. The same was also true of Magnus, however. His robes were shredded and almost entirely covered in deep scarlet. Blood drenched his face and one of his arms looked almost entirely unusable. Kysaar Magnus was a big man, however, and even though his knife was still embedded in the side of the Neodactyl, he was not backing down and now appeared determined to fight the creature with just his bare hands. He hunched low like a brawler and the Neodactyl screeched threateningly.

Cyrus saw the two slam into each other but a blinding pain in the side of his face drew his attention away. The Alchemist was back on his feet and intent on finishing Cyrus himself.

"CYRUS RUN!" Nel's voice echoed across the field and Cyrus's blood chilled. He didn't know what was more alarming; her unprecedented use of his real name or the tone in which she screamed.

Under the impression they had the upper hand in the ensuing chaos, Cyrus wheeled around in terror and immediately saw the reason for her panic. Magnus had broken free of the Neodactyl's slicing talons and was sprinting back in the direction they had come. He was going for the tridents and once he had retrieved them, nothing would be able to stop him from reigning terror down on the entirety of the Fire Fields. The

Neodactyl had given chase, but it would never be able to stop him in time.

Cyrus looked at Nel, her face pale and her eyes wide, and they both began to run. Cyrus was leaping deftly over every bit of shrapnel and debris in his path. He was confident he had never run so fast in his entire life, but it wouldn't be enough. They hadn't gotten more than fifteen feet before a deep, roaring vibration began to fill their ears from behind and a quick glance over his shoulder showed Magnus holding both tridents aloft and a positive hurricane of brilliant flame rising up around him. The Neodactyl was still attempting to find a weak point but Magnus's power with his weapons in hand was unparalleled. Cyrus whistled and the creature abandoned its attack and turned to flee.

Nel and Cyrus were within twenty feet of the treeline when the firestorm began to engulf their path ahead. Cyrus felt the heat splashing against his face and the embers biting against his clothes. Ten feet from the treeline and the pain became unbearable. A shriek from behind made Cyrus turn and the Neodactyl, still fleeing after them, was suddenly consumed by fire. There was no outrunning this. As Cyrus gasped and choked, he realized he couldn't see a thing ahead and he was running blind, likely towards his own death. He put on a fresh burst of speed all the same, closed his eyes against the pain, and pushed on.

He was smacked in the face by something hard but pliable and he winced as he buckled forward and smashed into the mercifully soft earth. He opened his stinging eyes to find he had made it through the inferno and reached the forest, but his pant leg was on fire and beginning to melt into his skin. Nel was on him before he had time to react, batting at the flames with her own hands. She scooped cool dirt from the earth and began shoveling it over his leg until the fire was finally stifled. Cyrus rolled over and looked out at the Fire Field, almost entirely obscured by deep black smoke at this point. He had thought the Neodactyl might have managed to survive and would come bounding out after them, but all was silent. It must have fallen prey to Magnus's wrath after all. It felt strange to feel pity for an animal that, until several minutes ago, had been an enemy of his, but maybe that was just it; creatures didn't take sides, they followed the orders of those that trained them.

Cyrus shook his head and turned to Nel. She was bloody, burnt, covered in ash from head to toe, and grimacing slightly against the pain… but she was smiling. Cyrus had never understood Nel, and he found that to be doubly so now. For every incomprehensibly bad decision she had made, for every time she had stabbed him in the back and betrayed him, she had without a doubt just saved his life.

Explanations would need to be provided and questions would need answering, but for now, Cyrus Dorn and Nelida Yore, the most unlikely pair on the island, got slowly to their feet and began to limp deeper into the forest, beginning the long and arduous trek back to camp.

CHAPTER THIRTY–NINE

THE HOST NEVER SURVIVES

I f Kat had been expecting they would simply walk down the road and speak with this mystery man that Nick insisted could provide the answers they sought, she was painfully disappointed. Nick had a way of drawing out a task that was as infuriating as it was unnecessary. He had agreed to help, but he still possessed a blatant lack of concern over whether they succeeded in their mission or not and he wasn't shy about shrugging off such petty annoyances as time delays. In fairness, a rainstorm had descended upon town square within half an hour of their tavern fight, but Kat still wondered how necessary it was to seek refuge indoors until it passed. Nick insisted it was the wisest choice, but upon entering an inn for the night, he proceeded to drown himself once again with copious amounts of ale, to the point that Kat wondered if this were his only true reason for delaying their departure. Once the sun had set, however, there remained no more reason to argue the point, so Dean and Kat settled reluctantly into a table across from Nick in the dining area of the inn.

It was a small place that thankfully served food and, as Nick noted before entering the establishment, drink. As with every place within the Kingdom, the interior was lit with pleasantly dancing candles and torches giving it a cozy feel that contrasted heavily with the dangers of the rest of the island. Unlike the tavern, there did not seem to be gangs of militants patrolling the inn, which Nick explained was due to the dining area and bar being reserved for guests with rooms booked for the night. Nick was able to arrange this with pieces of gold he had lifted from the dead assailants of earlier. The rest jangled around in a small satchel he had also procured from their victims, which now hung across the back of his chair alongside his ornate broadsword. Nick was a bit of an enigma, if Kat were being honest with herself. Where he came across as bullish and angry when they had first met, away from the constraints of kings and legends and responsibility, he was actually quick to laugh and eager to regale them with tales from his life. Arrogant he most definitely was, but there was an easy charm behind the bravado that was strangely endearing. Even so, Kat couldn't dismiss the obvious fact that Nick was only in it for himself and nothing he ever did was for the greater good. If he was helping them now, it was because he saw some benefit for himself. Kat didn't have a problem with that; they could use each other until they both achieved their goals.

As Nick finished a story of fighting for his country, though he had left out which country that actually was, Kat just smiled and shook her head. Nick noticed the response and furrowed his brow.

"What's funny?" he asked.

Kat shrugged. "I… just can't imagine being so willing to leave your entire life behind. There's really nothing you want to go back to?"

Nick smirked. "What's to miss? Being hunted by the authorities day in and day out? Sleeping in rat-infested holes in the wall hoping for a big break? Oh, or maybe it's having your closest friend shoot you in the chest just to really fuck up your day? I have no place back there. I have no place anywhere."

It wasn't lost on Kat that Nick thought himself the victim in every one of his stories, but she kept this to herself. "Doesn't this place, I don't know, change your perspective a bit?" Kat pushed. "I mean, we're talking about alternate realities, foreign worlds, despots and kings. You're an adventurer, aren't you at least having a little bit of fun?"

Nick laughed. "You're something else, ya know that? You almost got murdered in the street not two hours ago and you're having fun?"

"It was terrifying, of course," Kat agreed softly, "but I don't know. I've never been on a real adventure before. I've never felt my blood pump like that."

Dean looked aghast at her admission but Nick grinned. "Makes you feel alive, doesn't it? Yeah that's how it starts. Before long you're seeking it. It's how you *feel* the world."

"I'm not looking for trouble," Kat backtracked, "I just mean maybe you shouldn't piss your life away so willingly. You're seeing things that most of humanity will never get to see, no matter what reality they're from. That has to mean something."

"Sure it does," Nick nodded, "it means that it's all pointless. We fight tooth and nail for our own tiny scrap of the world only to find out that our actions don't really mean anything. If I screw up in this world, there are endless others to make different choices in. If realities truly are infinite, it means there's just as many versions of myself out there saving their worlds as ruining them. So what's the point? If there's a heaven or hell out there waiting for each of us, you really think they're going to begrudge me drinking myself into an early grave in this reality? For that matter, which version of me is getting judged at the pearly gates? Nah, those are all just bedtime stories to make us behave. Do right in this world and your soul will be saved in the next. But whoever wrote those bedtime stories never saw behind the curtain like we have. Embrace what you've learned, Kat; you've been given a free pass to live however you want."

Kat couldn't tell if she bought Nick's defeatist persona or not. *He* wanted to believe what he was saying, but she wasn't sure he entirely did. "That may all be true," Kat responded, "but I still choose to live with morality. And no matter what's happening in other realities in far off places, I can still care for the people I see before me. I can't change what's happening in worlds across time and space, but I *can* change what happens to Annica and Jack, Dean and Cyrus... even you. These are people I can help, here and now, so that's what I'm going to do."

Nick smirked. He emptied the last of his mug and slumped backwards heavily into his chair. His eyes looked unfocused but she suspected this wasn't solely because of the alcohol. "That's a young answer..." he finally replied, his voice deep with contemplation, "but maybe there is some truth in it."

*****

Nick woke both Dean and Kat surprisingly early the next morning considering how much he had drunk. The sun, weak as it was through the heavy opaque fog blanketing the damp streets, had just begun to rise on the new day. Nick explained this was the safest time to travel as most of the militants would still be sleeping off their revelries of the night prior. Sure enough, the formerly boisterous town was now silent as the grave with only the empty drinking vessels, occasional spatter of blood or the odd puddle of vomit as reminders of the prior night's frivolities. It was eerie in its quiet, but Kat vastly preferred it this way.

They moved quickly, creeping along the road without speaking, avoiding the larger pools of gathered rainwater as they went. Every sound seemed to echo in the still air, inviting the eyes of anyone willing to gaze out a window, but they went uninterrupted. The town was deceptively large given the cramped, claustrophobic quality of the winding streets and it took them a good ten minutes to arrive near the outskirts. The edge of town proper and the end of the designated neutral zone was not hard to identify as not a single building extended beyond a certain point. It was as though an invisible line had been drawn separating the communal safe space from the wilds of the rest of the island. In the morning's fog, the area beyond the last structure on the road was incredibly ominous and uninviting; sparse and desolate with several lone trees as barren as skeletons cutting through the white curtain with their spindly silhouettes. Kat thought of old maps and how they would inevitably end abruptly where the last of the known world had been drawn in. The idea made her shiver just slightly.

"Don't worry," Nick answered before she could ask if this was the path to their destination, "we're here."

Nick had stopped at one of the very last buildings at the edge of town; a run-down sandy-beige home nearly identical to all the rest. He eased up to the wooden door and gently gave it several soft taps. Unsurprisingly, nobody stirred within. Nick seemed to consider this in frustration for just a moment before he shook his head and rapped loudly with his fist. A sudden commotion could be heard behind the door involving a loud scraping noise, a dull thud, and quite a bit of swearing. But these were not the only sounds violating the silent morning air. It seemed people all up and down the street had been disturbed by the knocking, for the road was suddenly alive with coughing and groaning from inside the many homes. As Nick looked around uneasily, the door before them opened just a crack and a small, sleepy eyeball peered out at them. Nick, not waiting for an invitation, forced his way through the door, pushing the hidden occupant aside as he went.

"Get the hell outta the way, Lee," Nick snarled as he entered the dark interior, pulling Dean and Kat with him, "think I wanna be standing out there exposed?"

"Nick?" the man grunted in confusion, shutting the door swiftly behind them.

"Light a torch, will ya," Nick demanded as though he hadn't just woken the man from his slumber.

The man did as he was told and the miniscule room was soon glowing with brilliant orange firelight. He was a middle-aged man with frayed greying hair, a chiseled angular face and a right leg that ended in a wooden stump. He looked tired beyond all reason, and Kat could tell it had little to do with Nick's rude awakening.

"What are you doing here?" the man grumbled, "it's the middle of the night. If you've got my money, it could've waited til..."

"Wrong, it's a new day," Nick answered, peaking out through the shuttered window, "and you can keep dreaming about your money." The man rolled his eyes at this. "Brought some people who want to talk to you."

"This couldn't wait?" the man asked, rubbing at his eyes groggily.

"Dean, Kat," Nick gestured, "this is Leonysis, a brawler, a drunk, and a piss poor gambler. He also happens to be a fellow world traveler if you take my meaning."

Kat shook her head. "I really don't."

Nick sighed in exasperation. "He's not from here, just like you and I. He came to this world through a portal like we did."

Kat was failing to see the relevance. "I'm sure plenty of people aren't from here," she said dryly, "in fact, I'm starting to think everyone fell through one portal or another."

"Sure," Nick agreed, "the difference with Lee is, he helped create the portal that brought him here."

Kat paused. She looked at Dean who seemed just as shocked.

"What do you mean you helped create it?" Kat asked, now turning her full attention to Lee.

Lee looked down at his feet. "I came from another world…" he admitted slowly, "in the company of Magnus and Kalanoma."

"Kalanoma?" Dean asked.

"You might know him as the Alchemist," Lee explained, "we traversed countless realities together, the three of us. Always searching for that tantalizing perfect world."

"Perfect world?" Kat questioned, "what do you mean?"

Lee shrugged and eased himself against the wall. "It's a dream, a fantasy. If there's endless realities out there, the opportunities are endless. We thought we could keep trying, keep learning from our mistakes, keep experimenting until we finally found ourselves on top."

"I don't understand," Kat pushed.

Lee closed his eyes as though he were in pain. "Magnus had dreams of total domination, and I'll admit it was a tempting idea. The world I came from was broken, had been for a long time. When Magnus invaded my reality, it didn't seem so bad to me. Sure he was brutal, but if you could look past your morals just a bit… I tell ya, I could really see a future for myself. So I joined him. Joined him on his search for his perfect world."

"What was wrong with all the worlds you passed through?" Dean asked.

Lee laughed but it held no humor. "I didn't know at first. I mean, why couldn't we get it right? Even with an increasingly heavy fist, these worlds just shook us off. And I tell ya, we weren't afraid of tightening our grip, but every world ended in ruin."

"Just like this one," Kat nodded.

"Just like this one," Lee agreed. "You see, we decided we needed to find a world that would bend when we applied pressure… bend, but not break. Magnus became obsessed with the idea that the key was Cyrus Dorn. He was this king from a long time ago who willingly exiled himself to save his people."

"We've heard of him," Kat answered softly.

"Well Magnus began hearing rumors of a reality where Cyrus actually returned after his exile. He had this notion that such a legendary ruler could be used to control the hearts and minds of the people."

"Why would that help him?" Dean asked.

"Well you see, the trouble we kept encountering wasn't rebellion. It was just the good old-fashioned collapse of society. And that's where I began to question what we were doing. Being conquerors was exciting, but the problem wasn't the worlds… it was *him*. It was Magnus. He's a disease on any world he touches. He knows nothing of ruling, only of taking. But every reality has limited resources."

Silence hung, stifling and uncomfortable, for just a moment.

"Wait but how is he doing it?" Dean asked. "I mean, I think we can all agree that what Magnus has done is despicable, but how is he able to jump from world to world willingly?"

"Kalanoma… er, the Alchemist is the one that figured it out," Lee answered, "he built Magnus his tridents. I'm not sure if you've gotten a good look at those things, but they really are a marvel. Hewn from the fragments of each of our conquered worlds."

"They're made of the scepters, right?" Kat asked.

"That's right," Lee said with a nod, "it was the Alchemist that worked out a way of channeling the raw power of the scepters into a useable instrument. The catch is, you need a fragment of scepter from the reality you wish to travel to. Not easy to obtain, as you can imagine."

"Wait," Kat said, "you need to enter another reality in order to… enter another reality? How does that make sense?"

"It doesn't," Lee admitted, "or it shouldn't. There are ways of speaking with people from alternate realities, they call it opening a *window*, maybe you've heard of it. The Alchemist has been using that ability to persuade other worlds to grant us access. Once he's able to reach through that window and procure a fragment from that other world, he melts it into Magnus's tridents and adds it to our collection of worlds we can traverse. Does that make sense?"

Both Kat and Dean shook their heads slowly.

"It doesn't have to," Lee said supportively, "you don't need to understand the specifics. What you need to know is that Magnus's tridents are made up of countless fragments of scepter from other worlds. If you want to journey to a different reality, you need to have a piece of scepter from that reality. Melt it into the trident, touch the two together on that point, and voila, you've opened your very own door."

When Dean and Kat looked skeptical, he shrugged.

"I wish I had more to offer you, I really do. Perhaps this knowledge can provide you with a way home. I don't have a way of defeating him, but I can tell you this; he's not all-powerful. He's a man, just like anyone else. But if he's come to your world, I fear it's doomed to the same fate as this one. I was banished for disagreeing with him, left behind to watch our most recent conquest collapse around me." His eyes rose to the ceiling, flitting around as though he could see beyond the crumbling walls to the sky above. "And collapsed it has. You see, the most successful disease is the one that leaves its host intact, allowing it to multiply and spread and take over. The less successful diseases decimate their victims to the bone, leaving no more fertile ground to conquer. These diseases need to abandon their hosts in a hurry, lest they're dragged with them to the grave. Kysaar Magnus is this sort of disease, and once he's embedded himself in a world… well let's just say the host never survives."

Lee's words were incredibly ominous, but strangely, Kat only felt a fresh surge of resolve at hearing them.

"Our world *will* survive," she stated defiantly.

"Kat," Dean began, his voice full of pity, "I know you've come to care for these people, but you can't save everyone. I mean, we're not here to join a rebellion, we were brought to this world against our will. This knowledge, that could be our ticket home."

"At what cost?" Kat protested in exasperation, "I mean, knowing everything we know now, about Cyrus and Annica and the war for the Kingdom, doesn't that change things for you? Can you really just go back to your classroom and close your eyes to it all?"

Dean looked exceedingly guilty as he slowly shrugged his shoulders. "It's not our war, Kat. You're just a kid… maybe you don't need to be concerning yourself with such things. If we can find a way to get home, maybe closing your eyes to what you've seen isn't such a bad thing."

Nick and Lee were studying the exchange in silence, their expressions entirely masking their thoughts on the topic.

"I don't know how you can say that," Kat retorted with a shake of her head, "our people are…"

"But they're *not* our people!" Dean finally snapped. "This isn't our world. I need you to see that. I'm sorry I brought you into this, you have no idea, but I have a responsibility to bring you back. You're young, idealistic, and I get it. It's only natural to feel for these people and their plight, but this isn't your problem to solve. You're not seeing things clearly." He turned to their silent audience and pleaded, "Nick, help me out here."

Nick looked stricken at being asked to weigh in. He bowed his head and nodded. "Actually," he began slowly, "I think Kat is seeing things more clearly than any of us."

"Oh come on!" Dean spat, "You have no loyalty to anyone, this can't be how you want to spend the rest of your days. It's survival for these people every hour of every day. You think this started with Magnus? Have you two even been listening? Cyrus Dorn's Kingdom is a kingdom at war, it always has been. These people don't know how to live beyond scrambling for petty freedoms that our world offers easily. All I want is to take you back there."

Kat found herself rather disgusted with Dean at the moment. She knew his words came from a place of fear, but she still found them difficult to excuse. "That's not what I've seen," she answered softly. "What I've seen is a resilience of spirit, even in the face of oppression. I've seen people living real lives even as their world threatens to crumble. I've seen people refusing to be cowed into submission even when all hope seems lost. *That's* what Cyrus Dorn did. And I'll be damned if I close my eyes to that. Mr. Pyrene... Dean, this is where you decide who you're going to be, because you don't have to be a fighter to be a warrior."

Dean looked stunned into silence. Nick had raised his eyebrows and a grin was spreading across his face.

"I don't know how I ever left you two," Nick said in amusement, "you're just way too much fun. And D-Man I've just gotta say, your protégé here..."

Dean held up his hand and Nick went silent. He looked tortured in his expression, eyes winced against the sting of her rebuke. Nobody spoke for a long time.

"I hear you," Dean finally said. "I'm not used to this, you know. I have a routine; I teach, I go home, I read... hell I thought I was practically a different person when I flew to the Museum of Antiquities in London. Getting on a plane to visit a museum, *that's* an adventure for me. This? I'm so far out of my element here I can't even stop my head from spinning."

"Nobody's asking you to be a hero," Kat insisted softly, attempting to remove the previous harshness from her voice, "but we can't be cowards either. I'm not letting us turn our backs on this."

Dean seemed entirely stunned into silence. He gave a jerky nod that wasn't quite a commitment but at least showed he didn't intend to argue any further.

Kat just nodded back, but her blood was still pumping uncomfortably fast. It was like the adrenaline from her impassioned speech was still coursing through her body, sending tremors through her arms and legs and into the ground and walls around her... except the vibrations in the walls didn't stop. Small bits of dust were dislodging from the tattered corners and softly cascading down to the floor. She looked at Nick and Lee who suddenly appeared alarmed. There was a definite tremble running through the earth below and if she didn't know any better, it was getting stronger. No, not getting stronger, getting *closer*. Something was approaching on the street outside and if she had to guess, it had wheels.

Nick ran to the shuttered window and brought his face close, peering out. Kat couldn't see what he saw, but his expression filled her with dread.

"What is it?" Kat whispered breathlessly.

In response, a spine-tingling screech cut through the morning air from just beyond the door.

CHAPTER FORTY

ENEMIES AND ALLIES

What did he really want to happen here? As much as Alec wracked his brain for an answer, he kept coming up frustratingly short. For the life of him, he couldn't decide what outcome would best suit his position in the Kingdom. Midday had come and gone and, despite Annica and Jack scrambling for hours to ready a rescue mission to free Cyrus from the clutches of Kysaar Magnus, the team had yet to begin the journey. Alec had a suspicion their window for success had already come and gone, which possibly meant his brother was already dead. This was another prospect Alec wasn't sure how to feel about. Cyrus Dorn was his sworn enemy and easily the most problematic obstacle in his ascension back to power, but it would be a lie if he said there wasn't something uncomfortably final about the thought of him being truly gone. Cyrus had been pushing against him since their arrival here and, in a way, that had given Alec the permission he needed to seize his destiny in such spectacular fashion. He doubted very much that he would have found the resolve to rule if he hadn't had an equal rising up in opposition. His brother made him who he was and his absence would leave a hole. That being said, Alec would never be able to seize power in the Kingdom again while Cyrus was around.

Jack nudged by him rather roughly, pulling Alec away from his thoughts. He was carrying an assortment of weapons and shot a withering look as he passed. Alec was not welcome here in camp, that much was clear, but he was also not welcome to leave. It was another one of those strange dynamics where Alec was not quite a prisoner but far from a free man. As Jack dropped the arsenal into a steadily growing pile, he again turned to Alec with perceptible fire in his eyes.

"Something to say, Jack?" Alec hissed, "perhaps you should look around at the state of your Kingdom before you look down at me." Of course they were on opposing sides, but Alec was getting tired of his treatment as a second-tier citizen. After all, even in kingdoms of ancient times, opposing rulers were still spoken to with respect, even fear where warranted. It seemed to him his desperation upon entering camp this morning was giving everyone the false impression that he had lost his teeth.

Jack studied him for a moment, apparently taken aback by the question. "Bold as ever, eh Alec?" He paused a second before continuing, seemingly having an internal debate as to the benefit of the conversation. "Ya know, he'll never admit it, possibly doesn't even know it himself, but your brother's still waiting on some level for you to snap out of this. Give up your bid for power and return to the man you were. Find your way back. But he doesn't get it... too close to see things clearly. But *I* see things clearly, and you wanna know what I see? I see a man who's not lost at all. You left the path intentionally in favor of the shadows. So I'm not buying this desperation display; if you've come here on your knees, it's because you have something to gain." Jack shook his head in disgust. "Good thing your brother can't be let down any further by you."

"You're right," Alec snarled back, "his days of righteous disappointment are numbered if not over already. His light is fading as fast as it ignited, and soon his memory will be just that... forgotten in the past. And you're letting that happen without much of a fight."

Jack cocked his eyebrows and waved his arms at the surrounding preparations for war. "We're doing exactly what you wanted us to. We're racing towards a rescue mission despite deep reservations about the source of this intel. But sure, I'll bet you'd love to see us charge forward unprepared and fall into whatever trap Magnus has set."

"I'm telling you," Alec insisted, "Cyrus's time is dwindling faster than you can possibly imagine."

"And why would you care?" Jack demanded, finally taking several paces forward and bringing his face close to Alec's. "That's where I'm having some trouble because last I checked, your most desperate desire was to supplant Cyrus Dorn as leader of this kingdom. If Magnus is well on his way to making that a reality, why come to us to stop it?"

Alec was struggling with this himself. Would it not be best to leave his brother to his well-deserved fate and deal with the fallout in the Kingdom after? Why was he having so much trouble with this?

"I didn't leave Cyrus to die," Alec spat, "whatever he has coming to him, Kysaar Magnus doesn't deserve the satisfaction of ending my brother's life. *We* started this. *We* as a group. You, me, Cyrus, Nel, Dalton... but Magnus isn't one of us. If you don't want my help, fine, I'll consider myself dismissed. But I'm telling you the truth and it has nothing to do with Cyrus's wellbeing. It means nothing to me if he dies, but it *does* mean something if Magnus wins." Alec blinked and stepped back a pace after his speech, trying to deduce for himself if his words were true.

Jack nodded his head thoughtfully. "Now that's something I can actually believe."

"So can I," came a voice from behind them.

Alec turned and his jaw dropped. Cyrus was striding into camp with a wry smile on his face and a shallow limp. His clothes were scorched and melted and he looked even more bloodied than when Alec had departed, but people along the path were gasping in awe all the same at the sight of him.

"Cyrus," Jack exclaimed, staggering towards him in shock and taking in his numerous injuries. He patted Cyrus's arm with a shake of his head and Cyrus pulled him into a hug. Alec looked away. His eyes scanned the mindless and excitable throng of townsfolk descending on their one-time leader when they fell upon Cyrus's companion. Covered in soot and dried blood, she was almost unrecognizable, but her unblinking gaze was an easy giveaway. Nel smiled almost sheepishly at Alec and all the color drained from his face.

"What the hell is she doing here?!" Alec roared.

Jack suddenly seemed to notice her presence as well and appeared to have the same question. The crowd was suddenly alive with angry buzzing and hushed accusations. Ydoro and Noma had made their way to the front and their beaming smiles at Cyrus's return instantly soured. Nel seemed to shrink just slightly as she studied the mob with unease but suddenly a loud click brought silence to the scene. Annica had appeared behind Nel and cocked a bolt launcher aimed directly at the back of her skull.

Cyrus raised his hands. "Okay stop, everyone!" he declared. "I need you all to listen to me very carefully."

When Annica did not drop her hand, Cyrus approached her slowly and placed his own on top of hers. "I have to insist Annica," he whispered. It was gentle, even fatherly, but laced with authority. Despite whatever the dynamic between the past and current ruler was, this was a command. Annica nodded her head just slightly and holstered her weapon.

Cyrus turned to the group, looked as though he were about to speak, but then laughed slightly to himself before beginning. "I realize how confusing this all is, with changing loyalties and survival on the line." He paused for a moment, searching for the right words. "Nel saved my life. There's no other way of saying it." Excitable murmurs spread rapidly around the camp. Alec's chest tightened just a bit. "I would not be here before you if Nel hadn't acted. We've been enemies before… hell, we're still enemies now, but she risked her own life to save mine."

Alec's heart was hammering in such a way that his vision was blurring with every beat. He could feel his hands shaking and his jaw clench shut. What was happening here? Nel was still staring at him but her expression was shifting from embarrassment to confusion. Her brow furrowed as she studied Alec from over Cyrus's shoulder. She shook her head silently as if to ask Alec what was wrong.

"The same goes for Alec," Cyrus continued, "he didn't leave me behind. We escaped together, *worked* together. And if him and I can do that, everyone can." Cyrus paused, scanning what seemed to be every single face in attendance. His gaze lingered when it landed on Alec. "The truth of it is, we're up against something bigger than any of us. Nel understands that, and given my brother's presence here today, so does he. We can't continue to squabble over who leads this kingdom because very soon there won't be any kingdom left to lead. The situation *is* that dire and Kysaar Magnus *is* that dangerous, but I have a promise for you..." It seemed the entire crowd collectively held its breath to hear. Cyrus nodded his head in satisfaction and grinned. "He's not long for this world."

The crowd erupted in cheers and applause. Alec looked around in mild disgust. How dare his brother show up here with Nel in tow, flaunting her newly bought loyalty and using Alec's name as a spark to rally his people. That familiar white-hot serpent uncoiled painfully in his gut.

As Cyrus's people surged forward to congratulate themselves on their newly-promised but entirely unearned victory, Nel worked her way through the crowd to face Alec. She looked taken aback by his cold reception and rather than tread lightly with him, she squinted her eyes suspiciously and demanded, "What?"

"You betrayed me," Alec spat. All hope of rational thought was out the window now that he was this close to her. He *knew* her presence here meant the treachery with Magnus had been a ruse and he *knew* she had done it for the good of them all, and yet he couldn't let it go.

"I had no choice," Nel responded hotly, "if I hadn't pretended to turn on you, we would've both ended up in chains. It was our only chance."

"Or maybe you saw an opportunity for yourself you couldn't pass up," Alec snarled.

"Then why would I be here now?" Nel demanded, "if I wanted what Magnus had to offer, why would I have risked everything to free Cyrus?"

Alec shook his head in contempt. "Yeah, that is interesting that you'd risk it all for Cyrus but not me."

"*Cyrus* was going to be executed!" Nel practically screamed and their argument finally began to attract outside attention. "Would you rather I had let him die?"

Again, Alec didn't know the answer to this question. He felt ill… and confused. He backed up a step and his gaze traveled over the crowd, most of whom were attempting to act like they weren't listening to the conversation. But then his eyes found Cyrus, whose attention was unabashedly fixated on the drama unfolding. His expression was that of deep thought and piercing observation, like a scientist studying the social dynamics of a foreign species. Alec loathed him in that moment, and Nel along with him.

Unable to play the game any longer, Alec turned and stalked away through the crowd. He had thought he had lost it all; his last ally and staunchest supporter, not to mention his one true friend. So now that he had it back, why was he so angry? Was his disgust at Nel justified? Perhaps she had acted just a bit too well during her theatrical betrayal. Perhaps he couldn't get over how familiar she had looked cozying up with Magnus. Both probably true, but no; what was truly unforgivable was the simple fact that she had returned here in the company of his brother.

CHAPTER FORTY-ONE

STANDOFF

S hit, shit, shit, shit," Nick began muttering as he pulled his face away from the tiny gap in the window boards. Kat instantly rushed to take his place, bringing her eyeball right up to the miniscule crack between pieces of wood. What she saw made her heart practically stop.

What looked like nothing short of an army had gathered in the street right outside Lee's door, but it wasn't the twenty-some people that were causing her panic. Amongst them were four battle-hardened chariots, each tethered to its own Neodactyl. While the beasts seemed well-trained, they also appeared mildly abused and extremely ill-tempered. Unlike the bird that Kat had seen in Alec's company, which remained calm in the presence of its master, these creatures were disciplined but at the same time violently wild... they were instruments of war. Three of the four animals looked quite similar in plumage and coloration, but the fourth stood out. It was larger than its companions by a couple feet and in place of the vibrant multicolored feathers, it was a sleek brown with mottled, indistinct striping along its back. Its head was larger as well with a bit of a horn jutting out from the top of its beak and its eyes, while still yellow, were splashed with flecks of deep maroon and angry red. Kat didn't need to be told; this was the female of the species.

From the chariot of the female stepped a man Kat recognized. He was the same pockmarked militant who had harassed them in the tavern upon their arrival. He looked far more clear-headed in the early morning hours but just as unpleasant. The scar that split his face appeared to practically glow in the harsh sunrise. He walked heavily forward; not quite a stagger but certainly a laborious gait, like his boots were too heavy to fully lift from the ground. He wore a hideously sharp machete on his belt and absent his intoxication from the day prior, he appeared as an incredibly imposing threat. He squared himself up with the wooden front door and pounded a fist roughly into its surface causing the entire panel to tremble. He then leaned forward so that his forehead was practically touching the outer door and his ragged breath could be heard from within. His female companion from the tavern cozied up next to him, cackling slightly with a toothy grin. The remaining mob stayed back, their hands each resting on a machete of their own.

"I told you we'd meet again," the scarred man growled through the door.

Lee looked wide-eyed at Nick who attempted to shake his head as though he didn't know what was going on.

"What the hell did you bring down on me?" Lee hissed in whispered panic.

Nick waved his hands like he couldn't be bothered with such questions at the moment, then planted himself on the inside of the door as a would-be brace.

"Uhhh, who is this?" Nick called in feigned confusion, but it was a weak attempt.

"You're not gonna talk your way out of this one," the man on the other side of the door roared. "King Tyka's never heard of you. Neither has King Noros."

Nick's eyes were darting back and forth, chasing futile possibilities for an escape. "Ummm… we're in the neutral territory, friend," Nick finally said, "I don't know what your beef is with me but…"

"You tore up the town last night," the man shouted, "you thought that wouldn't have consequences?"

"Uhhh…" Nick was barely able to hold the conversation while simultaneously scanning the room. His eyes finally widened and he pointed hastily behind Kat. "You town marshal now?" Nick called through the door distractedly. "Man of your talents? I would've pegged you as more of a… beast of burden type."

The insult was met with a powerful bang from the other side of the door. The brittle wood quaked but held true. Kat looked wildly around to see where Nick was pointing and her eyes fell on his newly acquired broadsword. She lifted it to Nick who nodded wordlessly and grasped out with his hand.

"Keep playing games," the man snarled, "once I have you in my grip, you're dead!"

Nick attempted placing the sword against the door as a brace, but this failed almost instantly. Instead, he pulled a small knife from his pocket and began working it in between the slats at the center of the rickety door. Kat had no idea what he was planning.

"I… I think you might have the wrong guy," Nick called, attempting a tone of innocence. He continued to feed the knife in and out between the boards of the door, twisting here and there. He seemed to be trying to widen the gap slightly. "Tell you what, why don't you go down the road, have a bit of breakfast, and we'll meet you in a bit to talk this out?"

Another loud bang against the door.

"Either you come out here or we're coming in!" the man yelled.

Nick pocketed his knife again and picked up the broadsword.

"Hmm, doesn't sound like there's any pleasing you," Nick called in an obnoxiously placating tone, "I'm gonna have to suggest we just go our separate ways."

He brought the sword to waist level, held it horizontal and fed the tip carefully through the gap in the door slats he had just widened. He twisted it back and forth carefully until the blade began to feed through easily.

Another bang rocked the door. Nick clutched the hilt of the sword.

"Okay I can tell you're in a mood and honestly, that's no time to make rational decisions," Nick called. "I'm not coming out so if you wanna talk… well you're just gonna have to bring that ugly stain you call a face in here and make me."

With that, the man launched himself full-bodied into the door and shattered the ancient wood straight off the hinges. His companion cackled as he made such easy work of the barricade, and her laughter was so exuberant that she at first didn't hear the gasping wheeze coming from her friend as his lung deflated. Nick's sword had run him straight through, directly between the boards of the door, into his gut and out the other side. The man's eyes bulged as he attempted to draw breath but all that he could manage was a horrible, high-pitched gurgling like a balloon being deflated underwater. The woman had finally realized something was wrong but couldn't seem to make sense of the fragments of door inexplicably clinging to her comrade's torso. It was only after a moment that her face dropped and she saw the sword glinting between the shrapnel, feeding through the man's abdomen and ending in Nick's unwavering hands. Her face twisted horribly and she bellowed in rage. Her hand went for the machete on her belt but Nick was quicker. He withdrew the sword from the scarred man's stomach and slashed out at the woman, cutting her deeply across the arm and chest. She recoiled and fell backwards into the street.

The rest of the small army had remained in the road during the exchange and were understandably confused about what had just transpired. It was only once their leader slumped to the ground, the remaining bits of door clattering down around him, that they seemed to get wise to the situation. Without hesitation, Nick grasped at the lantern that Lee had lit upon their arrival, a glass-encased oil burning device. His hand must have scorched horribly from touching it but he didn't show any pain. Instead, he launched the lamp like a grenade at one of the chariots, which instantly exploded into a raging fire.

"C'mon!" Nick yelled and he dove headlong out into the street. Kat and Dean followed, their machetes drawn but unsure how they would fare against such a large number of adversaries. The militants, however, were entirely distracted by the flaming chariot and quick turn of events.

They were so distracted, in fact, that they allowed Nick to leap onto the platform attached to the large female creature unincumbered. The Neodactyl shrieked and attempted to snap behind itself but the reigns and harness made that impossible. Dean and Kat scrambled aboard behind Nick, who grabbed the tethers and gave an authoritative whip. As the militants began to realize their lapse in judgement, the chariot lurched forward with the enraged Neodactyl launching into a sprint. Nick twirled his sword high over his head and, with a fluid slice, managed to cleave the head of one of their adversaries clean off.

Kat and Dean quickly gripped the metal handle as the chariot sped up and Nick leaned out over the back.

"Sorry about the door, Lee!" Nick called out, "I'll pay you back for it next time I'm in town!"

With that, he gave the reigns another whip and the chariot tore off down the street. Kat looked back and could see the remaining group scrambling, barking orders and devolving into chaos. Several of their number jumped aboard the two usable chariots while others attempted to stifle the flames on the third.

"They'll be coming!" Nick called over his shoulder as the Neodactyl flew around a corner with an angry screech. "Tell me where we're going!"

"Tell you?!" Kat yelled back, her hair flying around her face like it was caught in a storm. "Didn't you have a plan?"

"My plan was getting us out of there," Nick responded while giving the tethers another snap, "now your job is to get us back."

"Get us back where?" Dean asked.

"Back to Cyrus and your queen," Nick explained as the wheels below them skidded precariously on a loose bit of sand. "Find me your door, we're going home!"

CHAPTER FORTY–TWO

INDOMITABLE

C yrus was tired. Exhausted even. It was no real surprise, of course, after everything he had been through. But as he eased himself into a seated position against a large tree at the edge of camp, he found he couldn't quite quiet his mind either. A change of clothes and rinse off in a nearby stream had done wonders, but now he desperately needed to be alone with his thoughts. He felt as though he had barely caught his breath since returning to the Kingdom. Would this be the legacy he leaves behind? One of war and sacrifice, sweeping victories and crushing defeats? He had taken on the mantle of king not for this sort of glory, if one could call it that, but to show the people a better way. To show everyone that the true power lay with them, and always had. He led by inspiring, not fighting. And yet, the majority of his rule had been spent clashing with one enemy or another. The people saw him as a warrior so that's exactly what he ended up becoming for them. But it was sobering, debilitating, and above all exhausting.

"You can't solve all the world's problems on your own ya know."

Cyrus turned and saw Jack approaching, a bottle of brown liquid in his hand. He smiled broadly, despite his desire to be alone.

"I can try," Cyrus replied heavily as Jack eased himself into the dirt beside him. "Some of the most effective leaders in history didn't win conquests and battles and elections by reacting. They won by seeking the quiet and thinking. Thinking." Jack studied him but didn't say a word. "Magnus is a monster but he's just a man. I'm tired of reacting, Jack. He wins by keeping us desperate. By acting so boldly that our only course of action is to scramble. It means that we're constantly playing defense while he plots his next move."

Jack nodded his head. "It's not fair, is it. We do our best, build something real here, and then watch as it all gets torn down. After Mora, Irias... Alec... you'd think we'd have earned peace by now." His voice was downtrodden and morose, and he sounded just as tired as Cyrus felt. Then suddenly, he uncorked the bottle and shoved it into Cyrus's hand. "But ya know what," he continued with a sudden strength in his words, "we don't get to feel that way. We're leaders for a reason. They chose you just like they chose me. And that means we don't get to feel sorry for ourselves. Our personal ambitions, even happiness, are secondary to theirs. That's what it means to be a true leader. And you know that. It's what led you to leave the Kingdom in the first place, and it's what made you come back."

"It wasn't my actions that brought me back," Cyrus corrected him, "it was your fancy repair of the scepter that did that."

Jack shook his head. "That's *how* you came back, that's not why."

Cyrus thought a moment but couldn't come up with a response. "What would you have me do?"

Jack smiled. "Drink with me, for a start. Then help me think of a way through this."

Cyrus chuckled softly and took a swig. Whatever the liquor was, it burned at the back of his throat and popped his sinuses, not unlike the sensation of traveling through an anomaly. "I don't think I ever thanked you for bringing me back here."

"To this?" Jack laughed, "Your Kingdom at war, literally burning around you? I think you were better off where you were."

"I wasn't," Cyrus answered seriously and Jack dropped his smile. "I was in hell, Jack. Watching my life paraded before my eyes by my brother. Searching desperately for recognition in the gaze of my one-time wife and knowing that it was a stranger who stared back at me. Realizing deep down that I had turned my back on the one place that I truly belonged."

"I didn't know," Jack said softly.

"You saved me, Jack," Cyrus responded. "Whatever happens now, I can die knowing I'm the person I'm supposed to be."

He passed the bottle back to Jack. There was silence for a long time.

"So you're married now," Cyrus finally said and Jack laughed aloud.

"I am," he said with a shrug. "Sorry you couldn't make it. Your invitation must've gotten lost with the damn inter-dimensional post office or something."

Cyrus smiled. "But you're happy?"

"I am," Jack stated, "I saw an opportunity to carve a life out for myself and I took it. It's another world perhaps, but living is living. And I feel like I've lived."

Cyrus had spent so much of his own time fighting against that notion that he found it refreshing to see someone embrace it so entirely. Of course his own situation was slightly different.

"In my time in the alternate reality with Alec, he tried so hard to hurt me, to break me, but nothing stuck. It infuriated him to watch me go through the motions without cracking. He wanted to see me bleed but all I felt was numb." Cyrus closed his eyes, remembering his time in exile, then slowly opened them again. "There was one exception. One thing that truly hurt me, and it was nothing to do with Alec. We spoke to an old colleague in yet another reality, and she said something that still haunts me. She said that the Cynthia from her world never stopped looking for me. That she hired search parties and sent expeditions out in search of answers. That even as she moved on, she never gave up. How can I live my life knowing that *my* Cyntha never knew what happened out there on the ocean. That she spent her money, her time, and her life scouring the world for me without knowing that there were infinite worlds separating us. I can't just accept that. I'm torn in two because I know it was my own doubts that held me back from becoming the person I was meant to be in the Kingdom and now that I'm back, I can't help but make the same mistake again. Because it would mean giving up on her… giving up on someone who never gave up on me. How do I justify that?"

Jack looked down. Cyrus hadn't expected him to have an answer, and it was wildly unfair to dump this amount of hopelessness onto his shoulders.

"You justify it by accepting that you have a greater responsibility now," Jack finally replied. "You're not doing it for yourself, you're doing it for your people. They look to you to show them the way. So sit here, take your time, *think*; but don't you dare lose your conviction. Not now. Not after everything we've been through."

Jack was right, and Cyrus needed to hear it. He took a deep breath and nodded firmly. "No more self-pity," Cyrus agreed, "we find a way to reclaim what's ours."

"There we go," Jack urged. "So how do we gain the upper hand?"

"We need to assess what advantages we have," Cyrus said, "we have the numbers, that's a certainty."

Jack suddenly looked away from Cyrus, gazing down the trail leading out of camp and his jaw dropped just slightly. "That we do," he mumbled.

Cyrus turned to see what he was looking at and found himself staring at a band of about fifty people shuffling down the path in their direction. Some were limping, many were bloodied and burnt, but they looked angry rather than beaten.

Cyrus stood up and scowled in confusion. "Where did you come from?"

The foremost woman in the group, a palm pressed over a wound in her temple, smiled broadly. "The rumors are true! You've returned!" When Cyrus only stared blankly back at her, she explained, "We're Easttown, my King."

"Easttown?" Cyrus repeated. But suddenly he recognized some of the faces. They were the shop owners, the merchants, the fishermen… his people.

"I thought everyone had moved to the Fire Fields," Cyrus continued.

"Many did," Jack answered, "we created the new Temple as a symbol of unity between the split Kingdom, but Easttown and Westtown still stand."

"No longer," a man from the group reported. "Easttown has been burned to the ground."

"Burned to the ground?" Jack repeated in horror. "How?"

"It was a man," the woman answered, "he didn't say anything, just walked into town and it all started coming apart."

"Easttown is nowhere near the Fire Fields," Jack exclaimed to Cyrus, "how could his weapons reach all that way?"

Cyrus didn't have any answers. Until now, he had been under the impression that Magnus's power ended at the perimeter of the Fire Fields. After all, it was frozen fire that his tridents reacted with to cause such destruction.

"How bad are we talking?" Jack asked the woman.

In response, she shook her head. "There's nothing left, my King."

Jack looked disgusted. "For what purpose?" he asked Cyrus.

"It's a message," Cyrus answered softly. "Retribution for my escape. He's telling us that his reach extends far beyond the center of the island and that we're not safe, even here."

Jack looked too stunned by the news to effectively guide the new arrivals, but luckily Annica joined them soon after and began the process of welcoming Easttown into camp. The rest of the original refugees also flooded out to greet the Eastern townsfolk, but whispered panic began spreading amongst the crowd at hearing the news of the town's destruction. Accusations were flying before long and, while they were said in hushed voices, Cyrus found them impossible not to overhear. People wanted to know if Magnus would be coming to camp next and whether Westtown was aware of the potential danger. Upon seeing Alec and Nel amongst their ranks, they also wanted to know if Westtown would now declare as their enemy again. Confusion was palpable and Cyrus wasn't sure what to do to settle everyone. Noma and Ydoro began weaving through the crowd, comforting those who needed it and helping to haul what belongings they had managed to salvage. Cyrus himself felt useless. What was he supposed to do to lead them? Give another uplifting speech? Promise them that a plan was being formed when no such plan existed?

Cyrus shook his head at himself. There was no more room for doubt. These people needed action, but what to do? His eyes scanned his allies, desperately assessing their strengths. Annica was strong, possibly the strongest of them, but her transition to a leader had left her crippled with self-doubt. Suddenly she seemed to feel the need to earn the people's permission in some way, making bold decisions impossible that had come so naturally to her before. Jack was capable but no real leader. He was rational, cool-headed, and clever, but he wouldn't make decisions for the group, despite being their current king. Noma and Ydoro were no fighters, and that truth only confirmed itself further as Cyrus watched them struggle as a team to lift a woman's bag onto their shoulders. Then there was Alec, who was walking amongst the new arrivals with fresh contempt written all over his face. He couldn't even hide his disdain for the people. It was clear that what he valued most, the ability to fight, was sorely lacking from this particular group. But wait, something was missing from his brother; his ever-present companion. Where was Nel? A quick scan of the crowd found her. Rather than skulking amidst the throng with Alec, she was trailing behind Jack and Annica, who were doing their best to ignore her. Indeed, as she tried to elbow her way into their company, they intentionally kept their backs facing her direction. Cyrus couldn't blame them of course, but what she did next struck him as odd. Rather than give up where her aid was clearly unwanted, she stooped to help one of the Easttowners with his small bundle of salvaged belongings. She didn't appear to know anybody was watching her, she was just... helping.

Cyrus nodded to himself, filed this bit of information away, and began studying the rest of the group. They were scared, desperate even, yet not defeated. Tears had dried on many of their cheeks at seeing their homes and lives burned to the ground, but they had picked themselves up, brought themselves here, and even showed joy at the sight of their old king. When faced with such indomitable spirit, how could Cyrus possibly allow himself to give in to despair. It wasn't right, it wasn't fair, and it wasn't who he was going to be. His jaw clenched and his lip curled in disgust. No, he decided; his legacy would not be one of war. His legacy would be one of victory against all odds and hope in the face of uncertainty. His legacy would be one of triumph.

CHAPTER FORTY–THREE

CHARIOT RACE

L EFT LEFT LEFT LEFT LEFT!" Kat screamed as Nick threw all his weight against the reigns trying to force the chariot to turn. The Neodactyls eyes bulged as it let out a horrifying shriek and attempted yet again to snap at the occupants of the vehicle tethered behind it. The carriage bounced and skidded along the road and only veered away from the approaching wall at the last second, scraping against the stone and ripping wood and iron from the railings and wheels. Kat winced against the spray of dust and turned her attention to their pursuers; two overcrowded chariots tied to ruthlessly sprinting Neodactyls. The militants had far better control of their creatures than Nick did his, but they were weighed down by the sheer volume packed into each vehicle. Nick looked precariously over his shoulder, his long hair snapping in the wind.

"Their gaining on us!" he shouted unnecessarily.

He attempted to coax an extra bit of speed out of the furious creature but it wasn't enough. One of the enemy chariots was already pulling up alongside them and the five shouting militants began slashing out wild-ly with their machetes. Kat and Dean leaned away towards the far side of their own platform trying to avoid the blows, but their shifting weight caused it to tilt violently and they just barely avoided spilling out altogether. Kat swung her own weapon through the air trying to deter the men from boarding, but it was futile. One of them reached out and grasped the mangled remains of the chariot handle and used it to pull the two speeding vehicles close. The pair of Neodactyls, now brought level as they ran, began hissing and spitting at each other, their eyes flashing angrily and their beaks snapping. Nick looked over his shoulder again and swore. The man with his hand on their chariot tightened his grip and jumped from his own platform to theirs. The entire wagon lurched to the side as he attempted to steady himself; his legs flailing trying to avoid getting caught in the spokes of the wheel. Kat hacked forward with her machete and landed a clean shot directly into his neck. The man howled and released his hold on the railing to staunch the flow of blood, causing him to drop. He fell between the two jockeying chariots and was pulled under the wheel of his own. The cart bounced sickeningly as it ran him over and made a horrible splintering sound, yet it seemed to hold together.

The remaining four militants, having no intention of suffering the same fate, began surging towards them as group. The closest of the men reached over the railing with both hands, one grabbing at Kat's wrist while the other clutched her by the throat. She attempted to twist the machete away from his grip but he was far stronger and looked positively murderous. She tried slamming her forehead into his, just like she'd seen in the movies, but the result was her vision exploding into stars while her aggressor largely dodged the impact.

Wham! Dean punched the man out of nowhere and his grip loosened immediately. *Wham!* Dean hit him again and the man staggered back into his people. The enemy chariot careened sideways and its occupants temporarily lost their hold on the railing. Dean whooped loudly in excitement and actually let out a manic laugh at his own bravery. But their victory was short lived. One of the four militants had retaken control of the reigns and was pulling their Neodactyl sideways, back into combat range.

"D take the wheel!" Nick yelled.

Dean scrambled to swap places with Nick, who had already relinquished control and was drawing his broadsword; but the switch was poorly timed and their chariot sideswiped an old vendor's stall in the narrow street. The stall exploded into pieces upon impact, sending shrapnel flying in every direction. Both chariots tilted violently as they ran over fragments of wood and falling baskets, twisting dangerously beneath their wheels. The female Neodactyl screeched angrily and made a fresh snap at the male, still matching her speed.

"Level us out, D!" Nick screamed as though it wasn't he who had dropped the reigns prematurely.

Dean attempted a response but was forced to duck quickly to avoid being decapitated by a shredded awning. The road they were on was far too narrow for two chariots and they were running out of space fast.

"Form up! Form up!" Nick shouted to Kat.

Kat, having no idea what he meant by this, raised her machete and prepared to meet their assailants, who were no doubt about to attempt a second boarding. Sure enough, the militants drew their chariot close once again and all four of them charged forward. This time, rather than stagger their assaults, all four launched themselves in unison onto the chariot driven by Dean. The carriage sank dramatically to one side and threatened to upend entirely. Nick tried to swing his broadsword but in such close quarters there simply wasn't enough clearance. Two of the men dove for Nick while a third wrapped a wiry arm around Dean's throat from behind. The fourth snatched at Kat's machete and tried to wrestle it from her grip. She twisted and tugged desperately but the man was overpowering her. He gripped each end of her weapon and pushed her bodily towards the back of the carriage. She scrambled to keep her footing but a large piece of the wooden platform shattered away beneath her boot and she fell legs-first off the back of the racing vehicle. The only thing that stopped her from being dragged off into the street was her grip on the machete, which was also firmly in the clutches of her attacker. She could feel her pant legs shredding as they were dragged along in the dirt and her knees were howling in pain on every rock they hit.

A raucous chorus of jeering erupted from behind her and she turned slightly to see the second chariot gaining on them. Their own Neodactyl was only feet away from her dragging body and already snapping hungrily at her heels.

Her assailant suddenly seemed to realize that the only thing keeping Kat attached to the chariot was the machete in his own hands. As the recognition sank in, he grinned at her, winked, and released it. Kat's upper body slammed down and she grappled with her arms trying to find purchase. She found it in the militant's pant leg, which she seized desperately. Her other hand had refused to release its grip on the machete, which was now solely in her control. The militant tried stomping at her fingers to loosen her grip. Instead, Kat heaved herself forward and stabbed the blade down hard into the man's foot. Unfortunately for him, his boots were old and seemed to be made primarily of some sort of cloth, for when the machete pierced the top, it ran straight through and buried itself in the wooden platform below. The man screamed and bent to pull it free. Kat seized the opportunity and snatched a handful of his hair. Off balance, the man toppled over and fell headlong into the street out the back of the chariot. His foot, however, was still pierced to the floor of the vehicle so he ended up bouncing along beside Kat, being dragged just like she was, but in reverse.

Kat clutched the hilt of the machete like a handle, trying to use it to pull herself back onboard. Finding she didn't have the upper-body strength to fully hoist herself, she clambered on top of her flailing assailant, still being kept in place by his trapped foot. The pursuing Neodactyl hissed and surged forward, finding the alure of two dangling pieces of prey impossible to ignore. Kat scrambled over the man, digging her boots into his abdomen as she went. He screamed as she finally boarded the chariot once again, turned and tugged the machete free from both the floorboards of the platform and the man's foot. His body was instantly ripped backwards onto the speeding ground and swept into the clutches of the ravenous Neodactyl. The creature set upon him with the speed of a striking snake, ignoring the fact that it was pulling a careening chariot along with five riders. The entire vehicle flipped upon hitting the bird, smashing onto its side and skidding along through the street.

As Kat steadied herself back onto the platform, she turned to her allies, still in the heat of their own battles. Dean was batting wildly at his assailant, who had him in a crushing headlock. Nick had managed to mostly untangle himself from his own two militants but was still unable to land a real blow in such close proximity. One of the men punched him across the face and he buckled slightly, trying in vain to raise his sword. Suddenly, the other grabbed him by the legs and flipped him off his feet, causing him to pitch over the side of the railing. A loose-hanging bit of awning off one of the passing buildings snagged him and he became twisted in the ancient fabric. Kat tried to reach out but their chariot had whipped by faster than she could blink, and she looked back to see Nick disappearing into the distance, working desperately to untangle himself. With the last glimpse she got before they rounded another tight corner, she saw Nick climbing the hanging cloth in an attempt to reach the roof.

With Nick out of the way, the two militants he had been holding at bay turned their attention towards Kat. They both looked a bit worse for wear but still ready to fight. Kat took a deep breath and held her weapon out before her.

Suddenly the man grappling with Dean roared in pain and released his hold, clutching at his face instead. It seemed Dean had managed to jam a thumb into his eye. Using the distraction, Kat charged forward and slashed with her machete, but she was easily blocked. The other chariot, now unoccupied but still running parallel to their own, hit a rough piece of ground and bucked alarmingly. Could Kat possibly make the jump to the other platform to get out of this close quarters combat? Not without abandoning Dean, she decided.

Their Neodactyl made a sharp turn down one of the winding roads and every one of them smashed into the left railing. Kat again tried to use the distraction and stabbed her blade forward, but again she was blocked. She was exhausting herself and it wouldn't be long before she was overpowered.

In the blink of an eye, Nick was back on the scene, leaping down from one of the flanking building roofs and landing hard in the unoccupied chariot beside them. It wasn't graceful and he looked to be in a great deal of pain, but he scrabbled over the quickly deteriorating chariot and propelled himself back onto their own. His stunt entirely unbalanced the militant clutching his eye, who was lost in a blur over the side. Nick twirled his blade high over his head but was still far too close to effectively swing it. Instead, he used the hilt to whip the closest militant in the side of the head. Dean was back at the reigns, attempting once again to gain control of the careening chariot and the enraged Neodactyl.

"I think we're almost there!" Dean yelled.

Kat looked ahead and sure enough, she could see the familiar clearing that represented the wasteland surrounding the Fire Fields. The last of the buildings whipped past them and they were out, flying across the dusty, lifeless terrain.

Nick punched at one of the men who staggered backwards into Kat, waiting with her machete. She stabbed it straight through his midsection without thinking twice. As he fell off the back of the wagon and was claimed by a cloud of dust, Nick grasped the final assailant by the shirt collar and hoisted him off the ground. He then threw the man, screaming and kicking, into the neighboring chariot.

With the platform now cleared, Nick gave his sword a wide flourish and brought it down hard on the reigns tethering the militant's chariot to the Neodactyl. They didn't snap right away but he hacked at them again. And again and again. The militant panicked and attempted to jump back towards their vehicle, but he was too late. With a final slice, the reigns gave way and the Neodactyl sprinted free of its bindings. The chariot, without the creature to stabilize it, dropped its front axle and tongue, which pierced into the rocky ground below. The vehicle launched up into the air, hurtling fragments of iron, splintering wood, and their final assailant.

Kat didn't see the shattered remains hit the ground, as they were consumed by a wall of dust, but she could hear the screeching and smashing as the frame twisted and the platform obliterated.

Nick let out a quick sigh of relief but immediately turned his attention back to Dean, still steering them onward.

"We must be close!" Nick shouted.

"I think it's just up here!" Dean answered back.

They were approaching the abandoned remains of the village they had first entered through, but how would they possibly find the right building?

"There it is!" Dean exclaimed and he turned the reigns hard to the left. When Kat saw it, she suddenly remembered; the chalk-white mark that Dean had left on the outer door.

Supremely grateful for his quick thinking, Kat braced herself with what remained of the railings as Dean pulled back on the reigns to bring their ride to a halt.

"Don't stop, don't stop!" Nick yelled, "we're going straight through, creature and all!"

"Are you crazy?!" Dean shouted back.

In response, Nick pulled the reigns free of Dean's grip and steered them violently towards the door with the chalk on the front. The Neodactyl screamed loudly in protest but rammed head-first into the door all the same, which slammed open from the impact.

"The scepter!" Dean shouted, throwing himself towards the back of the ruined chariot as they entered the house.

Kat seized his wrist just as he extended out and snatched the gleaming scepter from the far corner of the room. No sooner had she wrenched him back onto the platform than she began to see double and the light around them began to expand into brilliant streaks. They had reached the pocket around the doorway Magnus had opened and the world was dissolving around them once again.

The air began to darken and slip away, making her feel serene and somehow weightless. The Fire Fields were gone, the abandoned town was gone, and all that remained was endless, expansive nothingness.

CHAPTER FORTY–FOUR

TO WAR

Now this was what a real community looked like, Cyrus thought to himself. Rather than project frustration at the arrival of fifty new mouths to feed with their already meager rations or annoyance at needing to find fresh supplies to expand the encampment, the people of the Kingdom wasted no time in getting to work. New tents were erected, old tents were split to accommodate added occupants, trees were cut down to create roofs, and their population ballooned. It had been one day, and the people had simply made it work. Given another month, Cyrus had no doubt that the canvas tents and tarps, leaning branches and shelters made of leaves would give way to real structures with thatched overhangs, permanent walls, and real roads. But that would not be their future. No, the Kingdom was more than just resilient in hard times. They had worked relentlessly for a level of stability and they had earned a place in a real, functioning society. Cyrus knew he may not have a place in that society, but he would give everything he had to make sure his people had that opportunity.

It was funny how much a simple conversation with his oldest ally on the island had helped him find his purpose once again. It was now clear to Cyrus that Alec had taken more than just his freedom when he trapped him in that alternate reality. He had taken his confidence, too. He had made him forget that he was a leader… that he was a king. Magnus wanted him to forget this as well. He painted him as a relic from a bygone time, someone who had made his mark on the pages of history and then faded into the past. But that's because he was scared. He was scared of what Cyrus could do if he found his place again. He was scared of a Cyrus who embraced what he was supposed to be.

"They don't take setbacks sitting down, do they?" It was Jack, who had appeared next to him and was smiling while he surveyed the progress being made at camp.

"They don't," Cyrus agreed, "but they were beaten into submission once before, and it will happen again if we're not careful."

Cyrus was thinking of the people he had first encountered when they arrived on the island. That was six years ago now, but they were a people that had forgotten their strength entirely. They had once been strong, but their spirit had been stomped out by dictator after dictator. Once one freedom is given away, it is shocking how willingly the next is discarded.

"That won't happen," Jack stated flatly. "I won't let that happen… and you won't let that happen."

Cyrus nodded his head as he watched the work being done in camp and smiled just slightly. "Damn right."

Voices suddenly rang out through the forest and everyone began muttering and scanning their surroundings for the source.

"Right right right right! C'mon, work with me here!"

Whatever approached, it sounded like it had wheels and was moving incredibly fast.

"Help me out, D-Man! Put your back into it! Put your back into it!"

From the trees near the edge of camp erupted an enormous creature, a third larger than the Neodactyls Cyrus was used to, and it was pulling a chariot occupied by three familiar faces.

"Shit!" Nick Satterall yelled as he wrenched back on the reigns attempting to stop the creature from barreling over one of the outermost tents. He managed to avoid it, but only just, and the chariot gave an alarming crack as it pivoted sharply.

"Ropes ropes ropes!" Nick screamed as the Neodactyl skidded to a halt and hissed in agitation.

Several townsfolk rushed forward and flung ropes and harnesses around the thrashing creature, which lunged and snapped at them angrily.

"Tether it to that tree!" Nick instructed, leaping down from the platform and hoisting one of the ropes himself. "This thing is no friend to us, trust me!"

The Neodactyl screeched but the fight was over and its leads were knotted off against the sturdiest-looking trunk they could find.

"Whew!" Nick shook his head with a grin. "That'll wake you up!"

Dean and Kat both dismounted, looking wobbly-kneed and shaken.

"You're back!" Annica exclaimed, forcing her way to the front of the crowd.

"You're alive!" Kat beamed. "We were so worried after we went through the door!"

Annica shrugged off their concern, only slightly favoring one shoulder. Kat's eyes wandered to Cyrus and the smile continued to spread across her face. "And my King," she expressed softly with a bow. "It's good to have you back."

"Oh we're starting this again, eh?" Nick said with a roll of his eyes. But he offered Cyrus a forced smile all the same.

"I can't thank you enough for taking on this mission," Annica said to Dean and Kat, placing a hand on each of their shoulders. "You have earned your place in this Kingdom. Now tell me, what did you find?"

For the next half-hour, the duo recounted their time in a world wrung out and disposed of by Kysaar Magnus. A world with no rules, no laws, and no leader. They explained how this was not Magnus's homeworld, rather one of many realities that he had attempted and failed to conquer. They spoke of an old ally of his who had followed him from one world to the next in search of a single reality they could bring under their command. And most interesting of all, they explained that Magnus's tridents contained pieces of all his many conquests and that accessing those realities was as simple as smashing the weapons together at the point of repair.

"He's not all-powerful," Kat finished, "he's strong and dangerous, but he's a failure. He's here because he's failed in every other world he's tried to seize."

"He's here because he thinks this is the Kingdom at its weakest," Cyrus agreed. "He thinks this moment in this reality is the crack that he needs."

"That's what Lee said," Kat nodded, "that your return here gave him an opportunity to control the people in a way he hadn't been able to before." She looked down, slightly embarrassed. "That your return was the weakness."

Cyrus smiled, something that would have seemed impossible only a day ago. "Thank you Kat, Dean. It's a miscalculation that will be his undoing."

Kat grinned.

"And what of Magnus now?" Annica asked. "Did he try to stop you in the Fire Fields?"

"He wasn't there," Kat reported ominously. "We didn't pass anyone on our return trip."

Annica, Jack, and Cyrus exchanged wary glances but elected to not push the subject in such a public forum.

As the townsfolk worked on getting Dean, Kat, and Nick resettled, Cyrus left them to do a walk around the perimeter of the camp. He didn't quite have a plan, but he had confidence now, and that somehow seemed like enough for the moment. They had weapons, they had the numbers, and now they had information. If there was a time to strike, it was quickly approaching.

"So are we doing this?" came a voice from behind. Cyrus turned to find his brother, the last person in the world he expected to be following him.

Cyrus studied him for a long moment and finally decided there was no backhanded venom to his question.

"We're doing this," he answered. Then he turned and faced his brother head on. "And Alec, I need to know… we don't have to like each other, in fact I'd prefer that there was no *us* at all... but I need to know that you're with us on this. Because I can't be looking over my shoulder waiting for a knife in my back when I square up against Magnus. If you're *with* us, if you're for this Kingdom, then stand with us. No more games, no more double-crosses. We stand together now... or we all die. Do you understand?"

Alec looked to be in physical pain. Cyrus could see his lip visibly twitch as though it wanted to smirk or find some hostile retort. His eyes seemed to light up with flame and pulse with hatred, but it didn't last. It burnt out as quickly as it had ignited.

"I despise you, brother," Alec finally answered. His tone was soft but carried a weight that few of his words did. "I've come to hate everything about you, and I don't expect that to ever change. There will be a reckoning for us, of that I'm sure... and on that day, I hope you're ready, because I will be. But you don't have to worry about me coming for you now. The enemy is out there, plotting our destruction as we speak. I'll stand with you until that enemy is gone, if you'll stand with me."

Cyrus surveyed Alec, his kid brother whom he had shared a life with. There wasn't a time he could recall where their lives weren't deeply entwined. This was a person he had shared everything with; not just conversationally but experiences. Their lives were shaped by one another, and yet, there was no relationship here anymore. Cyrus found he despised Alec just as much in return.

Cyrus extended his hand, offering what small bridge he could. Alec thought a moment before grasping it.

"To bringing this bastard down," Cyrus growled, "we finish this, you and I."

Alec smiled. It was his hungry, vengeful, conqueror's smile, but Cyrus found he didn't mind it so much in the current circumstances. "To war," Alec answered.

Cyrus left Alec's side soon after, preferring the company of those he could fully trust. Strangely, however, he found he did believe the understanding he had just forged with his brother, as impossible as it seemed.

"There you are," Jack exclaimed as he saw his approach. Annica was with him and wore a serious, almost somber expression that gave Cyrus pause.

"What is it?" Cyrus asked in concern.

"Annica and I have been talking," Jack began, "and while we anticipate resistance from you, we're just going to skip past that."

Cyrus narrowed his eyes suspiciously.

"Cyrus, we don't care who's labeled as the king or the queen," Annica jumped in, "I think the reason we were chosen is because we don't put much stock in such titles."

"Fair enough," Cyrus said, "but I don't…"

Annica turned to one of her nearby guards and retrieved from his grip the repaired scepter that had brought Cyrus back to the Kingdom. She held it crosswise in front of her, the gleaming bronze fissure in the center of the staff catching the light and dancing across her face. Her palms were open, bearing the weight of the weapon with cautious reverence, and she nodded her head just slightly as she extended her arms towards Cyrus.

"Titles aside," she said softly, "we both feel this belongs to you. This is the weapon you banished the King of the West with and it's the tool that brought you back to us. We don't expect you to fight Magnus on your own, but when you do face him, it would feel wrong were you not armed with the weapon of a king."

Cyrus didn't know what to say. His first instinct had been to dismiss the importance they were putting on the scepter, but as she spoke, he changed his mind. He was reminded of his early days in the Kingdom, and how Alec had spoken so vehemently about the significance of the weapons. Cyrus had scoffed, regarding them as little more than symbols with which past kings had seized power. Not only did they end up being enormously powerful objects, but Cyrus had come to recognize the importance of such symbols. Elevating a leader wasn't just about finding a head to follow, it was about finding something to believe in. The townspeople erected that statue of the Guardian not to immortalize Cyrus, but to look up at the sky and be reminded that they fought for something greater. This was bigger than him. This was for the King-dom… and the Kingdom would be watching.

Cyrus reached out his hand tentatively, willing it not to shake, and grasped the cool, blackened bark firmly. He hadn't held the damned thing since returning, but the power he felt course through his body at gripping it was hard to ignore. He was certain that feeling was not, strictly speaking, a physical sensation, but that didn't make it any less real. Cyrus brought the scepter vertical and planted it in the earth, a small tremor of firelight flickering through the staff as it made impact. He looked to Jack, who offered him a wink, and then to Annica, who brought a fist to her chest and bowed her head in their old salute.

"We're with you," Annica said, "we're all with you."

CHAPTER FORTY–FIVE

STAND AS ONE

J ack could feel his control of their situation unravelling, slowly but steadily, like a bit of yarn caught on a nail. Perhaps the situation needed to unravel, perhaps that was the only way to move forward, but the six years of peace that himself and Annica had fought for suddenly seemed so very far away. Their camp not only housed everyone from town proper but was now home to all of Easttown as well. Not only that, it currently sheltered both Cyrus and Alec Dorn, two of the most formative and destructive leaders in Kingdom history, an admittedly gun-shy but unpredictable Nel, and four transplants from an alternate reality that had been caught up in the crossfire. Things were ready to blow; all anyone seemed to be waiting for was word that they were declaring war on Kysaar Magnus. Yet that ball seemed to be rolling without Jack's help.

He watched from the sidelines as Cyrus made his way through camp. He looked suddenly far older to Jack. His shoulder sloped as though beneath an immense weight, his formerly joyful, even arrogant eyes now hosted an apprehensive, world-worn quality, and his old firm, business-like gait was now that of a weathered general. He spoke with every local who wanted his ear, and while his words were lost from this distance, he nodded his head in grim understanding of their woes. This was someone who had resigned himself to the will of the people, and while it was commendable, Jack couldn't help but feel a bit sad all the same.

Ydoro seemed to notice Jack's contemplation as he walked past, for he stopped and took a place at his side.

"Remember those chess pieces you made, Ydoro?" Jack asked.

"Of course," Ydoro replied, "it's just a shame we never got to play with them."

"But you didn't really make them to play with, did you?" Jack asked, though it wasn't really a question. He was still watching Cyrus, now clasping a woman's hands in his own in a protective, fatherly way. "How did you know, even then?"

"How did I know?" Ydoro asked.

"How did you know who Cyrus Dorn would become? You saw him... you saw all of us through a lens I can't quite understand. But here was a man who, for all intents and purposes, was self-serving, egotistical, and wanted only to leave this place and get home, yet you saw him for something more. You stayed neutral in the Kingdom for ruler after ruler, never taking a stand, until Cyrus Dorn came to you and asked for help. What did you see in him that the rest of us missed?"

To his surprise, Ydoro laughed just slightly. "I wish I had an answer for you, my King, but it's truly an impossible question. You're asking me to define the undefinable. I don't know the difference between a good man and a great one, and I don't even know which one Cyrus Dorn is. What I can tell you is that he was exactly who we needed in that moment, and I think he's exactly who we need in this moment too. I carved him into stone because too often it's the violent and ruthless who become memorialized... the conquerors that history remembers. We rarely celebrate the peaceful listeners, the critical thinkers who quietly shape the world into a better place. Cyrus Dorn doesn't always believe in himself anymore... but I still believe in him."

Voices started rippling through camp. It started as whispers but was quickly becoming excitable and chaotic.

"Oh hell, what now?" Jack exclaimed, certain that any tidings at this point would be unwelcome news. Indeed, the locals all seemed visibly rattled as they pushed further into camp.

Jack began to walk towards the perimeter, Ydoro right at his heels. Cyrus had noticed the commotion as well and was approaching fast with his scepter ready, but none of them could get far before a wall of Annica's militants had formed up in a defensive blockade.

"Stand down," Annica called.

It was only once her fighters began to reluctantly ease their formation that Jack could see the source of the distress. In a moment almost perfectly mirroring the one from the day prior, Jack found himself facing a large group of men and women, each carrying a variety of objects and belongings. The clear difference here was that most of the items cradled by this group appeared to be weapons. Jack recognized several of the faces easily; these were the inhabitants of Westtown.

There was no other way of looking at it; Westtown were the outcasts of the Kingdom, even if Annica and Jack had strived for unity since the Battle of Westtown Square. These were the locals who had fought alongside Alec and Nel, and while some had elected to relocate to the Fire Fields and try their luck in the new society, many had stayed behind, either out of anger or possibly shame. They still traded with both town proper and Easttown, and had long since ceased to be a military threat, but further contact was limited. Seeing them now filled Jack with considerable dread. He could think of only two reasons for their journey; either they had finally heard of Alec's return and were here to swear their loyalty once again, or Kysaar Magnus had destroyed their homes, same as the East.

Annica seemed inclined to think the latter, for she made her way to the group and said, "Does Westtown still stand?"

"It does, my Queen," a short, hardened-looking woman in the front responded.

The use of 'my Queen' encouraged Jack just slightly, but he couldn't help but notice their collective eyes glance towards Cyrus, then to Alec.

"Then what's happened?" Annica asked.

"We heard of the destruction of Easttown," the woman in front announced, "so we've come to offer what aid we can."

"Aid?" Annica repeated. It appeared the gesture had taken her so off-guard that she was having trouble processing the meaning.

"We feel the time has come for the Kingdom to stand as one," the woman continued. "We have our differences, have fought one another and died at one another's hands, but we will not let an outsider with no claim to our lands destroy us. We've earned the right to fight amongst ourselves; this newcomer has not."

Annica scanned the group, each nodding their head in silent agreement and tightening their grips on what weapons they had.

"We appreciate the support," Annica finally said, her shoulders slumping just slightly, "but we don't have a plan. All we've managed to do so far is survive."

Cyrus stepped forward. It brought silence to everyone gathered.

"And that's not nothing," he said. His voice suddenly held the same cadence it used to when he would address his people. The voice that Easttown had followed six years ago. "With you here, this now represents the population of the Kingdom. The *entirety* of the Kingdom… against two men." Cyrus smiled, and it was his old, confident grin that lit his face. "I like our odds. What's more, our enemy's running scared." As murmurs of disagreement and exasperation spread throughout the crowd, Cyrus laughed. "No, it's true. He's running scared. He left the Fire Fields for Easttown which means he's done waiting for us to play into his traps. He's gone on the offensive which means his patience has run dry. It means his plan isn't working the way it should."

"But what if that means he's coming here next?" someone from Easttown asked.

"I'm certain that he is," Cyrus answered, and panic began to bubble amongst the people.

"Then what do we do?" asked another.

After a pause, Cyrus said, "I don't know yet." At this, the panic began to boil over, but Cyrus remained calm. "I don't know yet," he continued through the din, "because this isn't a speech to rouse your morale, and this isn't a speech to convince you to fight for me. In fact, this isn't an address from your leader at all… this is a war meeting. You've all proven yourselves, time and again, and while you've often been on opposing sides, you know this Kingdom better than anyone. Better than me, better than my brother, and better than Magnus. You want to know the plan? Here's what I have so far; Magnus attacked Easttown two days ago. He wasn't in the Fire Fields as of this morning when Kat, Dean, and Nick passed through, and he wasn't seen along the road to Westtown either. That leaves the forests to the south. That's where he'll approach from."

There was silence until Ydoro finally broke it. "So do we hit him from the road before he gets here?"

Cyrus nodded slightly. "Or we let him come, lure him into a trap."

"But we have nothing that can stand against those tridents of his," Annica chimed in.

"Those won't work so far away from the Fire Fields, will they?" It was Alec this time, and his words were met with buzzing whispers from the crowd.

"They will," Cyrus insisted, "somehow. He managed to destroy Easttown with them." Cyrus upended his scepter and stabbed it roughly into the dirt. The ruby ribbons within the shaft pulsated brightly and then dimmed just as fast. Several people from the crowd gasped. "These scepters only glow in the presence of frozen fire. There must be more than just dirt beneath our feet. I'd be willing to bet there are rivers of that stuff cutting through the ground below us. This scepter isn't strong enough to access it, but it seems Magnus's tridents are."

"Then he'll always have the advantage," Noma said, dejected.

Cyrus smiled again. "Here's the thing about fire. It's powerful, it's destructive, and it's nearly impossible to fight. But it's also nearly impossible to control." He paused a moment, thinking. "Alec," he finally said, and his brother looked surprised at being addressed, "At the Battle in Westtown, you rigged your chariot with some sort of explosive compound…"

Alec's eyes lit up. "It was from the Temple, that green powder."

"Powdered Dreamwood," Annica stated. "It's volatile stuff, though, and you don't wanna breathe it in."

Jack nodded his head in fervent agreement.

"Volatile may be exactly what we need," Cyrus said. "With Westtown here, the road to the old Temple is open. What if we retreated north, through the valley and up that hillside, forcing Magnus to follow us."

"But Magnus destroyed the Red Temple like it was made of kindling," Annica pointed out. "The old Temple may be bigger, but even so…"

Cyrus shook his head. "We're not fortifying the Temple because Magnus will never make it that far. We rig explosives along the road using the Dreamwood, let him follow us, then confront him at the place of our choosing. When he uses his tridents, the Dreamwood will light the entire place up."

People began muttering their general satisfaction with the plan but Annica was shaking her head. Many of the gathered crowd were already talking amongst themselves about procuring Powdered Dreamwood and discussing what belongings could be hauled on the road. Annica used the opportunity to approach Cyrus privately, and Jack rushed to follow.

"That's a risky move, Cyrus," Annica said quietly while the excitable crowd around them paid little attention. "Not only is that compound incredibly unpredictable, but this would require someone agreeing to face Magnus head-on."

"We don't have a choice in facing him," Cyrus insisted, "he's making that choice for us. But I'd strongly prefer meeting him on the road where our people won't be caught in the crossfire."

"You're not standing against him alone," Jack pushed.

"No," Annica agreed, "we face him together."

Cyrus's head gave a noncommittal shake. "Back in Easttown, during my time as king, you made the hard choice that I couldn't make. You fought the West without my aid and without my consent, knowing that if you were to fall, I would be alive to carve a future for our people.

Now it's my turn. As the new King and Queen, it's your time to make that hard sacrifice."

"Sacrifice?" Annica scoffed, "it sounds like you're the one sacrificing…"

"The sacrifice," Cyrus interrupted, "is *not* fighting. The sacrifice is putting our people first."

As Annica fixed Cyrus with a wary look, Alec made his way through the crowd and joined their conversation, followed by Nel.

"I know you don't like it," Cyrus continued, now talking only at Annica, "but you know I'm right. You're a fighter at your core, but now you're a leader too. Lead our people. Alec and I are relics of the past… leave the fight to us."

At this, Alec smiled, nodding his head slightly in agreement. At first, Jack wasn't sure what to make of the reaction. Possibly Alec just liked the idea of fighting for glory. But no, Jack finally decided, it was having something of importance to do that was appealing to him.

"We can help too," came a voice out of the crowd.

Kat emerged, apparently having been eavesdropping the entire time, followed by Dean, Ydoro, Noma, and a reluctant-looking Nick.

Cyrus was shaking his head before they had even stopped walking.

"We appreciate the gesture, but we've got this covered. More people would only be a hinderance."

"You'll need someone to rig the Dreamwood," Noma pointed out. "Dr. Garse has a stash in his medical supplies, but you'll want my help making sure it ignites in the right direction."

Cyrus sighed. "Okay, Noma and Ydoro, you help set the trap along the road, and then you get clear. But Dean, Kat, Nick, I don't want you anywhere near the fighting." As Kat began to launch into an argument, Cyrus put up a hand. "What you *can* do is ride that chariot up to the Temple ahead of the group. I don't know if Magnus has a way of controlling that Neodactyl, but I don't plan to find out." As she started to respond again, Cyrus interrupted her. "No more arguing, any of you. This is our best shot. You all have a job to do." He suddenly paused, realizing one of their company did not, in fact, have an assignment just yet. Nel looked back at him expectantly, but then her head dropped just slightly as though she knew she was about to be told to stay out of the action. Cyrus appeared to be considering just that, for he took a long moment studying her. "And Nel..." he finally said, "you're in the rear guard with Alec and I."

She smiled in surprise and nodded her head to him. Jack wasn't sure he agreed with this idea for her, but he decided not to argue.

As the group split apart, each preparing for the mission at hand, Ydoro stayed behind at Jack's side, watching Cyrus depart.

"Well," Ydoro said in a quiet, almost somber tone, "I think Cyrus Dorn finally believes in himself again."

CHAPTER FORTY–SIX

SHOWDOWN

The exodus had begun. It had been impossibly hard for Cyrus to bid farewell and good luck to Jack and Annica; leaving them to lead their people north into the hills and eventually to the old Temple. While he had hugged each of them and assured his old allies that this wasn't goodbye, a bit of destiny seemed to hang in the air on this particular morning. It was hard to put a finger on, but the gravity of this moment in time somehow clung to the forest around them like a blanket of mist. This was what he had been running from since he had found the Kingdom. As uncomfortable as the truth was, this was where Cyrus was meant to be.

The trek was slow-moving, with over a hundred people of varying degrees of fitness and health lumbering along the road. The pace felt even more painful from the back, where Cyrus, Alec, Nel, Ydoro, and Noma could only move as fast as the slowest of the group. An order had been given that no wagons of belongings and no personal items would be carted to the Temple. This had been met with some brief resistance, but they couldn't risk further delay. There was no telling how much ground Magnus had covered since he was last seen.

As the hike wore on, midday came and went, and the blistering afternoon sun was only now starting to dip behind the trees and offer some small reprieve from the heat. Cyrus found himself running through endless scenarios in his head for the majority of the journey, wondering whether he was correct in guessing Magnus's next move and dreading what it meant if he were wrong. They had planted a few canisters of Dreamwood in several of the tents left behind at camp on the off chance that Magnus showed up and decided to light the entire area on fire. No explosions had been heard all day, however, so Cyrus knew this likely never played out. In truth, he had no way of knowing for certain that Magnus hadn't cut north through the interior of the island and wasn't waiting for them at the old Temple. It was possible the entire population of the island was currently walking into one last trap, and that this gamble meant the extinction of the Kingdom. But no, Cyrus had to tell himself that wasn't the case. He was learning to trust his instincts.

The clouds above were beginning to turn a deep scarlet before Cyrus began recognizing landmarks indicating the approach of the Temple. They still had a mile left to go, but Cyrus indicated to the rest of his team to hold back, allowing the tail-end of the procession to gain some distance.

"I think this is our spot," Cyrus announced to the tired and road-worn crew. "We have a bend in the road up ahead, another quarter mile of forest, then it's all uphill to the Temple. This would force him into close quarters with us, and there's plenty of places to hide the powder."

Everyone nodded in agreement and began searching their surroundings for the right placement.

"I think here and here," Alec said, indicating flanking positions along the road. "Jars of powder could be stashed beneath the leaves and he'd never know."

"I think a third one there," Noma said, pointing out a position further down the road they had just travelled. "I can set it so that it blows primarily his direction once it's lit. But this entire place will become an inferno real fast. Be ready to run once this stuff is ignited."

"We hear you," Cyrus acknowledged gravely as Noma and Ydoro set to work placing the Dreamwood.

Cyrus paced along the trail, watching them work. He thumbed at the scepter in his hand apprehensively, watching the forest for movement. Alec and Nel did similar, each armed with a machete and a small dagger for close encounters. It felt strange preparing for a fight they knew they couldn't win. The battle would be a distraction to get Magnus to destroy himself. The trick would be staying out of the firestorm that he would no doubt conjure.

Cyrus passed Alec on one of his many laps around the center of the road and caught his eye. Alec looked ready, and committed to the plan, but Cyrus still found himself searching his gaze for any hint of betrayal. Lest he forget, this was still the man who had turned on him too many times to count, and his sworn enemy in every way that mattered. Alec just stared back at him; a calm intensity set on his face.

"I can count on you for this, right?" Cyrus found himself asking, and Nel peered between them curiously.

"You can count on me," Alec answered with a confident nod. But was it too confident? Was Alec so calm because he knew something that Cyrus didn't? Alec kept walking the perimeter of the road, and Cyrus just watched him. He glanced at Nel instead, who returned his look with a stony, resolute expression. Was this all a trap?

"How we doing, Noma?" Cyrus called, desperate to move things along. This was going to work, he thought to himself. This had to work.

"We've got this one placed," Noma answered, still crouched over a pile of brambles now hiding the explosive powder. "And that one behind you is already done, so that just leaves the one further down the road."

Ydoro nodded in agreement and indicated behind Cyrus, back the way they had come. "We're thinking just…"

Ydoro stopped talking. His face went ghostly white.

As a shiver ran down Cyrus's spine, he turned apprehensively to look down the road behind them. And there he was. Kysaar Magnus was standing twenty-some feet from them, both tridents grasped in his fists and the Alchemist slinking a few paces behind him. It was over. Before their plan had even started, it was over. Magnus's eyes scanned each one of them until they finally landed on Cyrus last. He grinned.

"All this for me, King Dorn?" Magnus snarled with a mocking smirk.

Cyrus glanced at Alec and Nel, each looking just as dumbfounded as he felt. He then looked at Ydoro and Noma, still crouched in the road with their mouths hanging open in disbelief.

Magnus nodded his head slowly as if to show he found what had to be done distasteful. It reeked of insincerity of course. He upended one of his tridents and said, "Perhaps you should have just died when you had the chance."

He moved before Cyrus had time to react. With one sweeping stab through the air with his nightmare weapon, the ground before him ruptured, carving a deep channel of violent, screaming fire into the road. Frozen fire was forcibly ripped from the depths of the earth below, carving a trail of brilliant flames straight down the path towards Ydoro and Noma. They had no time to flee. The path of fire reached their trap of Powdered Dreamwood just as the duo began scrambling to their feet. The resulting explosion was so immense that both men were launched through the air amidst flying debris and comets of embers; the tremor through the earth was such that Cyrus, Alec, and Nel all fell to their knees where they stood.

There came a shout of anguish that Cyrus was certain had escaped from his own mouth, but it hadn't. It was in fact the Alchemist, who looked wide-eyed in horror at the destruction. Strange that he would develop a conscience now. But no, his concern appeared reserved only for Noma, who was barely conscious and attempting to crawl feebly behind the trees, his clothes smoking and singed to his skin.

"You promised," the Alchemist screamed at Magnus, attempting to force his weapon away from the ground.

Magnus shoved him harshly and his eyes bulged with rage.

"I warned you," Magnus bellowed. "Now this is your doing!"

Magnus began to stalk forward towards Noma, still attempting his slow crawl to safety.

But Cyrus was back on his feet and began to move with such sure-footed precision that he surprised even himself. Alec and Nel seemed to have vanished from his side in the chaos, but Cyrus didn't have time to think about that. He also didn't have time to register Ydoro's crumpled form near the edge of the road and wonder if he still lived. All that mattered now was himself and Magnus. Everything else was falling away. Cyrus extended his scepter out to his side and raked it across the newly created chasm in the street. As had happened during his duel with Alec, red-hot embers began to rise up out of the earth and spiral around the staff-head like a rotating pinwheel of fire.

Cyrus saw Magnus's sneer falter as the jet of glowing particles shot through the air and exploded against his shoulder. Magnus had managed to dodge the worst of the hit but he still roared in pain and batted at his shirt before it could ignite. Remembering how the tridents had torn the scepter from Alec's grip with such ease upon their arrival, Cyrus had no intention of giving him that chance. He sent another blast in Magnus's direction followed immediately by another. Magnus blocked each of these with his own weapons, but they were near misses. His smirk was entirely gone as he ducked behind his crossed tridents and readied for the next assault. Cyrus was still moving along the road in a wide circle, sending blast after blast smashing into his enemy. He knew one wrong step would cost him his life, but he had no intention of making a single wrong move, not this time.

Magnus raised one of his tridents crosswise in front of him like a shield while the other he extended out behind himself. The ground began to vibrate and buckle once again and Cyrus knew the next attack would be devastating. He charged forward, fueled purely on instinct, knowing only that Magnus would lose his advantage in close-quarters combat.

Suddenly Alec had reappeared, sprinting out of the forest behind Magnus. He held his machete but that wouldn't be enough. In a split-second decision, Cyrus threw his scepter up into the air, past Magnus and to his brother's outstretched hand. Magnus turned just in time to see Alec grasp the weapon and drag it across the burning earth. The fireball created was so immense that, despite desperately attempting to turn and block the attack, Magnus was struck in the chest and thrown from his feet onto the steadily dissolving road. The next attack he managed to block, even from the ground, but that last strike had taken its toll.

Nel raced out from the treeline in the same direction Alec had come, but her quarry was the Alchemist. He attempted to turn and flee but Nel slashed at him with the curved blade of her machete and he began bouncing on the backs of his heels to avoid her. He pulled a small blade of his own from beneath the folds of his clothes and attempted to defend himself, but the duel was going to be short lived.

As Alec advanced further towards Magnus, Cyrus tried to move in with a machete but was blocked by a fresh jet of fire. Magnus regained his footing and began backing up swiftly, twirling his weapons before him in a manic frenzy. Once he had both Dorn brothers out in front of him once again, he tossed one of the tridents off to his left where it landed amongst the grass and shrubbery. He then spun his remaining trident in front of himself like a baton from hell, showing off his newly gained mobility with a single weapon. He bared his teeth like a wild animal and audibly roared as he stabbed the three-pronged staff through the air and opened a fresh chasm that rocked the earth and sent Alec and Cyrus diving for cover. He then spotted Nel, who had the Alchemist by the collar with her blade to his throat.

"Drop it!" Nel screamed at Magnus.

Magnus just laughed, but his bloodshot, bulging eyes betrayed his desperation. He then stabbed out again with his trident and a blinding gouge appeared across the ground with flames popping and spitting up around it. Nel tried to fling herself out of the way but the blast hammered into her midsection and sent her careening against a nearby tree. The crunch was sickening as she fell to the ground motionless, but the Alchemist had taken the full brunt of the attack. Instead of being launched backwards into the forest, he had attempted to duck out of the way of the inferno. This meant when the trench opened in the ground, he stumbled forward and fell onto his hands and knees. His screams filled the air as the flesh was scorched from his face. A twisted, bony arm reached out from the flames one last time before it collapsed into the ground and was consumed by steam.

Alec looked terrified at Nel's lifeless body but he didn't let it distract him. He renewed his attack on Magnus but was easily blocked this time. Magnus had regained the upper-hand and was gleefully summoning fresh bouts of fire from the earth, filling the air with embers, ash, and smoke. This destruction was impossible to combat and very soon fire would consume the entire area, including their fallen friends. They had to move.

As a blanket of billowing, choking black smoke temporarily obscured Magnus from view, Cyrus ran to Alec and yelled, "We have to fall back! Follow me!"

Cyrus ran up the shattered remnants of the road in the direction of the Temple with Alec readily following.

"Stay close!" Cyrus called as his eyes burned and he coughed through the fumes.

Cyrus looked over his shoulder and his heart dropped as he saw Magnus appear from behind the wall of putrid glowing smoke. Seeing their retreat, Magnus grinned; a diabolical, wild grin. He then lurched forward and began a full-tilt sprint in their direction. He began stabbing his trident madly through the air in front of him as he ran, causing fissures to rupture with every wild step they took. Cyrus snatched the scepter back from his brother and started launching storms of frozen fire down the road, praying that just one would make contact.

There was no hope of outrunning this man and the formerly forested path was quickly becoming a flaming tempest impossible to navigate. Even as it occurred to Cyrus that they should be leading Magnus *away* from their retreating townsmen, not towards them, the explosive trenches blowing open in every direction made finding an alternate route suicide.

The burning trees opened up ahead and as Cyrus and Alec slammed through a flaming thicket of branches, the Temple finally loomed above; across a small clearing and nestled at the top of a sloping hillside. The sun was nearly down by now but squinting through the shadows, Cyrus was horrified to realize that the doors of the Temple were not closed. The exodus hadn't finished yet. There were still dozens of people making their way up the gravel pathway, many of them the older, slower-moving members of the company. Upon seeing Cyrus and Alec erupt from the treeline, Magnus and his roaring storm of fire right on their heels, the remaining townsfolk panicked and began scattering in every direction.

Arriving at the base of the hill, Cyrus decided he couldn't let Magnus any closer to the Temple without risking him destroying the entire structure. He turned, swept his scepter across the ground and shot a blast towards Magnus that he had to stoop to avoid. It was enough of a distraction that he was able to change course and put several additional feet between them.

"Alec!" Cyrus screamed as Magnus raised his trident into the air and unearthed an enormous tendril of flame that came crashing down around them. Alec looked expectantly back at him. His face was scorched with black soot and tiny burns; his eyes were squinted half-shut from the blinding light of the surrounding fire. "Run to the Temple and load the chariot with Powdered Dreamwood!" Cyrus yelled as a deafening rumble from below caused the ground to shake beneath their feet. "Ride it back down to me and I'll finish this!"

Alec looked back at him in exasperation. Whether he disagreed with the plan or had something else he wanted to say, Cyrus wasn't sure.

"Just go!" Cyrus yelled.

He smacked Alec's shoulder, who sprinted off up the hill in the direction of the Temple, then turned and held his scepter ready as Magnus prowled through the glowing steam. The smile was back on his face.

"They'll submit one way or another," Magnus growled in his horrible, drawling voice. "They'll either accept the new world order in the Kingdom..." he paused and looked up at the Temple, then back down at Cyrus, "or they'll burn."

Cyrus whipped the scepter forward like the quick draw of a pistol in a gunfight and sent another jet of embers through the air. Magnus blocked the attack, then gave his trident a powerful jerk. To Cyrus's horror, the scepter in his hand wrenched forward and threatened to slip straight out of his grip. He held fast, but only just. Magnus grinned broadly and gave his trident another sharp tug. This time, the scepter was pulled through the air as though magnetically attracted to the trident, but Cyrus refused to let go. His feet buckled beneath his body and he was dragged violently across the fiery expanse towards his opponent, embers biting and slicing at his face. Magnus had not been expecting Cyrus's grip to remain true, however, for he looked shocked to find himself within a foot of his enemy. Cyrus reached down in desperation and tugged the machete free from his belt. He slashed it brutally across Magnus's chest, who screamed and tilted away, clutching at his shredded shirt. Cyrus fell to the ground hard and gasped for air, willing the breath to return to his body. Magnus stumbled a few more paces, then spun around with deranged, furious eyes. His gaze fell on the Temple above. People had begun pouring back out through the front doors, though Cyrus could not guess why. All he could see was movement swarming around the front of the structure, and Magnus saw it too. He raised his trident again, but this time it was slow, powerful, and deliberate.

Cyrus would have guessed the very core of the island had ruptured given the noise that suddenly emanated from below his hands and knees. The vibration was so strong that Cyrus's vision went blurry and he thought he might temporarily lose consciousness. The inferno that ignited from the earth was horrific and it tore up the hillside like a knife slicing through fabric. Cyrus could follow the blazing path of the fracture like a snake as it cut through the ground, up through the grass, and finally burst against the front wall of the Temple. Outer stones, each the size of a grown man, were shattered into oblivion or launched through the air. People screamed and dove for cover while others ran for the protection of the forest. It was hard to see through the sickly smoke, but it looked like the right side of the front wall had a newly formed crater in it.

Cyrus staggered back to his feet. Clouds of smoldering ash were now overtaking the entire area blanketing everything in deep, claustrophobic shadow. Fires continued to blaze freely in all directions, piercing through the din and casting dizzying silhouettes all around him. He couldn't be sure where Magnus was anymore, but the sounds of terror and agony drifting down from the front of the Temple were unbearable. Not only would Alec never be able to find his way back with the chariot, Cyrus couldn't be sure he had even survived the most recent assault.

His feet could barely move, his knees were wobbly and his head was spinning. All he could think to do was get to the Temple and take control of the chariot himself. He began limping uphill, towards the direction of the screams. More than once, his footing failed him entirely and he smashed forward onto his hands, each still gripping a weapon. Putting one foot in front of the other had never been so difficult in his entire life. A tickling along the side of his face told him that blood was running freely from his forehead. Even by the flickering light of the surrounding flame he could see his hands were blackened with soot and charred by the millions of flying embers. He almost fell again but caught himself on his scepter, which he was now using as a brace to get himself up the hill.

Out of the swirling haze ahead, two shadows came running towards him. They were calling out to others but Cyrus couldn't understand what they were saying with his head spinning so badly. They each grasped him under one arm and heaved him further up the hill. More figures came into focus near the base of the Temple and to Cyrus's relief, they were gathered around the clear outline of the chariot. There was just one problem; the Neodactyl was nowhere to be found.

CHAPTER FORTY–SEVEN

MY KING

Nick dabbed gingerly at a cut along his left cheek and winced. His fingers came away bloody. That last blast had nearly done him in. He had seen the trail of flame coming, but there had been very little he could do to avoid it. It had torn an enormous hole in the side of the stone structure behind him, and he had almost been buried by the resulting avalanche. Minutes before the strike, Alec Dorn had come running up the hill out of the hellscape below screaming that he needed more Powdered Dreamwood to load into the chariot. Someone had gone running into the Temple to retrieve it and come stumbling back out with the King and Queen on their heels. They had the Dreamwood in hand, several canisters full of it, and had just loaded it into the chariot when the explosion occurred. Now Nick was spinning in a circle foolishly, trying to get his bearings. Dean and Kat had sprinted off down the hill into the dark cloud, though for what purpose he couldn't imagine.

The situation was falling apart. Nick was always ready for a fair fight, but that's not what this was. This was a war... or perhaps more accurately, this was a massacre. This sort of destruction could only have one result; the total annihilation of a people.

"He's here! Help us!" It was Kat's voice and it rose out of the smog in a strange, echoing fashion. The King and Queen rushed forward as Kat and Dean limped back into view supporting Cyrus Dorn between them. He looked like hell; bloodied and burnt and blurry-eyed, but he was still walking mostly on his own. He clutched in his hands the scepter that had brought them all to the island and a gleaming, curved machete.

The King and Queen began instantly interrogating Cyrus about his condition, but he shook them off.

"I'm okay Jack," Cyrus insisted, extracting his arms from the shoulders of his aids and taking a few wobbly steps on his own. "I need the chariot, Alec…"

Alec, who had been bent over the chariot wagon, turned to his brother with a horrible, deflated expression.

"The Neodactyl's gone," Alec reported, holding up the singed end of the ropes that had been tethering the creature to the mount. "That last blast must have… it's run off."

Cyrus looked like he would fall to his knees, but to his credit, he remained standing. He looked around wildly; his eyes showing such terrible defeat that Nick almost felt the pain himself.

As another flaming trench threw the valley below into temporary light, Nick could see the tyrant Magnus gleefully spinning his weapon before him. People could be seen streaming down the hill in all directions, attempting to get to the safety of the trees. Magnus could pick each of them off if he wanted to, but it was clear he had eyes only for Cyrus.

"What do we do now?" Kat cried out. Her tone was heartbreaking. It seemed her unsinkable spirit was waning at witnessing the defeat in Cyrus Dorn's eyes. Dean, likewise, was shaking his head in terror and putting a bracing hand on Kat's shoulder.

"We still have the Dreamwood," Alec offered, but there was no real conviction in his voice anymore. "It was undamaged in the cart. If he makes his way up here, maybe we can, I don't know…"

Cyrus was looking down at Magnus, only his outline visible now amongst the billowing smoke and fire overtaking the hillside. He had planted his weapon in the earth beside him and appeared to be waiting. The message was clear; it was Cyrus's move.

"He can't win like this," Cyrus grumbled, but he seemed to be in a daze. He shook his head forcefully, but if Nick had to guess, Cyrus didn't have much fight left in him.

People had started to clamber their way back out of the Temple, probably concerned about its structural integrity against such attacks. Some of the more militant citizens were lingering near the front, but many were fleeing into the wilds beyond the structure. The ones who stayed behind looked down at the machetes in their hands, realizing how useless they were against such power. Cyrus spun in a shallow circle, looking at the meager defenses of his people and his shoulders slumped further.

As Nick studied him, Cyrus tilted his head upward towards the sky, closed his eyes, and began mouthing something to himself. It was incredibly worrying to see, and for the first time since returning, Nick found himself contemplating the distinct possibility that they may not make it out of this. The rest of the group let the former king take his moment in complete, respectful silence.

Finally, Cyrus's eyes reopened, and he tilted his head back down again.

"Praying?" Jack asked in concern.

Cyrus shook his head, looked at Jack and forced a feeble smile. "No," he responded, "trying to talk myself out of something. Convince myself I'm crazy."

"Crazy for what?" Annica asked anxiously.

"For one last stand," Cyrus answered.

Nobody spoke. Jack opened his mouth a couple times but ended up shutting it again. Annica was shaking her head but appeared unable to argue. It was Kat, however, who drew Nick's attention. As he watched, he saw the light temporarily return to her eyes. Like the hope of Cyrus having one last plan to save them was enough to rekindle a tiny bit of that fire she had.

"Jack, Annica," Cyrus began firmly, "those are our people running scared. Go with them. All of you, go with them. Magnus will come to me, and I'll buy you as much time as I can."

"You can't survive this," Jack insisted.

Cyrus shook his head morosely. "I don't plan to, but I'll do my best to make sure he doesn't either." Jack gaped but words again seemed to fail him. Cyrus continued before he had a chance to find them. "There's no time," he said, "give our people a future. Give our Kingdom a future."

Nobody argued. Nobody said a word. They all just stared at him. Kat's mouth was open just a bit, her eyes glinting with tears, but also with faith once again. And at long last, there it was. Nick finally understood the importance of such a man. Cyrus Dorn wasn't the perfect leader, and it wasn't status that had earned him a towering statue of stone. He inspired others to be better. He inspired hope when there was none. His conviction gave Kat the confidence she needed to battle in the streets, gave Jack and Annica the ability to guide a kingdom, and gave the countless people around them something to fight for. He was a great leader not because he was remarkable, but because he inspired the remarkable in others.

Cyrus looked around for another moment; at Annica, then Jack, then Kat and Dean, and even Nick before finally landing on his brother. He paused on Alec, who stared back only briefly before looking down, unable to meet his gaze. Cyrus then smiled; a sad, yet accepting smile, and turned away.

Nick found he couldn't quite take his eyes off of him. Cyrus Dorn strode away down the hill; the fires below casting his shadow far and wide behind him like a dragging cloak. His dark silhouette against the burning countryside and rolling smoke was a more powerful image than Nick could ever remember seeing in his life. Cyrus drew his machete, slowly and deliberately, and threw it into the ground as he walked. With his other hand he extended the scepter out away from himself; a simple act that made his challenge clear. He stopped then, having arrived at a flat piece of land, and as Nick watched, Cyrus crouched low, placed one hand against the smoldering earth and stretched his glowing scepter out behind him. One last stand for the King of the East.

Magnus was much too far away for Nick to see his expression, but he could imagine him smirking. He lifted his trident, releasing a roaring tempest of flame, and charged. He looked like a demon from the deepest depths of the nightmare realm as he sprinted towards Cyrus, the glowing inferno howling along at his sides. It was horrifying to watch, and yet Cyrus Dorn did not flinch. He stayed crouched; the Kingdom's protector one last time.

"My King," Nick muttered softly to himself, and Kat turned to him with tears in her eyes. He looked back at her; this warrior who had found her place because she had a leader to believe in, and his mind was made up. Nick suddenly smiled and Kat's brow furrowed.

"Keep fighting the good fight, Kat," Nick said to her, and her brow only pulled together further. "You're a warrior… and don't you ever forget it."

With that, Nick turned and snatched two machetes out of the waiting guard's hands. They both protested but he paid them no mind. Instead, he ran to the side of the crippled chariot, wrenched it sideways until its wheels pointed downhill, then threw his weight against the back until it began to roll. Even over the rocky terrain, the wagon started to gain momentum incredibly fast. Nick pushed along beside it, then jumped onto the moving platform. Now it was really picking up speed. As the vehicle careened downhill, Nick threw his body weight this way and that, doing his best to steer the thing. He passed Cyrus, still waiting stoically for his enemy to reach him, and would have offered a salute if he had a free hand to do so.

Magnus was still sprinting up the hillside but seemed to finally register that something was wrong. His attention was ripped from Cyrus as he saw the chariot speeding over rock and fire towards him. He raised his trident and conjured a new funnel of flame from the earth, but Nick was almost on him. As the blazing storm smashed against the side of the wagon, Nick launched himself off the front, both machetes at the ready, and flew headlong into Magnus. At the last second, Magnus had attempted to drop his trident and pull a blade from his belt, but it was too late. The rusted machetes in Nick's hands impaled him through the stomach up to the hilts. Magnus screamed, and Nick could feel the hot, fresh blood of his enemy pour over his hands. A horrible, tearing pain in his stomach told him that Magnus had landed a blow as well. Sure enough, as Nick looked down, he saw barely an inch of steel sticking out from his midsection. But it didn't matter. None of that mattered.

As Magnus fell to his back, Nick on top of him, Nick yelled... howled... roared at Magnus. He could hear the chariot obliterating as it crashed to the earth around them in shattered pieces; the flames of the field licking against every surface. But Magnus was strong... stronger than Nick could ever imagine a person being, and he rolled over, forcing Nick onto the ground and giving the blade in his gut a horrible twist, even while the machetes remained in his own.

Magnus looked deranged with a solid rope of blood twisting out of his mouth, but he sneered all the same and smashed his forehead into Nicks.

"Why do you fight so hard for them?" Magnus snarled, but there was a definite gurgling noise accompanying his words. "Yes I know of you; self-serving to the bone. Growing a conscience in your final days doesn't earn you anything." He brought his face close, so close that Nick could smell the sweat and blood caking his features. "You have nothing but *hell* waiting for you."

Nick started to laugh. He couldn't help himself. Even the pain in his stomach seemed strangely far away. In his final moments... in a make-believe kingdom on a mysterious island in an alternate reality, Nick Satterall couldn't think of any better way to go out or anything more appropriate to do than laugh. And Magnus was rattled by it. His sneer turned to a grimace, then to a scowl.

"What could possibly be funny right now?" Magnus demanded.

Nick continued to laugh, even as he felt the heat from the fire creeping in towards them. "It's just that I've been to hell already," Nick answered, offering up one last broad smile. "At least this time... I'm taking you with me."

Magnus blinked, opened his mouth, then turned to run.

BOOM!

The chariot's contents ignited in a flash so intense it lit up the sky. The canisters of Powdered Dreamwood sent shrapnel flying fifty feet in the air. Brilliant streams of golden fire so powerful they dissolved the ground below shot out in every direction. For the second time in his life, Nick Satterall left the land of the living; this time, however, he passed with a smile on his face.

RECKONING

Cyrus still wasn't positive he had truly seen what he thought he had. The explosion at the base of the hill had been incredible and Magnus had been right near the center of it.

Cyrus stood, feeling like he was in a strange dream, and began to walk down the hillside towards the still raging fire. He saw movement from within, and held his scepter at the ready, but the figure that emerged from the flames was beyond fighting. Kysaar Magnus staggered forward, his mind clearly not comprehending the defeat to his physical form. He dragged half his body like it was dead weight, a bone stuck out at his knee, and his face was ravaged and blackened with burns. He only appeared to have use of one eye and his right hand now ended in a twisted, shattered claw.

He fell suddenly, landing on his knees, and then somehow willed himself back to his feet. His one eye stared straight at Cyrus with unbridled hate, and it looked like he wanted to say something, but only a steady stream of blood dribbled from his mouth. Cyrus continued walking towards him slowly. There was no more reason to rush. People were starting to peer out from the treeline, and Cyrus was fully aware of the audience on the hillside. And yet he didn't speed up. He moved slowly… methodically. And then Alec was at his side. He too, moved with a quiet, almost somber gait as they closed in on their enemy. Alec drew the machete from his belt and extended the hilt towards Cyrus, offering him the weapon. Cyrus took it without looking and continued his approach. Alec veered right, giving his brother space, then stopped near Magnus's side just as Magnus stumbled to his knees again. He attempted to stand once more but Alec put a hand on his shoulder and forced him back to his knees. He then stepped back a pace as Cyrus came level. Magnus opened his mouth once more, attempting to force the words through the blood choking his throat, but Cyrus was done listening to anything he had to say. He barely broke his stride as he swept out with Alec's blade and cleaved Kysaar Magnus's head from his shoulders. As the body crumpled and his blackened head bounced into the dirt and rolled away, Cyrus handed the machete back to his brother and closed his eyes.

It was over. It was hard to imagine, but it was over. People began trickling out of the forest and down the hill from the Temple. There was a strange silence in the air that felt both peaceful and powerful. He heard Jack's voice, though he had no idea what he said. He heard Annica, but likewise her words seemed distant and muffled. Cyrus finally opened his eyes again and found what appeared to be the entirety of the Kingdom closing in around the site of the execution. They were giving Cyrus a respectful amount of space but openly gawking at Magnus's decapitated body. Their eyes showed a mix of wonder, awe, terror, and relief. He saw Dean, his mouth hanging open at the carnage. He saw Kat, tears having settled on her cheeks, peering hopelessly at the smoldering wreckage of the chariot. And then, limping to the front of the crowd, he saw Nel. She was cradling one shoulder and looked mildly dazed but otherwise okay.

Finally, Cyrus's eyes travelled to Alec, standing in the center of the circle with him and seemingly in deep contemplation. His gaze was locked on the smoking ground, making it impossible for Cyrus to look him in the eyes. Alec had just helped him defeat the greatest threat the Kingdom had ever known, and he had done so *following* his brother. For the briefest of times, Alec and Cyrus had worked as one once again... had come together and fought together when their people needed them most. Was there hope, after all this time, that they could put their differences aside? What was Alec thinking? Cyrus found himself yearning to see his brother's stare, if only to assess who he was dealing with. Had Alec changed at all, or now that Magnus was defeated, would the King of the West come roaring back to life? Cyrus studied him for a long time, trying to will his desire to see his brother's eyes, his *old* brother's eyes, into reality.

At long last, Alec raised his eyes and looked intensely back at Cyrus. Cyrus's hope extinguished.

"I told you there would be a reckoning for us, brother," Alec hissed. His eyes shone like fire and a sneer was playing at the corner of his lips.

"Don't do this, Alec," Cyrus pleaded, "not here. Let the Kingdom rebuild... let them heal."

"You'd like that, wouldn't you," Alec responded, "for me to step aside and let you reform this place in your image. I saved these people every bit as much as you did."

"I'm not fighting you again, Alec," Cyrus stated firmly. He could barely stand upright at the moment, but more than that, the Kingdom deserved better than two squabbling siblings endlessly dueling for the right to rule. The gathered crowd was watching the exchange uneasily, visibly worried that a fight could explode at any moment.

"Okay then," Alec said, and a smile broke across his face. "Maybe we let the people decide."

"You're not king anymore, Alec," Cyrus insisted, "and neither am I. We had this contest before, but our time has passed. Given the circumstances..."

"Westtown!" Alec called out, cutting Cyrus off mid-sentence. "You rose up with me once before. Now the threat to our lands has been neutralized and our Temple still stands. Who wants to see our kingdom returned to its former glory?"

Cyrus bowed his head in crushing disappointment. He had thought maybe, possibly, Alec had changed. But no, that had been foolish. His hate simply ran too deep. But something *was* different than last time.

As Cyrus looked around, Alec's invitation was met with silence. Several in the crowd shifted uncomfortably, many looked at their feet in shame, but nobody moved to join him. Perhaps Alec hadn't changed but it seemed, maybe, the Kingdom had. Even Nel just stared back at her former ally. Her face was passive and exhausted, but her feet stayed firmly planted where she stood. Alec nodded to himself and the smug confidence slid from his features. But then he forced a smile again, turning in a wide circle.

"Okay," Alec said, "okay."

But there was something else different as well. Something different about Alec's defiance. If Cyrus didn't know any better, he would have guessed Alec was play-acting. Putting on a performance that his heart wasn't really in it. In the past, Alec had raged against perceived threats to his power with such fervor that it became alarming even to his closest followers. In this moment, he almost seemed to be grasping at that power again because he felt like he was *supposed* to. Like he was somehow destined to play the villain. It was possible Cyrus was reading into things, but they had just worked side-by-side not moments ago, just like old times. This bold display now seemed jarring in contrast and suddenly, Cyrus felt sure he could get through to him.

"Alec," Cyrus offered gently, "it doesn't have to be like this."

Alec turned to him, raised the machete in his hand, and walked towards Cyrus. He only stopped his advance once the tip of the blade was directly over Cyrus's heart. He paused there, staring him in the eyes. Cyrus didn't move. He just stood there, staring back at his brother, willing him to make the right choice. Alec's hand began to shake. His lip trembled and his jaw clenched. But he seemed unable to follow through on his threat. The Kingdom watched as one, nobody making a move to intervene, not even Jack. It seemed everyone realized the time had come to resolve this, one way or another.

Alec's hand began to quiver violently. He was losing control, and perhaps his conviction as well. Finally, at long last, he pulled his blade away with a grimace.

"Okay have it your way," Alec hissed. He began to back up through the crowd, which parted to let him leave. Once again, Cyrus had the distinct impression that Alec was doing this because he felt he had to. That his legacy as a conquering tyrant would somehow be tarnished if he were to give up his power so willingly. Cyrus supposed that's what power did to some people.

"Westtown," Alec announced, "I'll be around when you change your mind." He continued to walk backwards, adopting a swagger that Cyrus felt sure was a forced show of confidence. "And you, brother," Alec growled, locking eyes with Cyrus one last time and pointing the machete in his direction, "*you* I'll be out there waiting for, mark my words."

Cyrus didn't have a choice; he had to let his brother leave. He had to let him make this decision for himself, as self-destructive as it was. All he could hope was that time would chip away at his stubborn resolve.

Alec had almost reached the edge of the crowd when he suddenly let out a strange noise. It wasn't quite a gasp, more like an involuntary bit of air escaping from his mouth. But he looked stunned. Confused. Cyrus knew something was wrong before most of the crowd did and he began to step forward. Alec turned on the spot slowly, and as he did so, Cyrus caught the glint of a knife protruding from his lower back. A person was standing behind him, though Cyrus couldn't make out who it was through the dark. Whoever it was, Alec was looking right into their face, and what he saw was enough to extinguish the remaining fight he had left.

With an audible gasp from the crowd, Alec fell. First to his knees, then onto his hands. Finally, his head dipped, his shoulders slumped and he rolled onto his side.

"Grab them!" Cyrus called as he ran forward. The townsfolk as one all seized the attacker, who put up no struggle at all, but Cyrus was headed for his brother. He was at his side in a second, but Alec's eyes were already beginning to cloud over. Cyrus cradled his head and began to reach around to pull the knife from his body, but the amount of blood that came away on his hand was enough to confirm it was too late. Cyrus didn't know what to do. Did he start shouting for a doctor? Did he attempt to cauterize the wound himself? It couldn't end like this, could it? Given everything that had happened, Alec Dorn was supposed to go out in a blaze of glory, not quietly like this. But he couldn't move. Some part of himself knew this was the last time he would see his brother, so he did nothing but look down into his face. Alec looked back at him with an odd expression. It started as hate, loathing even, but then began to soften. It was almost like he was trying to force a scowl of defiance that wasn't coming naturally. His mouth twitched and formed into a sneering grimace, but it didn't quite reach his eyes. His eyes remained soft, perhaps even kind. Finally, the weak grin relaxed further and settled into an almost friendly smile. And there his face remained as the life left his body.

Cyrus just stared down at Alec. He couldn't make sense of it. He couldn't make sense of this end for his brother and he certainly couldn't make sense of his feelings about it. It was like every emotion at once was suddenly trying to burst forth, and because each contradicted the other, he just felt numb. He raised a shaking hand slowly and gently closed Alec's unseeing eyes for the last time.

Then Cyrus was on his feet. He had no memory of standing, but he must have done so. The townsfolk were all looking at him with intense concern and giving him a wide berth as he turned around. A solid mass of people were gathered near the edge of the crowd, all holding the murderer, concealed behind their many hands. Cyrus wasn't sure he was ready to face who had killed his brother. The emotions coursing through him were so intense he thought he was likely beyond understanding them. But he walked forward, summoning all the strength he had left, and motioned for his people to release their captive.

As their grip relaxed, Cyrus first saw a mane of wild, tangled hair. Then a large beard came into view and tattered, dirty rags for clothing. Cyrus knew the man right away. This was the mysterious, nomadic stranger that Cyrus had first encountered in that alternate reality. He had somehow come to the island, likely by finding the scepter shard that Cyrus had left behind in his world, but why travel all this way just to do Alec harm?

Cyrus stepped forward a few more paces until he was face to face with the man. He didn't know what he wanted to say, or what he wanted to do. Instead, he just looked into his gaunt, emaciated face, the sunken sockets housing surprisingly intelligent eyes. Piercing eyes. *Familiar* eyes.

Cyrus backed up a step. He felt suddenly dizzy. What sort of a sick trick was this? He turned away, then turned back. Those eyes. They were the same eyes he had known his entire life. The same eyes that had watched him through every major moment in his career, had watched him jealously as he courted Cynthia, had smiled with him when they took the Kingdom, and grown hateful when they grew apart. They were the same eyes that Cyrus himself had just helped close for the last time.

"How?" Cyrus managed to say, but deep down he knew. This man standing before him was the answer to the burning question Cyrus had been desperate for an answer to. *This* was the Alec Dorn from the alternate reality his brother had hijacked. Cyrus always knew there had to be an original whose life Alec stole. Cyrus had thought he'd been killed, but thinking back, he wasn't sure Alec had ever confirmed that. When Cyrus had first banished his brother to an alternate reality after their duel in the Fire Fields, Alec had a seven-year head start. He must have travelled to their old hometown, found an alternate version of himself living there and abducted him. Sure, it would have been cleaner to simply kill the version of himself currently occupying that life, but Cyrus guessed he couldn't bear murdering his own self. So his solution had been to send this *duplicate* to yet another alternate reality where he could live out the rest of his days away from prying eyes. There was only one problem; the world he had sent him to was desolate. Alec likely never knew, but from what Cyrus had seen during his brief visit, this alternate Alec was the only human occupying that world. Cyrus winced just thinking of the crushing isolation of being marooned alone in a strange land for seven years.

Cyrus vaguely registered Jack and Annica at his side and was slowly becoming aware of the buzzing, conspiratorial whispers of the crowd suddenly filling the air, but he only had eyes for this... *stranger*. Even looking at him now, he couldn't quite bring himself to refer to him as Alec. He was familiar yet somehow different. He returned Cyrus's gaze with defeated, accepting eyes. Like he had used his last bit of willpower to kill his alternate self. He looked confused as well, though his expression gave the distinct impression he didn't much care to have his questions answered. It occurred to Cyrus that he likely had no idea what was going on in this Kingdom or in fact where he even was.

Cyrus nodded to the man, then placed a hand on his shoulder, beckoning him forward. He still didn't know how to feel about his brother's death, but he found he couldn't quite blame his killer for doing what he'd done, either. He guided the stranger forward, who accepted hesitantly, like a frightened animal worried it was being led into a trap. The crowd parted widely as they passed, all looking at the man with unchecked disbelief. Jack and Annica joined as they cut through the onlookers and started their way up the hill towards the old Temple. Cyrus didn't know what was leading him this way, all he knew was he wanted to find somewhere quiet.

They made their way through the heavy front doors, across the dank and cavernous entry hall and finally found themselves in their old dining quarters. This was the room where Ydoro had reported on their popularity in the Kingdom after Mora's death. It was also the room where Cyrus and Jack had laid out plan after plan, theory after theory about how to get back to their own world. Now, it was dark and shadowy with only a single recently lit torch along the wall. Puddles of cloudy water had gathered in the shallow recesses of the cobblestones and a steady dripping on the oak table echoed rhythmically off the ceiling. Cyrus guided the stranger to the wooden bench along the table where he encouraged him to sit. He then stepped back and found himself studying the man for a long time. He didn't know what to say or how to proceed. This man had known *a* Cyrus Dorn long ago, but not the one standing before him now. How much did he understand of this place or the life they had built? Did he despise Cyrus the same way the other Alec did? Did he even know they had been enemies?

Finally, with a lengthy sigh and a small nod to himself, Cyrus extended a hand for the stranger to shake.

"We haven't met," Cyrus said, "my name is Cyrus Dorn, and I come from a world far from here."

CHAPTER FORTY–NINE

CONFLICT BUILDS GREATNESS

A full day later and Cyrus still couldn't quite process the events of the past twenty-four hours. He was enormously grateful to have Jack and Annica taking charge of the Kingdom as king and queen because he didn't feel he had the stability for it at the moment. The people were frightened, of course, and most of them had lost everything they ever owned. The rebuilding was going to be a painful process for the island's inhabitants, but at least they were finally safe.

As if the Kingdom itself wanted to wash away the stain of Kysaar Magnus, rain had begun to fall late that night and continued into the next day, extinguishing the remaining fires and leaving behind only the charred, blackened aftermath. The dead were being gathered and prepared for burial, but Cyrus had his brother brought to him first. He spent a long time sitting in private with his body, not with any real agenda, just reflecting. His gut told him that Alec had changed at the very end; that despite his public hostility, a part of his old self had maybe started to win out just a bit, but he would never know for sure. Was that last smile he had offered a look of kindness to mend their broken bridges or simply the neurons firing off at random as he died? Cyrus would never know the truth, but he found he could live with that.

His conversation with the *alternate* Alec had been amongst the strangest experiences of his life. He had tried his best to explain everything that had happened leading to the moment last night, but he still felt he wasn't doing the story justice. The man listened intently but continued to give the impression that he didn't much care. Cyrus supposed he couldn't blame him for that; after living in isolation for so long, it was understandable that his one and only focus had been to kill the person responsible for taking his life. Once he was brought to the island after retrieving that scepter shard that Cyrus had dropped, he spent his days navigating the surrounding forests alone, something he was quite adept at of course. He hadn't known where he was or who the many people were inhabiting the island, but he did quickly notice that Alec, the one who had imprisoned him years ago, was amongst them. From that moment on, Alec's days were numbered; the stranger just had to find an opportunity.

Cyrus also found it supremely odd being in the old Temple again. The torches had all been relit of course and the place was starting to feel a bit more occupied, but there were undoubtedly some painful memories associated with it. He found himself walking the halls aimlessly, unsure of what he wanted to do, who he wanted to speak to, or what his future would look like. He ended up lowering himself onto his old bed in his old quarters and resting his face in his palms.

"You don't look like someone who wants company," came a voice from the hallway.

Cyrus looked up to one of the most welcome sights he could hope for in such times. Ydoro came limping into the room, badly bruised and battered but still with an eager smile on his face.

"Dr. Garse did a good job," Cyrus commented, standing and helping his old friend into the room. He sat him on the bed next to him and returned to his original spot.

"He knows his craft," Ydoro agreed, "of course you remember from experience. And Noma is up and moving around too, bit worse for wear, but he's young."

"How are you feeling?" Cyrus asked, taking in the burn marks along his cheeks, forehead, and neck.

"I've had worse," Ydoro responded dismissively, though it was clearly not true. "I'm more worried about you."

"Me?" Cyrus said with a small laugh. "I'm beat up plenty but I'll survive."

"That's not what I mean," Ydoro pushed thoughtfully. "You've been through a lot, more than most people ever will. And you just lost your brother."

Cyrus shook his head. "I lost my brother a long time ago."

Ydoro stayed silent a moment before continuing. "You know, it's okay to feel something for him. He did plenty bad in his time, but I don't think that was his whole story. Even if you don't celebrate him, perhaps it's okay to *remember* the whole person, not just his best and worst deeds."

Cyrus smiled. "He used to be so wide-eyed, enthusiastic. I mean, growing up we wouldn't leave each other's sides. A couple science nerds just catching frogs, exploring the neighborhood... learning how the world worked. When I first graduated, he was so happy for me. We celebrated all night, made fools of ourselves if truth be told, despite the scoldings from our mother. But it's like she always knew we couldn't get into too much trouble if we were together." Cyrus paused, his expression darkening as he remembered more current times. "I don't know when things changed in him. This place certainly tapped into the worst of his tendencies, but those feelings... that hate came from somewhere. It was living in him that whole time just waiting to be ignited. And I do wonder how much of that fault lies with me and my actions. You know, stories would have you believe that relationships are durable things; bulwarks that stand against the hardships of life. But the truth is that nothing can fully withstand the pressures of time, and the bonds between people are amongst the most fragile of things. Fractures that form can be nearly impossible to mend, and even the most solid foundations can rot away beneath our feet."

Ydoro again let the silence play out. To his credit, he did not appear uncomfortable with the heavy conversation but simply knew when to talk and when to reflect. It was a long time before he finally replied. "Alec considered you his worst enemy," he said, "but that's only because he couldn't bring himself to blame the person truly responsible for his life. He was always his own worst enemy, Cyrus. And if you don't believe me, just look at the way he died."

"Now there you might have a point," Cyrus agreed with a brief smile at the irony of the statement. "With how much we now know about parallel realities and parallel versions of ourselves, I guess I should find comfort in imagining alternate worlds where we didn't do all these terrible things to each other. Where we built each other up, made each other better, rather than tore each other down. Where we found peace with each other."

Ydoro nodded his head slightly, but it wasn't an agreement. "I can understand that. But conflict builds greatness. If Alec hadn't become what he was, you wouldn't be what you are today. And that would be an absolute tragedy. The world would have lost one of its greatest leaders."

*****

Cyrus felt better after speaking with Ydoro. He didn't know if it was his advice or simply being able to say aloud some of the things he was feeling, but it was cleansing. He found he could suddenly walk with a purpose again and make decisions with a clear mind. He wanted to seek out Jack and Annica, who ended up being quite difficult to track down. The Kingdom was a big place after all, and while the injured were using the old Temple as a site for rehabilitation and healing, the rest of the island's population were busy planning for the future. He eventually found them in the Fire Fields, assessing the decimation of their former town.

"Good to see you up and about," Jack called with a grin as he saw Cyrus approaching.

Workers were already weaving through the charred piles of debris with carts and wagons, clearing paths and searching for anything worth saving. It was remarkable, as always, how quickly the townsfolk got to problem-solving.

"You sure you're not pushing it walking around like this?" Annica asked, though she would of course be the first one up and about after an injury of her own.

"I'm fine, really," Cyrus assured her. "Just processing it all."

"How's our friend?" Jack asked skeptically. "You know, alternate Alec?"

Cyrus frowned slightly. "Hard to say. It's like speaking to someone who's just achieved their life's one ambition. They're victorious, but somehow hollow now. I don't know that he's thought about much else other than survival and revenge since he was marooned."

Jack gave a shudder at the idea but then rolled his eyes slightly and said, "It's still Alec, though. I mean, that's some poetic justice right there. He should have kept his counterpart alive, the two deserved each other."

Cyrus just smiled mildly but didn't quite share Jack's assessment. Jack didn't truly understand, having never encountered anyone he knew from an alternate reality. Cyrus understood all too well. It had been so incredibly painful and confusing being in the company of Cynthia and even Diana from that reality Alec trapped him in. It was difficult to explain, but there *was* a palpable difference in these people. They looked the same, and in many ways acted the same, but small deviations in their choices had changed the course of their lives. The Alec with them now; the malnourished, bearded *stranger* as Cyrus kept calling him, was a truly different person than the King of the West. This man hadn't been shaped by the island, hadn't made the choices the other Alec had made, and for all intents and purposes was a different person because of it.

"We do have one thing we want to discuss with you," Jack said with an uncomfortable shake of his head. "The Nel problem."

"What's she done now?" Cyrus asked.

"Well, nothing," Jack admitted, "that's sort of the problem. She helped you escape from certain death with Magnus, fought beside you at the end, and even declined Alec's offer to rebuild his empire... but it's Nel. She's unpredictable and dangerous. I know you remember her actions during your reign, but you also have to understand what's happened over the last six years. She was the reason our times of peace came to an end. We would never have been playing around with those scepters at all if she hadn't staged a military incursion against us. We never saw the damage she was doing from hiding, but it was six years she was quietly working against us. We were preparing for her trial when Magnus arrived."

Cyrus sighed. It certainly was a complicated situation. "Then maybe that's the solution..." he said grimly, "we have a trial."

They were interrupted by two of Annica's loyalists approaching fast with a small cart in tow. "My King, my Queen! We found them!"

Cyrus was left playing catchup, but Annica seemed to know what they were referring to. "Both of them?"

"Yes, my Queen," one of the men answered as he pulled the cart up beside them. He walked around to the back, reached in and tenderly pulled away several overlapping pieces of fabric to reveal the two tridents of Kysaar Magnus. They had been carefully placed and wrapped as though the workers had been afraid to touch them with their bare hands. The infinite gold repair sites wrapping around each staff like spiderwebs gleamed blindingly in the afternoon sun. Jack extended a hand and ran it through the air just above the surface of the weapons as though feeling for their power.

"We didn't want these falling into the wrong hands," Jack explained.

"Mmmhmm," Cyrus said thoughtfully. "And what about using them?"

"Using them?" Jack asked in alarm. "Magnus and the Alchemist visited more realities than we can count. Every one of these fractures is another decimated world, what would you be looking for out there?"

"I'm not interested in his worlds," Cyrus explained, "I'm wondering if they could open a door with *our* scepter." When Jack and Annica just stared at him, he said, "I made a promise. We all did. We need to send Dean and Kat home."

CHAPTER FIFTY

WHAT YOU TAKE WITH YOU

I t had been a week since peace had been returned to the island, yet Kat still felt like a lost orphan. Everywhere she stepped, she seemed to be in the way. The Kingdom was trying to rebuild itself around her; simply moving on from the horrors that had recently occurred, but she was finding it somehow distasteful to heal so quickly. How does one bounce back from something like this? She had been a college student, worried about her social status and her timeliness to classes. Now, she didn't really know what mattered. Whenever she closed her eyes at night, she kept seeing Nick Satterall. He winked at her, gave her a smile, and said 'keep fighting the good fight, Kat.' After everything they had been through together, she wasn't prepared for that to be the last time she would see him. He gave his life to save this place, these people, and she still didn't understand why. Nick wasn't the selfless type, why would he have done that? Despite having already died once, Nick was someone always so full of life that it seemed wrong for the world to move on without him in it. But move on it had.

Poor Dean was trying to provide comfort for her but was pretty far out of his depth. He had come yesterday with Nick's broadsword, retrieved from the rubble at the front of the Temple, and presented it to her with a bracing smile. He suggested that Nick would have wanted her to have it. It was a nice gesture, but she felt certain Nick wouldn't have cared who took his sword after he died. She could imagine him saying, 'Doesn't matter to me, I won't be using it anymore.' The thought made her smile just slightly.

She was currently sitting on the grounds near the front of the Temple, her legs dangling over the edge of a large rock from the ruined outer wall. She held Nick's sword in her hand, absent-mindedly turning it over between her fingers and staring out at the busy hillside below. The field remained blackened even now, but much of the debris and carnage had been cleared, the dead all put in the ground.

She heard footsteps crunching through the dirt behind her and winced slightly, knowing it must be Dean in another attempt to cheer her up. She really wasn't in the mood.

"The sword suits you," came a voice that was distinctly not Deans. Kat turned and was shocked to see Cyrus Dorn himself standing behind her. He was studying her with a mix of concern and warmth that felt supremely genuine, and she was once again struck by how much he truly cared for his people. Was she one of them?

Cyrus walked forward slowly and helped himself to the seat next to her on the rock. She had spent very little time with Cyrus Dorn, and never one-on-one. She found herself strangely intimidated after seeing the reverence in which he was treated in the Kingdom.

"It's not the first time this Temple has seen battle, you know," Cyrus reflected. "My brother stormed these gates once to rescue Nel from the clutches of the prior king. It's funny, that was six years ago now... feels like a lifetime... and yet it's only been a matter of months for me. Strange how time works like that."

Kat smiled but didn't quite know what to say.

"Something's bothering you," Cyrus stated bluntly. "I don't know you well, but you've been quiet since the battle. I know you were close with Nick..."

"It's just," Kat began, "nobody cares what he did for them. Nobody even knows who he was. He saved the Kingdom and it looks like he will just be forgotten. And, I mean no disrespect to you, but nobody's going to be building a statue of Nick, but why not? He gave his life so all of them could live. And it's not just Nick," Kat admitted, finding she couldn't stop now that she had started. "It's everything. I don't know how people just get over this sort of thing. I mean, you remember Mauretz? The man who came here with Nick? Well, nobody could find him after the battle, so Dean and I went looking. Turns out he was killed when the outer wall collapsed, and no one even knew. You think about it, he barely said two words to anyone since arriving here, stayed to himself, and yet he was apparently there with us, right there, watching Magnus destroy everything. He must have just been scared and thought he would stay close to the rest of us newcomers, and we didn't even notice. And yet he was the one to kill Nick the first time, so I feel guilty for even feeling bad for him."

"You never have to feel guilty for being a decent person," Cyrus said gently. "I was recently told that it's okay to remember the whole person, not just their best and worst deeds. I think that can apply to everyone."

Kat looked down at the sword in her hands again, somewhat embarrassed to be talking about loss with a man who had just lost his brother. "What was he like?" she finally asked, "Alec?"

Cyrus smiled. "Intense," he responded. "I wish he had a happier life, but he had his own demons to battle. I guess we all do."

Kat found herself staring at Cyrus as he looked out over the horizon. He was battle-hardened and weathered by his experiences, and while he still seemed to hold a bit of apprehension for the power he possessed, it was becoming more and more a part of him.

"You're a great king," Kat found herself saying, and Cyrus looked at her in surprise. "I know you're not king anymore, but this place looks to you when they're most lost, even Jack and Annica. That may not be what you wanted from your life, but I don't think you should ignore it."

Cyrus smiled appreciatively. "You wanna know a secret?" he asked. "I still don't feel like a king. I go to bed every night feeling like an imposter."

Kat laughed lightly at the admission. "That might be why you're good at it. Don't forget, I know you from my world's history, as a decently successful professor who vanished into oblivion. And if it means anything at all, when I look at you, I don't see that professor. I see a warrior king who fights every day for his people."

Cyrus nodded, "It means a lot." He then shook his head with a laugh and said, "but I was coming here to make you feel better, not the other way around. Isn't it supposed to be me imparting wisdom?"

Kat smiled and shrugged. "Never stop learning from your people and you'll always be a great leader."

Cyrus raised his eyebrows in an impressed sort of way. "That's not bad. You could make a powerful leader yourself one day."

"Here?" Kat asked.

"Well that's the other reason I came to see you," Cyrus said, "Noma has been working with Magnus's tridents... Kat, they can reopen doors that were previously closed. We can send you home."

Kat's first feeling was elation. It was what had kept her going, kept her fighting all this time. The hope of returning to her normal world and her normal life. Yet for some reason, her mouth refused to smile. She just stared back at Cyrus, whose own excitement for her began to fade as well.

"What is it?" he asked.

Kat wasn't sure she knew how to put it into words. "It's just, how do you go back to a life so... ordinary... after what we've seen here? It all seems so... unimportant now."

To her immense relief, Cyrus nodded in understanding. "There are infinite realities out there, Kat. You know what that means? This one isn't so special. You helped us save our world. Now you get to bring what you learned back to yours. Because what you learned about yourself doesn't stay behind... you get to take that with you. Go live your life. Become the leader you didn't know you could be before."

Kat smiled, but it was in a somber sort of way.

Cyrus took note. "The good news," he added, "is that the manufactured tridents are far more predictable than the scepters ever were. If it makes you feel any better, we'll travel to your world from time to time...

check in on you. Make sure you're still the person you're supposed to be."

Kat's smile grew just a bit. "I'd like that." But suddenly something occurred to her. "Does this mean you can go home too?" she asked excitedly.

Cyrus's smile faded a bit. "Unfortunately, we only have access to your reality because of that fragment that brought you here, which is safely reattached to the scepter. The fragment that connects to my world is long gone, lost in the Fire Fields is my guess. It would take about a million years to track down that tiny little shard."

Kat looked down at the ornate handle of the sword again. She knew how desperately Cyrus wanted to get back to his homeworld and his wife, but she secretly couldn't help but feel that this was where he belonged. She kept this to herself, however. She felt certain that Cyrus knew this already, even if he didn't like saying it out loud. She finally looked back up at him, then moved her fist to her chest and bowed her head as she had seen the citizens of the Kingdom do.

"Thank you, my King," she proclaimed softly.

Cyrus smiled and shook his head. "You don't need to do that, Kat. You helped save this place as much as I did, and as much as Nick did."

Kat considered this, thought of protesting, but then decided against it. Instead, she extended her hand out and said, "Okay, then it was good to meet you, Cyrus."

Cyrus took her hand in his and replied, "It was good to meet you too, Kat."

THE TRIAL OF NELIDA YORE

How horribly formal this felt. Asking Jack even a few weeks back what should be done with Nel, his answer would have been far different. Things felt uncomfortably complicated now. She had been instrumental in winning them back the Kingdom, and yet she was impossibly dangerous. The leaders, advisors, and trustees of the Kingdom had been meeting behind closed doors for the better part of a week trying to decide what to do with her. She knew the deliberations were taking place, though she was not jailed while her future was being decided. It had simply felt wrong to lock her back up after everything she had done.

Everyone had an opinion about Nel, that much was to be expected. But Jack felt all points and counterpoints were weighed appropriately and given respectfully. Ydoro had come out in favor of giving her a second chance, pointing out that half the Kingdom would be guilty if they began prosecuting everyone who had followed Alec in the past. But in Jack's opinion, and others as well, Nel had done more than just follow. She had been instrumental in his rise to power and shameless in her manipulation of a susceptible individual. There were those that still wanted her hanged for such treason.

A decision had finally been reached, though whether it was the right one, Jack could not say. They had been deliberating within the walls of the Temple, which in itself felt wrong. Himself and Annica had gone to great lengths to do things differently from their predecessors, purposely vacating this building for one more grounded amongst the people. It felt like a step backward to be deciding the fate of a citizen in such a place.

"It has to be done," Cyrus assured Jack as they exited their final meeting. "I don't like it much either, but we don't have a choice. Anything else wouldn't be fair to the people."

Jack just nodded but couldn't think of a response. This was the sort of firm-handed decision making that he struggled with, and probably why the crown didn't fit him as well as it fit others.

"I've known her a long time," Jack said. "We sailed together quite a few times before that last voyage. She was always so..."

Cyrus waited several seconds while Jack struggled to find the right word. "Cunning?" Cyrus offered.

"Fun," Jack admitted with a small laugh. "She would be laughing, drinking, fighting with the best of them. She was a force, but usually, in that sort of rough environment, it was welcome. Then we come here and..."

He trailed off and Cyrus just nodded.

"She made her decisions," Cyrus said, "we all did. Doesn't make ours now any less hard."

*****

Nel was brought in that afternoon to stand before her peers. Nobody wanted to make a show of it, so the public was not invited. She was again allowed to walk into the Temple freely, no chains or ropes or bindings of any kind. The general consensus was that she would not attempt to flee.

The room selected was a medium-sized empty space on the main level that had chairs and tables dragged in. It looked much like a courtroom, though more one-sided. There were seats along one wall for the King and Queen, Cyrus of course, and a handful of their top advisors, Ydoro included. Then across the room, facing the panel, stood a single wooden chair.

Nel, for her part, looked resigned as she stepped into the room, as though she anticipated what the decision might be. She had been helping with the rebuilding process and her pants were covered with flecks of dirt and dust. Jack wondered if this was intentional as a reminder of her willingness to contribute. She walked forward with straight-backed confidence. Someone else might have chosen a more contrite, respectful posture, but that simply was not Nel's way. Her calculating eyes scanned the room quickly as she found her chair but chose not to sit, electing instead to stand in front of it.

"Nelida Yore," Annica began, "we've gathered as a council to decide what should be done, in light of certain…"

"Oh come on," Nel interrupted, and Jack winced slightly. "I'm sorry, I mean no disrespect, but I know why we're here and I'd love to forgo the formalities. Just be straight with me."

Annica's eyes flashed with frustration but she composed herself quickly. "Nel, we felt the formalities were important to convey that this was deliberated extensively."

"I appreciate that," Nel insisted, though her tone lacked patience. "I'm just better with directness."

Annica looked exasperated and sighed heavily, but she finally conceded. "Very well, you want directness, here it is. You're dangerous, Nel. You helped build an empire to rule over our Kingdom in violence and fear, but worse than that, you did it by being manipulative, destructive, and, in all honesty, you did it with palpable glee. You saw both Alec Dorn and this place as playthings for your own personal amusement. The real-world consequences of your actions never seemed real to you. The amount of blood on your hands is staggering, the body count incalculable. If I were talking solely about the Battle of Westtown Square that would be one thing, but it never stopped there. And given the chance at freedom, you raised a rebellion against the democracy we were attempting to build and in doing so, allowed some of that same poison to spread out into other realities."

Nel had begun nodding her head halfway through Annica's speech. "Okay, okay," Nel interrupted with a slight roll of her eyes, "I get the picture."

Annica took a deep breath. "The Kingdom is indebted to you for what you did for Cyrus. He wouldn't be alive were it not for your actions, and nobody discounts the stand you took with our people against Kysaar Magnus."

"Can I say something?" Nel asked, and Annica looked so befuddled by the request that she just exhaled deeply and nodded. "I've made mistakes, we all have. But you don't see me standing here singing Alec's praises. Maybe I hitched my wagon to the wrong horse, I can admit that. But this place is all about second chances. I mean, we each got a fresh start when we came here, and in all honesty, I've never been anywhere that I've felt more alive. This is my home, more so than anywhere I've ever lived. Haven't I earned my place the same as all of you?"

Annica looked down at her hands and Jack was feeling extremely uncomfortable. But then Cyrus stood up, and silence fell. Official rankings aside, nobody had a thought to interject if Cyrus were about to speak, not even Nel.

"Nel," he began, his voice strong and level, "I will forever be in your debt for saving my life. And while I appreciate your admission that you chose the wrong person to follow, that statement doesn't hold up to scrutiny. You didn't *follow* Alec, you bent him to your will. I don't minimize Alec's sins, but you were right there with him for every decision he made. And honestly, the fact that you're now willing to discard your loyalty to him so quickly only serves as a reminder of how cheap your devotion truly sells for. You were the right hand of the devil, Nel. I say that not out of anger but out of profound disappointment."

Nel was silent, her face unreadable.

"You can't stay here," Cyrus concluded, "that is the decision of this council. We appreciate that this feels like home to you, but you've had many chances to *start fresh* as you say, and you've seized shockingly few of them. Personally, I hope this newly grown conscience you've developed is genuine, and if it is, I think you have a chance to finally build a successful, respectable life for yourself... but not here. We're sending our transplanted friends back home to their worlds... and you will be joining them."

"Joining them?" Nel repeated.

"There are different doors along that timeline for you to choose from," Cyrus insisted. "The one that this new... that *Alec* will be using is close to a time period you know. You can start a new life there."

Nel looked like she wanted to respond with any number of hateful retorts, but she held her tongue. Eventually, she gave a shallow bow of her head and said in a slightly mocking tone, "My King, my Queen... the rest of you."

She turned and strode out of the room.

"Should we be worried that she might..." Jack began.

Annica shook her head. "I think the Kingdom's looking to heal. She won't find much support if she tries anything."

"She'll be okay," Cyrus said confidently. "She was bound to have a reaction, it's Nel after all. She couldn't lose face by acting too respectful."

CHAPTER FIFTY–TWO

GOING HOME

While Kat struggled with the idea of returning home, Dean of course needed no such coaxing. At hearing the news that a door could be opened, he was practically pushing people aside to get to it. A part of her rolled her eyes at his eagerness to leave, but she had to remind herself that not everyone was meant for such adventures. The surprising lesson she had learned, however, was that *she* was meant for such adventures. Who would have known? But the adventure had finally come to an end.

They were being escorted across the Fire Fields, their procession somber and purposeful. A crowd had gathered up ahead, presumably at the spot where their doorway would be created. Cyrus was leading them while conversing quietly with a still skittish alternate-reality version of his brother. The latter still wore the enormous beard and long hair, making him look very little like his deceased island counterpart. Kat wondered to herself what they had to talk about, but it was none of her business. What mattered was that they were distracted, and Kat had one last thing she wanted to do before she left the Kingdom.

As they made their approach, Kat slunk away and walked towards the edge of the forest. Upon entering the cover of the trees, she began scanning the area for the perfect spot. Her eyes fell on a prominent stone and she cocked her head. There was nothing particularly interesting about it, but it drew her attention all the same. She approached slowly, thinking it would do nicely for her purposes, when she realized it had some old etching carved into its surface. Moss and algae growth had softened some of the tooling edges, but the letters were still clear: *Dalton Sydney*.

Despite the name sounding mildly familiar, Kat didn't know who the man had been or why his gravestone was buried in such an unremarkable spot in the forest. But it would work just fine.

She stepped carefully to the other side of the stone and began to dig a shallow channel with her hands. Once it was wide and deep enough, she lifted the broadsword, *Nick's* sword, and placed it gently in the earth. Nick would probably howl with laughter at seeing her bury a perfectly good weapon, but it made her feel better knowing that a part of him would be treated with the respect it deserved. She cupped handfuls of dirt and slowly shoveled them back into place, letting the particles cascade over the ornate carvings of the hilt and hide the beautiful artifact forever. Once the final bits were patted down, she placed her hand on top and bowed her head just slightly.

"Thank you, Nick," she said.

With that, she stood, exited the forest and jogged back to rejoin the group.

"Where did you go?" Dean asked upon seeing her breathlessly return.

"Just something I had to do," Kat answered vaguely. "Nothing to worry yourself about, Mr. Pyrene."

Dean laughed. "Mr. Pyrene? Does that mean you're my student again?"

"I don't know," Kat teased, "your classes might be a little intense for my liking."

They had arrived at the apparent site of departure. Noma had an assortment of tools and devices spread across the ground and both the scepter and one of the tridents had been stabbed into the earth causing the area to glow warmly. Ydoro stood off to the right along with Jack and Annica. Nel stood to the left, flanked by militants who weren't quite guarding her but wouldn't let her leave either.

"Now I've tried this myself," Noma announced, likely noticing the skepticism on all their faces. "The tridents really are a marvel of ingenuity! The designer actually implemented some of the ideas that I had been working on for the scepters. When I tap the staff of the trident against the repair site of the scepter, it allows us to access the door to *that* reality. The good news, unlike the doors created by breaking the staff, these will deposit you more or less where you were when you last touched the fragment in your world. You can navigate a little bit, and it won't be as painful as some anomalies of the past. Keep your eyes open, you'll see streaks of color and displays of light, but through all of that, you'll see worlds start to form. They won't all be familiar… take your time, allow them to pass by you; you'll know yours when you see it. When you do, ease yourself forward. The wormhole will do the rest."

Noma made it sound almost magical and Kat again wondered if she would ever experience this sort of awe again in her life.

"I think we'll start with you sir," Noma said, though it was unclear who he was speaking to. "Sir, sir," he continued, looking in the direction of the *stranger*. Nobody seemed comfortable referring to him as Alec.

The man stepped forward apprehensively. He turned to look at Cyrus who gave him a comforting nod, then briefly scanned the rest of the people and the surrounding landscape. He didn't seem overly unhappy about leaving, just passively curious about the strange land he was vacating.

A flash emanated brightly from behind him and Noma stepped back out of the way. He had tapped the two weapons together and a brief pulse of golden light had erupted from the site. As it dissipated, a small disturbance in the air could be noted around the *door*, but otherwise, you'd never know.

Alternate-Alec wasted no time making his way towards it, only offering one final glance at Cyrus as he went. Kat found herself wondering what sort of world he was going back to. From what she understood, Alec had forcibly taken over his life seven years ago and been working his job, living in his house, making a future with his wife. And then the husband she had been living with up and vanished several weeks ago. How would he ever explain all of that? For that matter, had they even been married the last time he saw her? Kat didn't know the timeline, but it was entirely possible they were only dating when he was abducted. None of this was her business, of course, but the mind certainly wandered.

There was no flash of light or real noise as he passed through the anomaly. His form simply became indistinct and slightly blurred around the edges, the way things look from a distance along a hot road. Another blink of the eye and he was gone, returned to the world he had been snatched from long ago.

"Now do we have to worry about accidentally stepping through that wormhole?" Jack asked, eying the slightly dancing mirage skeptically.

Noma tapped the trident and scepter together again and the air returned to normal. He then smiled. "As I said, King Jack, these tools are really quite impressive. They can close doors too."

As Jack nodded in acceptance, Nel suddenly stepped forward towards Noma, placed a gentle hand on his shoulder and began whispering to him rapidly. Cyrus, Jack, and Annica all looked concerned by the exchange, but Noma held up a finger to them.

He continued to listen to her frantic whispering, then shook his head slightly. "That's not somewhere you want to be," he insisted, but Nel nodded fervently.

"Please," she said.

Eventually, Noma nodded in agreement to her mysterious request and began running his finger over the gleaming fractures of the trident. Kat noticed Jack and Cyrus exchange a wary glance but they said nothing.

There was another flash of light as Noma tapped the two weapons together, opening a second door. He then nodded to Jack.

"This is you, Nel," Jack said, "and I can't quite think what to say."

Nel laughed slightly. "That's okay, Jack. I wouldn't expect you to find eloquent words in the moment." When Jack looked offended, she clapped him on the shoulder. "I'm joking, big guy. Never change." She then turned to Cyrus, who offered her a stiff half-smile. "Doc, it's been fun," she said.

She gave him a lazy salute, then turned and began to strut confidently towards the door. Both Cyrus and Jack seemed torn about watching her go, as though they couldn't believe this was truly the last time they would see her.

Nel appeared far less torn. She raised her hand up as she went, providing a dismissive gesture of farewell over one shoulder. She never paused once as she was claimed by the void and vanished before their eyes.

And with that, Nel was gone. Cyrus and Jack, the last two remaining members of that doomed voyage from the thirties, both looked somberly at the ground.

"What did she whisper to you?" Cyrus asked Noma.

Noma looked at him guiltily. "I am sorry, I didn't think it would harm anything, and she asked so nicely."

"What did she ask?" Jack pushed in concern.

"She didn't want to go back to her world," Noma admitted with an embarrassed shrug, "she asked to be sent to the reality Magnus came from... the one that Dean and Kat explored."

"What?" Jack practically yelled in alarm, "She... why would...?"

But Cyrus started to laugh.

"You think this is funny?" Jack demanded of his friend.

"Of course she wanted to go there," Cyrus responded, still chuckling. "It's the wild west... chaos. It's a world tailor-made for her."

"She'll... but what if she..." Jack continued to stammer.

"That's a world that can't be harmed any further," Cyrus assured him, "and hell, if there's one person who can bend that place into submission, it's Nel."

Jack shook his head, but then thought a moment and began to laugh as well. "Good luck to her, I guess," he said.

"Good luck to *them*," Cyrus corrected with another chuckle.

As Jack turned and began to playfully scold Noma for making such a decision without consulting the king, Cyrus turned to Kat and Dean with a warm, bracing smile and Kat's heart dropped just slightly. It was finally their turn.

"One more left," he said to them. "Remember, it's not leaving, its returning. Returning to where you're meant to be."

Dean smiled and shook his head in disbelief. "Cyrus Dorn," he muttered to himself. Kat knew he must be reflecting how this was the man they had tracked through history. Who would have ever imagined this was where their curiosity would take them.

Annica and Jack stepped forward and each shook their hands.

"Thank you for everything," Annica said warmly. "The Kingdom will forever be in your debt. Now go live your own life. You've both earned it."

Kat smiled as another flash of golden light announced the opening of a third door. She didn't know if she was ready or not, but she would have to be. She took another look at the island, the surrounding trees, the vibrant Fire Fields, and the people. Some waved, some bowed, but Cyrus alone seemed to fully grasp the feeling that was currently consuming her. And of course he understood, he had made the same choice once before. The difference was, this was where *he* was meant to be, not her. He beamed at them and nodded encouragingly. It was the strength she needed to take those final few steps. She smiled back, turned away, and took a deep breath. She then looked at Dean, her reality-hopping travel companion, who returned her gaze with a bit of his old smile again.

"Let's go home," he said to her.

They didn't look back as they strode forward; it would have been too painful for Kat to do so. It was several paces before the light around them began to streak and a vibrating sensation began to fill their heads. It wasn't unpleasant, just disorienting. Kat let the wormhole take her, lifting her feet from the ground. The weightlessness she felt was almost comforting as everything blurred around her, moving faster and faster. Then up ahead, if one could call it that in this world between realities, she could see a room beginning to form. There were desks, a laptop, a vacant podium, maps on the walls, a forgotten pencil on a table, and sol-id floors. Remembering Noma's instructions, she leaned in, allowing the wormhole to guide her. The swirling around her slowed, her vision be-came more focused, and the weight began to return to her body. As her feet touched the ground softly, she barely staggered at all. Her head spun a bit but it didn't last. Instead, she found herself turning and look-ing behind her, hoping that somehow, some way, she would still be able to see the door and that other world hidden behind it. But no, there was nothing. No indication that a tear in reality had just occurred and no sign that infinite other worlds were just a step away. They were back. Back to the mundane. Back to the unremarkable. Back to normal.

CHAPTER FIFTY–THREE

IN THE END

C yrus hadn't revisited the battlements atop the old Temple until today. There had never been a reason to ascend the precarious ladder up to the roof of the building. The last time he had done so was when he fought King Mora... the day he had won the right to lead the Kingdom. He couldn't explain why he wanted to be up here now other than the fact that it was removed from it all. He simply wanted to get away for a moment and not be responsible for making tough decisions or putting on a brave face for the benefit of the uneasy townsfolk. Perhaps that was selfish, but mentally he needed it.

There was a time when these walls would have been manned day and night by a collection of loyal guards, watching the perimeter for enemy movement. That was years ago by Kingdom time and the deep green lichen growth on the rocks proved it. It still made Cyrus's head spin just a bit thinking how time here had moved on without him.

He walked right up to the edge of the worn stone ramparts, climbed atop them and dangled his feet over the edge of the wall. It was dizzying to look down at the countryside from this height, but also incredibly peaceful. A Shrieking Bat called out from somewhere in the forest, an echoing, haunting noise that carried far and wide across the land, and it made Cyrus smile remembering his first encounter with the creatures. He found himself wondering where that Neodactyl from Magnus's world had gone and if they would ever see it again, but he somehow knew it wouldn't give them trouble. It was wild after all, how it was always meant to be.

With the exception of the charred open areas directly below, most of the island seemed to be in an active phase of growth. The recent rains had brought a lushness and vibrancy to the forests that glowed magnificently under the midday sun. From this vantage point, the deep cobalt ocean could be seen beyond the rolling hillsides, the Kingdom's natural border and its unyielding separation from the rest of the world. What a strange thought to consider; that there very well could be yet another Cyrus Dorn in this very world, out there beyond the sprawling sea. The Kingdom had always felt like a world of its own in this reality but there was no way of knowing if that was true.

Cyrus could hear footsteps on the ladder rungs and knew someone approached. Even before his face climbed into view through the door in the floor, Cyrus knew of only one person it could be.

"I know you don't want to be around anyone right now," Jack said, hauling himself through the opening, "but I don't count."

He brought himself to his feet, began rifling through a satchel he had hung from his shoulder and produced a large bottle of brown liquid. Without asking, he hoisted himself onto the battlements beside Cyrus and let his legs dangle freely over the edge next to him. He then uncorked the bottle and forced it into Cyrus's chest.

"I thought you probably needed it," Jack said as Cyrus took a sip.

"I'm fine, Jack," Cyrus insisted, handing the bottle back.

"Yeah I know," Jack responded, looking out over the vista himself.

The two shared the silence together for a bit. They knew each other well enough by now that some things were able to be left unsaid.

Finally, Jack looked at Cyrus with a soft smile and said, "Hey, remember when I insisted there was nothing to find out there on the ocean when we started the expedition?"

Cyrus just laughed.

"Dalton, Nel… Alec," Jack counted off on his fingers, "just you and me left. Who would've guessed it."

"Who would've guessed any of it," Cyrus answered, to which Jack raised the bottle in agreement and took another swig. "I hope what we've done has mattered," Cyrus continued. "I mean, we didn't come here to overthrow tyrants or start a revolution. We were just looking to survive."

"It's mattered," Jack stated confidently. "There will always be more work to be done, new problems to solve and all that, but that's just life. Now these people know what their world can be and if I had to guess, they're never going back. They won't be beaten into submission again."

"Maybe that means my work is done," Cyrus said. "A wartime king in peaceful times."

Jack shook his head. "You were never a wartime king. You were the king that ended the wars. Now the real hard work starts." When Cyrus looked questioningly at him, he continued with a shrug, "New potential leaders and future kings and queens are growing up every day. Now it's our job to teach them by example. I'm honored to have been elected, and I do my best every day… but you were born for this, Cyrus." As Cyrus pulled the bottle back and took a drink, Jack finished by saying, "And I've got your back… always do."

Cyrus watched the workers below, wheeling wagons this way and that, hauling materials and stones and carts of tools. His gaze followed the path to the treeline where it disappeared behind the dense vegetation of the forest. Beyond it, visible past the soft valley of trees was Westtown and the bustling town square. A Shrieking Bat flapped out from the canopy and gave another shrill call.

"Hey Jack," Cyrus said, still with his eyes on the horizon, "thanks for bringing me back."

Jack took the bottle and looked out at the island himself. "Don't mention it," he responded softly.

From up here, one could barely tell the trauma the Kingdom had endured, and maybe… with a little luck and a bit of time, the wars could become a distant memory. It would take work, Jack was right, but it was work worth doing. And if he was sure of one thing, it was that the Kingdom was up to the challenge.

But those were problems for tomorrow. For now, Cyrus was content. And what better way to pass an afternoon than sitting on top of the world… drinking with his friend.

EPILOGUE

I t's a funny thing about time. It never quite erases the past, but it certainly softens its edges. It can be impossible to tell which lessons will permanently stick and which are destined to be learned again. It can be equally impossible to tell who and what will leave its mark on history and who and what will be forgotten. But one can never know what their legacy will be in the moment... only time can reveal that.

Ydoro ended up living a long time. Just over a hundred years when all was said and done. The Kingdom changed, as things often do, and he was there to bear witness. These changes, however, weren't unnatural power upheavals or disturbances to the natural order, they were changes that flowed with purpose and grace; the spoils of a hard-fought campaign to create a real, functioning world. They weren't won with battles and war; it was simple growth and evolution. Ydoro was lucky enough to see their work fulfilled and the Kingdom become what Cyrus Dorn, Jack Viana, and Annica all envisioned it could be.

A year on from the devastation of Kysaar Magnus was cause for reflection in more ways than one. Ydoro spent the night drinking with Cyrus, Jack, Annica, and Noma on Cyrus's porch. The home had been built much in the same style as his lodging in Easttown during his brief reign, complete with a deck that overlooked the bustle and flow of the town roads around them. They drank and laughed with their feet up on the railings, reminiscing about harder times and long-lost friends. It was also a year since Alec had died; a date that nobody celebrated, mourned, or even acknowledged in any way except for Cyrus. He quietly remembered his brother, the good and the bad, while surrounded by his friends. He didn't spend much time talking aloud about his feelings on the subject, but Ydoro could see it hidden behind his eyes. He supposed those conflicted emotions would haunt Cyrus for the rest of his life. But it was also a year since Cyrus had been returned to them on the island, and as far as Ydoro was concerned, that was cause for celebration. All that was missing was a chessboard and it could have been a night from years past.

But time had moved on, as it always did, and it continued to do so at an unyielding pace. Two years removed from Magnus's assault proved that the unity brokered on the island was meant to last. With Easttown destroyed, the decision was made to expand Westtown down into the valleys and surrounding forests, creating a single, unified thoroughfare where people lived and shopped and conducted their business. For obvious reasons, nothing was ever built on the grounds of the Fire Fields again. The old trade roads became obsolete as the Kingdom moved forward as one, but they still functioned nicely as trails leading out to the various worksites around the island. The Temple was shuttered and abandoned for the second time, allowed to fall into disrepair and ruin over the years. Annica and Jack had modest accommodations built within town-proper and seemed to enjoy the close proximity to the people who had elected them.

Cyrus would never again serve as king, though there were many in the Kingdom who pushed him to do so. He preferred to function as an advisor or guide of sorts, mentoring new and up-and-coming trailblazers on the difference between ruling and leading. Jack and Annica never seemed to mind his presence and indeed included him in every decision made. They would eventually go down in history as the longest-serving monarchy the Kingdom would ever know, and while their time would be widely regarded as successful, they would never quite attain that level of reverence that Cyrus enjoyed.

As time again moved forward and Ydoro eased into middle age, he came to understand some things that he had never quite appreciated before. He found himself watching Cyrus one day, speaking with a young couple and laughing jovially at something they had said. He placed a hand on each of their arms and greeted their newborn with appropriate enthusiasm. But as soon as the couple turned away, Cyrus's face dropped just slightly and Ydoro felt he understood why. He had never truly appreciated what Cyrus Dorn had given up by staying in the Kingdom. He had recognized who he was supposed to be and stopped resisting his destiny on the island, but that didn't make the sacrifice of his former life any less painful. He talked of Cynthia less and less as the years went on, but Ydoro knew she was never far from his thoughts. He asked Cyrus about her one day and found him happy to tell old stories about their life together in their little house near the university campus. He said he missed her desperately but found comfort in the history that had been passed on by Dean and Kat years prior. They had spoken of a Cynthia Dorn who had eventually remarried and found a life beyond Cyrus. While this specific story was from a different reality than the one Cyrus had come from, he felt he could count on something similar for *his* Cynthia.

Not to say that attempts hadn't been made by Ydoro and Noma to find Cyrus his long-lost *door*. The two had spent years combing the Fire Fields looking for that original fragment of staff that had brought the team to the island. They thought perhaps by using the tridents, which seemed to attract the scepters, they might have a chance of locating the shard, but no such luck. They never told Cyrus of their hunt, not wanting to give him false hope.

As the years stretched to decades, the young grew older and became the new generation of leaders; learning how to do so based largely on those that had come before. This was where the legacy of Cyrus Dorn would start to become apparent. People who had watched him fight for the Kingdom when they were young now found themselves trying to emulate what they saw in their youth. They searched for ways to make their mark on history the same as he had done.

By the time Annica and Jack did eventually step down, elections were held and the voice of the people was respected. Ydoro didn't always agree with the king or queen of the day, but he made sure his voice was heard either way. Cyrus was the same. He never appeared to struggle with no longer being in charge, partially because his words continued to carry more weight than anyone in the Kingdom. He was unabashedly vocal with his support and equally so with his disagreement. But he taught people to discuss their differences rather than fight over them.

Still, even the most legendary of leaders have their time, and so it was with Cyrus Dorn, who eventually faded from relevance and became a relic of wars long past. That's the beauty and tragedy of a new generation finding its way; they aren't scarred from the past, but they don't remember it either.

Jack and Annica retired from public life with grace, remaining respected individuals who no longer took part in the running of the Kingdom. The older they got, the happier they seemed to be, basking in the success of their past deeds.

And still time moved ever onward. Ydoro passed middle-age and became an old man; one who people still listened to but now with more than a hint of skepticism etched on their faces. He supposed that was just a part of aging; that the younger generations began to regard you as a product of a different time. The wars of the past sounded like a million years ago to the young, and what a glorious gift for them to be given. They didn't have to think much about the cost of their fully-functioning society, they were able to just accept it. Ydoro didn't begrudge them this, he was just happy to have been a part of the fight.

It was once he had finally reached his eighties, on a cool, overcast day with the skies above threatening a storm that Ydoro overheard news in the street that he had been dreading for a long time. Somebody mentioned to their friend, in a casual, conversational way, that an old king of the past had died. Ydoro's heart sank. It could be any number of past kings, of course, but he somehow knew it was his old friend.

Sure enough, a week later, Ydoro found the winding streets of town packed to the brim with townsfolk making their way to the Fire Fields to pay their respects and acknowledge as one the passing of a king. Old and removed from leadership he may have been, but Cyrus Dorn could still draw a crowd.

The older generations took the news hardest, of course, having known the man in his prime and seen him in action. Many of the younger crowd still felt the loss deeply after having modeled their own leadership styles after his teachings. It was the youngest folk who turned up without much knowledge of who they were bidding farewell to. Ydoro planted himself towards the back of the crowd and discovered he was directly behind a trio of such people. They each appeared to be in their early twenties and were appropriately respectful and somber in demeanor, but eavesdropping on their conversation, Ydoro wanted desperately to tell them who Cyrus Dorn had been. They asked questions like, 'so he fought in the wars?' or 'was he the one with the brother?'

Ydoro let his eyes wander to the rest of the gathered crowd. It was immense, practically stretching to the edges of the field and into the forest. At the center of the area was Noma, middle-aged and greying now but still working right in the heart of the Kingdom. He was delivering some sort of eulogy but Ydoro couldn't hear from so far back. Off to the left he could see Jack and Annica, elderly and white-haired, sitting in specially designated chairs. A woman stood next to them that he thought he recognized, though at first he couldn't place her. She wore a stoic expression but her eyes shined with tears. And then it hit him. It was Katalina Killion, the young student who had helped them reclaim the Kingdom years ago. Her hair was still fiercely auburn and wildly untamed, and while she certainly looked older, he felt he could still sense her fighting spirit, even now. Ydoro hadn't seen her in decades, but he had heard rumors that Cyrus checked in on her from time to time.

Noma must have reached the end of his talk, for he bowed his head low and raised his fist to his chest in their old salute. It hadn't been used in countless years, but the crowd followed suit all the same. Ydoro noticed the young trio in front of him struggle just slightly as they saw their neighbors participate in the unfamiliar gesture. Ydoro himself closed his eyes as he saluted, allowing his mind to travel back.

When the tribute had ended and the crowd dispersed, Ydoro decided he didn't much feel like being alone. Instead, he wandered into a tavern along the main road, one that had been standing for nearly a hundred years at this point. It was dank and dark and stale inside with the weakly flickering torches along the walls struggling to illuminate the deep, shadowy corners of the room. He sat at a table in one of these corners and ordered an ale. He could have gone to check in on Annica and Jack, or perhaps gone to say hello to Kat Killion, but he decided he wanted to be amongst the people most of all.

Considering it was midday, Ydoro hadn't expected much of a crowd, but it seemed the funeral had coaxed people out of their homes and out of their routines. The place was packed, mostly with young folk but a few slightly older. He recognized the trio he had been standing behind at the service. They stood around a table a short distance away and were conversing loudly.

"I don't think he was the one with the brother," one of them was saying. "That must have been before his time."

"No it was," said another. "I'm telling you, that was Cyrus Dorn. He fought his brother in the Fire Fields, right where we were standing. There used to be a statue of him, before we were born."

"Exactly," agreed the third. "That's where the City of Dorn gets its name."

"Well yeah, I know that," the first one said, "I was just trying to remember what he did, that's all."

"Don't you three read history books?" snarled a rather drunk and disorderly denizen from the next table over. "That was *the* Cyrus Dorn we were just saluting. Have some respect, he killed his own brother to save all of you. Then fought off King Mangus when he tried to turn everyone into his slaves."

Ydoro smiled to himself at the attempt, wincing only slightly at the inaccuracies in the story.

"So you were there for the wars?" one of the youths asked the man.

"Well… not *there* exactly," the man admitted, "but I've heard stories."

"What was his brother's name?" the first of the youths asked curiously.

The man grumbled slightly. "Alex I think it was. Yeah, I think that was it."

"Alec," Ydoro corrected him before he could stop himself.

The group as a whole turned, understandably surprised to find an old man listening to them from the shadows.

"His name was Alec," Ydoro repeated.

The group collectively studied him, then seemed to decide he was worth listening to.

"Were you around in those days?" one of them asked.

Ydoro nodded slowly. "Those days and before."

"So, Cyrus Dorn," one questioned, "was he like… the first king?"

Ydoro smiled. "The first real one, maybe. He's the reason you have the Kingdom you do today. The reason people aren't dying in the streets or afraid to leave their homes… he was a great man."

Two of the three nodded slightly but it was clear they didn't know how seriously to take the old man or how much time they should give him. The third, however, looked more intrigued.

"You knew him," the third said thoughtfully.

"I did," Ydoro admitted.

"Well I'm sorry for your loss," he said, and though it was clear he meant it, an interesting thought suddenly occurred to Ydoro. He would be amongst the last generations to truly remember Cyrus Dorn as a person. Moving forward, he would claim his well-deserved place as a legend one reads about in history books, a story told to children.

"Well how 'bout a toast," the young man said, "a toast to your friend. Let's hear something about him."

Ydoro shrugged mildly but with the encouragement of the other two youths and a few onlookers from the surrounding tables, he eventually pushed himself out of his chair and stood upright with his glass in his hand. He began to raise it but then realized he had no idea what to say. He wanted to tell everyone listening what a great friend Cyrus had been. Or perhaps what a great leader he had been. He wanted to tell them of his many feats in battle and his many feats in politics. About the way he had banished his brother to another reality, or fought Kysaar Magnus one on one. Or maybe of his overthrowing of King Mora or the way he had inspired Easttown to rise up against Irias.

But no. In the end, Cyrus Dorn wouldn't have wanted to hear about himself. He would have wanted to hear about his people, about his teachings living on. About the times of peace that he had fought for and years of peace still to come. About the power of the locals and the strength they still housed. About his allies and critics. Virulent opponents and staunchest supporters. The community that he helped give a voice to. That's what he would have wanted to hear about.

A smile crept across Ydoro's face as he remembered his friend, and while he could have regaled the tavern with story after story, he decided to keep them all for himself. Instead, he raised his glass into the air and in a soft voice, uttered a single sentence.

"To the Kingdom."

AUTHOR BIO

Photograph by Katie Stukel

A storyteller at heart from a young age, Ryan Freerksen grew up filming intricate (and absurdly long) Claymation movies on his old Hi-8 camcorder before attending college for filmmaking. Almost a decade would pass before he realized his love for film was not rooted in its technical aspects but rather the crafting of a captivating tale. He found his narrative voice once again with *Somewhere* and decided he should have been writing all this time. He currently lives in Illinois with his wife Katie.

If you enjoyed this book, please consider leaving a review on Amazon and/or Goodreads. It's the best way for indie authors to get their books in front of a wider audience.

And for the latest updates on future books, find me and follow me:
linktr.ee/authorrfreerksen